HEGEMO

SULLIVAN'S RUN

BY:

ANDREW VAILLENCOURT

This is a work of fiction. Similarities to real people, places, or events are entirely coincidental.

SULLIVAN'S RUN

First edition. June 13, 2019.

Written by Andrew Vaillencourt.

Also by Andrew Vaillencourt

Hegemony
Sullivan's Run

The Fixer
Ordnance
Hell Follows
Hammers and Nails
Aphrodite's Tears
Dead Man Dreaming
Head Space
Escalante
The Fixer Omnibus

Watch for more at www.AndrewVaillencourt.com.

CHAPTER ONE

Warden First Class John Sullivan's day began with a hangover. This was neither novel nor unexpected. When one drinks as much as Sullivan was wont to, a hangover is to be expected. But his day then proceeded to take a nice big step off the cliffs of serendipity to subsequently plummet like a lawn dart into the rich loam of utter chaos.

The hangover would have been manageable. His list of things to accomplish for the day consisted of watching one suspected genetic modification facility and counting the known scumbags who went in and out. Sullivan suffered from hangovers with depressing frequency, so even with a sour stomach and a pounding headache, he felt secure and confident in his ability to sit at a window and observe a building.

Of course, because the universe hated John Sullivan, the local constabulary decided to assert their presence, and that is when a spirited shooting match began. Sullivan found both police and gunplay to be annoying under the best of circumstances. Today, the staccato cracks and chattering of attempted murder bothered him even more than usual.

The violence itself was no issue. Knowing that the shooting was premature, stupid, and the result of over-eager, trigger-happy morons with no respect for the work it took to get an investigation this far is what turned the roil of irritation in his stomach into impotent frustration. Sullivan had predicted this outcome beforehand to anyone who cared to listen. The irony of his pessimistic nature, he supposed, was that the only thing more annoying than being wrong was being right.

"G-team, this is G-one. MLEOs jumped the mark," he called into his team's channel, "as expected."

"Copy that, G-one," came the reply. "What's the play?"

From his vantage point in a second-story apartment, Sullivan scanned the scene unfolding across the street. The stately white marble facade of the building flickered with the jarring pyrotechnics of muzzle flashes. A dozen guns spat yellow fire from as many windows down to the roadway below. Ricochets spun sparks from the armored surfaces of two black vans now hopelessly pinned down by the shooters' superior position. "Chicago Metro Law Enforcement" had been emblazoned across the dark panels with reflective paint, so each tiny explosion sparkled like orange lightning across the sides of the vehicles. Detecting the commotion, all the streetlights and signs flashed in blue and red while recessed bollards ascended from the street to block off the scene. Information screens for blocks around would be informing pedestrians and passengers of the detour, and exhorting folks to patience while the municipal traffic grid rerouted them toward their destinations.

"Well, the wagons are completely skewered," Sullivan opined. "But the street is secure, at least. Looks like we got shooters entrenched in most of the upper floors. I'm just going to assume they've got all the ammo they need, too."

"They're sure as hell shooting as if they brought enough, G-one," came a reply as exasperated as Sullivan's.

"How close can we get a drone, Fagan?" In his irritation, Sullivan forgot to employ regulation signal discipline and used his partner's name. He noted this in passing and discovered he did not care at all.

"Stand by," the voice muttered.

While his teammate sorted out the drone, Sullivan rose and headed for the stairwell. A flood of stress hormones and endorphins washed his hangover away by the second step, replacing his malaise with sharp focus and frigid calm. He moved fast. Greedy strides gobbled up the intervening distance between himself and the main stairwell door. He took the stairs three at a time, turning at each landing with a hand on the rail to preserve his momentum. Eight seconds later, he burst through the rooftop access gate. The mangled handle and lock spun free of their moorings to skip the landing, victims of his headlong charge and the indiscriminate application of too much muscle.

On the roof, his earpiece crackled to life. "I got a drone up now, G-one. Guess what I see?"

Sullivan looked up and around, squinting into the pre-dawn light of the cloudy sky. He found the hovering quad-copter after a second or two and extended a middle finger in its direction.

"Please tell me you aren't going to do anything stupid?" The voice in his ear did not sound hopeful.

"Define 'stupid.'"

"Whatever it is you are thinking of right now..." the man sighed, "... is probably stupid."

Sullivan chose to ignore that. "Have that drone find me rooftop access, Fagan." Sullivan peered over the side of the safety rail to judge the distance. The street was fifty feet wide, and the other roof three stories below his. He juggled his chances of success with the potential consequences of failure and started to back up.

"Sully!" Fagan sounded angry now. "Even if you make it, you're gonna be stuck up there with two broken ankles!"

"With the height difference, I can do it." Sullivan dismissed the concerns. "But it won't mean a thing if I can't get in. Find me some access."

After three seconds of quiet, Fagan's voice returned. "You have two roof access points. One north and one south. If you are determined to pull this idiotic stunt, then I'm going to kick in the back door and try to make some noise to cover you. I'll meet you in the middle."

"I appreciate that," Sullivan replied, surprised by his own sincerity. "Tell those MLEOs to do something useful and draw fire."

"Copy that."

"I'm going now."

"Don't die."

"Okay," he muttered. When Sullivan had backed up as far as his roof would allow, he paused. Taking a deep breath, he started to run. The gravel rooftop ballast kicked up in his wake like the rooster tail from a power boat as each footfall drove him forward with more force and greater speed. Three feet from the edge, he leapt.

The street opened beneath him, a distant and deadly black demise beckoning from far below while a single madman hurled himself across the fifty-foot chasm. As physics demanded, Sullivan's horizontal trajectory came with a distressing drop in the vertical. Each yard of the gap he crossed brought him closer to the river of asphalt underneath and the abrupt death it promised.

Despite his external confidence, Sullivan experienced an instant of doubt. For the first nanosecond of his leap, the destination seemed too distant and his descent too extreme. With no other options, he windmilled his arms and bicycled his feet with Satan's own tenacity. To his benefit, he had misjudged his own velocity. Even as he decided he was not going to make it, his heel struck the black membrane of the distant rooftop.

Instantly, Sullivan brought his other foot down, braced his knees without locking them, and allowed the jaw-cracking impact to throw him into a headlong tumble. He rolled twice before the energy of his landing spent itself against hard rubber. Sullivan rose with caution, testing his joints for damage before trusting his full weight to them.

"I made it, Fagan," he said into the channel. "Feel free to start kicking the doors down."

Not waiting for a reply, he trotted to the north side of the roof and found the promised hatch. Sullivan scowled at the intimidating girth of the locking bar and the robust padlock holding it shut. Not wanting to look for the other entrance, he gripped the aluminum lid on each edge and pulled, but the lock refused to yield. Sullivan entertained no illusions that his own strength would ever be enough to snap a well-made padlock. However, the building owners had made a common mistake in securing the roof hatch. The lock was merely the strongest link in a chain of many weaker ones. Most of the hatch components were constructed from more mundane materials, and as such were not immune to Sullivan's prodigious musculature.

The metal square flexed and warped out of shape as Sullivan pulled. The simple hinges groaned like old men before a rainstorm, but held. Sullivan growled through his teeth and pulled harder, peeling at the corners as much as lifting. He changed directions, searching for signs of weakness in the closing mechanism. On one such twist, the groan became a wail, and then died with a loud clang as some interior part of the mechanism snapped. The door flopped off its hinges, still clinging to the hasp by the tenacious padlock. Sullivan had to work and warp the broken thing a few more times to bend it clear of the opening. When he had forced a gap large enough for him to slip through, he grabbed the top rung of the ladder and dropped into the narrow scuttle leading inside.

His feet struck tile in a dark room. Prudence demanded he wait for his eyes to adjust, though the delay sparked an indeterminate fury in his chest. It passed without incident, as it always did. Sullivan's frustration evolved from simple impatience to a deeper irritation with his inability to truly experience his anger.

As the rectangle of the door began to take shape, Sullivan wondered if today would be the day. He knew the situation. He sensed the genesis of fear and anger in the chill prickling across his skin. If he were normal, this would grow into a cold sweat and a gradual loss of fine motor control. A regular man might descend into a panic. A warrior might slide into a feral rage. Either reaction would be normal.

Sullivan did neither. These emotions all died in the neurochemical womb, drowned in a heady rush of sensory information and an eerie, unnatural calm. Blessing or curse, it did not matter. Without exception, stressful situations never failed to crystalize his thoughts and feelings into an infallible lattice of grim stoicism. When others got scared, Sullivan grew determined. When lesser men became angry, Sullivan achieved laser-like focus. When terror turned a normal person's feet to clay, Sullivan grew wings.

He hated it.

But he loved it, too.

He took a long breath, exhaled it, and charged. The door to his closet flew from flimsy hinges, hurled by his foot into the hallway beyond. Sullivan himself burst into the corridor with his weapon raised to eye level immediately after. He swept the muzzle left to right, searching for targets. The tiny blip of disappointment he experienced when he saw no one bothered him, though he did not dwell on it. With more important things to worry about, Sullivan ran down the beige corridor toward the distant sounds of gunfire. That he did not get lost was a miracle considering how repetitive and unoriginal the endless passages were. The harsh pounding of muffled gunplay guided his path. Scant seconds later, he stood outside an office door jumping and rattling in its frame with the roar of unrestrained violence from the other side.

Sullivan smashed through the door with speed defying comprehension. Distracted as they were by their own targets and the overwhelming noise of full-auto fire, no one inside realized a large man had entered the room behind them. All enemy eyes remained fixated on the street, all attention consumed by the scampering Chicago cops below. Seeing the backs of three men leaning out to shoot through broken windows, Sullivan had precious few heartbeats to make a choice. He should have first identified himself as a federal agent and then commanded them to surrender. Sullivan considered their apparent commitment to killing all law enforcement officials in the vicinity before dismissing such action. Playing it straight and heroic looked to be more risky than even he liked.

Shooting them all in the back was an option. He had the drop on them, and he was a very competent shooter. That would have been the most efficient strategy. Effective or not, he supposed this might be a bridge too far in the other direction. He could not shake the feeling that just slaughtering them where they stood was... unsporting.

So he holstered his pistol and charged. His first two steps sent him into the unsuspecting man at the closest window. A big right hand swatted down to slap the rifle away from its wielder, eliciting a cry of pain and shock. Sullivan's left elbow followed, and the satisfying crunch of a jawbone breaking told Sullivan it was safe to move on.

Leaving the first shooter to slump against the window frame, Sullivan spun on his heel and booted the second man away from his perch. The struck man caromed into the third, spoiling the latter's aim and sending a string of bullets across the ceiling in eruptions of chipped plaster. Before either regained their feet, Sullivan was upon them.

He relieved them of their weapons, disarming his foes with practiced twists of wrists and elbows. He might have finished them with ease, but he wanted more. More *what* even Sullivan could not say with certainty. He just knew that this was not enough of whatever it was he needed, and he intended to extract his due. The first man went for a blade at his waist, and the deft movement sent ripples of excitement across Sullivan's unearthly calm. Though only a mere taste of intensity, the subtle blip of fear teased Sullivan with the *more* he hungered for.

The second shooter leapt, an uncoordinated and undisciplined charge that Sullivan swatted aside as an afterthought. The man was clumsy and unskilled. Sullivan wanted no part of that. He redirected the tackle with a single arm and tangled the man's boots with a choppy kick to his leading foot. The impact of chin striking floor tiles gave off a wet slap, punctuated by the click of teeth breaking. Sullivan did not care.

The knife-wielding man commanded his full attention now. There was danger in the enemy's practiced stance, and easy confidence. The man held the blade in a firm fencer's grip, the knife's tip swaying in arcs designed to hide an incoming strike. The enemy's right shoulder dipped, and he slid forward on the balls of his feet to send the blade at Sullivan's throat. He was well-trained, the strike fast and smooth. His aim was flawless, and Sullivan watched the dull glint of the blade's edge as it parted the air between them. For his part, Sullivan felt nothing, and he parried the slash with his forearm. Annoyed, he stepped back to let his foe try again. He knew this was wrong. It was stupid and wasteful and made no sense. Nevertheless, he could not stop himself. He wanted the man to try again. Sullivan searched within himself for even a faint hint of fear. He wanted to feel something, to let fear become anger. He wanted to indulge the anger, encourage it, feed it. He did not know why he wanted any of these things, but the need of it drove him to greater heights of recklessness. Sullivan waited, steel-blue eyes daring his opponent have another go.

His foe danced forward, his body extending in a graceful line behind the tip of his weapon. He feinted a slash at Sullivan's abdomen, twisting at the last instant to send the blade upward. The knife hissed past Sullivan's ear without biting flesh. The skillful thrust had been meant for the face, though Sullivan's reflexes mocked the attempt. The man never had a chance, and therein lay the problem.

Sullivan gave up. He had wasted too much time on this already. Despite a personality rife with unpleasant traits, he was no fool, and playing with these men took time away from finishing the job and helping Fagan. The cops pinned down in the street would not appreciate his dawdling, either. He accepted that what he was looking for would not be found here. A dejected Sullivan ended the charade with two jabs so fast that the bladesman thought he was still fighting even as his legs stopped supporting his weight. The knife swayed lazily in his hands as he sank. Sullivan completed the journey into unconsciousness with a rising uppercut that stood the falling man back upright for an instant. Eyes empty and muscles limp, the last gunner joined his friends on the tile with identical broken jaws and matching concussions.

Sullivan was in the process of cuffing his victims when the cracking of gunfire below told him that Fagan had engaged the enemy as well. He resumed his sweep of the top floor and found no further opposition. "Top floor clear," he called into his throat mic. "You think maybe we can convince those MLEOs to stop hiding and help, G-two?"

"Twisting their arms now, G-one," came Fagan's slightly breathless response. "Second floor is clear. Four tangos down."

"I have three down up here," Sullivan answered. "Left them breathing, but they'll need medical. Have MLEOs hit the first floor, and I'll meet you on three."

"Gimme a sec, G-one," Fagan growled. "I can't run like you."

"I'll start without you, then."

"Asshole."

Sullivan was already moving. He cleared the stairwell of hostiles before descending to the third floor. Weapon ready, he peeked out into the open space of the lobby and found it empty. Shouts from the street and a steady pounding told Sullivan that the cops were finally doing something useful and bashing their way inside. This might have been a relief but for the sound of muffled expletives and shuffling boots moving closer.

Three armed men trotted into the lobby from a side entrance. They stormed across the carpeted expanse, oblivious to the man peeking out from the stairwell as they took up fighting positions at the main windows. Sullivan realized they were trying to get a shooting angle on the men breaking down the front door. Sullivan threw the stairwell door open and took his pistol in a two-handed grip. With nothing but ice water in his veins and the blank expression of an automaton, the warden advanced and fired. He saw only his gunsight's reticle, felt only the pressure of his index finger against the trigger. When the weapon erupted to life, he almost did not notice the stippled backstrap of the grip biting into the web of his thumb. The target and the sight disappeared for an instant, obscured by the flash of burning gas and the jolt of recoil. As if wielded by a machine, both the sight and the muzzle realigned for subsequent shots even before the previous fireball dissipated. A man's chest stood framed in the reticle with a glowing green dot over his sternum for a fraction of a second before the thunder of a gunshot and the lighting of a muzzle flash started the whole process over again. Six times, his ten-millimeter service pistol barked like a demon hound. All six shots creased the air with hypersonic ripples within the space of two long seconds. He placed each round with care, double-tapping every enemy center-mass as he had been taught. He felt nothing, of course. Punching life-draining holes into the fleshy sacks of meat and fluid that a millisecond prior had been living, breathing men was the sort of task he had been created to do. The intensity of this firefight only drove him further away from his emotions, deeper into the black tunnel of focus and determination.

Sullivan canted his weapon to the side to assess his work while sliding into cover behind the receptionist's desk. He already knew his shots were good. The only real question was whether the enemy wore body armor sufficient to withstand his marksmanship. He doubted it, though training and discipline were both hard to shake when his brain chemistry was responding to intense danger. A quick perusal of the front of the lobby confirmed his suspicions. All the men were down or dying noisily in a writhing heap, bleeding and gurgling with equal enthusiasm.

From somewhere off to his right and a good distance away, a horrific crashing and bashing commotion was shaking the walls. Sullivan had not been working with Patrick Fagan for a long time, but he recognized the signs of his partner's handiwork. Gunfire, screams, and the rolling rumble of wanton property damage alerted Sullivan to Fagan's imminent arrival. Choosing care over haste, Sullivan remained under cover and dropped the half-empty magazine from his pistol. Unthinking, he caught it as it fell and slipped it into his coat pocket. The noise grew closer as he fished a fresh one from his belt. With his emotions starting to slide back in, a smile touched his lips. No one would ever accuse Sullivan of being a team player, though it was hard not to like working with Fagan. As he seated the fresh magazine and ensured a round was in battery, the sound of wood splintering startled him enough to nearly drop his weapon. The top half of a man protruded from the now-ruined door to his left. His arms hung limp, and his head lolled in a manner that did not indicate good things for any of the associated vertebrae. Another crash followed, and both man and door hurtled inward, propelled by an impact that made nearby furniture jump and knocked a vase of fake flowers from its perch atop a bookshelf.

A giant stepped into the lobby. Bent over to fit through the door, Patrick Fagan looked like a mythical troll lumbering out from beneath a bridge. When he rose to his full height, this picture did not improve much. Somewhere in the fight, the sleeve of his jacket and shirt had been torn away, revealing a hairy arm as thick as a big man's leg. His tiny eyes blazed under a heavy brow, and massive shoulders heaved with each wheezing breath. A dense black beard hid a simian slab of a jaw, though Sullivan saw his teeth bared in a ferocious frown. Fagan's pistol looked like a child's toy in his gargantuan mitt, and Sullivan could tell by the upright position of the mag catch lever that Fagan had run the thing dry in getting here.

"Over here!" Sullivan called with a wave from behind the desk. "It's clear, I think."

Fagan crossed the lobby at a brisk jog. At the desk, he reloaded his pistol and pointed to his bare limb. A shallow cut ran along his triceps, weeping crimson into the coarse hair of his upper arm. "Fuckers were using knives, man. Who the hell uses knives in this day and age?"

"Where was his gun?" Sullivan asked, his curiosity genuine.

"He, uh, might have dropped it when I threw something at him."

Sullivan began to check the men he had shot for survivors. Over his shoulder, he asked, "And what exactly did you throw?"

Fagan was cuffing the inert form of the man he had put through the door. His reply came with more than a little pride. "A vending machine."

Sullivan shook his head. "Of course." Satisfied that his three targets were well and truly dead, he looked back to his giant partner. "What's ridiculous to me is that after having the vending machine thrown at him, he still decided that coming after you with a knife was a viable strategy."

"That's what I'm saying, man. A guy ought to know when he's beat."

Gunfire and explosions from below ended the conversation. A prolonged bout of shooting and shouting wafted up from the first floor. Both men rolled their eyes and checked their pistols.

Fagan spoke first. "Guess we ought to go help out the local yokels."

"Goddamn amateurs," grumbled Sullivan. "Might as well. My head is fucking killing me, and I'd like to wrap this up in time to grab a beer."

CHAPTER TWO

If the Chicago Municipal Law Enforcement Office detachment thought the wardens would be grateful for their assistance, Sullivan's frank and unvarnished assessment of their contribution to the raid disabused them of such immediately.

"On what planet, Sergeant," he fumed into the reddening face of the MLEO squad leader, "does 'secure the perimeter and contain' become 'pull up to the front door in marked vehicles?'" Sullivan was a full six inches taller than the policeman, and he glared down upon his prey in a manner most disconcerting to the shorter man.

"My office said to hit the place if it looked like high value targets were inside. I had orders."

"So on the authority of the Chicago Municipal Law Enforcement Office, you elected to preempt a Genetic Equity Enforcement Department operation?"

Sullivan's incredulity sounded a lot more like smoldering rage to the sergeant, who met it with his own growing irritation. "You're two guys in suits from Albany. You swoop in and tell us that there is a major criminal element financing and producing illegal genetic modifications in our backyard. Then you tell us to sit on our hands and do nothing?" The sergeant sneered back up at Sullivan. "On what freakin' planet do you think the mayor and the governor are going to let a pair of G-men actually run that show? You know how that makes them look?"

"It makes them look fucking incompetent or corrupt," Sullivan growled.

"Likely both," Fagan added, ever helpful.

The sergeant shrugged. "Well, now you know why I got the orders I got."

This did not satisfy Sullivan, who needed to vent his irritation. "Christ, you're an idiot. All they did was transfer the embarrassment."

The sergeant bristled at the insult. "The fuck you talking about?"

Fagan continued to be helpful. "Now *you're* the one who looks incompetent or corrupt, Sergeant."

Sullivan explained. "You jumped the gun on an eleven-month GEED investigation, dumbass. There was nobody here all that important. Yeah, we'll get some accountants and some street muscle locked up, but no big players. You just spooked all the bad guys, blew an expensive investigation, and started a firefight on a busy street right before rush hour." He began a slow, derisive golf clap. "Oh bravo, Sergeant." Then he stopped clapping. "And what, pray tell, do you have to show for it all?" He held his hands out the sides, encompassing the wrecked atrium. "Dick-all. Well done, Sergeant. Well done. I figure the over-under on you getting fired is eight weeks." He looked back over his shoulder to the giant behind him. "You taking that action, Fagan?"

"I'll take the under for a hundred. The mayor is going to want to get far away from this screw-up fast. Especially once Horowitz starts shrieking."

Sullivan winced. "Oof. Yeah. I should have thought that out more. Definitely less than six weeks. Damn. I'm gonna be out a hundred bucks now." He returned his attention to the sergeant, stepping closer to loom over the man. "So if you are looking for gratitude, numb-nuts, you can fuck right off."

The two men locked gazes, and the policeman's jaw worked in silent fury at all the implications of his folly. He growled his response through teeth pressed tight together. "Now you listen here, you suit-wearing Fed motherfucker. My boys and I came in here to enforce the law, and maybe to help you guys out. Without us, it would have been you two freaks against the whole goddamn building. Maybe we moved too early, but you still got your bust, and without our help, you'd have nothing. So I don't want to hear anything but 'thank you' out of that pretty little GiMP mouth of you—"

Sullivan's hand darted forward to clamp over the sergeant's face. The palm crushed his lips and nose with an ugly slap, and the sergeant found himself unable to breathe. Sullivan squeezed and pushed downward, driving the man to his knees while he struggled to force air through Sullivan's fingers. The dozen or so MLEOs wandering around pretending not to hear the argument suddenly turned toward the commotion, twelve hands resting on the butts of twelve weapons.

"Sully..." Fagan's tone carried a warning.

With a snarl, Sullivan released his captive. The sergeant crumpled to the floor, coughed twice as he caught his breath, then heaved himself back to his feet. His face glowed red, and spittle flew from his mouth as he sputtered, "You piece of shit GiMP motherfucker!" The policeman stepped forward as if to hit Sullivan, then thought better of it when he saw the warden's face. It was like an internal switch had been flipped, and now a different person sat behind the wheel. Sullivan wore no expression at all. He stood blank-faced and relaxed. Those eyes that had burned with anger now sat ice-cold and level. Hands balled into fists only seconds before now hung loose at his sides. The irritation was gone. The anger and frustration had fled his body. The sergeant had never seen anything quite like the warden before, but he knew what that look meant.

"Fagan," Sullivan said in a frigid voice. "Can you please finish debriefing the sergeant, here? I suddenly need some air."

"Yeah, go take a walk, Sully," Fagan said. "I'll sort the good sergeant out."

Sullivan moved away from the tense knot of policemen and wandered back into the main foyer of the building. The MLEOs had made a mess of the place with an uncoordinated breach and sloppy contagious fire. The burned-chemical smell of smoke grenades still lingered, the salty tang of it tickling his nostrils with the slight chance of a sneeze.

In truth, he was not all that angry with the sergeant. Beyond the general baseline stupidity of jumping the gun, the man had not really done anything all that wrong. Sullivan's irritation had more to do with the consequences. That one stupid mistake had cost Sullivan and the department a lot of work, and this meant big headaches for everyone involved. Sullivan accepted that his outburst had more to do with an unspecified desire to ruin the sergeant's day than any real loss of temper. The sergeant's blunder irritated him, and he wanted to punish the man for it.

Sullivan did not like the implications of this, as it placed him in the role of the bully. It was a role he had played before, almost always when his stress response weakened his otherwise ironclad self-control.

The lapse was understandable. To be mean was his nature, hard-wired into the fiber of his brain chemistry at birth. Nevertheless, he bristled as he stalked down a hallway. The voices of his instructors echoed in his head, rebuking him for his moment of childish indulgence.

You cannot control your feelings; therefore, it is useless to try. You can control your behavior, and therefore you must. Your emotions are a consequence; your actions are a choice. Learn to feel without acting, and to act without feeling, and you will master both yourself and your enemies.

It was an old mantra, beaten into him across years of training at the hands of skilled instructors. These same lessons had saved his life and livelihood more than once, and he always felt like a fool when his frustration got the better of him.

His feet thumped as he paced the halls, lost in his own thoughts. His walk appeared to have had purpose, though he merely needed something to do with his body while his brain sorted through its laundry list of recriminations. Adrift as he was in his own ruminations, the small shuffling sound coming from behind a closed door almost went unnoticed. If the eerie quiet of the building had not been quite so complete, he might have missed it and walked on. Yet, without the hum and bustle of a normal workday to mask it, the screech of metal on floor tile pierced his mental fog like a bullet.

Sullivan stopped and cocked his head to listen. The sound came again. A scraping noise, soft and tentative, from the other side of a door that looked like it opened into a closet. Sullivan cast about to get his bearings and discovered he had wandered into some deep and secluded corner of the facility. He did not recognize his location, and there were no signs that the battle had meandered anywhere near this particular hallway. He listened some more, and the scraping continued.

He toyed with the idea of calling for backup, then decided against it. The fuming warden would now add the poor job of clearing the first floor to the long list of complaints he intended to file with Chicago's Municipal Law Enforcement Office, and the thought of MLEOs bungling this operation any further turned his stomach. It also felt like it might be a good idea to keep Fagan on the sergeant for the time being. It did not seem sensible to revisit that interaction anytime soon.

His right hand brushed his jacket away from his holster and drew his pistol. He listened for another few seconds to make sure he heard nothing that sounded too strange or dangerous. The scraping and scratching continued, and Sullivan thought he heard some huffing and grunting as well. Satisfied that the door did not hide a squad of heavily-armed goons, his left hand reached for the latch. With a yank, he almost ripped the door off its hinges. The reticle of his gun-sight amplified what small quantity of light there was in the chamber beyond, and Sullivan saw a small man trying very hard to move a large cabinet.

"Federal agent!" Sullivan boomed. "Hold it right there!"

The man squeaked and dropped to the floor, arms raised above his head in a pose of abject surrender.

"Don't shoot," he cried. "I give up! I give up!"

Sullivan assessed the scene for a moment. The cowering man was short, thin, and terrified. He wore a suit that looked expensive, though somewhat worse for wear. He appeared pathetic and quite harmless, so Sullivan holstered his sidearm and stepped farther into the room. If there was a gun somewhere under that jacket, Sullivan supposed the twerp could go ahead and try his luck. He said as much to the trembling man.

"If you're armed, either drop it or make your move. It's all the same to me."

"I'm unarmed!" the man gasped.

"Good. Get up. Keep your hands where I can see them."

The man complied as best he could. Dragging himself upright, he strained to see who had caught him. Narrow eyes squinted at the warden, then widened with a mixture of fear and awe. "You're Sullivan, aren't you?"

"Am I that famous?"

The man shuffled his feet in a nervous tic. "In some circles, yes. Your reputation, ah... precedes you. As does your father's."

Sullivan was not sure he liked how that sounded. "My father is not your problem right now. Does my reputation say what I'll do to you if you give me a hard time?"

He replied with an emphatic nod. "Oh yes! Don't worry. I'll cooperate!"

Something felt wrong to Sullivan. He could not place it right away, and a scowl striped his face with deep lines. "That's real accommodating of you, Mister..." he left it hanging with a raised eyebrow.

"Mortenson. Sam Mortenson. Are you going to arrest me now?" The face hardened. "I have a good lawyer, you know. You better not try any rough stuff."

Sullivan's doubts gathered momentum. "You sure seem in a rush to get locked up, Sam. Just what the hell are you hiding?"

"I was hiding myself!" The warden was unconvinced with this answer. Mortensen tried harder. "From all the shooting! It was bedlam out there!"

Sullivan looked past Mortenson to the cabinet he had been pushing. The size of an armoire, the rectangular metal box was otherwise uninteresting. Sullivan might have assumed it held files or office supplies if not for the obvious effort his captive had been putting into moving it.

"What's up with the cabinet, Sam?" he asked.

Mortenson swallowed. "A hiding place, you know?"

"You weren't trying to open it, pal. You were trying to move the damn thing." Sullivan walked up to it, ignoring Mortenson as he passed the man. Mortenson eyed his now unobstructed path to the hall with naked hunger, and Sullivan chuckled. "If you think you can make it, give it a shot," he said without turning.

Mortenson stayed put, his round shoulders slumped in defeat.

Sullivan wrinkled his nose at the piece of furniture before his eyes. "Now, why the hell is a spindly little thing like you trying to move such a big, heavy thing?"

"Just wanted to hide," Mortenson sighed.

"Bullshit." Sullivan grabbed the cabinet by the edges and dragged the whole apparatus away from the wall without so much as a grunt of exertion. Mortenson bolted for the hall as soon as it started to move. Sullivan whipped around and shot an arm toward the fleeing man. With a handful of Mortenson's collar in his grip, the warden yanked his prey off his feet and threw the mousy man into the closest wall. "Not today, Sammy." With a sharp cry of pain, Mortenson slumped to the floor, where he settled into a panting and groaning pile of limbs. Satisfied, Sullivan examined the section of floor formerly hidden by the cabinet. Nestled into the tiles was a square metal door, twelve inches on a side. A control panel with a numeric keypad and a screen sat atop it. "Well, now," he said with a knowing chuckle. "What do we have here?"

Mortenson said nothing.

Sullivan looked over to the crumpled heap of man, a dark smile on his face. "I don't suppose you know the combination to this here vault, do you?"

Mortenson remained silent.

"It really doesn't matter. We have people who can hack it. I'm just giving you a chance to cooperate. It will look better if you do when it comes time to cut a deal with the prosecutor."

At last, Mortenson looked up and met the warden's eyes. "You don't want to open that door, Warden."

"Sure I do," Sullivan said.

"No, you don't," Mortenson said. "There's nothing in there but bad news, and once you open it, your life won't be worth shit." Mortenson's pleading was making Sullivan uncomfortable. "Take my advice, John. Walk away right now. Arrest me, take down this operation, hunt us all down if you must. But leave that door closed, for all our sakes. For your own sake!"

Sullivan considered this for a moment, then he stomped over to Mortenson and grabbed him by the lapel. A flick of his arm sent the smaller man flopping over to land atop the hatch.

"Open it."

Mortenson's fingers trembled as he punched keys. "You don't understand, John. I'm trying to protect..."

"Shut up," Sullivan barked. "You call me 'Warden Sullivan.' Only my mother can call me John, and I think we both know I don't have a mother."

A loud click indicated the tiny vault was unlocked. Mortenson slid away to lean against the wall. "Have it your way, then." He made a weak hand wave toward the door. A cheerful green light blinked on the panel. "It's open."

Sullivan lifted the hatch, revealing a small recess filled with data cards.

"Christ..." he breathed at the sight of them all. "That's a lot of evidence, isn't it?"

"Enough to damn us all," Mortenson said. "Every last one of us."

CHAPTER THREE

"The hell with it. I'm going in."

The statement, bland and unadorned as it was, carried the weight of finality and the promise of dire administrative consequences for all involved. Sullivan cemented his folly by stepping into the black river of shimmering heat waves warping the air above the asphalt of a busy Hartford street. A half-dozen vehicles lurched to an abrupt halt as dozens of sensors registered the living creature crossing their path. Those same vehicles, upon uploading the brazen jaywalker's infraction to the transit grid, received immediate confirmation that, despite the flagrant disregard for safety and egregious disrespect toward the sanctity of traffic law, the tall man in the brown jacket had all the authority necessary to bring traffic to a halt without consequence. Several lawyers, one stockbroker, and a lone software developer found their ire both impotent and ignored. The combined sputtering and blustering of the jostled passengers died like a mild breeze before the hurricane of official state business.

One brave soul, sounding tired and resigned, made the requisite attempt to rein the stalking man in.

"Oh, come on, Sully!" Even through the earpiece, Fagan's admonition wore the heavy cloak of a man who had endured this conversation several times before and was rather tired with repeating himself. "What the hell are you doing, man?"

"I'm going in now, Fagan," Sullivan said. "I'm sick of waiting in this heat. It's just the one guy. I'll get him to come in on his own."

"Sully," he pleaded, friendlier this time. "Come on, man. You know this doesn't ever work in your favor. Just wait for the wagon like you're supposed to."

"Like in Chicago?" Sullivan replied. "Not in the mood for that shit again. This guy and this bust are way too important. I'll just be a minute. Sullivan out." He pulled the bud from his ear and let it dangle over his collar. He still heard the irritated exhortations of Fagan on the other end of the line, though he found these much easier to ignore now that they had been reduced to incoherent buzzing. He supposed it matched the incoherent buzzing of the fragmented thoughts limping across his booze-soaked synapses. Maybe it was the lingering after-effects of too much late-night hotel drinking enhancing his discomfort, or an artifact of his hyperactive metabolism. Either way, it remained painfully obvious that he had not dressed properly for the mid-July heat. Connecticut was supposed to be a cool place. Why no one had mentioned that this picturesque New England town might scorch like the sixth ring of hell, the warden could not say. He suspected that people just liked to watch him squirm, then dismissed the thought as frustration-induced paranoia. No matter where the responsibility for his misery lay, his lack of sartorial flexibility had placed him in a situation where an otherwise normal day at work was rapidly deteriorating into an arduous afternoon of roasting in his own juices. He was desperate for this to be someone else's fault. He searched his memory for a suitable scapegoat, though no quantity of mental gymnastics seemed up to the task of producing one.

There was a pattern to his woes, a common denominator to each nagging misfortune that only the most obtuse of morons could miss. His many personality faults notwithstanding, the warden refused to succumb to self-delusion. If his day was going poorly, he had no one to blame but himself. No one had forced him to drink himself unconscious the night before, and no one had forced him to oversleep.

It was he who had failed to invest ten seconds in checking the weather before throwing on yesterday's clothes and getting out of his hotel room. Sullivan was miserable because his own choices made him late, and left a naked woman in his bed with a name he did not remember and a face he did not want to. He recalled heavy breasts, gin, bleach-blond hair, beer, and regret. Not necessarily in that order, either. Dejected, angry, and acutely uncomfortable, the warden marched up the concrete steps of the Hartford County Municipal Courthouse secure in the knowledge that the architect of his bad mood was none other than his own damn self. This was as it should be. This was his normal.

His face a mask of minimally-contained aggravation, Sullivan passed through the main doors of the brown stone building like a rolling thunderhead. His pace did not alter for doors or turnstiles, and brisk steps through the vestibule moved him into a wide, sunlit lobby. The open space was noisy with the dull rumble of voices pitched to a quiet yet conversational level. Before him, several neat lines of angry-eyed people shuffled and ambled through assorted security checkpoints. Sullivan scanned the sea of humanity, looking for signs of his quarry or perhaps the first indications of burgeoning trouble. He realized that a little trouble might serve to improve his mood, and then dismissed this as unhelpful. The last thing he needed was more headaches.

What he saw was the laborious plodding of a hundred faces, all cast into defeated expressions of impotent frustration. One by one, uniformed personnel manning the checkpoints ignored their dignity in an age-old act of fruitless security theater. Pockets were emptied, bags were searched, and as a final insult, the patrons of this municipal administration facility were made to step through a multi-threat scanning arch.

Sullivan nodded to himself, satisfied that if nothing else, the security meant he was unlikely to encounter any weapons upstairs. He brushed his way to the front of the line, drawing scowls and muttered expletives from the grouchy crowd. No one tried to stop him, of course. Each growled protest directed to his rudeness died when the affronted saw the height and width of the antagonist. None of those inclined to object understood exactly who he was just from looking at his retreating back, but Sullivan seemed to possess an indisputable air of authority. He exuded a particular species of institutional arrogance that cowed the crowd just like the cars on the street outside. A more perceptive observer would see this presence for what it really was: a personal shield of placid menace wreathing the big man like a dense fog of restrained violence. An angry lemming stuck in the interminable security line might not understand why their guts chose this moment to freeze into a block of ice, yet there was no question at all who was to blame. Each person, even through the obscuring haze of his or her own anger, ascertained in that instant that the rude man in the brown jacket was best left to his business.

Sullivan relied upon this phenomenon to maneuver himself without incident to the checkpoint. He did not bother to empty his pockets, nor did he deign to submit to the scan. He gave the doughy security marshal both a bland look of condescension and his ID. Then he merely waited for the underpaid rent-a-cop to comprehend what he was looking at.

This took four seconds, if one included the time wasted on a gape-mouthed double-take. The guard almost spoke, probably to blurt something stupid and guaranteed to panic the crowd, so the warden stopped him.

"Shut up," Sullivan said. This confused the guard, for he had not spoken yet. The warden did not care and pressed on. "Don't say a word. Just nod, look down at your screen, and wave me through. Don't call anyone or do anything, clear?"

"Got it," the man said, and he waved him through.

"I told you not to talk." Under more normal conditions, Sullivan would have blasted the incompetent oaf with a scathing diatribe, but his heart was not in it at the moment. He walked through the arch without bothering, content to let the clanging and pinging of the scanner startle the guard back into doing his job. Sullivan had a very good idea as to where he was going. He found his way to the stairwell and trotted up two flights. At the third-floor landing, a helpful sign illuminated the path to the office he needed, and moments later, the warden stood outside an old wooden door.

Here he paused. His hands went to his waist, fingertips just brushing the worn kydex holster on his right hip. His thumb slid along the retention strap and dragged across the knurling of his sidearm's grip scales before giving the gun a gentle press to ensure it was well-seated. It was an old habit—a bizarre affectation he had acquired over the years. It might be considered an understandable nod to caution. It was logical to check one's weapon before an arrest. Arrest and detention were inherently dangerous things. However, the tiny tic carried the insecure edge of something uncomfortable and incongruous. When other wardens checked their pistols before moving on a target, they looked like dedicated professionals ensuring a beloved tool was in its proper place. When Warden Sullivan patted his holstered sidearm, he seemed like a zookeeper making sure a dangerous animal remained securely locked up. He could have left the gun at home, he knew. The lack of it would have no impact on the outcome of this operation. Thanks to the mountain of intel recovered in Chicago, Sullivan had arrived quite secure in the knowledge that no guns would be needed today. Nevertheless, the uncomfortable weight of his pistol sat there as it always did. Two pounds of metal dragging one side of his pants down and chaffing his side raw through the sweaty cotton of his shirt. He had no intention of drawing the pistol or using it, and his conviction helped the small surge of anxiety pass almost unnoticed.

With a quiet grunt of resignation, Sullivan pressed his ID against the door panel and stepped through when it beeped. Inside the sparse office beyond, a man looked up to greet him. He sat at a table, papers strewn about and a digital notebook open. The man at the table was of medium height with an athletic build. His face was average-looking, wearing an ethnically-ambiguous tan and no other particularly striking features. His suit was dark and tailored, his hair brown and combed to perfection. The warden had to concede that if lawyers had a prototype, this guy was it.

"Excuse me?" The implied question came with an imperious tilt of the chin and sounded more than a little annoyed. "I believe I have this room today. But I only have one hearing left. It starts in twenty minutes, so you can use the room when I'm done."

"Don't need the room, counselor," Sullivan said. "Came to see you."

Something about that put the lawyer on edge. "Then you can make an appointment with my office. If you'll excuse me?" He gestured to the door with his stylus. "I'm very busy."

"It's okay. I've cleared your schedule, Mr. Langley." The warden had not meant for this to sound so menacing. Hearing his own words made him wince. "Sorry for the inconvenience and all that, but I think we should talk for a bit."

The man at the table put his stylus down and fixed his tormentor with an even glare. "You cleared my schedule? That's an interesting choice of words. You want to tell me who you are and what's going on?"

The warden leaned against the door, only incidentally blocking the only exit with his body. "My name is John Sullivan, and I am a Warden, First Class, with the Genetic Equity and Enforcement Department."

Sullivan always paused at this moment to gauge the reaction. Not every person he brought in even knew what they were, and the universe could not possibly send anyone worse than Warden John L. Sullivan to reveal so catastrophic a truth. This was not his fault. He was neurologically disinclined toward empathy at a very fundamental level.

The lawyer's response came with a tiny flinch, sparing Sullivan any further wasted efforts on this front. His tone was flat, calm, and professional. "I do not currently represent any GMPs, Warden Sullivan. If you have a complaint or a warrant for one of my clients, you could have simply taken it up with the office."

"That's true," Sullivan said with an affable nod. "But I'm not here for one of your clients."

"Then I can't imagine how I might help you, Warden."

That was the moment Sullivan knew that the lawyer understood his own status and the nature of his clientele. He was too cool, too detached. He gave too much away with this affected calm. First Class Wardens did not go on milk runs or do generic investigations. An innocent man would be confused and terrified in this situation. A low-level GMP often gave up at the first sign of someone like John Sullivan. Langley did no such thing. The lawyer held his ground, a challenge inherent in his stone-faced resistance to the obvious. Sullivan respected the attempt and returned the glare with his own level gaze.

Far more comfortable with the emerging paradigm, Sullivan switched tactics. "Track and field was a good call, Mr. Langley. Too many football players get tested. Track will still get you that good scholarship without attracting the wrong kind of attention. I'd have held off on setting the state record in pentathlon, though. Second place would have kept your scholarship without all the risk."

Langley's mouth twitched, an involuntary reaction that he covered by speaking. "So this is about me? You believe I have been modified for advantage? That is a serious charge, Warden Sullivan. I am happy to submit to whatever tests you would like to administer, but I must advise you I am deeply offended by your department's lack of procedural decorum in coming here to do it. You can expect my office to file a grievance with—"

"Oh, shut up," Sullivan interrupted with a wave of his hand. "I get that you think I'm here to test you. But I'm not. You'll test negative, anyway. Just like you did when you took the bar."

"What then? I am both confused and quite annoyed." Langley's eyes narrowed. "Answer carefully; your career depends upon it."

"If you don't mind, I'll do the threatening, counselor," Sullivan said. "You don't have the vocabulary for it. So now you think I sauntered up here to shake a confession out of you? The old 'I got my eye on you' routine? Maybe a little oblique departmental intimidation?"

Langley said nothing. Sullivan pressed on. "You aren't that lucky, counselor. I've done this dance so many times, I teach the steps at a local community college. I'm here because it's time for you to come in. Now, I'm willing to put you down as 'no prior knowledge' if you don't turn this into a big mess. We both know that's bullshit, but it makes no difference to me whether you do time before you enter state service. It's your clients we really want, anyway. You aren't shit compared to them."

Langley played his last card. "Do you have a warrant, Warden? Because if you don't, you have just pissed off the wrong lawyer." Sullivan assumed Langley thought this to be impossible. This was an understandable error. There were no SWAT officers blocking the exits, no containment wagon parked on the street. None of the usual elements of a GMP apprehension were present, so a bluff on the warden's part was not out of the question.

Sullivan himself would be the first to admit he lacked the imagination to bluff. In this case, he did not have to.

"I do."

Langley sat back in his chair, defeated. His lips parted, and a tiny "How?" escaped. He placed his head in his hands for several seconds, then managed to speak with volume. "It was supposed to be undetectable."

"It was. Your modifications were minor enough. No one was ever going to catch you with tests." Sullivan let a wan smile turn the corners of his mouth. "We got lucky. Two days ago, I raided one of your best clients' facilities. Included in the evidence we collected, there was a complete record from the lab your parents used. Your genotype was one of about six hundred still on file. Once we bounced the records from the lab through the database..."

"You found the match from my bar exam test," Langley finished. "Well done, Warden."

"It's the job." Sullivan stood up straight. "How do you want to do this? I didn't bring the wagon or a bunch of SWAT guys. If you want to do this cool and calm, I don't mind. No sense in making a scene. Like I said, I'll write you up as NPK. You are going to have to turn on your clients if you want to keep it that way, though. Nothing illegal about being a lawyer, so you won't hang for their crimes if you play ball."

"What happens if I don't want to go? I worked hard to get where I am. I've got a couple of mild athletic enhancements is all. Just enough to get me a full scholarship to a good school. Everything else I did on my own." The lawyer's composure was melting. "I earned this! I don't want to go be a prosecutor or public defender."

"What about the kid who didn't get the scholarship because you beat him for the spot? What's he up to these days?" Sullivan shrugged. He had heard all these arguments before. "Rules are rules, counselor. You have an unfair advantage, and you're supposed to know better."

"It's not fair." The man was whining now. He had lost, he was trapped, and his life would never be the same. For now, he was afraid, though Sullivan knew fear would yield to anger soon enough. "I didn't ask to be born this way. I never had a choice."

"You do now," the warden offered, not really believing it himself. "You can do a lot of good with your gifts. Help a lot of people. You will be the key to bringing down a lot of bad guys."

"I don't want to help people! And those bad guys will kill me!"

There it was. The anger. Sullivan welcomed the gravelly sound of rage-bitten invective like the old friend it was. It meant that this would be over soon.

"Well, I'm sorry then. But it's still time to come in. Can I convince you to walk out of here with your head up? Or are you going to try your luck?"

Sullivan watched the calculations going on behind Langley's eyes, saw conclusions drawn, decisions reached. It was the same every time. They all did the math, they all weighed the consequences. For some, it was easy. Those with nothing left to lose found the calculus quite simple, while people with much at stake had more to consider. In most cases, the result was the same, and Langley proved to be no better than a hundred others before him.

Langley leapt from his chair and surged toward Sullivan with a speed that was a credit to the lab that birthed him. The warden let him come, let the headlong tackle slam him into the door with a crash. He felt the bruise blossom across his ribs, hissed when the electric sting of his elbow striking the door frame followed. He smiled at the hot rush of pure fury that pain brought, the spike of danger that filled him with liquid heat and violent desire. Dopamine and endorphins flowed through his body in response, and his pain receded like the sea after a tsunami. This left only the joy of his boiling rage and the searing flush of a swelling bloodlust. He knew it would not last, so he hesitated, absorbing clumsy punches from his untrained opponent just to see if he could still feel them. He did not, and this bothered him far more than the lawyer's clumsy assault.

It was always this way. Sullivan's anger, his fury, his rage, were too ephemeral. They beckoned like a willing lover with a promise hot and sexual. He longed for the crescendo of emotion and the ecstasy of explosive physical release. Yet no matter how hard he tried, he could not get there. Something kept coming between them, soaking the heat of combat in a damp mental fog. It smothered what should have been a torrid embrace, converting it into the clumsy fumbling of teenagers.

His need to feel something normal amidst the intensity of a fight pushed him to new heights of recklessness. Just like the man in Chicago with the knife, Sullivan dared Langley to hurt him. Another punch connected with his temple. He could have stopped it, but he wanted something, *anything*, to hurt. A gaudy class ring dug into the flesh of Sullivan's head. This brought enough pain to send a blip of adrenaline through the calming layer of dopamine. For a tantalizing moment, he tasted the response from his amygdala. It lasted only an instant, this flash of anger seasoned with a dash of fear. Too quickly it faded, as all such moments did. What he wanted seemed so close, though the mere act of trying to seize the prize drove it away every time. The futility of it all maddened the warden, so he let the lawyer hit him a few more times in frustration.

Realizing that his quarry presented no answers for his deeper issues, an unsatisfied, unhappy, and bored Sullivan gave up on chasing satisfaction. With a defeated grunt, he stopped another sad punch with his palm and spun Langley into a choke hold. Twelve seconds later, Langley was unconscious.

CHAPTER FOUR

Sullivan left his department-mandated debriefing in a very different mood than was typical. Getting through the meeting was always a chore, though the well-meaning administrators usually decided what to write down before he even started to talk. This made it easy to tell them what they wanted to hear so he could leave without getting reprimanded. This meeting had not gone the way so many others had. He had given Langley too many free hits, he knew. The reviewers had not seemed pleased to hear about him eschewing procedure and going in solo, either. Sullivan accepted that the whole idea had been stupid and careless. He had been indulging these whims more often these days, and clever people were starting to notice when he acted out of character. He only barely understood why he behaved this way himself, and the last thing he needed was the department brass asking pointed questions about his actions. If what he suspected about his own brain chemistry turned out to be correct, his career and his life would end the moment anyone found out. For what felt like the thousandth time, Sullivan resolved himself to buckle down and get his head in the game. He refused to be a psychopath, no matter what his genetics said about it.

"Sully!"

The shouted greeting ripped the warden from his own thoughts and brought him back to the stark reality of his surroundings. He looked up to find a man of robust build and even more robust beard barreling down the bland, cream-colored hallway toward him. A clerk, being either too slow or too oblivious to take evasive action, bounced off the approaching giant. With a startled shout, the hapless man spun to the side, a cascade of papers spilling from a thick file to cover the floor.

"Erm, sorry," Warden First Class Patrick Fagan mumbled to the sprawled clerk. He even managed an apologetic wince.

The downed man seemed ready to let fly a scathing retort, but thought better of it when he saw the massive paw being extended his way. In preservation of his dignity, the clerk declined the offered assistance and set to collecting his scattered documents. Fagan shrugged and continued to head for Sullivan.

"You are going to kill someone someday, Fagan," Sullivan said.

"Well, I didn't pick the acromegaly life. My parents sort of picked it for me. Even with all those illegal optimizations, I don't have any fancy agility tricks like some people I could mention."

Fagan belonged to a select group of individuals who could both look Sullivan in the eye and make him appear small. He did this now, tilting the craggy mass of his heavy forehead toward the leaner man. "How much shit you in this time?"

"About the same. Brass is pissed at me for going off track again. They're happy I got the guy without a ruckus but..." He shrugged. "They aren't real big on my style."

Fagan snorted, rustling the whiskers of his prodigious beard. "Nobody is. Why you don't just do things by the book, I'll never know." He shook his head. "You've got to start letting me know when you want to go in without the full crew. You know I'll back you up. But I can't help you if you go off half-cocked."

Sullivan nodded his agreement. "Oh, I know, Fagan. I really was going to play this one straight, too. But it was so goddamn hot out there that I really wanted to get into some climate control. I kinda lost my temper a little, jumped the gun."

"Bullshit. You were hung over and impatient, and that's all it was. You'd think all your fancy genetic crap would give you a better tolerance for the booze."

"My tolerance is fine, buddy. The hangover is non-negotiable, I guess."

"Says you. I never get 'em," Fagan said with a shrug.

"You weigh like five hundred pounds, Fagan. Big-ass freak like you doesn't even get drunk like a normal person."

"Who are you calling freak, runt? At least I have two parents." The jibe might have set Sullivan's infamous temper off, except that Fagan, a seven-foot giant with the bone density of an elephant, got away with many things others could not. Sullivan suspected that the department had saddled him with Fagan as a partner precisely because the man was one of the few people in the talent pool Sullivan could not bully. Every once in a while, Fagan took a moment to remind his partner that neurological excuses notwithstanding, Mama Fagan's favorite son would only tolerate so much of Sullivan's legendary bad manners. Having accomplished this, the big man changed the subject. "You seen the captain yet?"

"Nope. How bad?"

"She probably won't kill you. Probably." Fagan bobbed his head from side to side, as if weighing the odds of something. "Pretty sure she's going to try to fire you. Again."

"She does seem to enjoy making the attempt from time to time." Sullivan squared his shoulders and continued his trek down the hall. "Let's go face the music, then."

Fagan fell in next to him. "Over-under on your ass-chewing is eighteen minutes, by the way," he said. "I took the over. Try to drag this out for me?"

"And people say I'm an asshole?"

"You *are* an asshole," Fagan said. "But you are the only asshole I know of with an official exemption for being an asshole. The rest of us have to deal with the consequences when we act like jerks. You get to hide behind your disability."

"You really like being the only guy who gets to run his mouth at me, don't you?"

"Everybody needs a guy like me. It's good for you."

"Maybe one of these days, we find out if you are as safe as you seem to think you are." Sullivan's irritation had more to do with his impending confrontation with his captain than Fagan's jabs, though he entertained no remorse about giving the giant a hard time.

Fagan remained unperturbed. "Anytime you feel froggy, runt, go ahead and jump."

"Not today, partner. My dance card is all full up." Crossing the organized chaos of the main office floor, the pair arrived at the captain's door. For all the implied peril of this meeting, a plain white panel with "Captain Elaine Horowitz" illuminated at eye level did not convey the proper level of dread.

It seemed Fagan detected the same disconnect as his partner. "I don't spell so well, Sully," he said with a goofy smile, a thick finger pointing at the letters on the door. "Does that read as 'abandon all hope, ye who enter here' to you?"

"It should, considering the three-headed demon bitch waiting on the other side, anyway."

Fagan winced. "You said it, not me. Make sure you tip the boatman."

Sullivan looked away from his partner to examine the main floor. As his gaze wandered over the open office, he found a constellation of faces fixed upon him and his giant partner. Like prairie dogs, the tops of heads and blinking eyes of three dozen spectators peered over the edges of gray cubicles. Sullivan saw equal parts pity and horror there, his oncoming doom reflected in the awestruck wonder of peasants watching a royal beheading. He understood their expressions; he stood before a fate many considered worse than death.

Sullivan turned to address the eager faces across the room. His fellow wardens and support staff looked back, some anxious to see him fail, others concerned for his career, more than a few hoping to make a few dollars on the coming storm. He intoned with mock solemnity, "We who are about to die, salute you!" The accompanying salute was more of an obscene hand gesture, and he continued in his mock oration. "Okay, folks. Before I go in there to die in glorious battle with Lady Spitemaw, axe-wielding demon-queen of Premenstria, I want you all to know that I hate you and hope nothing but bad things happen to all of you."

This earned him a few chuckles from the crew and a groan from Fagan. The door speaker came to life with the irritated sounds of a woman who had heard every word Sullivan had just said. "Get your ass in here, Sullivan. Fagan, you can wait outside. Don't tell me the over-under, either."

Fagan looked to his partner. "I'd say it's been nice knowing you, but c'mon. We all know you're a total dick."

"Yeah, well, put flowers on my grave, all right?"

"Sure. Maybe. It could happen."

Sullivan palmed the door panel and waited for the click. When the door slid open, he stepped through. Inside the captain's office, a single desk sat on a boring white tile floor. A few file cabinets lined one wall, and a lone bookshelf stood against another. Several awards, citations, and framed letters from prominent citizens hung behind the black leather chair where sat Captain Elaine Horowitz.

Her back was ramrod straight, her hands folded atop the desk. Eyes the color of cafe mocha beamed pure disdain like lasers at Sullivan from under her short black bangs. She wore a gray suit, tailored to fit, though not particularly stylish. A narrower cut to the jacket would have showed off a lean figure; however, the need to keep her service weapon accessible meant a boxier silhouette had been selected. She may have been forty years old, or sixty. It was hard to tell, and Sullivan had never been brave enough to ask her age.

"Are you trying to get fired, Warden?"

She often began with a question like this. Sullivan found it tiresome, so he replied with a question of his own. "Are you going to fire me for bringing a GMP in without using a bunch of department resources unnecessarily?"

The look in her eyes told Sullivan exactly how she felt about this response. "I'd tell you not to be an asshole, Warden, but I guess you don't really have a choice, do you?"

"That sounded suspiciously like a violation of GEED's genetic sensitivity in the workplace policy, Captain. My personality is a function of my unique circumstances."

"File a complaint, then." The captain declined to rise to his bait. "I could use a paid week off after that shit you pulled."

"Help me out, Cap." Sullivan feigned confusion. "I brought the guy in, nobody got hurt, no big scene. What's the problem?"

"Procedure exists to protect both the subject and the department. We have no witnesses for what went on in there. What if he tried to sue? He could make up anything he wanted, and we couldn't deny it."

"I left my telemetry on—"

The captain slapped her desk hard enough to make Sullivan jump. "It was a courthouse, you fucking clod! Worse, you took him down in a lawyer's conference room! They jam everything for attorney-client privilege! There is no telemetry!" She stood, leaning across her desk to make sure Sullivan heard every word. "He's a lawyer. A very good, very wealthy one. We have no telemetry to back our side of the story. You brought no backup to corroborate your account. Do you know how many complaints, charges, and motions he's filed since you brought him in yesterday?"

Sullivan did not, though he recognized the rhetorical nature of the question. When he remained silent, the captain answered for him.

"Fourteen." She sat again, looking far more tired than angry. "Your union rep is already sorting through them. Nothing will stick, but he'll use them to plead into an NPK. Because of your stupidity, that perp will walk out of here a free man."

"Nothing free about it," Sullivan reminded her. "He's in the system now. No more cushy partner's office at his firm, no political aspirations, no big dreams of wealth and power." Sullivan met her eyes. "Just a government job and the satisfaction of knowing his gifts will help make society better for everyone. Before all his old clients have him murdered, that is. I give him a year at best."

"You know damn well what I meant, Sullivan. We had that bastard on a clean-as-you-please Cognizant of Modification Advantage charge, and CoMA charges are why you have a job in the first place, *Warden.*" She twisted the last word, injecting it with a merciless combination of sarcasm and derision. "We could have used the threat of a CoMA conviction to pressure him into flipping on his clients. Thanks to you, he's buttoned up tighter than a schoolgirl's blouse."

"Sounds like you and I went to very different schools," he quipped. The thundercloud rolling across his captain's face reminded him that his comedic timing needed a lot of work.

In a rare display of forbearance, Horowitz ignored his bad manners and plowed ahead with the berating. "We have no case and no leverage. If you hadn't tripped over that pile of evidence in Chicago, you'd be cleaning your locker out over this one. So if I was in your shoes, right about now I'd be trying like hell to demonstrate my value to the people who have a say in my career."

Something burned hot in Sullivan's chest. "And what the fuck does that mean?"

The captain matched his heat with her own. "It means there's a whole ton of people out there who think you are too dangerous to be on the street. It means that every time you act like the rules don't matter, you give them a reason to ship you somewhere where you don't cause so much trouble. It means that incidents like yesterday make me think those people might be right."

"My head's in the game, Captain. I can't believe I'm standing here getting chewed out for the crime of bringing in a GMP with no issues and little cost. I do the job, Captain. I do it better than anyone. I've never apologized for how I do it, and I won't start now. If the powers that be can't handle it, they can come down here and tell me themselves."

"Oh, spare me, Sullivan. Better than anyone else? I know for a fact your ass was hungover. Then, in a fit of uninspired stupidity, you took your grouchy, hungover self into that building without backup. On top of that brilliant play, you proceeded to get your ass kicked by a level one GMP who was good at throwing the discus."

The accuracy of her analysis disturbed Sullivan on several embarrassing levels. He thought he did a good job of covering his look of chagrin. He was wrong.

"Never pretend I don't know everything already," the captain said. "You aren't that clever. If you want to keep your job here, you need to get over whatever it is that has you self-destructing like a narcissistic teenager out there. People are noticing, and considering your unique circumstances, getting noticed is not a good thing."

"Nobody seems to mind when I get the job done, though."

"If that was true, Warden, then I wouldn't be sitting here staring at your new counseling schedule."

Sullivan's face turned dark. "I've been assigned to counseling?"

The captain accepted her victory with grace. "Absolutely. Straight from top brass and approved through your own union. Your new counselor is no county-level civil servant, either. They're sending professor Stephen Connors from Yale. He specializes in GMPs with neurological modifications for aggression. He was very excited to get to work with a famous chimera." She slowed her cadence, enunciating as if speaking to a dull-witted child. "There are a lot of very powerful eyes on you right now, Warden."

"I can handle him."

"No, you can't. But whatever. I'm supposed to inform you that your sessions with Doctor Connors are now weekly and mandatory."

"Weekly? What the hell?" Sullivan tried to protest further, but the captain silenced him with a wave.

"Your own fault, Warden. Furthermore, when you are on assignment, you are to have Warden Fagan with you at all times. That's from our lawyers, and it is non-negotiable. You want to run off and play cowboy? Then you take the bull with you. He understands procedure and will at least give a corroborating witness for whatever stupidity you end up compelled to inflict upon our poor department."

The muscles in Sullivan's jaw worked beneath the skin of his cheeks, and Horowitz smiled. The curl of her mouth was devoid of warmth, and she cooed with fake sympathy. "Don't like it? Aw, too bad. You wanted to be different? You wanted to do things your own way? Congratulations. This is what you get. Good luck with it."

Sullivan stared at the woman, judging the set of her jaw and the steely glint of her eyes. Her look was a challenge, a double-dog dare for a stupid teenager. She wanted him to be stupid, to say something actionable. He could sense it, and she did not care. When the stare-down had gone on far too long, the captain looked down at her desk. She stabbed her keyboard a few times with her finger and said, "You and Fagan are on the eight a.m. 'loop to Charlotte. The tech nerds are struggling, but they've busted into more of the Chicago files. Apparently, there is a good-sized facility there that's churning out GMPs. I want you two to surveil, assess, and if feasible, apprehend anyone involved. You will have Municipal LEO assets." She reaffixed her seething glare. "Use those assets if you value your career, Warden."

"Eight a.m. to Charlotte? I just got back—"

He wanted to push, to rant, to argue. She shut him down before he could get rolling with a sharp head shake and a curt, "The bad guys know we are onto them. They are going to start pulling up stakes and running for cover. You and Fagan need to secure as many arrests as possible before they do. So get your ass to bed on time tonight. Lay off the booze, and steer clear of any loose women, too. Now, head down the hall and meet the shrink. I suggest you try very hard to be impressive. He holds the keys to your career with the department." The captain did not look like she liked his chances. She added a final admonition. "Eyes are on your ass, Sullivan. Try to look like a professional for once." She waved to the door behind Sullivan. "Dismissed, Warden."

CHAPTER FIVE

"Am I boring you, Warden?"

Doctor Connors wore a crooked smile. His bright white teeth peeked between thin lips drawn tight, amused wrinkles framing his mouth with shadowed parentheses. Sullivan disliked the man immediately. He had that aloof sort of condescension that told you in no uncertain terms exactly how much smarter than you he was. For a psychiatrist, he looked fit. There were no signs that academic indolence had softened his features, nor had the sedentary life of a department shrink rounded his silhouette to any appreciable extent. It was strange and incongruous, therapeutic detachment paired with the physique of an athlete.

Sullivan deferred his initial rude retort and elected to complain. "Nah, Doc. It just feels like I've done this all before, you know? It's like deja vu."

The doctor's smile widened. "I bet it does. I apologize if I'm making you repeat yourself, but since this is our first session, I'd like to hear what you have to say about what happened."

"You read the report, so you already know what I have to say."

"Oh, don't be difficult, Warden. I'm a slave to my job description as much as you are. Let's just get through it, okay?"

"Fine."

Irritated, Sullivan leaned forward to assume a more comfortable posture for conversation. Though a large man, he was not enormous. Four inches past six feet tall, broad at the shoulder and narrow at the waist, he cut an imposing figure without coming off as gargantuan. A pale complexion and a dense field of sandy stubble on both his face and his head spoke of distant gallic heritage, and weary blue eyes gleamed with dull luster under heavy brows. His own expression was wry, as if the current situation amused him in some inscrutable and perverse manner. When he spoke, it was with a bored and practiced narrator's tone.

"I received confirmation that the suspected GiMP was inside the building at one-six-five Garamond."

The doctor interrupted. "Ah, Warden? I don't really approve of that term. It's derogatory and inappropriate."

Lips peeled back in a feral grin. "I get to use it. It's a GiMP thing. Don't worry, I'm hard to offend."

The doctor waved for him to continue, "Fine, then. Have it your way. Where were you again? The Hartford building?"

"Yes."

"Go on."

The warden leaned back against the couch and resumed his bland oration. "My reconnaissance indicated that the building was not fortified, and I noticed that the existing security measures precluded the likelihood of armed opposition. I elected at that time to enter the facility to attempt apprehension of the Genetically Modified Person." He layered the formal designation with feigned disdain.

The doctor let it slide. "You did not call for back-up?"

"I did not."

After an uncomfortable pause, the doctor gave an impatient wave of his stylus. "Care to elaborate?"

"Do I have to?"

"You aren't being investigated, Warden. I'm here to ascertain your mental health and your state of mind. It does not bother me one whit that you went in alone. I just want to know why."

Sullivan sighed. "Sure, you do. I went in alone because I didn't think I needed any help. The profile said this guy had minimal upgrades, a non-combative personality, and no special training. Hell,

I figured I could talk him into coming in without an issue. He was a one, maybe one-point-five, GMOD rating at best. Barely a decent CAPpie."

"Cappy?" Connors looked up from his notes. "You'll forgive me if I'm not current with your industry jargon..."

"Collegiate Athletics Package. It's what you buy if you want your kid to get a college athletic scholarship but don't want him to stand out too much. Really hard to detect."

"Ah, I see. Go on."

"I figured if I rolled up on him with a squad of SWAT guys and a wagon, he'd have bolted for sure. At least this way, he had a chance to come in without getting the crap kicked out of him."

"So you merely wanted to have a clean apprehension with a minimum of fuss?"

"Exactly."

"Even though that is clearly in violation of current department policy?"

"You've seen my file, Doc. I think you can figure out how much I appreciate department policy."

The doctor chuckled at this gross understatement. "Fair point. Back to you attempting to apprehend the GMP. How did that go?"

The tall man's eyes narrowed. "He chose not to come along quietly, obviously."

"I read as much in the report. Here is what has me confused, though." The doctor leaned forward now, eyes scanning the warden's face for clues. "This man had a GMOD rating of one-point-five at best. You said so yourself."

"Yeah?"

"The medical report says you suffered bruised ribs, a sprained elbow, and multiple contusions during the apprehension."

"Guy was motivated."

"Warden?"

"Yeah?"

"What is your current rating?"

The warden paused, lips pressed tight, eyes piercing. At last, he said, "Neuro-motor is like a seven. Physicals run between five and seven depending on which criteria you isolate for."

The doctor nodded. "Five through seven across several categories? I've been working with Chinese military GMPs for sixteen years, Warden. I've never met a seven in *any* category before." He glanced down at the papers on his desk and stated with bland authority, "Among your dozens of other illegal modifications, you were born with myostatin inhibition, hyperosteoplasia, enhanced neuroplasticity, neuromotor hyperkinesia, and a full suite of experimental neurological aggression tweaks." His eyes came back up to meet his patient's. "Warden, you were three times as strong, twice as fast, and much better-trained. How on earth did this one-point-five even raise a welt on you?"

"Like I said. He was motivated."

"In Chicago, you incapacitated three armed men with your bare hands rather than shoot them, is that correct?"

"I had the drop on them. Seemed more humane than gunning them down."

The doctor leaned back, satisfied. "I have a theory. Do you want to hear it?"

"It's your hour, too, I guess. As long as the department is paying for it, talk all you want."

"Thank you." The doctor folded his hands in front of his face and met the eyes of his patient. "You don't like to hurt people, do you?"

"Does anyone?"

"That's evasive. I mean you have a very strong aversion to violent conflict."

"I was created by a mobster to hurt people professionally. Violent conflict is sort of my thing."

"Oh, I've read the file, Warden. You are very good at violence, but you appear to go to great lengths to avoid it. Or to at least use the least amount possible."

"Is that a problem?"

"Not usually. But in your case, it makes me wonder. Your brain was modified to overproduce every aggression chemical we know of. Your acetylcholine numbers are insane, and your dopamine response to anger has been carefully altered to modulate your baseline aggression several standard deviations above the mean. Your GABA receptivity effectively makes you immune to fear or anxiety, even under heavy adrenal response. All these alterations were designed to make you mean as all hell without turning you into a rabid animal. You ought to love a good fight, but instead, I see a pattern of deliberate forbearance in your career. I would like to explore the reasons for that."

"Because me not wanting to mangle folks who can't fight back means I'm crazy?"

"No, because your aversion to operating at your full capabilities is getting you hurt. Since that aversion does not appear to be neurochemical in origin, I have to assume it is a deliberate choice to self-harm."

"You think I like getting beat up?"

"No. But I do think you *want* to get beat up."

The warden's lip curled in an ugly half smile that did not touch his eyes. "Now you sound crazy, Doc."

"I know it." The doctor's answering grin seemed genuine, at least. "But I requested your case deliberately because I think you need help, and we both know you were never going to ask for it."

"You're going to save the sad, crazy GiMP, Doc? This a charity thing?" The warden shook his head in a slow arc. "Let me save you some white guilt, pal. I don't need saving. Somebody put a lot of effort into growing themselves a vicious, hardcore killer." He gestured to himself with both hands. "What they got was me, Warden First Class John Sullivan, the department's most legendary grouchy asshole. Maybe I'm just saving my aggression for the guy who ruined any chance of me having a normal life. Maybe I just like knowing that while that piece of garbage rots in prison, I'm out here doing everything I can to not be the thing he spent millions trying to make. Every time I get punched by some low-level GiMP runner, it makes that jerk look even more stupid. Hell, doc, I have so much endorphin sensitivity, it doesn't even hurt that much."

"So to spite your father, you let people beat you up?" Something in the doctor's voice betrayed frank disbelief.

"Father?" The warden snorted. "Yeah, right. Exactly how much of his DNA did I actually get? You read the file. You know damn well I don't have a father. I have a financier. I was a product he paid for, that's it. Joke's on him, eh? Hope he kept the receipt."

"When did you speak to him last?"

"Mickey Sullivan? Why the hell does that matter?"

"Because maybe if you told him these things, you wouldn't need to get punched in the face so much." The doctor said this as if it was obvious.

The warden did not share his conviction, and spat back, "What? You want me to talk it out with the guy? Get closure?" The tall man barked a harsh laugh, an unhappy guffaw layered with contempt and scorn. "Oh, that's rich, Doc. The guy is a mob boss. He thinks buying and selling people is a game. He hurts anybody he wants to for fun and profit." The warden made a vulgar hand gesture for emphasis before continuing. "The sick bastard wanted the ultimate successor and paid to have me stitched together from a menu of other folks' DNA, just so he could have a son his rich friends would be envious of. He actually hand-picked the mixed bag of brain mods that has me spending my life perpetually pissed off." Sullivan seemed to collapse back into the couch, his voice trailing off even as his body sank into the cushions. "If I get anywhere near that piece of crap, I can't promise I won't kill him outright. Won't 'Dad' be proud then?"

If the warden's sudden increase in intensity concerned the doctor, he gave no outward signs of it. He remained distressingly composed. "I don't like to think in terms of closure, Warden. It's outdated as a concept, really. I'm talking about directing your anger toward the appropriate targets, and not turning it inward, as you seem so very intent upon doing. To put it simply, you don't need to hurt yourself to punish him. You could easily get satisfaction any number of other ways. I think you are smart enough to know this, so frankly, I don't believe your silly little 'I hate my dad so I misbehave' line. Even if my predecessors did."

The bluntness of the accusation startled the warden. The doctor noted this, and his eyes sparkled with glee. "Warden, I am aware you have had three other counselors before me. I have read all their notes, and I can see that you are very good at saying all the things they want to hear. Let's get one thing straight before we continue. What you need to start processing inside your angry little brain is that I can smell bullshit from a mile away, and brother, you stink of it. When we started, I wondered if you were bullshitting yourself, too, but now I'm pretty sure you aren't. That's good. I can work with that."

"So I'm full of shit?" The warden tried to sound confident, though the doctor heard the catch in his retort, a nearly infinitesimal moment of doubt.

"Up to your eyeballs, Warden. But I don't mind. This is my job."

"So you figure you got me pegged, huh?"

"I'm not even trying to 'peg' you, Warden. I just want you to tell me the truth and let me help you realize your full potential."

This seemed to strike sparks off something inside the warden. The big man's spine stiffened, and the muscles of his jaw worked in soundless rhythm for a long moment. When he finally spoke, the words came heavy with undisguised frustration. "My full potential,

Doc? So I can be a good little federal agent and do the best possible job for the benefit of society?"

The doctor managed to mask his sudden delight at getting a response that appeared real and not fabricated for effect. "That is generally the job description, yes." It was a goad. When the warden was angry, it seemed he lost his ability to obfuscate.

"What if I want to do something else with my life? It's got to be a government job, of course. Can't have GiMPs like me competing in the private sector, can we? I don't suppose they would let me work in child care. Or maybe I can get a gig at the DMV."

The doctor did not rise to the bait. "You lack the temperament for either. But there are many state jobs you would be suited for. You'd make a fine Executive Protection Agent, or perhaps a position with one of the anti-terrorism divisions. I can think of a dozen state departments that would kill to get someone like you on the payroll. Yet you stay with the Genetic Equity Enforcement Department."

"What can I say? I seem to gravitate towards my own kind."

Sullivan had caught himself before giving too much away. For all his loutish bad humor, the warden had a certain primal cunning. The doctor made a note about it in the file, then tried to push him some more. "How do you feel about your career? Do you like your work?"

"The work is fine, for what it is. Running down GiMPs is exciting enough. The office environment stinks. I figure you probably already got that much from my file."

The doctor chuckled. "Yes, your abilities in the field are far more impressive than your interpersonal skills."

Now, the warden grinned. "I was made to be an asshole. You try hanging around the office with my brain chemistry and see how you do."

"It's a fair point, Warden. How are you coping? I know how often my co-workers get on my nerves, so I can't imagine trying to manage it in your situation."

The warden shrugged. "Mostly, I try to keep my mouth shut. Back when dear old dad still had me, I got to spend lots of time with different teachers. Some of them were shrinks like you, some were weird, mystical, hippie Zen types. I learned a lot about keeping my eyes on the prize and letting stuff go."

The doctor nodded. "So you do deep breathing, mindfulness, that sort of thing?"

"Well, I also picture throwing a lot of people through windows. It relaxes me."

A slightly graying eyebrow rose at this. "Yet when the time comes to actually throw someone through a window, you hesitate. What stops you? What exerts control over your actions when that feeling comes?"

The warden intoned his reply with overwrought solemnity. "When you act in anger, you surrender your will to the thing angering you. If you allow that to happen, you lose the only thing that was ever really yours."

"Control," the doctor replied evenly. "Very profound. Was it a psychiatrist or a hippie who taught you that?"

Sullivan shook his head. "Judo teacher." When the doctor merely nodded at this, Sullivan elaborated. "The only guys who ever got me were the combat tutors. Big surprise there, right?"

The doctor agreed with a wry wink. "I am simply shocked to hear it, Warden. Did you find that you preferred the company of these, uh, combat tutors?"

"Of course." Sullivan said it as if this should have been obvious. "Picture me at fourteen years old, hormones surging, my brain literally drowning in aggression enhancers. I was already six feet tall and could bench 350. The only time I wasn't walking around with a throbbing rage-boner was when I got to train with those guys."

"Really?" Now the doctor felt like he was getting somewhere. It was as if Sullivan wanted to talk about this. "I would think that the training could be very dangerous under those conditions. You had the strength of a powerful man and the maturity of an angry child. What happened if you got angry enough with an instructor to hurt them?"

The warden looked at the doctor as if he had said something profoundly stupid. "Well, Doc," he replied with desert-dry inflection, "I'm guessing you have never rolled with a Brazilian jiu-jitsu champion before. Or boxed with a middleweight contender. Or played at singlesticks with an Escrima master."

"Well," the doctor matched the sarcastic tone with one of his own, "would you believe I haven't?"

"Yeah," Sullivan acknowledged. "I figured. There are levels to everything, right? At the time, I was nowhere near good enough to hurt these guys, physical advantages or not. Sure, I got away with a lot more mistakes than I should have because I was so big and athletic, but that wasn't enough of a boost to put me on their level. For all his bad qualities, the old man knew how to pick the right kind of instructors for me. If my aggression made me stupid, those guys were really good at reminding me of why I should try to be smarter."

"You sound happy about that."

"It was the only time I could cut loose, Doc. I could swing as hard as I wanted to, push as hard as I could without fear. They let me do it. Hell, they encouraged it. They let me explore my bad temper and didn't judge me when I lost control of it. If I went too far and lost my head, they slapped me back down to reality. They were on another level, and because of that, they had nothing to fear from me. I figured out that I really wanted to be on that level, too. The kind of level where nothing made you angry because you were just that damn good."

Connors made a surreptitious note of the warden's choice of words there. He looked up to see that Sullivan was not paying attention to him at all.

"They didn't care that I was a GiMP, either. I was just an angry kid who was never going to beat his frustration if he didn't learn to understand it. I needed discipline, and enough practice to make it stick. They made sure I got both. I started out hating them, but in the end, I wanted to be just like them."

The doctor sat back, at last understanding. "So that's why you let them hit you? You're trying to be like your old instructors?"

Sullivan shifted, a subtle and uncomfortable hitch that told the doctor he had won this round. The warden exhaled through his nose, the sound a soft, irritated snort of defeat. In the end, he simply told the truth. "Life as a Genetically Modified Person can be a prison, Doc. You didn't ask for the mods, but everybody hates you for having them. The government tells you where you can work, what you can do, and watches you like a goddamn criminal. Sure, we're not slaves, and it's technically illegal to discriminate against us. But let's be honest. We're second-class citizens with first-class capabilities. It can get to a guy, living in that kind of world. When runners see me coming, they know the jig is up. I try to give them one last chance to be themselves before they have to start being who the state tells them, too. Whatever they choose, I try to handle it as well as my instructors did."

The doctor took it all in with a furrowed brow. "And you can do this because they are not on your level."

The warden shrugged again. "You've read my file, Doc. You know they aren't."

CHAPTER SIX

"I don't care what she says, Fagan. This is some bullshit!"

Fagan did not deserve Sullivan's ire, though the giant found himself taking the brunt of it anyway. Sullivan understood this. He would feel guilty later, but his counselling session had put him in a black mood, and the tirade flowed without restraint. "Horowitz can't just ship me out on a whim because I pissed her off!"

"Yes, she can," Fagan said, though Sullivan was not listening.

"I just got back from Connecticut, and now she has me on a goddamn 'loop to Charlotte? I've been back less than thirty-six hours!"

"Mayhap it's not about you?" the big man offered.

Sullivan carried on as if he had not heard Fagan's sensible question. "She wants me to quit. She can't fire me, so she's just gonna keep pissing me off until I quit."

"By sending you on hugely important operations filled with opportunities for career-making busts?" Fagan shook his head. "Truly a wily strategist, our Captain Horowitz."

"She probably has it in for GiMPs, too. She's discriminating against me."

"Sixty percent of field operatives are GMPs, Sully. You're really reaching for this one."

Sullivan kicked his chair hard enough to flip it into the wall of his cubicle. Fully aware of his occasional tantrums, most agents responded with wry head shakes and returned to their work.

"Let's grab a beer," Fagan offered. "I figure you owe me for making me lose my bet."

With a start, Sullivan realized what sort of spectacle he was making. His face fell, and he spared a moment for a long internal rebuke. Once composed, he turned back to Fagan. "So, I owe you beer because Horowitz kicked me out of my own ass-chewing too fast?" Sullivan shook his head. "For a law-enforcement type, you sure have a weird sense of justice."

Fagan clapped the chagrined warden on a drooping shoulder. "Yeah, well, she had me in there for most of an hour, jerk. I got a list of things I gotta keep you from doing that's as long as my arm." Fagan extended a ropey limb for emphasis. "*My* arm, pal."

Sullivan started to head toward the exit. As was his way, he tried to hide his embarrassment from anyone watching by moving fast and looking straight ahead. "I still can't figure out why she's so pissed," Sullivan muttered as he fled the scene. "I got our guy, no big incident. The lack of telemetry just means he gets an NPK and walks. So what?"

As fast as he was, there was no competing with Fagan's gargantuan strides. The other man kept pace with ease. "She likes to get those CoMA convictions, man. It's why she's the boss."

They passed the bullpen at high speed. Sullivan's embarrassment receded when he noticed most of the staff had already left for the day. If only a few people saw him lose control, it became easier to pretend the outburst had never occurred. Oblivious to Sullivan's discomfort, Fagan waved to the few remaining people still pattering at their keyboards. One waved back without looking up. The rest ignored the pair, as was typical for anytime Sullivan's temper got the better of him. Fagan scowled at the perceived slight. Sullivan allowed that Fagan was a likable guy, and people snubbing him probably stung a little. A more sympathetic man might have experienced guilt over this. Sullivan did not. At the best of times, he enjoyed a very limited ability to experience sympathy, and under duress, it disappeared entirely. The elevator ride to the lobby was quick, and to Sullivan's delight, silent. The two men stepped from the car and into the wide atrium of the GEED main offices without saying a word. With hopes for a quiet walk to the bar soaring, Sullivan began an aggressive stalk toward the main doors.

Mere seconds later, Sullivan swept through the exit doors with his enormous shadow in tow, and upon the sidewalk, he voiced his unconditional surrender to the larger man's determined pursuit. "I'm not getting rid of you, am I?"

"Nope. I got orders."

Fagan's smile blunted the sharp finality of the uttered syllables. Sullivan wanted to be angrier. He was in a broody, grumbly, drinky mood, and the big man's damnable affability was ruining his chances for a proper sulk. Fagan was too fast to outrun, too big to fight, and too nice to stay mad at. Sullivan shook his head and growled. "You're killing me, man. I'm trying to be a dick here, and you aren't getting with the program."

"You're a dick all the time. I stopped noticing a while ago." Fagan slapped him on the back with an enormous mitt, staggering the smaller man. "I might be the only person in the world who will have a beer with you willingly, so an asshole like you might as well take advantage of that."

Sullivan turned and started to walk. In the height of summer, the five-thirty streets of Albany were still bright and warm. Like the GEED facility, most of the other businesses on their block were disgorging their employees onto the clean concrete of the sidewalks in earnest. The steady flow of relieved office drones as they filed toward 'loop stations swept along the rolling pedestrian lanes like a laconic flash flood. Others meandered on foot in the direction of food and drink, a swarm of eager-eyed faces moving as one hungry mass. Ever the determined misanthrope, Sullivan did not mask his disgust with what he saw. The average urban office worker lived a life rich in fast food and poor in exercise, and it showed. Numerous government programs designed to combat the first-world obesity epidemic had done little to blunt the appetites of the disheveled masses. Hundreds of portly middle managers waddled along red-faced and huffing, satchels clutched under flabby arms as they shuffled as quickly as they could onto moving paths. The paths would take them to trams or automated taxis. These would subsequently move them to their doorsteps without so much as a wayward footstep to risk elevating the labored beating of their atrophied hearts. Inside their efficient little hovels, each would sit in front of their screens and eat junk food until sleep took them or diabetes killed them.

Fagan saw the disgust on Sullivan's face, and having heard his opinions on the average citizen's dedication to fitness, the giant decided to let it lie. "Come on, runt," he grunted. "Let's go get that beer."

Speakers chimed the various transportation schedules to those who cared to listen, and the occasional obnoxious buzz announced the folly of those oblivious enough to step out into the streets before the all-seeing eyes of the traffic grid had given them leave to do so. One such interruption reminded Sullivan to turn his department identification card to "silent" mode. He tried and failed to accomplish this without his chaperone's knowledge.

"You aren't supposed to do that," Fagan pointed out. "You are already in trouble for your crappy signal discipline. Don't beg for more, man."

"Are you going to be like this all the time?" Sullivan groused. "'Cause that shit is going to get real old real fast." He tucked the ID card back into his inside pocket. "I'm not interested in having the department watching my every move, all right? I aim to get drunk, and I aim to get laid tonight. If I wanted Horowitz in on that, I'd have invited her."

"Okay, that's now in my head forever. So much for my libido." Fagan shuddered.

"Imagine the disappointment of all those women out there with sasquatch fetishes. I truly am a monster."

"There's truth in that," Fagan said. "They got websites and everything."

"Wow," Sullivan snorted. "Now my libido is gone."

"Imagine the disappointment of, well nobody, really," Fagan shot back, flashing a broad grin.

Sullivan snorted and ignored the remark. "I figure the captain has about as much interest in my bad habits as you do. Technically, I'm doing her a favor. Now she has plausible deniability, and the department doesn't get to keep track of who I bang after work."

"The data gets deleted after twenty-one days," Fagan pointed out.

"Sure it does, Fagan."

The usual GEED watering hole was a scant two blocks from their building and the wardens arrived after only a few minutes. This proved a welcome relief, and Sullivan stopped at the entrance. He did not pause to catch what his partner had to say, but to gesture to the door before them. Softly illuminated letters emblazoned across the wooden double doors beamed "The Black Hole" in warm red light. It painted an unhealthy crimson tinge to their skin in the fading afternoon sunlight. "We're here. If I buy you some beer, will you keep my personal life to yourself?"

"Only one way to find out," replied the bearded giant, who stepped past his partner into the pub.

The wardens pushed through the waiting crowd around the hostess station and picked empty seats at the bar. Sullivan was able to sit down, while Fagan took a moment to assess the structural integrity of the barstool. The smaller man eyed his giant companion before turning his gaze to the arrayed taps. "I hate drinking with you." Sullivan lamented with a weary head shake. "This is going to suck. I just know it."

"It's not my fault I don't get drunk like you do." Fagan, still standing, flexed like a bodybuilder. By some miracle, the seams of his jacket held against the sudden pressure of his nearly five hundred pounds of bone and muscle. He grinned like an idiot, completing his comical pose with a flourish before lowering himself onto the barstool. "My body is as much a curse as your bad attitude, man. Blame my parents."

Sullivan scoffed at this, refusing to acknowledge his partner's antics. "Having to shop at the big and tall stores is not the same as being angry at the whole planet every waking moment."

"You have any idea how much my joints hurt, all the time?" Fagan said, his tone much more serious. "Or how hard it is to do anything in a world designed for people half your size? I can't fly on commercial flights, I can't buy a regular car, I can't even use public toilets." He gestured to the stool below. "Christ, this thing is halfway into my colon right now."

Sullivan had to acknowledge that he had not considered any of that. "That does kind of suck."

"And yet, I keep my sunny disposition. You want me to tell you how I do it?"

"Can I stop you?"

"No."

"Do tell, then."

The big man signaled the bartender before proceeding. "Two of those IPAs please," he rumbled politely.

"I don't like IPAs," Sullivan said.

Fagan curled a lip, which made his beard wiggle. "They're both for me, dumbass. Order your own beer."

"I'll have a Stella," Sullivan said.

When the bartender had left them to pour the drinks, Fagan turned on his stool to face his partner. "You know what your problem is?"

"I have a three-page diagnosis that spells it all out."

"Not that shit. Your real problem."

Sullivan leaned back and spread his arms. "Why don't you save me a lot of grief and just tell me."

Fagan shrugged. "You're grouchy and angry because your old man fucked with your brain. But you are an asshole because you like being an asshole."

"Really?"

"Yup."

The arrival of their drink order interrupted the conversation. The bartender asked if they wanted food, and before Sullivan could decline, Fagan said, "Two of those giant pretzel apps with the cheese, a plate of the nachos, and uh... how about three dozen buffalo wings."

Wiser now, Sullivan asked, "Any of that food for me?"

"It's all apps. We can share those."

"I just realized we have something else in common, Fagan."

"What's that?"

"Appetite." Sullivan took a pull from his beer. "Between the severe myostatin inhibition making my muscles grow, and neuromuscular hyperkinesia jacking my metabolism, I'm always starving. If I don't eat six thousand calories a day, I start to shrink."

Fagan chuckled. "Yeah, but you get about half that in booze, I hear."

Sullivan accepted the barb with grace. "A third at most. How about you?"

"I eat between eight and ten thousand calories a day. But I'm a foot taller and two hundred pounds heavier than you."

Sullivan sighed and looked back to his glass. "Yet another perk of that sweet GiMP life, right?"

"See, that's what I'm talking about right there."

"What?"

"You're being an asshole when you don't have to be."

"Because I said 'GiMP?'"

"Yup. You know damn well that word hurts people. You *choose* to say it because you *want* it to hurt someone."

"I didn't think you'd be so sensitive."

"I'm not, but others might be. That's the point."

Sullivan turned away from Fagan to look across the bar. "It's not my fault some people have thin skin. It's just a word. A word only has as much power as you give it." He rolled his eyes. "If a word hurts your feelings, then you shouldn't be out where people might use them."

Fagan pinched the bridge of his nose. "That's exactly what an asshole would say." He changed gears. "You do this with everything, you know. You act like your point of view is the only one that exists. Which is weird, because it's tragically fucking skewed and pretty much irrelevant to the rest of the planet."

"What does that even mean? I'm allowed to have a point a view."

"Take how you were just looking at the people on the street. You get all pissy because somebody can't maintain a healthy weight, when you don't know shit about how hard it is."

"How hard is it to not eat yourself sick?"

"For you? Easy. Harder than you think for a regular person." Fagan looked like he was going to smack Sullivan across the back of the head. "You literally just told me you have to eat six thousand calories a day to not shrink. That's three days' worth of food for a regular slob. Your magic metabolism means you can eat whatever you want. You couldn't get fat if you tried. Hell, you'll starve if you don't eat all the time. What the hell do you know about maintaining a healthy weight?"

Sullivan had a retort but could not get it out before Fagan pushed on. "Let me answer that for you. You don't know shit. But you go ahead and judge 'em anyway. As if somehow, a guy literally designed to be a super-athlete at the genetic level could ever understand what it's like to have to choose between being happy and being healthy. You are the very definition of 'modified for advantage,' and your attitude is what makes norms hate us."

The ironic arrival of their first round of food saved them both from further repartee. This served Sullivan just fine. Fagan was starting to sound intense, and Sullivan did not think he wanted to get drunk with an intense Patrick Fagan. Both men tucked in with gusto, creating a terrifying scene as one large man and one enormous man proceeded to tear through five appetizers like starving gorillas. Sullivan met the bartender's disapproving gaze with a challenging scowl, and the beleaguered employee decided to find something else to do while the two men murdered their food.

Sullivan was beginning to hope that eating would spare him more of Fagan's intensity when the giant looked up and shook his head. "Sorry about the lecture, man. I was fucking starving, and I get weirdly irritable when I'm hungry."

"Eh," Sullivan shrugged. "Whatever. I suppose I need to hear that stuff from time to time, and you're the only guy I'm likely to take it from. I'm a dick by nature. I try not be, but constantly reining myself in is tough. I get into my own head too much, and then I piss people off."

Sullivan paused, his non-apology stalled by a tall blond woman seated at a nearby high top. She wore a plain gray skirt, fashionable and businesslike. It hugged her impressive curves in a Rubenesque arc while it raced down to the knees. Her shirt was white and starched, fitting close across a proud chest that commanded attention. The body crammed into the otherwise boring business ensemble grabbed Sullivan by the frontal cortex and held on for dear life. For an instant, their eyes met. Sullivan gave her his best smile, a surprisingly disarming schoolboy grin that had devastated female inhibitions many times before. The woman's face flushed, and she quickly looked back down at her menu. Sullivan returned to his food, satisfied that the hook had been set. He would reel her in later, and perhaps salvage some sort of fun for the evening.

As part of the dance, he darted his eyes her way one more time. As expected, he caught her stealing a surreptitious glance in his direction. He smiled again to keep the game afoot, and thereupon found his view obscured by the hairy and significantly less appealing visage of Patrick Fagan. The giant wiped his mouth and beard on a napkin and waggled a finger at Sullivan.

"Oh, hell no, Casanova," he rumbled. "None of that shit tonight. If Horowitz is going to send us to Charlotte tomorrow, I don't want you tangled up in somebody's skirt till the wee hours."

Sullivan licked wing sauce from a finger and tried to vaporize Fagan with a fierce glare. "She told you to back me up, not babysit me."

"She told me to keep your eyes on the prize and your head in the game. Which is also why I'm here making sure you don't get too drunk to get things done. I don't want you puking in the carriage, and I don't want you missing our gate."

"You seriously going to do this?" Sullivan grabbed a greasy pile of nachos and stuffed them into his mouth. Still chewing, he jabbed a finger at Fagan. "This is a serious breach of bro-code."

"You can back off now, or I can make sure that poor lady never looks at you like a man again." Fagan pointed to his crotch. "You're out of your weight class, runt."

Sullivan accepted defeat with his usual composure. "You are kind of fucked up, Fagan."

"I'd tell you to blame my parents, but that one's all on me."

Sullivan decided to change the subject before any more of his life could be wasted discussing his over-sized partner's genitalia. "Carriage? I guess that means we really are taking the 'loop, huh? Damn. That's a long-ass ride."

"I don't fit in planes."

"You mentioned that," Sullivan said. "Horowitz said this is more residual stuff from Chicago. Anything juicy?"

"Another lab, it looks like. Research facility, possible production creche, that sort of thing."

Sullivan bobbed his head and said with a sneer, "Could be some career-making busts in there, I figure."

"So you *were* listening to me. Wonders never cease." Fagan signaled for more beer. "Not to mention the opportunity for career-breaking screw-ups, too."

"Am I such a burden, oh brother of mine?"

Fagan ignored the disrespectful tone. "Nope. I actually like having you around. You know how to do the job, and you are good when things get hairy. Would it kill you to act like a team player once in a while?"

"Might just," Sullivan said into the top of his beer glass. Then he sipped to hide a soft frown. It was easy to forget that his own bad decisions often had consequences for others. Horowitz must have known this would rankle him, and that was why she had given Fagan orders to stay close. Sullivan's self-destructive nature was a known quantity, yet he was not the sort to drag others down with him.

Fagan shared his suspicions. "I figure Horowitz is using me to force you to play nice. She knows you're a dick, but you really only want to ruin your own day."

"Banking on my better nature, is she?"

Fagan scoffed. "You don't have a better nature. She's banking on your stubborn streak." He downed a pint of beer in one long pull, slapping the mug on the bar when he had finished. "And that, Warden Sullivan, is always a solid bet."

CHAPTER SEVEN

Dr. Sharon Platt stared at her screen.

Words scrolled alongside a gently spinning graphic. Twin spirals twisted around each other, annotated in helpful color-coded sections with interactive video presentations. They were wasted on her. She did not need any help understanding the implications of her latest test results. She understood what she looked at far better than most, and it both frightened and thrilled her.

"Is this for real, Joe?" she called over her shoulder. "Have we duplicated these results over a statistically-viable set of stochastic conditions?"

The man at the other lab station ducked his head in affirmation. "Sure is, Doctor. It's stable, too. Heterozygous, dominant, ought to be strongly selective, too." As an afterthought, he added, "If we can duplicate it in a non-chimeroid organism, that is."

"Can we?"

"Who the hell knows? This is the first one of these we've seen."

Sharon scowled at monitor. "This is insane. A stable, selective, and beneficial mutation. I mean, we figured she was special, but this is..." Her voice trailed off, her mind questing for a word suitable for what she saw on her screen. None came to her, so she simply sighed. "We deserve a Nobel Prize for this."

"I wouldn't publish just yet, Doctor. The current political climate isn't very positive toward illegal genetic research facilities."

"And mankind suffers for it," she said. "I want to run a few more testing packages before we send this up the chain, though. It looks good, but these things have a habit of ending up more complicated than they first appear."

"I hear you," the other man said. "Nobody wants another incident."

Platt shuddered. "Agreed. I'm going to go talk to her. She should know about this."

"Sure, Doctor. She's awake and eating right now."

Platt stood, turning the terminal off as she rose. She rubbed her face with her palms, running her fingers through the tangled mess of brown hair falling over her eyes. She realized that she could not remember when she slept last, or what her previous meal had been. "Shit," she muttered. "Maybe I'll take a shower, first."

"Yeah," her assistant chuckled. "You should probably clean up first."

She ignored this and left the laboratory. Exhaustion dragged on her steps and pressed her shoulders into a sad stoop as she walked. Close to forty hours in the lab without a meaningful break was just not the sort of thing she was equipped to handle. A true academic, only now did the intrepid Doctor Platt regret her diminishing physical fitness. She had been athletic once, and in truth, it was not so long gone a thing. Her mind wandered back to college, where she had been a promising gymnast, if not a touch too tall for anything truly competitive. For the hundredth time, she promised herself she would get her body back to some semblance of its former glory. If only to stay ahead of the crushing malaise these marathon testing sessions left her with.

So distracting were these thoughts, she did not hear the man calling her name from down the hall until he was nearly upon her.

"Doctor Platt!" came the breathless greeting. "Doctor Platt! Wait up!"

She paused, uttering a mumbled curse toward a universe either blind or unsympathetic to her needs.

The man caught up to her, and she faced the pinched visage of the lab technician she had only just escaped. "What is it, Joe? I'm beat."

"Main office just called. We have to go to an emergency meeting. Right now."

"Oh for crying out..." Platt was not proud of how petulant she sounded, even to herself.

"Sorry. It's all-hands."

The doctor threw her hands up in defeat. "By all means, then. Let us go and hear what our glorious leaders feel is so important."

As the pair walked through the stark white hallways of their research facility, Doctor Platt began to notice a strange intensity to the usual bustle of the faculty and staff. The lab was always busy, always humming with a thousand conversations and the murmurings of people and equipment. It was a large building, the floors populated with people much like herself and all the support staff the various types of research going on within the otherwise uninteresting facade might require. So while the magnitude of noise and activity she observed seemed no more voluminous than normal, the timbre of it all put her on edge.

People were not just talking while they walked as co-workers often did. They hissed and whispered as they moved down the corridor, furtive eyes darting back and forth as they exchanged hushed speculations. People who might otherwise be inclined to meander or mosey from the office to the cafeteria stalked the corridor with long, ground-eating strides. Individuals coalesced into clumps delineated by departments or research groups, the instinctive herding reflex of startled mammals subtly asserting itself and telling Doctor Platt that something was very much amiss.

"Joe, why do I suddenly have a really bad feeling about this?" she asked, not sure if she intended the question to be rhetorical.

"I don't know, Doctor, but I think you might be on to something."

The stream of humanity at last began to filter into the large cafeteria, and Platt found her way to the back of the room and a good spot to avoid notice. When Joe settled in next to her, she jabbed him in the side with an elbow. "Now I know it's bad." She tilted her chin toward the front of the room, where a large monitor screen sat, a typical addition to the room whenever management decided to have a chat with the rank and file but could not be bothered to actually visit. "Looks like management is too nervous to set foot in our dirty little den of iniquity for this one," she lamented with a sour grin.

"We aren't exactly in the kind of place these people can afford to get caught hanging out in," Joe replied.

"And we can?"

"Touché."

The room lights dimmed, and the screen snapped to life with the large "Free Research Collaborative" logo. The blue stylized Caduceus staff set inside a gold star blazed bright yellow for a few seconds before fading to reveal the company motto of "Crescat Scientia" in Romanesque block letters beneath it. The logo and motto sat on screen for ten seconds, just long enough to lend gravitas to the moment and allow the hushed conversations going on to die a natural death. Then the logo disappeared, and the face of yet another executive vice president whose name Doctor Pratt could not be bothered to remember graced the screen with a fatherly expression.

"Good afternoon, everyone," the man on the screen said. He even paused to allow a few mumbled "good mornings" to waft in from the crowd, which Pratt thought was a nice touch. "The rest of the board and I have called this emergency meeting to bring you all up to date on several emergent situations that will affect our work moving forward."

This statement sent a ripple of tension through the room, a palpable wave of apprehension that manifested as more than a hundred people shifting in their seats at once. It sounded to Pratt like some mythological giant preparing to blow a house over with a single breath.

"I won't sugar-coat it," the nameless old man on the screen said. "Our efforts to improve humanity and create a better world have been dealt a serious blow over the last ninety-six hours. As you all know, our sister facility in Chicago was raided and taken down by the Genetic Equity Enforcement Department. Many excellent researchers have been detained, and we expect criminal charges will number in the hundreds, if not thousands." The man on screen wiped his face with a hand. "But it gets worse, friends. We do not know precisely how it was accomplished, but GEED agents have succeeded in securing the records stored at that facility."

A collective gasp grew across the assembled people, and the first icy tendrils of real terror began to crawl up Doctor Platt's spine. Her name would feature prominently in those records, with inescapable legal ramifications.

The man on the screen continued his speech. Oblivious or uncaring that his previous sentence had just ended her personal and professional life, he droned on. "Yesterday afternoon, GEED agents apprehended Thomas Langley. As he is, or rather *was,* our chief legal counsel, we find our projects in a precarious position." The man on the screen held up a hand to silence the growing panic in the room. "We do not anticipate that Mister Langley will violate any attorney-client covenants, but his capture means several large-scale alterations to our operations are now necessary. Effective immediately, this facility will need to be closed and liquidated."

The tension in the room would not be contained at this, and it took several seconds for the exclamations to calm enough for the man to be heard. "All currently running experiments will need to be shut down, and the results encrypted for transfer to more secure facilities. Any products ready for deployment will be immediately transferred to their clients. Products and experiments in progress but not ready for delivery will have their materials collected by our operatives and transferred to a new facility, once again in a more secure location. Those of you in affected programs should see one of our project managers after this meeting to coordinate the transfer and receive new assignments."

Doctor Platt's breathing grew shallow and fast. The woman was neither stupid nor naive. Who her employers were and how she had acquired funding for the research she conducted here were not mysteries. She accepted the devil's bargain for the good of humanity, never really examining what the consequences might be until this moment forced her to consider them. The man spoke about living, breathing organisms like they were an unfortunate but acceptable loss of material. The language, the tone, the bland expression on his face all painted a picture of a man not particularly concerned with the welfare of those "experiments."

A truth she had assumed would never matter coalesced in her head, urging her to action with waves of guilt and urgency. With care, she began to sidle along the wall of the cafeteria toward the exit. Whatever the man on the screen had to say next was irrelevant to the panicked scientist. All that mattered was getting back to the lab before her Machiavellian overlords made a decision that could not be appealed or reversed. The growing swell of relief in her breast when she at last slipped through the door died screaming when she found her path blocked by a tall man in a black and gray security uniform. This was not the usual rent-a-cop she was accustomed to seeing. The imposing figure wore armor plates over his uniform, and a helmet that hid most of his face. His arms cradled a short gun of some variety, attached to his harness with a strap. Doctor Platt possessed almost no knowledge of firearms except that they frightened her. This one more than most.

A gloved hand halted her in place, the thick, black-clad palm pressing against her sternum as she tried to pass.

"Everyone is to remain in the cafeteria until reassigned by project managers, ma'am." The voice was dry and bored, though not rude. "Orders from management. Please return to the cafeteria."

Something about how he said it, the clipped cadence and the formal language, set her jaw. She let her eyes wander over him again. His posture was taut and wary, tense without looking agitated. His weapons and gear were immaculate, yet they looked well-used. The doctor realized she was dealing with a military man, or an ex-military man at least.

"I need to check on an experiment. It's, um, in a precarious state. If I wait too much longer, we could lose a lot of expensive data." She tried to sell it, but the guard was not buying.

"Your project manager will assess the needs of each project, ma'am. I understand this is stressful, but management will accept any losses this transfer causes. We apologize for the confusion."

Platt began to lose her cool. "You don't understand... I need to get to the lab. Now!" She tried to push past, and the politely firm hand became a firmer and less polite grip on her collar. She was about to scream when another voice intervened on her behalf.

"Doctor Platt, is it?"

The voice was rich and creamy, deep as a well and smooth as butter. She stopped struggling with the guard to look at who was speaking.

The man was tall and incredibly handsome. Brown hair coiffed to stylish perfection, blue eyes piercing, symmetrical face cast in an expression of sympathy and understanding, he stood to her right looking like a matinee idol.

"My name is Vincent Coll, and I'll be your project manager. I understand you need to get to your lab right away?"

"Yes," was her breathless reply. "We have a series of experiments running, and if we have to move them quickly, I'll need to close them out myself to not lose the data." To cement her urgency, she added, "I think we've just had a major breakthrough, and I don't want to lose it."

"Would that be EM-2115?"

Platt blanched. "Yes."

Coll placed his hand on the guard's restraining arm, and only then did Platt notice that in addition to height, Coll had a muscularity that rivaled the man in armor. His fashionable suit hid the thickness of his arms and width of his shoulders behind the crafted silhouette of what she assumed to be the work of an expensive tailor. In another time and place, Platt allowed she might have found a way to spend much more time with Vincent Coll.

He smiled, and this only enhanced his good looks. Then he addressed the guard. "I think we can let the good doctor go close out her work, Grady. But do me a favor and escort her to the lab. There are going to be a lot of agitated people scurrying about in a few minutes, and management would hate for anything to happen to EM-2115 or Doctor Platt. Everyone is going to be very excited to hear about this 'breakthrough,' after all."

"Copy that, sir," the guard said with a curt nod. "Lead on, Doctor."

She left the company of Coll with Grady in tow. Walking back to her lab felt surreal. The hallways swarmed with strangers. Security contractors identical to the eponymous Grady moved around in pairs, scary black weapons carried in conspicuous fashion. Suit-wearing project managers talked in tight groups, looking at tablets and gesticulating toward various offices and laboratories.

When they arrived at her lab, she turned to Grady. "You need to wait out here. You are not cleared to be inside, and you don't have the right inoculations to access the experiment." She intercepted his objections before he even started. "I just need to close the tests, gather the data, and then secure the materials for transport. There is a lot of weird biological stuff involved, and no offense, you are only going to taint the data." Then she set the hook. "There is no other way in or out of this lab, Grady. I need fifteen minutes, and you can stand right here the whole time."

This seemed to placate the man, and he replied with a terse nod and a grunted, "Fine."

"Thank you," she sighed. Then she palmed the door switch and swept inside the lab. She stopped at the terminals and work stations, grabbing hard drives whole and stuffing them into her pockets. Then Platt moved to the door at the far end of the room. With a cleansing breath, she tried to arrange her face and features in a calm mask of confidence. She could not say if it worked, and there was no time to make sure. Another palm press and a code unlocked the door, which slid to the side with a soft hiss.

Inside, an eight-year-old girl with blond hair and a bright smile was playing a video game. The VR goggles covered what Platt knew to be inquisitive blue eyes and cheeks flush with the glow of youth.

"Emilie," she called softly. The girl started, then pulled the goggles from her head to beam at the doctor.

"Auntie Sharon!" she squealed. "You're back! Are we going to get that ice cream you promised me?! I was good for the other doctors and did everything they said without fussing."

"I saw, dear. You were perfect and brave. But now we need to be brave just a little more."

The girl pouted. "But you promised!"

"I know, Emilie." She gave the girl her best conspirator's smile. "And we are totally going to get that ice cream very soon. But we have to pack up and leave right now for a little unplanned trip. It might be kind of scary, but if you are brave and good, we will have ice cream until you can't possibly eat any more."

This seemed to satisfy the girl. "Where are we going?"

"It's a secret," Platt whispered. "But you are going to love it there."

Emilie's eyes widened at the promise of adventure. "Really?"

"Yes," Platt said, her heart in her throat. "No more doctors, no more tests. You are all done with that forever, Emilie. But we have to play a little game, first. There are people outside who can't see us leave. That's the part where you need to be brave, okay? We have to sneak out without anyone seeing us."

The little girl saw through Platt's tone to the fear beneath it. Her voice shook. "This sounds scary, Auntie Sharon."

"It probably will be, dear." Platt did not have the heart to lie. "But if we are both brave, we will make it."

"Then ice cream?" Emilie asked, with all the hope and innocence in the world. It broke Platt's heart to hear it, because she knew the girl well enough to guess she was already figuring out how precarious her position was.

"All you can eat."

The little girl smiled up at the doctor, beaming confidence and trust directly to her soul. "Okay, then. Let's go!" Then she added, "How are we going to sneak by the bad people?"

"That won't be too hard," Platt said. She went to the back of the girl's room and entered her access code into an emergency exit door panel. "They aren't that smart."

As soon as the door latch released, the lights dimmed, and a baleful two-toned alarm began to howl. "Time to go!" Platt ordered, and Emilie scampered to her side. As the pair scurried through the escape hatch, a sound that curdled the blood in her veins hit Platt's ears.

Like the first hailstones of a summer storm, the distant staccato patter of gunfire could be heard over the shrieking of the alarm. Platt shoved the girl ahead of her into the narrow stairwell. She turned to slam the door behind her, tears filling her eyes at the first tortured wails of the dead and dying.

Genetic Equity Enforcement Division Selection Board Evaluation Expert's Notes for Case SUL-002

Dr. Sharon Platt, Ph.D.

The subject proved to be every bit as interesting as I thought he would be. His tendency to restrain his physical inclinations toward violent response when presented with the opportunity runs much deeper than previous superficial diagnoses. No disrespect intended toward my predecessors, but the subject possesses an extremely cunning nature. The hypothesis that the subject is engaged in some kind of adolescent rebellion against the man he believes is his father falls apart when placed under scrutiny.

During his sessions, it became obvious that the examiners' questions were irritating him. Of course, thanks to the nature of his neurological alterations, he is perpetually irritated. He engaged in all the behaviors my predecessors noted. Namely deflection, sarcasm, feigned incompetence, et cetera. It should be noted that even when angry, his control is excellent. He attempted several different tactics to deflect the examiners. His favorite is feigned incompetence, as he tried several times to show he was not smart enough to deceive them. It was clear he was playing to the ego to put them off the chase as he had done with his other counselors.

Persisting in the inquiries (employing a personal challenge to his deceptions... a calculated risk on their part) did result in a small breakthrough. He admitted that he identifies best with violent interactions, referring with great fondness to his training at the hands of several high-level "combat instructors." Those interactions obviously shaped his relationship with both anger and his natural proclivity toward violence. This is telling, but he shut down when he realized he had been goaded into revealing this information.

I have to admit that I feel the board is quite justified in their concerns. His behavior is aberrant and unhealthy. The adventure of his initial apprehension was a ludicrous display of a mind at war with itself. We understand so little about chimera brain chemistry, though. The subject's neurological feedback mechanisms have been twisted so far from what we believe to be healthy that it is hard to say what will become of him. If I saw these numbers in anyone other than him, I'd assume I was looking at a high-functioning psychopath. He should fight over any slight, kill without compunction, and be quite immune to issues of conscience or remorse. There is enough co-linear data with PRC soldiers to support this assertion. I have spent many hours with multiple types of aggression-enhanced GMPs, up to and including "berserker" class individuals with GMOD ratings as high as five. If I had not examined the videos personally, I'd be convinced he was destined for Fort Leavenworth and a life of heavy sedation. After reading all his files and speaking with the selection team, my impression is that this is not the case. For reasons I cannot fathom yet, he is either afraid, disgusted with, or otherwise averse to whatever it is that makes him want to fight. No, I need to amend that. He has no issues with fighting per se, but it appears that he is not comfortable with how he feels while thus engaged. It's not much of a distinction, but I think it may be important.

He avoids excessive violence, but once engaged, he will harm and kill without noticeable remorse. This is as expected for someone with his genotype. The interesting part is that whatever is making him hesitate or underutilize his gifts has to come from somewhere. We can assume the disincentive is not based on guilt or empathy, as his ability to experience either is quite limited. I remain convinced that this is an adaptive or habituated response. The problem with that is how easily altered that kind of mechanism can be. I defer to my colleagues in the psychiatric fields for more in-depth analysis.

In the end, I am forced to admit that the board is right to be concerned. I have worked with many GMP patients, most of whom were surviving PRC soldiers. I have seen enough hyper-aggressive brain alterations to know what should be there and how to fix it. The goal of all such sessions is to identify and rectify any dangerous antisocial tendencies in the subject. The problem, as I see it, is that the subject has many fewer antisocial tendencies than he should.

I have grave concerns with regard to this matter. The nature of chimeric genetic construction leaves me at a loss to explain his behavior. We have precious little data on how he was made, and I fear my work with other chimeroid organisms has not prepared me for this. It's not that the subject is unstable; rather, I find myself more and more concerned about how stable he appears. Has he beaten the condition, or is he so competent a psychopath that he fakes stability better than any I have heard of or seen? I know what ought to be there, how he should be behaving, how he wants to behave. Yet for reasons that remain a mystery, he refuses to conform to the profile. That is far more frightening than yet another violent GMP with aggression tweaks.

In a way, he is exactly what so many governments were trying to achieve with their various war-fighter programs before and during the war: a person with superhuman physical characteristics driven by a fearless and warlike personality. The board does not need my assessment to surmise that the subject would make an extremely formidable warden. But something isn't working in his brain, and that warrants further investigation.

I have submitted a requisition for his birth records and the unsealing of Michael Sullivan's case files. Hopefully, we will find some clues there. If whatever mechanism preventing the subject from giving in to his worse nature stops working, I fear for anyone around him.

CHAPTER EIGHT

Vincent Coll had grown accustomed to being treated a certain way.

It was more than just good looks and plenty of money opening doors that would be otherwise closed to him. People just seemed to love giving him whatever he wanted. He presumed it to be a combination of his chiseled appearance and a natural, easy-going charm. Though he also allowed that one could not underestimate the influence of his reputation, either. The reputation in question was a grim thing, and it often preceded his arrival and overrode any other impressions. He supposed it was his reputation driving the men securing the laboratory to scurry from his path like startled rodents, and not his pretty face.

His expensive Italian oxfords slapped the floor tiles with a brisk rhythm. He knew he should slow down. His aggressive pace betrayed his frustration and mounting irritation. The underlings would sense it and get antsy. He decided that this was fine. They should be nervous. One of their own had screwed up, and now they were all in trouble. He saw no reason to spare any of them his ire and the consequences of provoking it. Nevertheless, he did make a sincere effort to calm his features. He desired an expression of effortless calm to accompany his air of regal authority. It was something he always found difficult to achieve when his cortisol levels got elevated, and they were quite elevated at the moment. Vincent brushed past two armed men in the hall, sparing them a glance only as he passed. Recognizing a name tag, he stopped the trooper with a firm tug on the arm and barked, "Report."

The armored man replied immediately. "All offices are secure; all lab materials have been collected. Building is prepped for a burn, sir."

"Not all of them," Vincent corrected the man, and the officer ducked his head in acknowledgment.

"All remaining offices and labs, sir," he amended his report. "Once we have identified all the bodies, we'll be ready to clear out."

"Keep access and egress secure for now, and don't get ahead of yourself. We can't mop up until we sort out our runner."

"Grady's in the cafeteria, sir." The reply came crisp and sharp. The man was almost too eager to throw his squadmate under the bus, if only to rescue himself from Vincent's undivided attention. It was understandable. Vincent was in a dark and indiscriminate mood. He allowed that he was probably doing a poor job of masking his need to hurt someone or break something. He would need to work on that.

"Very good," he said, forcing some levity and calm into his voice. "Let's go see if we can't un-fuck this cluster, shall we?" He tried to smile, though the expression on the officer's face told him that he had likely missed the mark by a wide margin. With a defeated sigh, he turned and strode into the cafeteria where, just a few hours prior, more than a hundred brilliant scientists and staff had gathered for a meeting. The coppery tang of blood and the rancid stink of human filth filled his nostrils as soon as he stepped through the door. Vincent did not wince or grimace. If he told the truth, he would have to admit that he rather liked the odor of blood. Not in a sick or psychotic way—it merely smelled like results to him. Vincent Coll was all about results. Or perhaps it evoked the satisfaction of loose ends getting tied up. Either way, when Vincent smelled blood, it usually meant that he had done what needed doing, and it was time to get paid. It was most satisfying. He supposed some of this was likely built into his DNA. All his senses were extremely keen, and he acknowledged that when your nose was as good as his, one had better not be squeamish.

A sticky crust of dried blood stained most of the cafeteria floor tiles, shading the clean white squares with a rusty brown patina. Bodies riddled with holes and leaking fluids had been dragged to the corners, leaving streaks and stripes painted in the gory mess like muddy crop furrows. Dozens of blank faces stared with dead eyes into space with mouths agape and jaws slack. The job had been accomplished quickly and with professional attention to tradecraft. There were no mangled limbs, no gasping wounded. Clean hits and clean kills were the norm, and Vincent appreciated the professionalism of the men assigned to this mission. He did not always receive quality help, so it was a nice treat when he got to work with professionals.

All except one, he supposed. Standing in the room at parade rest was a large man in gray and black armor. His carbine hung from his harness by a strap, dangling at his side in a position suited to rapid deployment. He had removed his helmet, and Vincent noted that his eyes were clear and bright, his expression locked in an indifferent mask of stoicism. Vincent walked over to this man and looked him in the eye.

The man before Vincent did not flinch, though he seemed to shrink a touch before the cold gaze of his employer. This man understood the situation and knew Vincent's reputation well. The mercenary's body language made it clear he wanted to give the well-dressed man whatever it was he desired. This suited Vincent's intentions perfectly. However, the man in the black and gray armor did not have what Vincent wanted, and thus the man found himself in a position to experience Vincent's dire reputation for himself. To his credit, he showed no fear. Even protected by his false composure, nothing could stop the icy river of cold sweat from racing down the spine beneath that armor.

Vincent's current mood leaned very much in the direction of terrifying, making the armored man's reaction appropriate. When Vincent Coll wanted a man to experience fear, there was just no getting past it. The armored man was large and powerfully built. His shoulders spread even wider than Vincent's. He stood a half a head taller than Vincent, and he bore the tools and the scars of a man born and bred to war. To the casual observer, the scene might appear comical. A soldier, a warrior, a fighting man with intimate knowledge of battles both won and lost over a long career, squirmed like a child before the scrutiny of a single man in a charcoal suit.

Vincent stared at the man for a protracted moment, just letting his irritation wash over the hapless individual and soak him in dread. "There was only one objective even worth all this mess in the whole damn building, Sergeant Grady," he said at last. "A single project worth more than all the others here combined." Vincent swept his hand in a wide arc, encapsulating the limp piles of dead bodies still littering the cafeteria floor. "We killed more than a hundred people today, just so we could hide one experiment from any prying eyes. One. Millions in cryptcoin spent developing it, millions more spent to keep it hidden." The hand fell back to his side with a soft slap, a calculated and theatrical gesture of defeat. "And now it is gone. Off in the fucking wind to who knows where." Vincent picked a microscopic piece of lint from his lapel and worried it between a thumb and forefinger for a moment. Grady viewed this in silence, pretending as hard as he could that the tension was not driving him mad. As if suddenly remembering where he was, Vincent released the speck with a scowl and addressed the armored man again. "Now, Sergeant Grady, I'd like to understand how it is that you managed to misplace this thing. Keep in mind that as far as my client and I are concerned, that girl is worth *so* much more than your life will ever be."

Grady shifted his feet before replying. "She had a bolt hole, sir. I didn't know there was another exit from her laboratory." After a pause to evaluate Vincent's blank stare, he added, "I, uh, I think she suspected something like this would happen."

"You think?" A sculpted eyebrow rose. "Sergeant Grady, I do not believe 'thinking' is your strongest suit. I say this because despite your sudden insight into the good doctor's state of mind, somehow this twenty-nine-year-old woman convinced you," he gestured to the big mercenary with a derisive hand wave, "a veteran of some twenty years, to wait in the hallway while she bundled up a king's ransom in research and ran off with it."

"With all due respect, sir, she has three Ph.Ds." Grady's voice wavered. "She said I didn't have the right inoculations, and that I'd taint the experiment if I went in. I don't really have the expertise to argue that sort of thing, sir. It sounded like a plausible reason for caution."

Vincent's retort sliced like shards of broken glass. "And was it? Plausible, I mean."

"It was not, sir."

"No. It certainly wasn't," Vincent agreed with a condescending shake of his head. His voice acquired a strange, husky intensity. The frustration he tried so hard to mask leaked through his crafted calm and oozed into his rebuke. "And now she is gone, and she has taken a product worth more money than you can even imagine with her. Something I was paid to retrieve and manage, and now I look like a fucking idiot because you couldn't figure out that one tiny broad might be trying to run away from the scary fucking men with guns!" Impeccably manicured fingers moving faster than the eye could follow seized Grady by his weapon strap and snapped the bigger man forward and down. As Grady stumbled, Vincent turned and threw the man over his hip. With the rattle of armor and spilled ammunition, Grady crashed to the bloody floor in a heap. Before he could finish his yelp of pain and surprise, Vincent brought a knee down on Grady's ribs and yanked upward on the strap. Grady's breath fled his lungs with an expressive "whoosh" that ended in a coughing fit. Pinned by Vincent's weight, Grady could only gasp and squirm beneath the grimacing demon perched with one knee on his solar plexus and a monster's grip on his sling.

Once again, Vincent had lost his battle with the monsters in his head. His cortisol levels now exceeded his brain's ability to regulate his aggression. Malice filled Vincent from the bottom of his nice shoes to the top of his impeccable hair. This sort of thing happened to him with some regularity, and while he accepted that slipping into psychotic rages was probably a bad thing, Vincent possessed enough self-awareness to admit that he enjoyed these episodes. Killing Grady would accomplish nothing of value, but it also would cost nothing. Whether or not the incompetent sergeant lived out the day was something Vincent Coll felt deeply and irrevocably ambivalent about. Vincent left the decision in the hands of fate and pulled.

The synthetic mesh of the strap groaned in weak protest as Vincent began to haul Grady upward. Grady could not rise, however, because Vincent's knee still pressed him against the blood-smeared tiles. The arm pulled up, and the knee pressed down. It felt like Vincent was growing heavier and heavier as the strength of a single arm crushed Grady's chest. The pressure grew with each passing second, and little by little, Sergeant Grady's ability to breathe slipped away.

Grady clutched at Vincent's wrist, he squirmed and kicked at the floor, he bucked his body like a landed carp. Nothing worked. Vincent was too strong, his position too dominant. Grady was pinned and dying by degrees, and he knew it. The veteran killer's eyes met Vincent's, pleading for mercy from a man he knew to be merciless.

Now that he had the man's full attention, Vincent spoke with a devil's voice. "Every corpse in this room was worth more alive than you are, Sergeant Grady. Every one of them is dead now. Think about that. Think about how many brilliant people and all the expensive machinery our employer chose to scrap today. All of it sacrificed to cover up what Doctor Platt was working on." Impossibly, Vincent increased the pressure on the beaten man. Grady's eyes bulged, and his breath crept in and out in tiny, choking gasps. "And now I have to tell all those incredibly powerful people that the good doctor has managed to slip the net, and that it is your fault. How much do you suppose your little life is worth to them now?"

The sergeant knew in that moment he was going to die. He had never imagined his death could be like this. He always assumed it would be either an unseen gunshot that got him, or the unstoppable advance of old age if he managed to get to retirement. As motes of flashing light blinked across his dimming vision, Sergeant Grady cursed his job, his employer, and the over-coiffed asshole squeezing the life from his body. He refused to look away from Vincent. He saw feral rage in the man's eyes, an all-too-human malice tainted by an unhinged sort of glee as well. Consumed by incandescent fury, Vincent Coll was enjoying himself. The man's face glowed with madness, and that was going to be the last thing Sergeant Grady ever saw.

The sharp crack of Grady's sling snapping split the air like a gunshot. With the pressure gone, the sergeant's upper body flopped back to the floor with a thud, and his tortured wheezing filled the deafening silence of the cafeteria. Grady's world shrank to the sound of his own strained respiration and the roar of blood in his ears for several long minutes. When his vision stopped swimming, Grady looked up to see an irritated Vincent Coll standing over his body. The mask of insanity was gone. In its place, Vincent wore a small smirk of bemused disbelief. The intense blue-gray eyes stared at the length of weapon sling in his hand as if the failure of an inanimate piece of nylon constituted a betrayal both deliberate and personal. The carbine dangled from the end of the strap, swaying back and forth before Grady's blinking eyes like Poe's titular pendulum. When Vincent looked away from the strap and back at Grady, he did not appear so much angry as he did disappointed. With a cleansing exhalation, Vincent recomposed himself. The cold administrative demeanor returned, and the man in the suit released the strap without warning. Grady's carbine hit the floor inches from his ear with an ugly clatter, and the abrupt noise ripped a startled flinch from the downed man.

"Oh, pull yourself together, Sergeant," Vincent spat. "Grab a squad and start searching the premises for any other bolt holes. Have a team start identifying and cataloging the bodies as well. I want to be absolutely sure nobody else has managed to escape." Vincent produced a handkerchief from a hidden pocket and began wiping his hands on it. "Every nook, every cranny, every square inch of this facility is to be scoured, Sergeant. No exceptions. We can't afford any more mistakes. Your life depends on it."

CHAPTER NINE

The arrival of two GEED wardens sent a palpable buzz through the assembled Municipal Law Enforcement Officers and a ripple of agitation through the throng of onlookers.

No one in the Charlotte law enforcement community had believed for a second that GEED would not be all over the crime scene, though it was quite another thing to see the pair of large men arrive. They came in a full-sized police transport, and this led many to believe a swarm of black-clad operatives was about to descend upon the location. As intimidating as such a display might have been, most found the reality altogether worse. First, the big black van had to pick slowly through the burgeoning crowd of gawkers and assorted media streamers to avoid running anyone over. This allowed extra time for competing groups of boisterous protesters to rile up the masses with conflicting messages of pro- and anti-GMP rhetoric. Most of Charlotte's MLEO detachment found themselves relegated to the thankless job of keeping the chaos manageable.

When the doors of the transport at last opened, the throng of people roared their disapproval. The pro-rights contingent hurled cries of "Fascist!" and "Nazi!" at the men, while the anti-GMP cohort pelted the wardens with accusations of "collusion" and "abominations."

The two GEED wardens, inured as they were to such things, ignored it all and moved to the line of confused uniformed police officers working the cordon. Most of them stared gape-mouthed in their direction. Sullivan supposed he could excuse them a little bit of a gawk. He and Fagan made for a bizarre sight. The hirsute giant and the stern-faced curmudgeon were almost certainly the strangest couple of wardens the local constabulary had ever seen.

"Don't look now, Sully," Fagan said. "But I think they're staring at you."

Sullivan snorted. "Oh yeah. I'm the strange one." He scanned the group of uniforms until he found what looked like the supervisor. "Come on," he said to Fagan, indicating with his chin the selected target. "Let's find out what the hell happened here." The crowd of cops parted before the men as they made their way to the ranking officer. Sullivan noted the name "Brighton" on the aging man's ID badge. The lieutenant met Sullivan's eyes with his own weary orbs, then glanced at Fagan with undisguised apprehension.

"You guys the wardens?"

Sullivan did not get to deliver the scathing retort he had loaded and ready to go, because Fagan's voice rolled over his like an avalanche. "Yes," he replied in his affable manner. "I am Warden First Class Fagan, and this is Warden First Class Sullivan. We got word of the situation while en route."

"If your office wasn't too cheap to spring for a hopper, you might have made it in time to do something about it," Brighton grumbled.

"Unfortunately, my condition does not allow for air travel, Lieutenant Brighton," Fagan said. "Can you tell me what happened?"

"Sure." Brighton cleared his throat. "As soon as we confirmed it was the laboratory in question, we sent the information to your office. That was, uh..." he looked at his watch and squinted. "...forty-one hours ago." He looked back to the wardens, his scraggly brows furrowed. "About sixteen hours ago, a person or persons unknown entered this building and murdered every living soul in it."

Sullivan hissed through his teeth. "How many dead?"

"One hundred and nine. All hard drives, servers, and data cores are missing or destroyed. They torched most of the laboratory sections, too. It's a mess in there, but the fire suppression systems kept the burns from spreading." Brighton wiped his eyes. "The bodies were stacked in the cafeteria, so at least families will be able to identify their loved ones."

"Site was burned," Sullivan stated. "They were tipped off."

Brighton's face twitched in irritation. "We surveilled this place for two days before sending that intel to you guys. Nobody jumped until your office was told." The implication was clear, and Sullivan did not like it.

"You think we are compromised?" It should not have been a growl, Sullivan knew. But he had lost that battle early today.

If his feral tone bothered the lieutenant, the older man did an excellent job of hiding it. "What the hell else should I think? The only other option is that our communications are tapped. I got the nerds going over everything now, but so far, our signals still look secure."

Fagan decided to change the subject. "Who's inside now?"

"Just the lab folks and the coroner's guys. We have full AR capability, so you'll be able to see the scene as it was found."

Fagan nodded. "Very nice, Lieutenant. That will be a huge help. Come on, Sully. Let's go get a look."

Stepping into the lobby, Sullivan noted no outward indications of what had occurred there. The marble floors bore no signs of violence, the pristine columns stood clean and bright under the yawning skylights. It looked warm and inviting, and this bothered the warden. He was relieved when the illusion got destroyed by people wearing white plastic coveralls meandering about. Most carried bags of tools, and one was breaking down a pylon in the middle of the atrium that had been set up to take 360-degree scans for augmented-reality recordings. It was to this man that Sullivan went first.

"Hey man," he said, flashing his GEED identification. "Can I get some glasses?"

"Sure," the technician said. He reached into a tool bag and pulled out two clear plastic visors. "Just turn them in when you're done, okay?"

"Will do," Fagan replied. "Anything to see in here?"

"Nah," the tech said. "All the, uh... interesting stuff is on the fourth floor."

"Thanks."

The wardens found the stairs and went directly to the fourth floor. The aroma of stale smoke was the first thing both men noticed as they exited the stairwell and pushed into the lobby. Neither saw any fire damage, though the intensity of the odor indicated that the fires could not have been too far away.

"Shall we?" Sullivan asked as he settled his visor over his face. As soon as the device recognized a user's eyes, it snapped to life. Ghostly images materialized over the scene, recorded data overlaid onto the visible information. The lobby did not change much, except for the translucent image of a woman's dead body on the carpet. The wardens walked over to the shimmering corpse.

Fagan frowned at the ghostly image. "Looks like she almost made it."

"Almost," Sullivan agreed. "No blood on the carpet. She took the bullet through the heart from behind." He pointed to the tiny hole in the center of the woman's back. "Bullet severed the spine, then pulped the heart. She was dead before she hit the floor. She didn't even bleed."

"What are the chances it was luck?"

Sullivan sneered at the thought. "Yeah, right. Notice any holes in the walls?"

"Nope."

"Exactly. This guy fired one round and killed the target instantly. He hit exactly what he was aiming for, and he did not need a second shot."

"She was on the move, too," Fagan said. "This was a professional hit."

"Paramilitary," Sullivan clarified. "Hitmen are rarely this clean. Let's keep moving."

The hallways held more horrors. The bodies had been removed, but the visors revealed each corpse as it had been left by the killers. Sullivan again remarked on the cleanliness of it all.

"Six bodies in the hall. One bullet per corpse. Head, spine, or heart shots all around." He pointed to the tile. "We got boot prints in the blood." He focused the visor's reticle on the print, and data about shoe size, tread pattern, and probable manufacturer scrolled across his vision. "Name brand, commercially available, size ten," he said. "There's a whole lot of nothing to work with right there."

"Not a single stray bullet hole, man," Fagan said with a rueful head shake. "Goddamn uncanny."

"Fish in a barrel," Sullivan remarked as they continued walking. "These guys used low-velocity ammo, probably subsonic and suppressed to keep things quiet. They had time to pick their shots, too." He waved a hand around to encompass the four or five images of dead bodies. "These folks would have been panicking. I assume most of the people were in the cafeteria, so these were just stragglers." He whispered the next part. "Too easy, really."

"I guess it's time to check out the cafeteria, then," Fagan said.

"You ready for that?"

"Does it matter?"

"I can go in there without you. I, uh..." Sullivan stumbled, trying to explain. "My brain is less... sensitive."

Fagan smiled. "It's easy to forget how much they fucked with your head, man. I appreciate the offer, but I'll do my damn job."

"It's bad enough you have to babysit me, Fagan. You don't need nightmares on top of it. I am aware of my status as an asshole, but part of being that asshole is I don't get shook by this sort of stuff.

You are a nice guy, and there is nothing wrong with being a nice guy. You like people. That's good. The world needs people who like people. I'm just saying that I won't think any less of you if you don't want to go look at a hundred dead bodies."

"What's this? John Sullivan coming off all sensitive and considerate? You feeling okay?"

Sullivan saluted his partner with a raised middle finger. "I'm not insensitive, jerk. I'm just easily aggravated and struggle with empathy. I don't have to experience your feelings to acknowledge their existence." While true, explaining himself to Fagan put Sullivan on edge. He had never cared to spare anybody's feelings in the past, and he did not understand why he tried to do so now. He supposed it had something to do with the annoying fact that he liked Fagan. Or he liked Fagan as much as he knew how to like anyone...

"I love you too, pumpkin," Fagan said through a chuckle. Then he took a deep breath. "But it's my job, so I'm going in."

"Suit yourself. Don't say I didn't warn you."

The cafeteria was every bit as bad as Sullivan thought it would be. Despite what he said to Fagan, Sullivan was not immune to the sight of the massacre. The coroners had not removed all the bodies yet. Four men in the white plastic suits were pulling corpses from the stacked piles and putting them in body bags. The smell was a physical thing, a thick and cloying miasma that swam up the nostrils to settle in the back of his throat. Sweet and sour, acrid and foul, the stink tickled Sullivan's gag reflex. He nearly coughed, but resisted for fear he might never stop. The stink of death and violence set off a series of chemical reactions in his brain before Sullivan could stop them. His skin turned cold, and the hairs on his neck stood on end. His pupils dilated, collapsing his field of vision into a bright tunnel. Within this tunnel Sullivan could pick out tiny details with preternatural clarity. This proved unhelpful, as the details only enhanced his neurochemical overreaction. The cycle was going to drive him insane if he did not break it. Fear of this galvanized his will and Sullivan ground his teeth. Employing every trick he had been taught, Sullivan backed himself off the ledge of insanity. Relief came in waves. He addressed each surge of aggression in turn with the serene acceptance of a Zen master. It should have been impossible. However, the anger stayed below the surface, as it always did. Without the distraction of rage, he could focus on the calming process in a way others could not. His aggression surged with frosty intensity, and he crushed it with force of will alone. Nobody saw his conflict. In truth, the entire incident came and went in the span of five seconds, leaving no one the wiser. Sullivan noted that this time, he had beaten it fast, and this encouraged him.

Fagan's reaction turned out to be far more explosive. Moving into the room a second or two after Sullivan, he barely perceived the placid calm on his partner's face before the scene grabbed his full attention. He made the mistake of gasping, taking in a big gulp of the disgusting air and all the horrors it contained. A hacking spasm overtook the giant, and this was not insignificant considering his size and the power of his lungs. He needed several seconds to reassert control of his breathing, and the commotion alerted the coroners to their presence. One of them trotted over with hurried strides and pressed nose plugs into their hands.

"Jesus, you morons! Put these on before you puke and contaminate the crime scene!" The woman under the Tyvek hood shook her head in disbelief. "What the hell is wrong with you?"

Sullivan rescued his green-faced partner from having to respond with his own sharp retort. "You wanna watch that tone, lady?" He flashed his ID at her and gave her a moment to put together the relevant conclusions. "GEED just had us sit for six hours in a 'loop car because there are only nine First Class Wardens on the East Coast. We are tired, hungry, and most of all, really grumpy. You will just have to deal with the fact that my partner and I do not have the time to gently stroke your ego or fondle your sacred cows. You copy that?"

"Uh... sorry, wardens." The woman looked equal parts insulted and terrified. "I thought you were some kind of city inspectors or something."

"Got a lot of seven-foot government employees in Charlotte these days?"

"Go easy, Sully." Fagan had a modicum of his composure back. "Ma'am, we need to take a look around. We know how to avoid contaminating a crime scene." He turned back to Sullivan with watery eyes and a bloodless complexion. "Come on, man. Let's get this over with."

With a final scowl for the coroner, Sullivan followed the big man over to a corpse pile.

"Shit on me," Fagan breathed.

"Yup," Sullivan agreed. He was crouching for a better view of the dead. "More of the same. Shot placement is less precise here. Once the shooting started, the place got real chaotic. Still, most of the hits are clean kills. Couple of double-taps here and there. No over-penetration, no wild fire."

"Why'd they stack them?" Fagan asked, as much to himself as his partner.

"That, my friend, is a damn fine question," Sullivan said with a frown. "You can see where they dragged them over. Why? Why stack them neatly after shooting them?"

"Why does anyone stack something?" Fagan started to tick off reasons. "Storage, but that can't be it. Organization? Were they sorting the bodies? Why the hell would they sort corpses?"

"Inventory," Sullivan said.

"They were making sure they got everyone?"

"That's my guess," Sullivan said. "When the shooting started, speed was of the essence. There was no time to count or sort through them all. But after?" He nodded. "Well, then there'd be lots of time to match names to faces, wouldn't there?"

"Bastards." Fagan sighed.

"Here's the real question, my oversized amigo." Sullivan looked up at the bearded giant. "Did they get everyone? It seems even they weren't sure. Otherwise, why bother?"

"How would we figure that out?"

Sullivan stood and dusted his hands on his pants. "Is there a building log? Keycard access? Staff list?"

"Maybe. Possibly. Probably. In that order."

"Then let's start matching bodies to names, Fagan." Sullivan began to walk toward the exit and respite from the carnage. "With any luck, somebody made it out of here alive."

CHAPTER TEN

The wardens opted for a takeout lunch, not wanting to get too far from the crime scene. They found an outdoor table and benches in a nearby park and tucked into a mountain of food procured from several different local restaurants. Just as the intensity of their feeding frenzy seemed to peak, an insistent buzzing from Fagan's ID card interrupted their otherwise silent meal. The big man pulled his handheld from a pocket to check the message with a scowl.

"The only thing worse than you having a hunch," Fagan said, "is when that hunch turns out to be good." He snapped his secure GEED phone closed and turned back to his food. The second of three enormous hamburgers lost half its mass in a single enormous chomp from the giant, and his beard wormed and wiggled while he chewed his food with a thoughtful frown.

Looking up from his own lunch, Sullivan gave his head a rueful shake. "That's not always a good thing." He scooped up a spoonful of penne alfredo and pondered it before continuing. "But I assume we have a survivor?"

Fagan swallowed and gave his mouth a polite swipe with his napkin before replying. "Looks that way. We have a Doctor Sharon Platt who was keyed in that day. She never keyed out, and her body was not included in the butcher's bill."

"Abducted or murdered?"

"Can't imagine murder," Fagan said. "If that was all they wanted, they'd have left her with the rest. I figure they grabbed her."

Sullivan found no fault in that logic. "Next question is 'why?' Why kill everyone and run off with one doctor?"

Fagan shrugged. "The home office is pulling everything they have on her now. Maybe there's a clue in that. Off the bat, we know she is some kind of genetic engineering wunderkind. Multiple Ph.Ds., tons of awards, that sort of thing."

"Do we know which laboratory was hers?"

"Yes."

"Then finish eating. We have work to do."

"Give me five goddamn minutes," Fagan said. "If I don't eat now, who knows when I'll get the chance again. I go hypoglycemic pretty easy, and I'm too heavy to carry." He shoved most of the third burger into the gaping maw beneath his mustache and cycled his jaw like a lizard gulping down a whole rat. Bound by similar metabolic constraints, Sullivan matched his partner's gusto by hoovering an entree-sized portion of pasta into his face at a pace bordering upon reckless. A woman walking a small dog came upon them in the midst of this display. Her face contorted into a mask of pure disgust at the sight, and she hurried away from the wardens as if terrified they might try to eat her dog next. Her flight went unnoticed by the men, engrossed as they were in the act of eating.

Six minutes and forty seconds later, the wardens completed the annihilation of several lunches and made their way back to the laboratory. The cordon was still in place, and they found the crowd swollen to several hundred angry protesters. Charlotte MLEO had reinforced the barricade with a dozen more riot police. Each side of the issue eyed the other with wary animosity, and insults flew without restraint. Sullivan took it all in, eyes scanning the tinderbox with pessimistic intensity. While the whole atmosphere was tense and raucous, it looked like a full-on riot remained unlikely.

Or it seemed that way right up until the two wardens once again approached the line of uniformed officers. The reappearance of the controversial government agents birthed a roar that surged through the crowd like wildfire. Protesters surged in their direction, only to be blocked by the armored mass of riot police. News crews pushed to the front of the swell, cameras pointed like rifles at the intimidating men, while drones violated a dozen ordinances to whirl around their heads. Sullivan tried to hide his grimace at the affront. His hand went to a jacket pocket and emerged with his GEED handheld. Two swipes of his thumb later, the drones fell from the sky dead. He looked to one of the riot cops. "Collect those and charge the owners. That shit is dangerous and illegal!"

"Please," Fagan added with a sideways look to his partner. "He meant to say 'please' when he said that."

Reporters shouted questions at the pair, which both ignored. Fagan took a moment give the department-approved, "You can check our public relations site for an official statement when one is ready," speech. This had no effect on the journalists, whose questions only increased in furor and frequency.

It was inevitable, Sullivan mused to himself, that some brave soul would take it upon himself to escalate a bad situation into a worse one. On cue, a fist-sized chunk of asphalt sailed in their direction. Already on edge, Sullivan's reflexes were primed to deal with threats, and this prevented any injury. He reached out a hand and caught the improvised missile three feet before it struck Fagan in the head. He dropped the rock and pointed directly to the thrower. "Male, early twenties, five-foot-seven, maybe 160 pounds. He's wearing blue jeans and a yellow T-shirt. Brown hair, cut short. Go get him."

One of the riot police realized that Sullivan was addressing him and quickly relayed the information to officers better positioned to make an arrest. The young man in question, upon realizing he was significantly less anonymous than he thought he was, turned and bolted. This sudden activity shifted the crowd's attention away from the wardens, and the two men used the opportunity to complete their escape through the cordon and onto the relative safety of the gutted laboratory building.

"Just another day serving and protecting," Fagan said as they entered the lobby.

"Service is its own reward." Sullivan let his own tone match Fagan's dry sarcasm.

Fagan's laugh was honest and contagious. "It's a good thing the pay is total crap, otherwise a guy might start to feel guilty about living the life of a genetically-modified government employee." The shaggy head shook in resignation. "By the way, Sully, your reflexes are insane. I think that kid shit his pants when you just grabbed the damn rock out of the air."

"Everyone is a badass revolutionary when they don't think anyone in authority can see them," Sullivan replied with a small smile. "He won't be using this story to get tail from liberal arts co-eds, at least."

"Don't knock liberal arts chicks, man. Had a lot of good times back in the day..."

Sullivan wanted very much to retain his bad mood. The pulse of anger at having a rock thrown at his partner felt good, and he wanted to maintain the level of arousal even that small quantity of danger had sent through his brain. Fagan's irrepressible good humor killed any chance of that happening, though Sullivan could not bring himself to be mad about it. This confused him, yet he let it pass unexamined.

Sullivan was anxious to get to the laboratory, but his partner paused. With a thoughtful look hiding beneath his beard, Fagan asked, "What are the chances that was a Sons of Adam agitator? The crowd seemed calm enough before he showed up with his rock."

"That rabble looked calm to you?" Sullivan inquired with a raised eyebrow.

"Well, I mean, they were rowdy, sure. But I wasn't getting the riot vibe from them at all. He threw the damn thing right at me, too. Not the cops."

Sullivan pointed out an obvious answer. "You are kind of a big target. He was probably just going for the easy hit."

"I don't buy that. Most of the time, assholes throw the rock at the cops. They are in uniform, and thus they represent the authority. I was the only obvious GMP." Fagan shook his head. "I mean, you're a big guy, but I'm the one that really stands out as a 'GiMP,' right?" He made air quotes around the slur for emphasis.

"I don't know, partner," Sullivan said. "Sounds like you're seeing bogeymen where there aren't any. SoA likes big flashy ops, not grass roots douche-baggery."

"Ops like murdering a hundred scientists at an illegal genetic research facility?"

Sullivan stopped and thought about that. "Well, shit, Fagan. You just might be some kind of detective after all." He started to walk again. "One question there, though."

"Yeah?"

"Why go for the scientist? SoA is zero-tolerance on us abominations, sure. I'd make them for executing everybody, because that follows. But the scientist angle makes me think this isn't them. They'd shoot her in the head all day long, but honestly, they're more likely to burn a place like this to the ground than run a professional cleaning job like this. My gut says the assholes who did this were looking for that doctor specifically. It doesn't add up." They had arrived at the stairwell, and Sullivan realized he did not know where to go.

Fagan still appeared lost in his own thoughts. Finally, he grunted, "Well, it was a good theory."

"Don't table it yet," Sullivan said. "I've seen weirder shit. Let's just keep an open mind. Which floor do we need?" He used the question to put Fagan back on track.

"Sixth floor," the giant said. "Shall we?"

"Yup." Sullivan led the way to the stairwell and began to ascend.

Fagan starting groaning after just one flight. "My poor knees! What do you have against elevators?"

"Too slow, too cramped, no escape routes. It's like walking into a trap on purpose."

"You must have had one fucked up childhood, man."

"You don't even want to know."

Platt's laboratory door wore an official Charlotte MLEO evidence sticker, which the wardens tore away without a second thought. Inside, Sullivan made several key observations right away.

"No fire here." He extended a hand in the direction of a suspiciously barren workstation. "Desktop terminal missing."

"Seems like they treated this area much nicer than the others," Fagan said. "No bodies found in here. No gunfire or indicators of foul play."

Sullivan moved to a door at the back of the lab. He checked to see if it was secured. It was not, and he pressed through without incident. His eyes grew wide for a moment, then narrowed to confused slits while his brain processed what he was seeing.

"Fagan!" he called back over his shoulder. "Come look at this!"

The sound of the giant's footsteps clomping his way told Sullivan his partner was coming. The big man's voice followed. "What? The MLEOs miss somethi—"

Sullivan nodded his head at Fagan's forgotten question and responded with one of his own. "This look right to you?"

The men were looking at what could only be described as a child's playroom. The carpet beneath his feet was a soft sky blue, and the walls were lined with shelves containing books and toys. Where there were no shelves, fanciful children's characters had been painted in various states of play. In the dark quiet of the crime scene, the over-sized eyes and bright smiling faces of the cartoons abandoned all pretense of childlike whimsy and stared back with ghastly intensity. A twin bed sat against one wall, its pink sheets and comforter dull and muted in the poor light.

Fagan expressed a breathy, "What the fuck?"

Sullivan's reply was low and solemn. "What the fuck, indeed."

"They were keeping a kid in here?"

"I'm gonna go ahead and say that's a real distinct possibility, partner."

"There were no kids in the employee logs. Nothing on the visitor's list either." The big man rubbed his face with both hands. "I don't even want to think about why there was a kid here, Sully." Fagan's voice sounded shaky; the implications of finding children's things at an illegal genetics laboratory heaped a new layer of horror to what was already a horrific place.

Sullivan asked, "There's no production creche here, right?"

"Just R&D, according to our intel. MLEOs didn't find any incubators or birthing suites, either."

"So it's just a lab..." Sullivan scanned the room. He understood Fagan's fear. The list of viable reasons to keep children at a facility like this was short and included no pleasant options. His own hackles were rising, though he enjoyed the luxury of a more controlled reaction this time.

A sheet of cool began to spread across the back of his neck, and the contents of his stomach started to roil and churn. A fury both violent and sublime sent Sullivan's heart rate soaring without touching the clarity of his thoughts. He was not afraid this time. This was not the slaughterhouse on floor four. There was no pervasive stink of death to set his mind spinning toward madness up here, so he could relax and enjoy the benefits of his condition.

His brain had been a mad scientist's plaything, and his life a living hell because of it. This was his normal, yet the warden would be a liar if he said that his condition did not come without perks. Sullivan had been designed from conception to thrive under high degrees of mental strain. When it worked, knowing that stress made him better at everything brought him great comfort, and even joy. Sullivan was at his best in situations where others might break. In this case, his vision grew sharper, and his skin tingled with sensory input. He saw every subtle twist of a single floating dust mote, he felt the tiny currents that set it to dancing, and he heard it land on a flat surface. His wildly-dilated pupils moved from left to right, not actively looking, but passively absorbing all the information. If he thought about it, he could even perceive his sense of time itself stretch to accommodate the storm of neurotransmitters and endorphins soaking his gray matter. When he was calm, when the monster in his head did not bang against its cage and demand that he fight and maim and kill, Sullivan liked what his brain could do.

His gaze settled on the fire exit. There appeared no reason to give it any attention whatsoever. It sat against the wall, uninteresting, nothing more than a plain metal door at the back of the room. But Sullivan saw the disturbed dust and the fresh scratches on the non-hinged edges. A small smile turned the corner of his mouth at the sight of it. "Good news, partner. I think they got out."

"Who?"

"The lady doctor and the kid." He pointed to the fire escape. "Bet you a nice dinner that thing was accessed right around the time of the killings."

The men walked over and examined the door. The diagnostic records yielded to their GEED clearance, and soon, Sullivan's suspicions were confirmed. He shook his head. "Right on schedule. The bad guys must have shit their pants when the alarms started screaming." He peered into the escape stairwell, still lit with pulsing red light. "Straight shot to the ground floor, too. Easy as pie to grab the stuff and the kid, then get out before they realized she was gone."

"How do you figure that?" Fagan asked.

"Main area is not tossed or burned. The bad guys never got this far, or if they did, what they wanted was already gone. I'm guessing the doctor snatched it all when she ran."

"With the kid?"

"Looks that way. Want to know what else I'm thinking?"

Fagan nodded. "All ears."

"So the bad guys didn't torch this lab. They didn't do any shooting or killing outside of it, either. They wanted whoever was in here to sit tight while they did their jobs."

"Suppressed weapons, subsonic ammo, gathering everyone in the cafeteria first..." Fagan was putting it together as well. "It would have been real quiet up here. At first, anyway. They'd have gone hot when the fire alarm started."

"Whatever it was they were after, it was in this lab."

"And they killed everybody in the building to keep it a secret." An element of menace replaced the horror in the giant's voice.

Sullivan nodded. "You thinking what I'm thinking?"

"They want that kid. Shit. The doctor must be protecting the kid!"

"Or selling it to the competition," Sullivan countered.

"Christ, you got a dark mind," Fagan said.

"You don't know the half of it." Sullivan said with a sardonic curl of his lip. "Either way, my gut tells me that this kid is real special. A hundred people died over it."

"Her," Fagan corrected. "It's all unicorns and daffodils in here."

"That doesn't mean anything. Boys can like that stuff. Don't be sexist."

The giant pointed to a toy box with "Emilie" stenciled on the front. "I suppose a parent could name a boy 'Emilie,' too. But I'll play the odds on this one."

"Well, ain't you just the great detective."

CHAPTER ELEVEN

Lights streaked by the window like lasers.

Darting lines of bright white, yellow, green, and red flashed across the clear flat panel as the car hurtled toward Kansas City at nearly three hundred miles per hour. Each glowing signpost painted the interior of the swaying car in conflicting moods that varied from pensive to demonic, every color lending its own connotation to what was no more than the brown synthetic leather of aging seats. How much her own mental turmoil aided and abetted this effect, Platt could not say.

Emilie was asleep. For this, Platt thanked whatever gods still existed. The gentle vibration of the Hyperloop ride had lulled the terrified child into the slumber of the truly exhausted. Her tiny blond head lay in Platt's lap, and her breathing came in languid snores. Platt envied her the peace of sleep. She certainly did not expect to enjoy the gentle embrace of Morpheus anytime soon herself.

She still had not wrapped her head around what had happened in Charlotte. She had always been prepared to run, of course. Though she might be deficient in many areas, intelligence could not be counted among them. The parties who funded her work were far less mysterious than they tried to be, and she possessed enough imagination to guess what they were capable of when cornered. The importance of what she was trying to accomplish trumped any moralistic objections to the provenance of her research money, so the doctor had bitten down on her principles and kept her nose to the grindstone.

Running had been unavoidable from the start. She applied this claim to her bruised conscience like a soothing balm. She never intended for Emilie to belong to... them. Besides, it was inevitable that the money would run out, or the law would get too close, or her backers would realize she was never actually going to give over her research. Escape had been part of her plan since day one. Though in her darkest nightmares, she could never have imagined exactly how far those financiers would go to keep her.

They killed everyone.

She still struggled with the magnitude of that. In hindsight, she could not understand why the possibility of her employers resorting to wholesale murder never occurred to her. The horror of it was too much. Her mind lacked the depravity to even conceive such a course of action, let alone predict it. The bitter irony tasted like ashes in her mouth. Her inability to anticipate the ruthlessness of those she fled was a function of how insane they were and how crazy she was not. She did not like to admit that her naivete had just killed more than a hundred people, yet her intelligence was a curse that did not spare her such conclusions.

Those deaths are on me, she thought. *I may as well have shot them myself.*

Part of her understood this was not a fair assessment. That part was small and quiet and weak compared to the behemoth her guilt had grown into. She looked back down to the girl in her lap.

Please be worth it.

It was wrong to put a burden like that on the shoulders of an eight-year-old. The girl's potential belonged to no one. She was meant to be a gift to the world, an asset to the human race. Something inside the brilliant doctor scoffed at the lofty notion even as it crossed her thoughts. Her own stupid pride had kept this ludicrous conceit alive long past the point where her other childish dreams had died.

Almost none of the pristine luster of her idealistic youth survived. Ten years in the laboratory navigating the dark underworld of illegal research societies later, and the good doctor hardly recognized herself. Staring out her window and listening to the soft snores of a sleeping child, she was left to wonder at the consequences of her hubris. She hoped that the girl would not suffer because of her mistakes. Her former co-workers had already paid a high enough price, and Platt's conscience could not stomach any more.

She gave the child a gentle nudge, coaxing her awake with a flutter of eyelids and a murmur of confusion.

"It's time to wake up, Emilie," Platt said. "Our stop is coming up."

"Where are we?" the girl slurred.

"Just outside of the Kansas City Metro."

"Will we be here long?"

"I hope so," Platt said with a smile.

They exited the 'loop car, Emilie shuffling on tired feet and Platt darting nervous looks into every shadowed corner. They crossed the platform without incident. Few passengers rode this leg of the 'loop so late at night, and even fewer people roamed the station. A man in a dirty green jacket made eye contact with Platt, and the doctor's heart leapt in fear. She forced the terror down her throat and started to walk his way. The man smiled as they grew near and held his hand out in greeting.

"Doctor Platt?" His face was narrow. Piercing brown eyes were separated by a long nose and framed by thin eyebrows. He did not appear old, though the bloom of youth had fled his features some years prior. The fact that he knew her name was a good sign, though his casual use of it in public irked her.

"Don't say my name! It's not safe!"

The man's smile never faltered, and he gave no indications her rebuke had bothered him. "Oh, it's definitely safe in here," he said. "My teams have been sweeping the station all night. There isn't a soul in the station that is not one of ours, or being watched by one of ours."

Platt's eyes swept left and right, trying to find the hidden agents among the scant pedestrians. "You can do that? You have that kind of manpower?"

"For our little Emilie?" The smile turned to wash the girl with warmth. "For someone like her, I pulled all kinds of strings." He looked back to Platt. "I'm Porter, by the way. I'll be your conductor. The Railroad has cleared the route for you, and we have food, showers, and a bed waiting in the complex. If you'll follow me?"

Platt detected the first signs of relief begin to suffuse her aching muscles. She had been on edge for so long that she had forgotten what it was like to relax. "That sounds great."

Porter took her bag, and they started walking. The Hyperloop station was not large and the exit was not far. Platt found this station much different than the larger and busier versions she used in Charlotte. Porter noticed her expression and chuckled. "It ain't like your big coastal stations."

"It really isn't," she said. "Is it really that bad out here?"

"Bad? 'Bad' is kind of relative, Doctor. The Midwest still hasn't recovered from the war, much. The riots cleared all the respectable folks out a long time ago. Even after more than thirty years, the complexes are still pretty much a no man's land." He shrugged, a noncommittal huff escaping his lips. "You can't just build three hundred giant production facilities, empty all the towns of people to staff them, and then close them all overnight without consequences."

Platt knew the history. "But if they hadn't..."

"We'd all be speaking Chinese," Porter finished. "Still sucks for us, though. At peak, the KC Complex put out close to ten thousand drones a month. Quality stuff, too. My dad used to brag all the time that no matter how much the Chinese juiced their boys up, one of his drones could cut down any ten of 'em."

"Turns out there's no gene for bullet-proofing."

Porter shrugged. "You work with what you've got. PRC had lots of people, so that's what they used. We had tech, so we used that." Porter stopped at a banking terminal and added, "Tech won. Hold on, gotta grab some cash."

Platt put an arm around Emilie's shoulders. "How're you doing, kiddo?" she asked.

"I'm really tired."

"Me, too. You are doing great, though."

Porter turned away from the machine to give the girl a big smile. "The car ain't far. You'll be snug in bed toot-sweet, kid."

They resumed their journey, and a few seconds later, they were outside. An old car waited for them. It had chipped blue paint and the interior smelled of mold, but the seats were large and comfortable. Emilie snuggled against Platt's side and was slumbering within a minute of their departure. Porter drove the car manually, which made Platt uneasy.

"Is this safe?"

"What?"

She pointed to his hands on the steering yoke. Porter laughed. "Am I making you nervous?"

"A little."

"This car is not on the traffic grid. So I either drive it by hand, or we don't get anywhere."

"Not on the grid? Is that legal?"

"Out here? Totally. This ain't like one of your big coastal metros, Doctor Platt. You get more than five miles away from the 'loop, and there *is* no traffic grid." He saw her face go white, and his head shook. "You get used to it, Doctor."

"If you say so..."

Porter checked to make sure Emilie was asleep before changing the subject. "What happened in Charlotte?"

"Apparently, GEED found out about the lab. The backers sent people in to scrub the site except..." her voice faltered.

Porter picked up her thread, a sharp edge in his tone. "Instead of the usual 'pack-up-and-move,' they went for something more drastic?"

"They killed everybody."

"They do that sometimes," Porter said. Platt observed his knowing tone and wondered for the first time just where it was the Railroad had found this man. Then he gestured to the sleeping girl next to the doctor. "Is it true?"

"Is what true?"

"They say she is an honest-to-goodness mutant. A new species of human."

"Looks that way," Platt said. "Initial testing leads me to believe so, at least. Though not so much a new species but a new type of the same species, I guess."

Porter pounded the yoke with his palm. "Goddamn it, this is big."

"She's just a little girl," Platt reminded him. "We can't put too much on her. She won't understand."

"What can she do?"

"Nothing, yet. Her recall is significantly above average. Extraordinary even, considering her age. If it progresses as observed, I expect her adult memory to be near-savant levels without coincident neurological drawbacks."

"Intelligence?"

"Above average, but so far not exceptional. At her age, it is hard to benchmark."

"Mozart wrote his first symphony at five."

Platt hated that canard. At every progress meeting where Emilie failed to demonstrate genius level intellect, some project manager would drag that tired bit of trivia out and walk it around. Platt's bland reply wore the threadbare cloak of endless repetition. "No, he didn't. He wrote a minuet at five, and it's kind of terrible." More softly, she added, "He wrote his first symphony when he was Emilie's age. She doesn't like to play instruments."

"What does she like?"

Platt paused, not sure she wanted to answer. "She likes to read and draw and play video games, just like other eight-year-olds." Platt rubbed her face. "Emilie is not some kind of GMP messiah, Porter. She has one stable genetic mutation that is beneficial and just might be selective. It doesn't give her superpowers or make her a genius or anything, okay?"

"What does it make her?"

"Unique." When that did not appear to satisfy the man, she elaborated. "As far as we can tell, her telomeres don't degrade." The driver's blank stare pushed her to explain. "She will age very, very slowly once she matures. She won't get cancer, either. If she avoids high-risk lifestyle behaviors and takes care of herself, who knows? She could live two hundred years, easily. Maybe three."

Porter nodded slowly. "And this is selective?"

"Looks possible."

Porter gave a low whistle.

"Yup."

Porter asked, "Can you duplicate it?"

"I don't know. We were trying for improved memory and neuroplasticity, so this was kind of a surprise. The excess telomerase reverse-transcriptase was not a targeted augmentation. It's a mutation."

"The whatsahoosis?"

"The enzyme that protects her DNA from damage as she ages." Porter seemed no better off for knowing this. Exasperated, Platt simplified as much as she could without crayons. "She has a lot of the stuff, and hers works better than ours."

"Right," Porter said, as if he understood.

Platt rolled her eyes and went on. "We still have to reverse-engineer exactly which alleles expressed to isolate all the markers. Emilie is a chimera, so that is going to be really hard to do."

"But then you could duplicate it?"

Platt threw up her hands. "Who the hell knows? This is why it's called research and not omniscience, Porter."

"Right. I gotcha. First things first, we need to get you safe and away from GEED and the backers. The backers are going to come looking for you, and GEED will come looking for the backers." Porter ground his teeth together. "Word is they're sending Coll."

"Coll?" Platt blanched when she recalled where else she had heard the name. "Tall guy? Real good-looking? Nice dresser?"

"He doesn't do anything for me," Porter replied. "But yeah. Sounds like him. You've met the guy?"

"He was in Charlotte. He was supposedly my new project manager."

"That is no project manager, Doctor Platt. That guy is a mob cleaner. He's who they send to mop up messes when failure is not an option." Porter shuddered. "Guy's a bona fide bogeyman. No one knows who he is or where he comes from. But it's no damn secret what he does."

Platt felt her gorge rising. "And that is?"

"He makes problems disappear for very rich assholes."

Platt had more or less expected this kind of answer. "What are we going to do?"

Porter turned the yoke and pulled the car off the main road. The solid rubber tires crunched the uneven surface of a poorly-maintained surface street, making Platt shudder. "We have plenty of safe places. Bad news or not, Coll has no pull in the KC Complex. Neither does GEED. If either of them head this way, we'll see 'em coming."

"Then what?"

"We will figure it out. Coll's scary, not bulletproof" Porter made a good show of tough talk, though Platt thought perhaps he was trying to convince himself more than her.

Porter zipped down a dark street at speeds his passenger considered quite reckless. The asphalt was pock-marked and cracked, making the whole vehicle shake as each obstacle jostled the car. In a moment, Platt realized just how far from the 'loop station they had come. The looming specter of a legendary mob enforcer and the new and terrifying terrain began to claw at the edges of her exterior calm.

"How much farther?" She tried to keep the apprehension out of her voice. Porter glanced her way, and his expression made it clear she had failed.

"Just a little bit more to go. We'll use the Rosedale entrance, 'cause it's the closest. The KC Complex is way outside of town, for obvious reasons." He ventured a guess at the reason for her unease. "You've never been this far out of a metro before, I'm guessing."

Platt shook her head. "Out of a metro? Never. I've never even been off a traffic grid."

This dragged a rough chuckle from the man. "It's not so bad out here. We don't get all those nice services a metro can provide, but nobody bothers us, either."

"You make living on the edge of civilization sound almost nice."

"You'll get used to it, but I can't promise you'll love it."

Genetic Equity Enforcement Division Selection Board Expert's Notes for Case SUL-002-a

Dr. Sharon Platt, Ph.D.

WITH GEED ASSISTANCE, I have managed to acquire Sullivan's birth records. I must admit, they are very troubling. The subject's genetic profile is complex, even by chimera standards. His designers were well beyond experimental in his creation. I would use the words "reckless" and "negligent" with equal enthusiasm in this case. It is a miracle his embryo ever got past the zygote stage. Even so, absolutely no thought was given to his quality of life, and I expect his childhood was one long traumatic episode.

First of all, his level of myostatin inhibition is just not sound. I expect he had to eat every hour or have a permanent feeding tube installed simply to survive infancy. Since he was genetically inclined toward aggression, this must have made his first years a never-ending cycle of hunger-induced fear and rage. The records indicate that extensive pharmaceutical intervention was employed to keep his personality from collapsing during this period. It is unknown if he has any lingering damage from this.

We don't get any really good data until he turns twelve. His modified hormonal profile meant that puberty was early and aggressive. Records show he was sixty-eight inches tall and one-hundred-sixty pounds on his twelfth birthday. We have Michael Sullivan's orders for his tutelage and schedule from those later years on record, and they are enlightening. The subject had extensive instruction in foreign languages, military history, economics, criminal justice, business, and law. He was also subjected to a physical training regimen that would challenge a professional athlete. Even with his (frankly superhuman) physical gifts, I am sure the subject found it a grueling existence. (Personal note: Michael Sullivan still has ninety-four years to serve, and it does my heart good to know that he will die in prison. What he put that child through was monstrous.)

The subject's adolescent testosterone-to-cortisol ratio was well into the danger zone and beyond, but aggression and psychosis continued to be managed pharmaceutically. As his hormone profile stabilized, he was weaned off the drugs as he developed better control of his urges. He has been entirely drug-free since the age of sixteen, even though his t:c ratio remains dangerously high. For the record, when GEED finally acquired him at that age, he passed all relevant psychological tests without the aid of modern medicine. At 75 inches tall and 245 pounds, Sullivan at sixteen was too dangerous for foster care. While I don't disagree with the decision, I'm concerned that spending the last two years of his minority as a ward of the state at a youth detention facility may have had adverse effects. Testing at this time demonstrates his physical capabilities to be beyond what could ever be considered within the realm of unaltered human genetic potential. As a personal note, I have studied many GMP soldiers and athletes, and the subject's strength, speed, and reflexes are significantly superior to any of them. It stands to reason, of course. A chimera is a designer product, not a mass-produced item.

I'm still trying to find his creche index, but in looking for it, I found something interesting in his design profile records. Acetylcholine, norepinephrine, and serotonin levels in his brain are all linked to dopamine. To some degree, this is not all that interesting.

However, it appears that in this case, dopamine has been used as a rate-limiting step to reward his brain for avoiding hyperarousal and its consequences. More on that follows.

On my first pass, I could not understand why the subject was not more out of control. On paper, he ought to be flying into blind rages with some frequency. Even as a fully-developed adult, his t:c ratio rivals that of most psychopaths. Now, acetylcholine is critical for skeletal muscle activation, as it controls rate coding for myofibrillar contraction. It plays a supportive role in neurological arousal in general, and this synergistic action makes it a favorite among genetic engineers for producing athletic enhancements. However, it also plays a major role in depression, meaning one cannot just play with the levels willy-nilly without consequences. That brings us to dopamine. Now, dopamine can either enhance aggression or mitigate the impulsiveness caused by aggression, depending on the exact neurochemical environment and, most importantly, any existing habituated feedback mechanisms.

Thanks to an over-production of gamma-aminobutyric acid (GABA), the subject can tolerate absolutely staggering quantities of arousal without experiencing anxiety or a fear response. Either by design or happenstance, the reward center of his brain reacts to these situations with an increase in dopamine. Quite simply, the subject responds to stress by calming down. This is not conscious control. He simply cannot experience neurological arousal above a certain level without triggering a flood of dopamine and a corresponding drop in serotonin. The higher the stress, the calmer he gets.

It is easy to see why his designers thought this was desirable. His athletic enhancements coupled with his near-perfect calm and focus under pressure would seem to make him an ideal combatant. But that is where they were wrong. For some reason, the subject is almost pathologically averse to fully engaging in physical violence. When he does fight, he uses only as much force as it takes to resolve the conflict with minimal injury. Despite the efforts of his father, the subject is no bloodthirsty killer. (Not yet, anyway.) I will refer to my extensive experience in this field and assert that I know the signs when I see them.

Nevertheless, I am still very concerned. Because his baseline t:c ratio remains high, he lives his life in a constant state of unfocused aggression. The elevated acetylcholine protects him from depression over it, but the artificial rate-limiting step on hyper-arousal means he can never access or confront emotions like anger or fear. He can and does experience them, but they do not follow the sort of natural progression with which the human brain has evolved to process them. This is not conducive to good mental health. At best, he experiences flashes of intensity, only to have them slip away un-confronted and un-explored.

Most troubling, I see no indications that the system is foolproof. My initial impression of the subject indicates that he may be capable of overriding this dopamine trigger if he wanted to. It is possible, and even likely, that some combination of events or triggers could surpass the rate-limiting aspect of dopamine, or that he could become habituated to ignore it. Yet, the record on this matter is very clear: The subject is not (excessively) impulsive, and he is not (unreasonably) violent. Despite his unpleasant veneer and the spirited assertions of certain members of the Selection Board, he is the very model of iron discipline and self-control.

The next step is to explore his various habituated feedback mechanisms, as the answer may be found there. He has admitted to having positive interactions with his anger before. Namely during training sessions with various martial arts instructors. I am not a subscriber to the romantic "kung fu mental discipline" trope foisted upon us by cinema, and I do not believe his success has anything to do with fortune-cookie Zen silliness. However, combat sports can produce similar levels of arousal to actual fighting, and therein the subject probably had the opportunity to learn to deal with his condition. I will look deeper into this aspect of his development to see if he is as stable as he appears, or if we are all just being fooled by a bona fide psychopath.

CHAPTER TWELVE

The Charlotte Municipal Law Enforcement office smelled like burned coffee and detergent. Despite crinkling his nose at the overwhelming olfactory assault, Sullivan supposed a busy MLEO hub that did not reek of the unwashed masses and methamphetamine residue was a good thing. Sullivan and Fagan had been ushered into a cubicle farm adjacent to the main intake and processing area, and here they awaited what helpful information Charlotte Municipal Law Enforcement could provide. To this effect, a tired lieutenant handed Sullivan a tablet and stated, "Doctor Platt boarded the 15:50 'loop run to KC yesterday, Warden." The tablet's screen showed what appeared to be surveillance camera video of a thin line of people shuffling into a Hyperloop car. This by itself would be entirely useless and unhelpful. However, the lieutenant had marked one particular boarder with a helpful yellow outline. Sullivan paused the playback and tapped on the highlighted person. The face expanded to fill the screen, and several blue dots indicated where facial recognition software had identified defining characteristics. She was pretty enough, he supposed, if a touch harried-looking. Her hair was shoulder length and brown, her eyes bright blue. She looked young to Sullivan, though he suspected this was a function of his own jaded nature and not a reliable indicator of actual age. A box blinked into view next to the hollow-eyed woman in the 'loop station. This displayed a UCLA employee identification picture wearing identical dots. Though the woman on the security camera looked older, more tired, and substantially more scared than the fresh-faced girl in the ID photo, Sullivan immediately concurred with the station AI that this was the same person. His gaze also picked up the small blond girl holding the woman's hand. She looked no older than ten, and Sullivan's stomach heaved at the sight of her. He did not understand why, and he did not like it.

"That's our runner, all right," the warden said. He showed the tablet to Fagan, who grunted his agreement. Turning back to the lieutenant, Sullivan asked the logical next question. "We have anything from the KC station? Did they meet someone there? Did they have a car waiting?"

"Funny thing, that," said the lieutenant with a grimace. "It appears that the KC 'loop station had a weird malfunction right as that 'loop car arrived."

"Well, that's just really goddamn convenient for them, isn't it?" Sullivan sighed. "KC Metro Law Enforcement got anything to say for themselves on that front?"

The lieutenant answered with a snort. "Yeah. They say they're looking into it."

Fagan wiped a palm across his face and groaned, "They're in that complex already, aren't they?"

"Seems a safe bet," Sullivan said.

"Good luck with that, wardens," the lieutenant chuckled, earning him blank stares from the pair.

As was his nature, Sullivan seemed poised to deliver a response both ill-timed and inappropriate. Fagan preempted this with a massive paw to his partner's shoulder. He addressed the lieutenant before Sullivan could blurt out something that might harm his career. "Thank you, Lieutenant. Genetic Equity appreciates your assistance."

"My pleasure," the lieutenant said. "Good hunting."

Fagan dragged Sullivan from the chuckling cop's office and guided the quietly fuming man down the halls of Charlotte's main police station. Sullivan did not resist much. Fagan was clearly in the right, and a wise man would do well to follow his example. It would not do to have Fagan knowing this, so he put up just enough of a fight to communicate his displeasure without eliciting a more spirited response from the larger man. As they exited onto the sidewalk, Sullivan inhaled a deep breath and let it out as a long sigh. When he had cleared his lungs and purged his brain of the excess acetylcholine, he growled an expressive and emphatic, "Fuck."

"I hear you, partner," Fagan said. "Losing them in a complex is going to piss Horowitz off."

"You know damn well I don't intend to lose them," Sullivan said.

"Would you believe I had a real strong feeling you were going to say something like that?"

"I assume you are going to try to talk me out of it?"

"It really depends on how shitty your plan is."

"I'm still putting it together."

Fagan nodded. "So kind of shitty, then?"

"It's a work in progress." Sullivan wanted to be irritated, but as usual, Fagan had a point. "Let's go find food. I can't plan when I'm hungry."

"Oh, this is going to be good," Fagan chuckled. He pulled his phone from a jacket pocket and began to thumb through screens. "Let me find a restaurant that has booths my size. You can tell me all about your non-plan while I eat."

Several minutes later, the two wardens found themselves seated at a booth in a Japanese noodle restaurant. Fagan flipped absently through the menu screens, making his selections with satisfied grunts. When he was done, he looked up to see Sullivan doing the same.

"You ever been in a complex?" Fagan asked.

"Once. When I was a kid." Sullivan stabbed the screen with a forefinger without looking up.

"You were a kid? I thought you came out of the creche a fully-formed adult asshole."

"No. I was only a partially-formed asshole. Assholery at my level requires years of practice. Anyway, Mickey Sullivan took me into the KC Complex when I was fourteen. Wanted me to help with a negotiation." Finally, he looked over to meet Fagan's eyes. "You know, to teach me the family trade."

"Shit, man." Fagan tried to back-pedal. "I wasn't trying to get into your past..."

Sullivan waved him off. "It's no big thing. I mean, I was raised by a mobster to be a mobster. I've seen a lot of mobster shit. Sometimes, the only way to get some mobster shit done is to go where no one can follow."

"The complexes," Fagan said.

"Yup."

"At least you've been to this one before. That's a bit of serendipity, right? Any insights before we try our luck?"

Sullivan nodded. "These places are not as lawless as the press makes them out to be. They have rigid hierarchies and rules for keeping conflicts minimal. They will pretty much kill us on sight if they find out we are GEED, though. Lots of GiMPs run to the complexes to avoid government service."

"Better rule in hell than serve in heaven, huh?" Fagan opined.

"Serve or run. We all made our choice, partner." Sullivan continued his briefing. "But we won't stick out too much, at least. We will need convincing cover stories, but your size and my obvious good breeding won't throw them off if we spin it right."

"Then what?" Fagan asked.

"Then we have to find one woman and a little girl among a hundred and thirty square miles of abandoned and repurposed manufacturing facilities and their constituent support buildings."

"Before the bad guys do," the bigger man added.

"Before the bad guys do," Sullivan said. Then with a frown he added, "Bad guys we have yet to identify."

"Oh, I think once the rest of the Chicago stash gets decrypted, we'll have some good leads." Fagan winked at Sullivan. "I think we have a real good idea already."

"How do you figure?" Sullivan asked.

"Follow the money, runt. This operation was funded entirely in cryptcoin, which is no surprise. But how much did it cost, and how much did they lose by burning a whole R&D site?"

Sullivan pointed his fork at Fagan. "A metric shit-ton, partner. Possibly even two metric shit-tons."

"Exactly. We know that our top-secret project cost millions in volatile pseudo-currency, and we know that the backers were willing to burn all that investment just to hide it. What does that tell us?"

"These guys are rich in the kind of way that makes money meaningless."

Fagan pointed back. "Bingo! That means governments, megacorporations, and a few select individuals and organizations."

"Corps want no part of this," Sullivan interjected. "It's too much risk for too little reward."

"Governments?" Fagan offered.

"They're on the list. Especially all those Pan-Asian remnants."

"And finally...?"

Sullivan sighed theatrically. "The mob."

"See?" Fagan crowed. "Two solid suspects right off the bat." Then, with less enthusiasm, "How to narrow it down, though?"

"I have a plan for that," Sullivan said with a sly smile. "But you won't like it."

"Gonna want a good dinner, then," Fagan said with a grin as their beers and appetizers arrived. The men were just beginning to tuck into the first round when Sullivan's ID card buzzed.

"Shit," he said. "Horowitz is looking for me. What should I tell her?"

"Tell her the truth, dumbass. She's your boss."

"She is not going to want us going into the complex, Fagan."

"Well, duh. Guess you'll just have to convince her." A pork dumpling disappeared into the cavernous opening beneath Fagan's mustache. "Try being charming. Just pretend you want to get into her pants."

Sullivan scowled at the bearded giant, now chuckling into the foam of an enormous beer. In a rare moment of forbearance, he declined to fire an insult at his partner. He instead elected to focus on the herculean task of convincing a woman who did not like him very much to let him run an operation inside an impenetrable hub of criminal and terrorist activity. The strategist in Sullivan surmised that this would be enough of a challenge, and adding a fistfight with a legitimate giant to his list of obstacles did not sound like a good idea. Accompanied by the sound of Fagan's smug snickering, he pulled out his phone and keyed in his captain's code. Horowitz did not bother with a salutation. On the second chime, her acerbic voice simply barked, "Report."

"Good to hear from you, too, Captain. We're doing and fine, and hope you are as well. How are the spawn? Everybody hatch yet?"

Horowitz, who was never in the mood for Sullivan's version of banter, ignored him. "Cut the shit, Sullivan. What's going on down there? I have reports of a goddamn massacre and implications that our operations are compromised. Tell me you haven't screwed this up already."

"Well, Captain, you will no doubt be thrilled to hear that this screw-up has nothing to do with me. You can relax on that front." He paused to sip his beer. "But somehow, the bad guys got wind we were coming, and instead of their usual sweep-and-clear, they decided to go scorched earth on the whole facility."

"Why the hell would they do that? Killing a hundred people is a ton of risk to take on over one production facility."

"Well, that's the interesting part. It's not a production facility. A good chunk of it was straight up R&D. It looks like they had some kind of super-secret project going on that they wanted to keep buried."

An uncomfortable silence followed. Sullivan imagined Horowitz chewing her lip while she processed this information. Finally, she responded. "And is it buried?"

"Fagan and I don't think so. We have evidence that one of the researchers escaped, and we are pretty sure that whoever ran that operation wants their missing scientist back very badly."

"How confident are you of this?"

"This is what I do, Captain. I was literally born in a place just like that one. We know for a fact that one research lead bolted from the facility prior to the massacre. An emergency exit was activated just before the shooting started, and we have it on good authority the doctor was on a 'loop car headed for KC."

"So you assume this doctor is headed for the complexes?"

"Is there any other reason for a scientist involved in illegal genetic research to flee to Kansas City? It's the only place on the continent where both GEED and the mob struggle to operate."

Horowitz breathed a long, exasperated sigh into the phone. "I suppose you want to follow this lead?"

"That would be a safe assumption, yes."

"Even though it is a terrible idea?"

"All of my best ideas sound terrible, Captain. Fagan will vouch for that."

Fagan sputtered at this, spraying beer across the table. Sullivan tossed him a napkin and a dirty look and went on. "This whole thing smells wrong, Captain. Mobsters can be brutal, but they don't kill a hundred people on a whim, and they don't sink expensive operations for the hell of it. Whoever did this used well-trained paramilitary operators with clear objectives. We got plain damn lucky when that doctor escaped, and there is no guarantee we will stay lucky. If we lose this, who knows what else we'll miss."

"Do you have a plan?"

"I'm working on it."

"So that's a 'no' then."

"I said I'm working on it!"

"Don't take a tone with me, Warden. What does Fagan think?"

"He agrees with me."

"I never said that!" Fagan said, loud enough for Horowitz to hear.

Sullivan could almost hear the captain's eyes narrowing as she growled, "Tell him to key in."

Sullivan looked at his partner. "Nice job, wise guy. Now she wants you to key in."

Fagan pulled his own phone from a pocket and linked to Sullivan's. "I'm in," he announced.

Horowitz cut to the chase. "Is Sullivan off his meds again, or is this legit?"

The giant snorted at the ribbing but answered truthfully. "He's not wrong, Captain. The scene was ugly, and something stinks about the whole thing. I think getting into the KC Complex is going to be a very tall order, either way." He found Sullivan staring at him and added, "But yeah, I think we have to at least try."

"Christ," Horowitz moaned. "You're a bad influence on him already, Sullivan. Fine. You want to go infiltrate the complex? We can't do much to help you once you're in. I want your plan to infiltrate and extract this Doctor Platt on my desk before sunrise. I want schedules, contingencies, back-ups, fail-safes, and eject buttons spelled out."

Sullivan's face fell. "I was sort of hoping to scope it out before we locked in a lot of resources..."

"Bullshit. You were hoping to get drunk and climb up some poor, unsuspecting local's skirt tonight. Then tomorrow, you were going to get some sleep on the 'loop car before improvising your way through a no man's land of anti-government criminals far from any help we can provide."

Sullivan could not deny there was some truth to that, though he would never admit it. "Captain..."

"Shut it, Warden. Fagan?"

"Yeah, Captain?"

"If any part of this operation starts to look like Sullivan's usual one-man-army crap, you drag him out of there kicking and screaming. Copy?"

"Copy."

"Good. I look forward to laughing at your plan. You have till six a.m. Oh, yeah. Be sure to check in with Doctor Connors before you move if you value your career. Horowitz out."

The line clicked dead, leaving both men staring stupidly at each other with phones pressed to their ears. Sullivan dropped his to the table with a disappointed huff. "And they say I'm an asshole."

"At least she didn't pull us back," Fagan replied, putting his own phone back in his pocket. "I couldn't help but notice that you neglected to mention the small child to our esteemed captain."

"Thanks for not calling me out on that."

"You want to tell me why you left that part out?"

The waiter chose this moment to show up with four orders of ramen. Sullivan held his answer until after the man had left. "We missed our shot at her because somebody leaked that we were coming. I just don't want any more information floating around than strictly necessary. By holding some information back, I can get a better idea of the leak's source based on what the bad guys do and do not know ahead of time."

Fagan bobbed his head. "I'll buy that. But you really think our dedicated GEED comm signal is bugged?"

"Nope."

"So you suspect the captain?" Fagan stopped shoveling food into his maw to fix Sullivan with a stern glare. "That's a real big thing to suspect, Warden."

"Is it?" Sullivan replied, his tone even. "She told me, and I quote, 'I want your plan to infiltrate and extract this Doctor Platt on my desk before sunrise.' Any part of that sound weird to you?"

Fagan dropped his spoon, eyes wide and terrified beneath his bushy brows. "You never mentioned the doctor's name!"

"I did not."

The big man's head dropped into his waiting hands, and it shook slowly as he muttered, "Oh shit. Oh shit shit shit shit shit."

Indifferent to his partner's dismay, Sullivan resumed eating. "So either the captain is into some really bad stuff, or she has access to intelligence she doesn't want us to know about. Either way, it's fishy as all hell." He looked up at the still groaning man across the table and added, "We just can't trust her."

"It might be less sinister than all that, man." Fagan squared himself with a cleansing breath. "Maybe she has other sources and just doesn't trust us."

"You mean she doesn't trust me," Sullivan corrected over the top of his beer glass.

The giant did not contest it. "It's no secret she doesn't like you very much."

"It's a possibility, sure. But it changes nothing. We will need to do this run alone and as radio silent as possible." Sullivan turned deathly serious. "I can't really put that on you, so if you want to jump off this ride, I understand."

"No, no. I'm in. That little kid needs help, no matter what the hell else is going on." Fagan picked up his spoon again before adding, "And you are really not qualified to handle a child."

CHAPTER THIRTEEN

The heat of a Kansas City summer day made Connecticut feel pleasant in comparison. The thick air slapped the wardens across the face with a solid wave of sticky humid oppression as soon as they left the 'loop station and stepped onto the dirty concrete of the sidewalk.

"Ah, fucking hell!" Sullivan exclaimed when the shock of getting swamped with sub-tropical heat and humidity had subsided.

"Touch warm today, no?" Fagan opined with a subtle dryness that irked the smaller man.

"Jesus!" was all Sullivan could muster for a reply. "How are you not dying?"

"I'm pretty much always warm, so I stopped caring years ago."

"Lucky you. Let's flag a hack."

Sullivan seemed ready to step out onto the street. A not-so-gentle hand from Fagan stopped him. "You want the grid to flag you as a warden?" the giant asked. "Don't be jaywalking until we are clear of the traffic 'net, okay?"

"Shit," Sullivan hissed. "I don't do undercover shit that much."

"Imagine that," Fagan said. "Would you believe that I don't get much of that action, either? Feels discriminatory. I should file a complaint."

He extended a hand to the waiting line of cars, the first of which pulled forward to where they stood. Fagan looked at the medium-sized people-hauler and scowled. "This is going to suck."

The side door slid open with the whine of aging electric motors, revealing a dingy interior redolent of body odor and the acrid tang of methamphetamines. "Already does," Sullivan said. "You first."

"Thanks," Fagan said. With a pained expression, he then began the laborious process of wedging his enormous body into a vehicle designed for people half his size.

Sullivan used this opportunity to stash their bags in the cargo section. When he came back around, he found his partner taking up more than three quarters of the passenger cabin. Sullivan thus accepted his fate and set about jamming his own not-inconsiderable mass into what space remained. Fagan chuckled at his contortions. "At least we'll both be miserable."

"And this is a good thing?" Sullivan did not share in the humor. He turned to the driver's cab partition and shouted, "Hey! We need to get to Rosedale. You good with that?"

The driver said nothing, but he must have heard, because the car surged into aggressive acceleration. Fagan turned slightly pale at the sudden movement, and Sullivan took the opportunity to exact revenge on his partner. "Little fast for you, Fagan?"

"I hate it when people self-drive," was the curt response. Then he changed the subject. "What are the chances she's at Rosedale?"

"Slim to none, but it's the only way I know of to get into the complexes without attracting a lot of attention. Most GiMP runners get to the Rosedale Complex first. We will be a lot less conspicuous if we start there. Even you."

"You think she's moved on?"

Sullivan nodded. "She's too smart to run without a plan. I bet she had this whole thing worked out in advance."

"She has outside help." It was a statement, not a question.

Sullivan nodded. "Almost has to, right? She's an academic. No strong social ties, working in shadowy bio-med facilities on illegal projects all these years. No way she runs on her own without getting caught."

"You figure it's Railroad? Or maybe a rival organization?"

"Now that, my oversized friend, is an excellent question."

A viewing panel in the partition between the cab and the passenger compartment slid open with a tortured squeal. The driver's grizzled face appeared, and his wheezy voice stated, "Rosedale in forty minutes. Pay up now."

"You want dollars or 'coin?" Sullivan asked.

"'Coin works," the driver said. "No sense getting the government involved, right?"

"I hear that," Sullivan said, his tone artificially amicable. He placed a small black box against the payment panel and held it there while the two devices negotiated the transfer of untraceable electronic sums.

"All set," the driver said. "I'll drop you at the south gate. Most new blood will want to start there." The driver gave Sullivan a knowing look through the partition. "If you find yourself lost or needing help, just look for one of the Road Crew guys. They'll know how to manage any lingering obligations you might be avoiding. They'll spot the big fella pretty quick, so if they approach, you just be cool. The Road Crew runs admissions at Rosedale, so make sure you play nice. Nobody is going to worry about your GMP status, either."

"Thanks for the tip," Fagan said with a smile.

"Folks around our complex got no love for the Genetic Equity Act." The driver said this as if that was all that needed saying.

Fagan kept the smile on his face as the panel closed. Then he raised an eyebrow to Sullivan. "Well, that was mighty neighborly of him."

Sullivan shrugged. "People out here really don't like the federal government. They think America has sold out to the concept of globalism."

"They aren't interested in being part of our new Global Republic, huh?"

"They call it a hegemony. To them, it's just another bunch of political elites making decisions for people they don't actually represent."

"Well, I suppose they come by that honestly," Fagan said. "Where was the federal government or even the New Republic when they shut down the complexes? Three million people lost their jobs and homes overnight."

"Yeah. That was handled poorly."

Fagan snorted, "You think?"

"Too bad it's not that black and white, though. What options were there?" Sullivan shifted to try to get more comfortable. "I studied this quite a bit when I was with... well, when I was younger. Imagine you're the government. You got millions of people crammed into six multi-trillion-dollar industrial megaplexes cranking out drones and other equipment to fight a war against a hundred million genetically-enhanced Chinese super-soldiers. You've seized all production assets, federalized the economy of a whole country, and essentially conscripted half the population to either fight or produce. By the time victory was assured, the dollar was not worth printing anymore, secondary and tertiary economies had cropped up, and while you weren't looking, a massive class of organized criminals got nicely entrenched because you were too busy preventing Armageddon to stop them. The only tool you have to shift a giant economic machine away from a wartime footing is the dollar, and that's been getting the crap kicked out of it for most of a decade."

"But just firing everybody...?" Fagan left the implication hanging.

Sullivan barreled on. "So, you're stuck with a giant production apparatus and its workforce. But the problem is that none of it was ever designed to make a profit, and the marketplace for those goods died with the last bits of the PRC ruling class. It was a massive expense made necessary by the threat of goddamn annihilation." Sullivan, warming to his narrative, twirled a finger in a circle. "Worker housing, medical care, schools, and all those other services that these people enjoyed for years when the feds were buying were barely sustainable even when the dollar had some oomph, but without a war to fuel it? Hah! It was just one big unfunded liability driving a forty-four percent flat tax. And then cryptcoin hit in '33." Sullivan shook his head and sneered. "That shit killed it all. Now the rich criminals had a place to hide money that couldn't be found or taxed. Twenty percent of the circulating currency in the U.S. disappeared overnight. Most folks don't get how close to straight-up economic collapse we were in those days. The fed had to stop the bleeding before all the mobsters finished the job the Chinese had started."

"So they killed the complexes," Fagan said.

"They tried re-training and job placement. Historically, almost a third of complex employees found new jobs and careers within eighteen months. No one mentions that, of course. But a lot of the workers had gotten accustomed to the benefits of the complexes, so they refused to take the help. Others didn't have the aptitude to survive in the new economy and refused to leave. As a group, they tried to hold the government hostage by squatting. The government's response was, well, uninspired."

"The Rosedale Riots," Fagan nodded. "I watched them from my fifth-grade social studies class."

"I was home-schooled," Sullivan said. "But my tutors were thrilled to have the riots as a teaching tool. The mob always makes a profit when people are dying." Sullivan shook himself, as if to clear a bad memory. "Anyway. The riots were a classic example of a horrible situation made worse by stupid people on both sides."

Fagan interjected, "But the riots make it easy to see why the people here don't have a lot of nice things to say about the federal government, and why they have no use for the New Republic."

Sullivan accepted this with a nod before explaining further. "The U.S. would never have even agreed to the New Republic movement if not for the economic relief and the adoption of the dollar as global currency. The UN bought our military horsepower with that deal, and closing the complexes was just one of the terms."

"Can't have a member of our new world order with all those weapons factories?"

"Bingo."

"So there really was no choice?"

"There never is. But that's not exactly comforting to the folks who got fired. And they are correct when they call it selling out. It wasn't just about weapons. The U.S. had to shed all those unsupportable financial obligations to get the deal we needed to survive. It was that or total collapse."

"Ever notice how it's always the little guy who gets fucked the hardest when that happens?"

"Since the dawn of time. But it ain't all bad. Every once in a while, the little guy eats the big guy." A sly smile turned the corners of Sullivan's mouth. "But then again, that makes the little guy into the new big guy..."

Fagan adopted a theatrical tone. "And the cycle begins anew!"

"To everything, a season," Sullivan replied.

The car jerked to a halt, and Fagan gasped as the inertia nearly sent him slumping into Sullivan. "Fucking self-drive," the giant muttered as he composed himself.

"Welcome to Rosedale," the driver said through a speaker. "Good luck."

The door slid open, and the two men untangled themselves from each other and the car. As each uncoiled to their full height and stretched, a sea of faces turned to mark the newcomers. Fagan retreated to the back of the car to retrieve their bags, and Sullivan took the opportunity to look around.

The Rosedale section of the KC Complex stood a rust-brown monument to the desperation of a nation at war. Hundreds of identical gray concrete buildings sat in squat rows. None of the outer buildings rose taller than forty feet, each with three rings of narrow, bronze-tinted windows striping the above-ground floors. Sullivan knew that beneath his feet, every one of these ugly bunkers was connected to the other, and that the true size and majesty of the complexes was found well underground.

"They're like icebergs," he said when Fagan tromped up next to him. "You can only see the part that's above the water."

The giant clapped him on the back. "They say the part you can't see is what kills you."

"They aren't wrong about that," Sullivan replied. "You got your game face on?"

"Let's do this."

The men began the long walk from the cracked street to the main gate of the Rosedale Complex. A small crowd milled around outside. Some looked like garden-variety hobos, but most had the appearance of troublemakers. Sullivan saw how they leaned against bollards with bland expressions of malice and walked with a sort of sculpted braggadocio. Just like the street hoods and gangsters he had known as a child, these men and women only fooled the fearful. Even the fourteen-year-old John Sullivan had not been impressed with the type. His father had called them hyenas—tough in groups and when faced with weak prey, but weak and easily cowed when challenged by someone stronger. Mickey Sullivan's Boston accent filled his memories as Sullivan recalled his last trip to the complexes.

"They ain't lions, Johnny. They ain't like you. The lion ain't afraid of shit because he already knows who's the baddest thing in the jungle."

Even at fourteen, Sullivan had been irritated by all the things he knew to be wrong about that statement. He had pointed out in that sullen teenager's way that lions don't live in jungles and were afraid of many other savannah species. His father, as usual, was neither impressed nor appreciative of the input. "What the fuck is a cape buffalo?" the mobster had asked in response to his son's correction. "Buffalos ain't scary, Johnny. You gotta be the lion." The junior Sullivan had given up at that point.

Looking upon the arrayed buffet of opportunistic street trash, Sullivan could not find fault with his father's assessment beyond the generally inadequate understanding of African wildlife. These were low-level scavengers playing at being predators. Yet hyenas in large numbers were dangerous, so he locked his face in a scowl of streetwise aggression.

Sullivan approached the entrance as if he owned it. He had chosen a dirty brown hooded jacket over a white T-shirt and worn dungarees for his disguise. It had been necessary to ditch his service weapon, as the Beretta 10-millimeter automatic and its caseless ammunition were a dead giveaway that he was some kind of federal agent. Now, an old replica .44 special someone had modified to shoot caseless ammo rode in a cheap holster at the small of his back. He had found the revolver at a pawn shop for a pittance. The antique had twice the mass and cycled at a fraction of the rate of his Beretta, though Sullivan allowed that the bullets were large, and it would not malfunction no matter what he put it through. The trade-off seemed acceptable. He was letting his beard grow in, and with the hood pulled low over his forehead, the sandy stubble deepened the shadows of his cheeks and emphasized the geometric squareness of his jaw.

He heard Fagan fall in to his left and stifled a knowing smile. All eyes would be on the giant, and rightly so. If John Sullivan played the part of a lion, then Patrick Fagan would have to be a cape buffalo. Together, they stomped to the main gate without sparing the now-gaping crowd a single glance. Only when they had reached the huge brown metal doors did Sullivan look to either side. The crowd did nothing untoward. Each wandering miscreant seemed invested in their own concerns, or at least tried very hard to appear nonchalant. Quite a few young men stood close to the gate. These were arrayed in dense clumps, where they played games of chance while smoking various things from various implements. Sullivan quickly noted a general similarity in style and color of clothing among them, and surmised he was dealing with one of the local gangs. His suspicions grew when he caught several surreptitious glances thrown his way. He met these glances with his own narrowed eyes, while the remaining people shuffled about the business of being poor and not wanting to get harassed.

Addressing one young man in particular, Sullivan called out, "Okay. What's the deal with the door?" Meeting a blank look, he let his eyes touch each face in the courtyard, his gaze a challenge. "Nobody? None of you know how to get it open?"

One of the men in gang colors stood up from his dice game. He was of medium height and lanky, wearing stained brown leather pants and an orange vest. Sullivan picked out the butt of a pistol at his waist. The vest being too snug to hide the telltale bulge, it was clearly an intentional display. The man was no older than twenty, and he walked toward the wardens with a swagger only a young man could think was fooling anyone. "You want inside, buddy?"

Sullivan showed his teeth in what might have been a smile if his eyes were not saying something totally different. "That's right. What's the story?"

"Well," the gangster said, stopping about three feet from Sullivan. "There's the issue of the entrance fee."

"Imagine that," Fagan rumbled. The pure, unfiltered menace in his tone surprised Sullivan. The growl came in stark contrast to the big man's normally affable nature. The gangster flinched, and Sullivan could not suppress the snort of mirth that escaped his lips.

"I'll make you a deal, kid," he offered. "You get that door open, and I won't have the SOAP here break your spine like kindling. Sound good?"

The young man swallowed, his eyes glued to the seven-and-a-half-foot behemoth. The fingers of his right hand twitched, and Sullivan shook his head. "If you go for that piece, kid, I might just take it away and shoot you with it. The big guy is a genuine SOAP, and I'm a level five MINK. We're trying real fucking hard to avoid problems, but we aren't taking any shit, either. Just open the goddamn door." As an afterthought, Sullivan added an insincere, "Please."

The young gangster stood still for a moment. The eyes of his crew were on him, searching for signs of weakness or fear. He stalled. "What the fuck is a SOAP?"

"Selectively Optimized Acromegaly Package," Fagan answered. "I'm huge and strong, but my heart won't burst, and my joints don't tear themselves apart. I'm a real expensive morph, shorty. People will be looking for me, and I'd rather not get found."

"You're a troll?"

The street vernacular for Fagan's modification was not popular with the big man. "Call me that again, and you'll be shitting into a bag for the rest of your life."

"Easy, buddy," the young man said, far friendlier now. "No goddamn offense meant. I can waive the fee for a... what was that? A SOAP?" He shrugged. "Lots of folks will want to talk to you anyway. Cut me in on whatever action you get, and I'll make sure you get taken care of in there. Deal?"

"I'm amenable," Fagan said. "And you are?"

"Call me Skip," the young man said. Then he turned to Sullivan. "As for you..."

"Myostatin Inhibition with Neuro-Kinetic enhancement," Sullivan said quickly, anticipating the next question. "And yes, I really am a level five. You got an insulting word for one of those?"

"I know what a MINK is, okay?"

Sullivan doubted that very much. "Sure, you do. My buddy and I are really hot commodities right now, and we'd like to avoid a lifetime of government employment, you get me?"

"You're really a level five?" Skip sounded skeptical. "You got, like, proof or something?"

Like the beat of a hummingbird's wing, Sullivan reached out and flicked Skip across the bridge of the nose. Even as the gangster reached up to clutch at his face, Sullivan's other hand removed Skip's pistol from underneath the orange vest. Skip's hands stopped ascending to his nose and reversed direction to clutch for his stolen weapon. With a grin, Sullivan flipped the worn automatic away and up to eye level. When Skip again grabbed for the pistol, Sullivan dropped the magazine right in front of his eyes. As it fell, Sullivan caught the descending piece with his other hand. Well behind the action, Skip started to reach for the gun again, and Sullivan twisted it away from the clumsy movement. Somehow, Skip found himself clutching the magazine instead, and while he stared stupidly at it, Sullivan separated the pistol's receiver from the frame with a deft twist. He tossed both to the stunned youth, who instinctively dropped the magazine to catch the two pieces of his pistol. He failed. Magazine, receiver, and frame all fell to the concrete with a metallic clatter. Skip looked up from the mess to find that somewhere in the mix, Sullivan had procured a gun of his own. The ice-cold muzzle of an antique revolver pushed against his forehead with far more pressure than was necessary to make his point.

"Convinced yet?" Sullivan asked.

The crowd had ended all pretense toward other tasks and were watching the action with wide eyes. The rest of the gang seemed frozen by equal parts fear and indecision. Skip held up his hands, and they seemed to calm.

"That'll do, MINK," he said. "You guys wanna be called something or not?"

"Call me Suds," Fagan said. "The little guy is Sully."

"Suds and Sully, huh?" Skip pushed the muzzle of Sullivan's gun away from his forehead with a lopsided smile. "Cute. Okay. I'm gonna bring you boys inside to get set up. Y'all play nice, and we can get you all the action you want. You can stay here and make money, or move on when you want to."

"So long as we cut you in?"

"Everything's got a price, Sully."

CHAPTER FOURTEEN

The interior of the Rosedale section smelled like gear oil and burned copper. Sullivan and Fagan followed Skip through a large open foyer with a row of huge steel doors at the back. Skip doled out pertinent information as they walked.

"This is the main entrance for the Rosedale section, and it's how you get to the different zones, ya get me? Every section has one of these, and they're called 'exchanges.' During the war, this part of the complex produced mobile drone control relays." He pointed to the doors at the back. "Each of those doors leads to a separate section. Like where specific production lines were and stuff like that. What you guys need to know to avoid trouble is that each section has its own rules."

"Because different gangs run them?" Sullivan asked, already knowing the answer.

Skip sounded unperturbed. "That's one way of putting it, yeah. Rosedale is still pretty far from the central hub, so we don't get a whole lot of attention from the Council. They let us run things our own way."

"Council?" Fagan asked. "This place has government?"

Skip stopped to look up at the giant. "We got about a million people living in a metroplex covering like a hundred and thirty-five square miles. You bet your ass there's government." He paused to amend his statement. "Well, more like a bunch of really powerful crime lords that meet on a regular basis to sort shit out. Too much fighting is bad for business, ya know. The Council makes sure business stays good."

"And the feds don't do anything about it?" Fagan sounded incredulous.

Skip actually laughed out loud. "What can they do? They really gonna pick a fight with a million people dug into a fortified position? The structures go almost a thousand feet into the ground, man. They'd have to nuke us from orbit to have a chance, and even that won't get all of us."

Sullivan added his two cents' worth. "It's a risk versus reward thing. They could sweep the complexes clear if they really wanted to, but that would cost money and political capital. As long as the complexes don't make any noise, it's easier to ignore the squatters than it is to make war on your own soil. The U.S. position within the New Republic is too fragile for that kind of scandal right now."

Skip stopped and gave both men a stern look. "It's best not to talk about that sort of thing in here, okay? Lots of folks will pop right off if you go down that rabbit hole, you hear me?"

"Touchy subject?" Sullivan asked with a smile.

"Take a tip, fresh meat. The less said about The Hegemony, the better."

"Got it," Fagan grumbled before Sullivan could make the situation any more tense. "Don't talk about... uh... 'The Hegemony.' What about this Council? Anything we need to know?"

"Not in Rosedale," Skip replied and resumed walking. "Here, it's all gang turf." He pointed to the first of many doors. "That goes down to the Meat Market. You can get hookers and drugs and all sorts of shit down there. It's Tunnel Rat turf, so make sure you are right with the Rats before you try to get laid." He pointed to the next door. "Down there is Rosedale Station. It's the local hub for the trams that connect Rosedale to the rest of the KC Complex. The Road Crew..." he pointed to his orange vest and winked, "...we run the trams. That's why we get to man the gate. Traffic is our gig, so stay cool with us, and you can get anywhere you want." Skip pointed to the other doors in turn, "After that, you got the Reapers running the food production plant, the Devil Dogs at the power station, and the Pale Horses getting shit done at the mercantile. Those are your main players. Plenty of scrub crews run their own rackets all over, but they mostly stay out of the way of the bigger gangs."

"What keeps all these gangs from fighting each other for supremacy?" Fagan asked.

Sullivan answered before Skip got the chance. "Mutually assured destruction. If any two gangs get into it, the remaining gangs will pounce on the winner while it's still recovering. If all the gangs fight, a crew from another section of the complex will swoop in and take advantage." He looked to Skip. "I'm betting if it gets bad enough, this council of yours will step in and put a stop to it?"

"You got it," their guide replied. "Truth is, we all got a pretty good thing going on here, so there hasn't been a gang war in like fifteen years." He resumed his narration. "Up next is the dorms. Dorms are neutral turf, but I'll be real with you. If you are on anybody's shit list, 'neutral' is gonna be a real fuzzy concept down there. I'll take you there first and get you set up with a bed."

"For free?" Sullivan asked.

"Fuck, no. You chumps are gonna cut me in on whatever action you get in here. That's how it works. All the gangs will extend credit to newcomers in exchange for a cut of future earnings. My job is to broker those deals and get you started making money."

"For a cut."

Skip pointed a finger gun at Sullivan. "Damn right, Sully. And you two fuckers look like a damn good investment."

"We brought our own money," Fagan warned. "Don't get too excited."

Skip answered with a dismissive wave. "If you brought dollars, you wasted your time. If you got 'coin, great, but they don't spend real well this far from Hubtown. You need credits, man."

"I presume you will explain how that works?"

"A credit is equal to a single hour of unskilled manual labor. All debts in the KC Complex can be paid off with credits. It's like, an unwritten rule, y'know? A guy can choose not to take dollars, or 'coin, or barter if he doesn't want 'em. But he's got to take credits or the equivalent in labor if he wants to do business here. How do you think we maintain all the shit down here? Love of our fellow man?" Skip blew a raspberry. "Fuck that. The Council pays in credits for work done on the equipment. That way, the place doesn't fall apart."

Sullivan did not point out that this also meant that the Council controlled the value of their currency. He did not think that Skip would understand or care what that implied.

Skip was still talking. "The dorms in Rosedale only take credits, and the exchange rate for 'coin to creds is shit, I warn you now."

"Great," Sullivan sighed. "How about you just tell me where to find the Railroad, and I give you a bunch of 'coin?"

Skip stopped walking. "The Railroad usually finds you, but I can make it happen quick-like if you need it. How much 'coin?"

"Half of whatever number you're thinking of right now," Sullivan shot back. "To be paid after we have met with the Railroad."

"Five hundred," Skip said. "And you'll still need to get a dorm. The Railroad will want to vet you both before they come out to play."

"Fine," Sullivan said. "Take us to the dorms, then."

The wardens trailed the orange-vested man through one of the doors and down a long corridor. As they moved deeper into the complex, the hall sprouted offshoots and branches that Sullivan soon lost track of. With each step, the men began to see more and more people. They came in all configurations. Young and old, dirty and clean, big and small, the thickening tide of humanity seemed to eschew all notions of cultural identity. With the exceptions of gang members, there did not appear to be any sort of overarching fashion or theme to the denizens of Rosedale.

Skip led them to a wide lobby with a dirty office at one end. He rapped on the window with two knuckles and called "Hey! Hello? Fresh meat out here!"

A wizened old woman peeked from around a corner and squinted through the clear panel at the noise. "That you, Skip?"

"Yeah, Hazel. It's me. Got two new ones today."

The old woman shuffled to her side of the window and stared intently at the two wardens. She sniffed and remarked, "Big fuckers, aren't they?"

"You should see my sister," Fagan said. "I'm the little one in the family."

"Lots of work for trolls this month," the woman said. "I can get you a bed your size." Then she peered into Sullivan's face. "You got any skills, handsome?"

"Says he's a level five MINK," Skip answered. When Sullivan turned a searing glare his way, the gangster added, "And I fuckin' believe him!"

Hazel nodded. "Plenty of jobs for those, too. You guys need one bed or two?"

"Two," both men said in unison.

Hazel simply looked down at her tablet. "Ain't no business of mine either way. Eight creds per day for hot-bunking or twenty-four if you want your own pod. You're both going to be in demand, so I'll extend you one week in the pod. After that it's hard creds or nothing."

"We'll take a pod," Sullivan said. "If you take 'coin we'll pay in advance."

"I don't take 'coin," the old woman said. "But you can get it changed over at the Mercantile if you don't mind getting bent over and violated by the Pale Horses."

"We'll come back with credits," Sullivan advised the old woman and turned back to Skip. "Why the fuck didn't you take us there first?"

"I don't think you appreciate how bad the exchange rate is," Skip said with a knowing shake of his head.

"I don't think you appreciate just how much 'coin we have," Sullivan countered.

"I'd be careful who you mention that around," Hazel interjected with a sharp look at Skip. "Folks around here might think to take an opportunistic approach to a couple of nice boys who don't know the lay of the land yet."

Fagan beamed his friendliest smile at the woman. "Thank you, Hazel. You have been most kind. I'm sure our good friend Skip here will make sure that no one takes advantage of us. It'd be a real shame if he ended up a quadriplegic over an avoidable misunderstanding like that."

"Jeezis, you guys are intense!" Skip's fear sounded legitimate. "You wanna get fleeced that bad? Fine. I'll take you to the mercantile."

The trip to the Mercantile took longer than Sullivan would have thought. Being indoors made distances deceptive, and they walked for what felt like half an hour before emerging into a broad, vaulted cavern of a room. Sullivan estimated it to be a mile long and maybe half as wide. The space was crammed to the walls with storefronts stacked on top of each other. Skip saw the wide eyes on their faces and grinned. "The feds wanted the complexes to be completely enclosed and safe from bombing, so everything the workers needed was underground. Every section has plenty of shopping, restaurants, bars, recreation facilities, all that stuff."

"Take us to the bankers, then," Sullivan said.

"Yeah, sure." Skip failed to conceal the disappointment in his voice at Sullivan's dismissive tone. He led them past a row of clothing stores, inexplicably stocked with new products.

"Where the hell do you get all your goods?" Fagan asked.

"We make a lot of it. This place was always a production facility, so you'd be amazed at how much stuff we produce right here in the complexes. Beyond that, there is a real good smuggling network that gets new stock into the stores all the time. You're gonna pay out the ass, but if you got creds, you can get whatever you want."

"I never realized," Fagan said, his voice filled with wonder, "just how much of a functioning world there was down here. I learned about the complexes in school, but this is nothing like what I was taught."

"That's 'cause we make the feds look bad. As long as folks think we are a bunch of dirty, subterranean weirdos, they can ignore us." Skip led them to a gray metal door. "Here's the best Exchange in the area. Come on."

Inside, Sullivan could not suppress his bemusement at how organized the whole operation appeared. The place was clean and well-lit, the atmosphere quiet and professional. The only thing marring the otherwise benign appearance of the bank was the scruffy and openly aggressive nature of the patrons. Several people in wildly disparate outfits waited at a cordon for assistance from clerks seated behind a long counter. If Sullivan had to guess the occupations of the people in line, the answers would have included mundane things like laborer and waitress, as well as professional gunman and pimp. The disconnect between the environment and the occupants jarred his senses and put him on edge. Worse, he saw no private, computerized banking stations. Sullivan found this quaint, though he also supposed that the kinds of transactions going on here were best left off any official electronic records.

All eyes in the room turned to assess the newcomers, and as usual, they lingered over the pair of large men. Sullivan tried to keep his features neutral, and Fagan maintained the same look of genuine good humor on his face that he always did. Skip gestured to the line, and without a word, Sullivan took his place to wait for his turn. At the counter, a sour-looking man examined his 'coin vault with a handheld scanning device. Satisfied it contained no viruses, worms, or other hidden bits of nefarious software, he placed it into a slot on the counter and recited the exchange rate. If what Skip had said about a credit representing one hour of unskilled labor was true, then the quoted exchange rate was nothing short of revolting. The urge to throttle the smug little banker brought a flush of heat to Sullivan's cheeks. He squashed the flash of homicidal desire and withdrew enough credits to pay for their lodgings and have cash for bribes and other sundry things.

The banker slid a thin plastic rectangle the size of a domino across the counter with an admonishment that the credits encoded to it were untraceable and fully transferable. If he lost this chit, the money would not be recoverable, and he should not waste his time complaining to the bank about it. Sullivan answered with a glower and pocketed the money. He left the counter and rejoined his partner.

"Let's go pay Hazel and then figure out how to find the Railroad," he said when they were outside the bank.

"I need food," Fagan said. "I get irritable when I'm hungry."

"Can't have that." Sullivan's retort was sarcastic, though his own stomach added its own rumble to the conversation. "Fine. Food first."

"You buyin' lunch?" Skip asked. "I know a good place. Real meat and everything."

"Who are we to turn down real meat?" Sullivan shook his head at the implications that came with promises of 'real meat.' "Lead on, Skip."

The young man led the two wardens from the banking zone out into the larger retail areas. Within each bundle of storefronts, Skip pointed out the various clusters of eateries. Sullivan began to question the wisdom of consuming the offerings of many of these and despaired of ever tasting food again after passing the first few squalid establishments. As they moved closer to the center of the mercantile district, their options improved. The better neighborhood came with an assortment of places ranging from smelly, open-air stalls to free-standing structures bearing a promising resemblance to the kind of diners the wardens were accustomed to. It was outside one of the better-looking places that the trio ran into their first bit of trouble with the local color.

"Hey, Roadie!"

Skip's head jerked up at the sound of a man shouting. In a flash, his eyes locked onto the source of the cry, and his face hardened into a fierce scowl. A clump of men wearing identical black hooded sweatshirts detached from a larger group of people at a food stall. Sullivan counted seven in the group, and his trained gaze rapidly identified four more observing from secluded vantage points between stalls and stores. As the main group approached, Skip addressed them with a firm tone. "I'm working, boys." He gestured to the wardens. "All our stuff is in order. What's the issue?"

"You keep strange company, Roadie," the leader of the group said. "Word's come down through the Silk Road that a couple of hot GiMPs gonna be moving through. Major creds to the crew what finds them." The leader's eyes took in the two wardens. "Now, I gots a Roadie moving a troll and his pet MINK through the mercantile. Pale Horses need to know what's up, y'know?"

"Rules are rules, boys," Skip said. "These guys came through the gate like everyone else. You got a claim, you wait until the Road Crew gets them settled."

"This is Silk Road business, Roadie," the Pale Horse said. "Regular rules don't apply."

"Who's looking?" Sullivan interrupted. "What the fuck is the Silk Road?"

"Shut up, GiMP," the Pale Horse said. "We'll get to you when we're done with the Roadie."

Fagan spoke up next. "You know what? I'm getting real irritated with everyone here calling me a troll."

"Fuck you, troll," the Pale Horse said, his face a sneer.

Fagan's shaggy head tilted down at the leader of the Pale Horses. "A troll is someone who has been given acromegaly without any special modifications, little man. Now me?" Fagan showed his teeth in a big grin. "I ain't no damn troll. My acromegaly comes with myostatin inhibition, osteoplasia, and extra testosterone. Do you understand what all that means?"

The Pale Horse did not seem impressed. "Unless all that bullshit made you bulletproof, it means you need to shut the fuck up while me and the Roadie handle business, troll."

If the man thought the threat of being shot was going to settle the giant, Fagan disabused him of this immediately. "I'm trying to help you out here, tiny. I'm helping you see that you don't really have a good grasp on your situation, and I'd like you to reconsider your attitude before you lose control of it. I'm not a troll, and I'm not bulletproof. I'm stronger, faster, and tougher than any troll you've ever met. And I don't need to be bulletproof, because there's no way in hell you are ever going to get the chance to shoot me. Wanna know how I figure that?"

"Bitch, I don't give a fuck what the hell you think you are—"

Sullivan drew his pistol. The motion was subtle, executed with speed and precision well in excess of anything the Pale Horse could fathom. His mind was only just acknowledging that Sullivan had moved when the barrel of the warden's .44 filled his field of vision with the yawning blackness of its enormous bore. The other Pale Horses did not move. They never had the chance. The whole action had begun and ended before they could react to it. For a tense moment, nobody moved or spoke. Sullivan broke the silence with a wry observation. "You know, partner, I don't think this cockroach knows what the last two letters in MINK stand for."

With his humiliation at the gate still fresh in his mind, Skip addressed the Pale Horse with mock sympathy. "Don't feel bad. I didn't know either." He stepped out to the side so he could whisper into the Pale Horse's ear. "Turns out they stand for 'neuro kinetic.' Apparently, it's some fancy tech-talk meaning he's really goddamn fast." Skip looked to the rest of the Pale Horses. "Now boys, it seems this is all just a big misunderstanding, right? It'd be awful if the... uh..." he scowled as he tried to remember the word.

Fagan helped. "SOAP."

"Right. It'd be a shame if the SOAP ripped all your spines out over a little miscommunication, right?" Skip held his hands out to his sides, palms up. "Maybe you should check with your people before you do something stupid and get hurt."

The Pale Horse leader considered this, his eyes never leaving the gun pointed at his head. He tried to keep his voice level and calm, though success in this endeavor proved elusive. "You sure you want to play it this way, Roadie?"

"You're the one breaking the rules, pal."

"Rules change. Folks who want these GiMPs ain't losing sleep over any rules, man."

Sullivan let the barrel of his pistol dip so he could see the man's face. "Is that a fact? Let's just have a talk about who these 'folks' are then."

The Pale Horse shook his head. "Oh, don't sweat it, GiMP. It's already been called in. They comin' to see you right now."

CHAPTER FIFTEEN

"Called in? Called in to who?"

To Sullivan's ears, Skip sounded more apprehensive than the situation called for. This implied more was going on than he currently understood, and the realization started a fire of irritation in the pit of his stomach.

The Pale Horse kept his eyes on Sullivan, or more specifically, on Sullivan's gun as he answered. "Told you, this is Silk Road shit. You get what that means, Roadie."

The rest of the Pale Horses began to shift. In tiny increments, they spread out to put some space between each other. Sullivan noticed several hands inching toward waistlines, and he growled, "First one to go for a weapon dies." He saw doubt on some faces, indecision on others. He looked the leader in the eyes. "Talk to your boys. You best believe I can center-punch any one of your little minions and be back on you before they drop."

"Stay cool, crew," the leader said. "Ain't nobody got to jump stupid over this."

"Good call," Sullivan said. "Now, let's talk about this 'Silk Road' of yours."

"That ain't so good an idea, Sully." Skip's tone carried a warning. "We need to clear out of here. I can find out what's up, but not if we're all dead."

Sullivan weighed his need for information against the need to extricate himself from the current standoff. "What do you think, Suds?"

"I think discretion is the better part of valor," Fagan answered. "But I'm still hungry as hell, and now I'm pretty pissed off, too. Won't break my heart if we start beating information out of people."

Sullivan examined the burgeoning tension in his guts and decided to err on the side of prudence. "Okay, dumbass. You and your girlfriends here are going to drop your weapons to the deck. Then me and my associates are going to leave. Now, you seem like the kind of suicidal idiot who might consider this an opportunity to try your luck again. I'm telling you right now that I will kill every one of you if you do. Are we communicating, pal?"

"Sure thing, GiMP."

"It's 'Mister GiMP' to you. Now, slowly, everybody go ahead and get those pieces on the ground." Sullivan cracked a sick, predatory smile. "Or try to shoot me. Your choice, really."

As one, the gang members extracted their sidearms with exaggerated care. Once exposed, each pistol fell to the floor with a loud clang. When Sullivan was satisfied, he lifted the muzzle of his .44 from the gangster's forehead. "Good call."

"Be seeing you, GiMP," the Pale Horse said.

The parting shot rang hollow. Sullivan had dealt with enough street trash to identify the toothless barking of a beaten dog. The warden was content to ignore him. Fagan, however, was not. "Better hope not," the giant fired back. "Because the next time you and I meet, you are going to have a very bad time."

The wardens and Skip started to back away from the knot of Pale Horses. They walked backwards for a few yards, never taking their eyes off their enemies. The Pale Horses stood without moving, each observing the retreating trio with wary eyes. When Sullivan decided the distance was sufficient to deter any gunplay, he holstered his revolver, and the group pushed through the ring of curious onlookers that had gathered to see the action.

"Talk to me, Skip," Sullivan growled. "What the hell just happened?"

"You tell me! Just who the fuck are you guys, and who are you running from?"

Snarling, Sullivan grabbed Skip by the collar and hauled him into the narrow space between two shops. Skip stumbled and nearly fell, then turned to Sullivan when he regained his balance. Before he could say anything, the warden shoved him against a wall. "We didn't think we were running from anybody, Skip. We don't know shit about a 'Silk Road' or your gangs or whatever. We just want to find the goddamn Railroad. It's only after bumping into your scrawny ass that we suddenly have problems." Sullivan's gaze bored into the squirming gangster. "I'm going to give you ten seconds to explain what the hell is going on before I start hurting you."

"The Silk Road must be after you for some reason, man!"

Sullivan's voice became a low, throaty rasp. "I'm getting real tired of asking the same questions over and over again, kid. What is the Silk Road?"

"It's how we get most of our raw materials and stuff. It's a big network of companies that make sure we don't starve or run out of supplies. It's kind of an open secret that these are all legit corporations who do regular business out in the world. They can't get caught dealing with the complexes, so they use dummy corporations and shells to hide it."

"And they don't follow your weird-ass rules?"

"They're supposed to. They're supposed to answer to the Council, but nobody really knows if they do or not. They don't usually do anything down here at all. But when they do..." Skip made a helpless hand wave. "There ain't shit anyone can say about how they go about doing it."

Fagan, playing the role of lookout near the entrance to their alley, interrupted the conversation. "Heads up, guys. Pale Horses chatting with some real sketchy-looking bastards."

Sullivan released Skip with a muttered expletive and joined his partner at the mouth of the alley. As reported, the group of Pale Horses that had just accosted them could be seen in intense conversation with four large men in suspiciously tactical attire. Drab, military-style jackets covered telltale bulges at the belt line, and the quality of their combat boots belied their otherwise scruffy appearance. "Pros," Sullivan hissed to his partner.

Fagan's cheek twitched. "Not unlike the kind of guys who might get hired to shoot up a laboratory?"

"Maybe," Sullivan answered.

"What laboratory?" Skip asked.

"Shut up," both men said in unison.

"So, we got four armed pros and about ten armed gang-bangers out there," Sullivan mused.

"That's a lot of bad guys," Fagan noted.

"But also a lot of potential information," Sullivan said. "Hate to miss an opportunity like this. Skip?"

"What?"

"What happens if Suds and I decide to jump that crew?"

"If you survive, you mean?"

"Let's just assume the big guy and I can take them."

"You'll be pissing off the Pale Horses, and you'll probably get banned from the Mercantile for a while. But if those really are hired mercenaries, then no one is gonna have a problem with you shanking them. Folks down here don't like it when big shots send paid muscle into our backyard." Skip paused, then added, "The Silk Road already has it in for you, so that won't change. If you don't kill any of the Horses and you don't wreck any of the shops, you might just end up coming out all right." Another pause. "I mean, if you don't die, that is."

"I am not a fan of this," Fagan grumbled. "But I am fucking starving. Hell with it. If it gets me to lunch faster, I'll kill them all myself."

"I don't like the odds," Sullivan said, his irritation audible. "I'd like to make it easier. Let's tail the pros and see if we can't grab a few once they get away from the locals."

"I like that better," Fagan said. "One problem, though. I'm not exactly good at subtly tailing people."

"Okay." Sullivan was improvising now, and the words tumbled out. "Skip, you are going to lead Suds here out of this alley and toward the exit, or the Exchange or whatever. Move fast. Don't poke around."

"Somebody's gonna see us and call it in..." Skip protested.

Sullivan interrupted, "No shit. We want them to. Just get to the exit. I'll slot in behind the mercs when they start to follow you two. If they try to take you before you get out, I'll hit them from behind and pull them off. If you make it to the Exchange, Suds will show you how to turn a pursuit into an ambush." He looked to Fagan. "Sound good, partner?"

"Anything that leads to lunch sounds good."

Sullivan scanned the open square for signs of their pursuers. The Pale Horses were gone, presumably off searching for Sullivan and Fagan again. The mysterious men in military attire could not be found, either, and Sullivan assumed they had slunk back into the shadows to wait the wardens out. He grunted, "Okay, let's do this. I'll buzz your phone once you grow a tail. I'll buzz again when I move on them."

An apprehensive and unconvinced Skip led the giant from the alley and made a beeline for the far side of the Mercantile. Sullivan watched from the shadows. He inspected each pedestrian like a paranoiac, convinced that any one of them could blow the whistle. After sixty interminable seconds, he slipped from the alley and moved along the path Skip and Fagan had taken. It took him less than thirty seconds to catch up, since picking out Fagan's shaggy head bobbing above the throngs of meandering people proved to be a rather simple task. He hung back as far as he could, keeping plenty of distance between them.

In less than two minutes, Sullivan spotted the first Pale Horse lookout. This time, the gang member did not accost the big man and his guide, choosing instead to slink back into an alley. Sullivan presumed the skinny youth had slipped off to make a call to those mysterious mercenaries. When two men in dirty brown fatigues joined the flow of people two minutes later, Sullivan knew he had guessed right. Smiling, he tapped out Fagan's code on his phone from inside his own pocket. He did not pull his phone out or speak. He only opened the channel and let it buzz three times before shutting it down. Then he settled in to see how many pursuers showed up and how close to the exit they were willing to let the prey get.

Thirty seconds later, Sullivan decided they were not going to get out of the Mercantile without a conflict. He had expected as much. The Exchange was too open and too neutral for the enemy to let them get that far. It would be better for the mercs to execute a takedown where space was tighter and they had the nominal back-up of a local gang presence. When their numbers swelled to six, the men in fatigues began to close the distance. Sullivan saw them converge on each other and watched them briefly converse, then pick up their pace. Soon, the men began to fan out. Flankers walked even faster to get alongside the big man and Skip. Sullivan recognized the maneuver. The men in the middle would attack from behind, and when the prey tried to flee, the flankers would close the net and cut off escape to either side. To Sullivan's eyes, it looked like this group had done this type of thing before. The time had come to shut these jokers down, and Sullivan's body woke to the impending violence.

When the distance between himself and the mercenaries had shrunk to about twenty feet, Sullivan began to detect the cold prickling sensation of his adrenal response. His body went cool and hot at the same time, and he thrilled to the familiar rush of euphoria following the siren's call of approaching danger. The blood running in his veins turned to ice water at ten feet. The ethereal wisps of a norepinephrine buzz brushed the edges of his brain with electric feathers. Sullivan counted each hair on his body as they stood up. His heart began to beat harder, though not necessarily faster. Deep inside his hypothalamus, a desperate kind of fear began to push at the wet blanket of preternatural calm holding it down. There were six men to deal with, and he had the drop on them. He could not say if they were genetically enhanced or not. He did not know if they wore armor beneath those dirty jackets. He might be facing a half-dozen ex-special-forces GMP super-soldiers, or a ragtag group of regular-army dropouts. There was no way to tell for sure, and the potential danger filled him with giddy anticipation.

It was a strange form of madness, to court destruction like this. He hated this need for a release he could not understand, and he hated how it drove him to make stupid choices. Even though Sullivan had been through this a thousand times before, the dance never got easier. Worse, he knew better. He had already figured out that the promise was false, the seduction just a cruel trick that would leave him hollow and unsatisfied afterward. He was not going to get what he wanted out of this, yet part of his soul begged him to try anyway.

He considered circumventing the issue by drawing his pistol and shooting them all in the back. From his current position, the shots would be easy enough, if a little tricky due to the pedestrians milling about. He discarded this plan as a strategic dead end. They needed answers, not corpses. He then considered taking them on by hand. Even with his laundry list of modifications, Sullivan did not like his chances in a fist fight with six armed men all at once. If they were competent fighters or otherwise enhanced, victory would not come easily if at all. The real possibility of losing a fight sent a jolt of excitement through his body. Maybe then, he would finally experience what he had been missing.

Sullivan quashed the stupid thought before it gathered any momentum. He had a job to do, and getting killed meant that the doctors had been right about him all along. He refused to be insane. He was better than that. The instability in his head would have to wait for another day, because a lot of people expected him to screw up, and John Sullivan loved nothing more than disappointing those people.

With no time to discuss it with Fagan, Sullivan decided on a plan. While six armed men was too many to fight on his own if they were good, technically, he did not need to beat all six people by himself. He just needed to hurt a few and survive long enough for Fagan to pick up the slack. No one could deny that Fagan was an army unto himself when he got rolling, and combined, the two wardens were more than capable of handling just about anything.

Sullivan did not love any plan that required him to rely on other people, but he was out of time and options. Buzzing the big man's phone one more time, Sullivan squared his shoulders and got to work.

CHAPTER SIXTEEN

The main passage leading out to the Exchange hummed with enough foot traffic to cover his approach. Sullivan slid in behind the man farthest to his left. He was nearly on top of the target before the clueless man realized someone was behind him. At the first sign of cognizance from his prey, Sullivan pivoted on his right foot and clubbed the man in the side of the head hard enough to send him flailing into his teammate. Sullivan serviced the next with a straight right hand to the chin. A millisecond later, the second unconscious person flopped to the floor atop the first.

The third man, having enjoyed a full one-and-a-half seconds to assess the rapidly deteriorating situation, met Sullivan's charge with a raised hand. His other hand fumbled at his hip, searching for the butt of his pistol. The outstretched arm clipped Sullivan on the shoulder, spoiling the incoming punch and buying enough time for the weapon to clear its holster. The mercenary rotated the pistol without raising it, betraying some level of experience in close-quarters fighting. Sullivan slapped downward, shoving the muzzle offline and spoiling the first shot. The bullet threw sparks from the floor and spun away with a keening whine.

With the deafening report of a gunshot, the crowd evaporated with speed and organization alluding to frequent practice. As the battlefield opened up, the remaining mercenaries dropped back and drew their weapons with speed and organization that also alluded to frequent practice. Sullivan had begun with a confusing and shifting arena and the advantage of surprise. Now, he faced four gunmen in an open space with clear shooting lanes. The imminent danger drove lances of fear arcing across his nerves, each wave dying before it could gather much strength. The flood of neurotransmitters soaking his brain stretched his sense of time, while the soothing peace of dopamine kept him sharp and focused even in the face of what should have been certain death.

He dove to the side, drawing his own pistol mid-leap. His shoulder bit hard into the metal floor plates, though the pain of it came through his mental fog a mere shadow of its normal intensity. His ungainly dive transformed into a smooth roll when his muscles caught up with his brain. A hail of bullets hissed through the air where his body had been, the muzzle flashes lighting the faces of the mercenaries like flashbulbs. Sullivan squeezed off his first two rounds without lining up the sights. He fired instinctively, not caring if he made lethal hits or only suppressed the enemy's efforts. A mercenary jerked and gasped, standing with spine locked for a half second before folding his arms over his abdomen and sinking to the deck. Sullivan rose and fired again. He took a quarter second to get the stubby front post of his sight in line with the next man's chest and touched off a round. He did not stop to assess his marksmanship. Instinct and peripheral vision spoke in unison, and he threw himself backward. A streak of white-hot pain marching from his hip to his armpit told Sullivan that he had just taken a glancing shot to his side. There was no panic or recrimination that came with this understanding. He had no opinions on how it had happened, nor was there any indecision about how to handle it. The rage and fear that surged so desperately beneath the surface of his preternatural calm begged for release. It sang to him with promises of catharsis and closure. Try as he might, Sullivan could no more touch it than he could grasp a handful of smoke.

He hit the ground hard and scrambled for traction of any kind. When he felt the sole of his shoe bite into the floor, he hurled himself into another roll, jerking left and right to throw off any follow-up shots. The need to right himself and line up his own return fire drove him to new heights of athletic desperation. The enemy had him dead to rights, and only his speed and skill had kept him alive for just these scant seconds. To his surprise, the shots never came, and he guessed the reason for this long before he stopped his spastic tumbling.

Fagan hurtled into the remaining mercenaries with a roar like a mad bull. One warhammer fist pulped a foe's face even as the thug lined up his sights for a kill shot. Another gunman got yanked from his feet and tossed aside like an afterthought. The final enemy Fagan seized around the head and neck, yanking him bodily from the floor and swinging his flailing body in a wide circle. If Sullivan squinted, the pair could be mistaken for a small child roughhousing with a favorite uncle. At least until the giant brought the airborne man down against the floor with a grotesque crack, and the idyllic illusion shattered like so many vertebrae.

The man Fagan had tossed aside regained his feet with distressing speed and agility. His pistol came to bear on the giant in a solid, two-handed grip. Sullivan leapt from his crouch to hit him with a low tackle. Bolstered by surging adrenaline levels, Sullivan smashed his shoulder into the mercenary's ribs at top speed. The air split with the sound of ribs snapping, and the gun fell from nerveless fingers. Sullivan's charge lifted the shooter from the floor, and a rough twist brought him back down to earth with a hollow thud. From astride his opponent, Sullivan launched three brutal overhand rights. The first dashed all semblance of consciousness from the mercenary, but Sullivan's black mood demanded he take no chances. The second and third punches mashed the nose flat and fractured the jaw with a disgusting crack.

"Sully!" Fagan boomed. "That's enough!"

Sullivan supposed the big man had a point and stopped. Beneath him and breathing in thin wheezes lay one mercenary. His shooting, being of its usual quality, had rendered another man cold and motionless. The other gunshot victim writhed in a growing puddle of slick red blood, moaning and gurgling in a manner not at all encouraging. The muffled sounds of a man stirring and whimpering nearby accounted for another, and it looked to Sullivan like it would be some time before his senses returned to anything approaching normal.

Fagan's victims had fared no better. The recipient of the giant's first punch looked to be dead. Sullivan supposed he might be alive still, but if the man survived, Sullivan did not think he would ever be the same person afterward. The condition of the final mercenary required no special medical analysis. His body lay in a twisted pile, his back broken badly in many places. If by some strange miracle the mangled skull did not prove fatal, there still remained the issue of a spinal column splintered into what Sullivan estimated to be about a thousand pieces to contend with.

Skip jogged over, pale and huffing. "Holy shit! Holy Shit! Oh god, oh god... Holy shit!"

"Eloquent little man, aren't you?" Sullivan said, climbing off his man and standing. "Ah!" he blurted when the wound in his side reminded him of its presence.

"You hit?" Fagan asked.

"Got creased. No penetration. Gonna bleed, though."

"We gotta get outta here!" Skip cried, as if having an epiphany.

Sullivan concurred. Pale Horses were emerging from the shadows, and a running gunfight with the local gangs seemed ill-advised.

"Fagan, grab one of the sleepers!" The order came out harsher than he intended, though Fagan did not appear to take offense. The big warden leaned over and scooped up the first man Sullivan had punched and threw the moaning mass over his giant shoulder. "Let's go," he said, and began to trot toward the exit and the relative safety of Rosedale's Exchange.

Sullivan reloaded as he fell in behind Fagan. Skip bounced and flitted around them, exhorting the men to ever greater levels of haste. They made the Rosedale Exchange area without being accosted, whereupon Fagan deposited his fleshy cargo on the floor in a dark corner. A soft moan escaped the body when it hit the metal floor plates, disturbing a sleeping man who reeked of alcohol.

"Fuck off, hobo," Sullivan growled. The sleeper scurried away like a startled rat.

"Easy, man," Fagan said. "Your brain chemistry still out of whack?"

"Give me a minute." Sullivan tried to force the irritation out of his voice.

"It's cool," Fagan said.

"He okay?" Skip asked. His eyes were fixed on Sullivan, wide with fear.

"My man Sully has some testosterone issues," Fagan lied. "Getting shot can make him a little irritable. He'll be cool in a second."

Skip did not sound convinced. "He ain't one of those berserkers, is he? Like the Chinese used? I heard stories..."

"If I was," Sullivan replied, "you'd be dead, all those guys back there would be dead, and probably a bunch of other people, too. I got in a fight, and I got shot. I'm pissed off is all."

This was a lie. Something was not right, and he could not figure it out. His cortisol levels were holding, and adrenaline with them, both staying elevated far longer than normal. Usually, his combat tweaks settled down as quickly as they ramped up. The fight was over, so he should be coming back to baseline. His skin remained ice cold, his senses scalpel sharp, his vision reduced to a tiny tunnel.

"We need a place to hole up and interrogate this guy," Sullivan said. "Unless you want us to work on him right here?"

Skip virtually vibrated with fear and indecision. "I don't know man... this shit is getting out of hand..."

"Find us something!" Sullivan snarled, taking a half step in Skip's direction before he realized what he was doing.

"Sully!" Fagan snapped back, a warning in his voice that re-crystallized Sullivan's focus.

"Shit," Sullivan hissed. "Sorry. Whatever. Get us somewhere quiet, and I'll pay you 200 credits right now!"

The offer of what Sullivan suspected to be an exorbitant sum for the low-level gangster seemed to cure Skip's indecision. "I know a place. Come on!"

Fagan dragged their now semiconscious prisoner to his feet and wrenched his arm up behind his back. "Walk, or I start breaking things," Fagan instructed.

The mercenary complied in sullen silence, too wobbly to resist and too outnumbered to even consider it. Skip brought them across the Exchange and down through the door to the area previously referred to as the Meat Market. Sullivan had no eyes for the arrayed buffet of women and their tawdry come-ons. They lined the dim metal streets like signposts advertising earthly pleasures ranging from the blandly pedestrian to pure depravity. The lurid stares and plastic smiles disappeared as soon as the braver ones got close enough to see Sullivan's leaking side. He stalked behind Skip with his jaw locked in a smoldering grimace. The cold penetrated his skin now, leeching into his muscles and bones as adrenaline deadened his nerves. The fear, still wrapped in its wet blanket, writhed and heaved beneath it all. Sullivan could not shake the feeling it was trying to tell him something, but the insulating layers of dopamine and other chemicals muted the signal.

He did not recall paying the madame at the desk for a room. He could not remember her face or anything she said. He climbed the stairs in an irritated mental fog, grinding his teeth together at every interaction to avoid alienating people with the belligerent invective that waited.

It was when he opened the door to their room that he noticed something else. He was getting weaker. Sullivan had always been in tune with his capabilities. The training he had endured as a child and his continued dedication to maintaining his physical prowess granted him near-perfect proprioception. The heavy metal door and its ungreased hinges took more force than it should have to get open, and Sullivan's guts went topsy-turvy when he put it all together.

While Fagan secured their prisoner to a chair, Sullivan stole into the bathroom. With the door closed behind him, he stripped his dirty jacket off and wriggled out of his bloody shirt. With decent lighting, a good mirror, and no onslaught of raging killers to contend with, Sullivan at last got a good look at his problem.

The mercenary's bullet had dug a shallow furrow along his left side beginning at the hip. The seeping crease traced a line over his ribs before becoming a jagged open wound where the bullet had started to tumble. His arteries had been spared, so the blood only trickled from any single portion of the grotesque injury, making the damage deceptive. However, his was a practiced eye, and Sullivan now understood why his adrenal response refused to subside. The gash was nearly three feet long, and every inch of it wept blood. Because he could not feel it, the blood had managed to soak his shirt, run down his leg, and fill his left boot almost to the top.

"Fagan!" he called through the door. "Could use a hand in here!"

The door swung open. Fagan's figure blocked the entire door frame, and he needed to stoop to get inside. Preoccupied with navigating into the small bathroom, Fagan did not notice Sullivan's blood-soaked side and ruined pants at first. When he did, the big man gave an expressive grunt of frustration. "Ah, goddamn it, Sully!"

"Is my bleeding to death inconvenient for you?"

"It really is, man."

Sullivan could not keep his irritation from his voice. "Maybe I could bother you to help with that then?"

"Yeah, yeah," Fagan said. "Let me grab some towels and rustle up a doctor. Or whatever it is they use for doctors in here."

Sullivan began to strip out of his ruined clothes and sat down in the bathtub. Fagan handed him some towels, which were immediately pressed against the length of the injury. "Skip!" Fagan yelled.

"Yeah?"

"There's another hundred credits in it for you if you find us a good doctor who knows how to keep his mouth shut."

Skip beamed. "No prob, Suds!"

"In the next ten minutes," Sullivan added. Adrenaline reduced blood flow to surface capillaries, which kept Sullivan alive for the moment. He did not want to push his luck any further than he already had. Anyone else would have passed out by now, and once that happened, his blood pressure would drop, and death would be more or less inevitable. Sullivan could not say how much time he had before his condition proved fatal.

He should have been terrified. He was not. He felt tension. He felt apprehension. He was concerned. Still, the purity of true fear stayed chained well beneath the surface. He searched for rage instead, hoping his greater familiarity with that emotion would allow him to experience the sensation as others did. He was sure he was angry, yet when he dug into it, all he found was his normal frustrated belligerence. There was heat and a sense of impatience, though neither rose higher than an intense irritation. Even staring down death itself, he could not muster up a legitimate human reaction.

"You okay?" Fagan asked. He was squinting into Sullivan's eyes, as if trying to make out what his partner was thinking.

"Just leaking fluids, man." He tried to sound blasé. "You know, like you do."

Fagan reached over and placed a hand on the towel. He added pressure to slow the bleeding. "It's an ugly scratch, all right. But once you get closed up, it'll be fine. Nothing broken or punctured. Skip should be back in a few minutes with help."

"So I can die of an infection instead of blood loss?"

"You really are a 'glass is half empty' kind of asshole, aren't you?"

"Glass is broken and leaking, Fagan.

Fagan did not reply, but shifted to keep pressure on as much of the wound as possible. Skip returned in less than ten minutes with an aging woman in tow.

"That the doc?" Fagan asked.

"Sure," Skip said. "She's the doc."

"Not convincing," Sullivan said, but his voice was weak.

The old woman shoved past Fagan and sent him from the bathroom with a brusque wave. She peeled back the blood-crusted towel and gave the wound a disapproving tutting. She opened the lapel of her ruddy brown coat and pulled out a black satchel. From inside, she procured several bottles of antiseptic, bandages, and what Sullivan presumed to be a staple gun. With strong, well-practiced hands, she began to pull the sides of the gash together and tape them. She looked into Sullivan's eyes after a few inches of the gash had been thus closed and asked, "You want something for the pain?"

"What pain?"

The woman did not seem impressed. "Okay. The big, strong man wants to gut it out? Fine by me."

Washing as she went, the old woman applied a long bead of dermal adhesive to the length of his wound. Sullivan felt the sharp chemical sting, muted and distant, through a dense shield of endorphins. The doctor's eyebrow rose when he did not flinch or gasp. Then she picked up the staple gun and asked, "Ready?"

"Do it."

She did it. It took sixty-one staples to knit the whole thing closed, and Sullivan never so much as hissed for the long sixteen minutes it took to apply them all. When she finished her work, the woman stood up with a grunt and brought her tools to the sink.

"You are very strong, Mr. Sully," she remarked as she began to clean. "I've had tough men pass out at half the pain as you just took."

"What can I say," Sullivan said, his voice drowsy. "I'm a bad man."

"You are very nearly a dead man. It is a good thing you are so densely muscled. That myostatin inhibition saved your life, you know."

"Yay, me."

"You need to rest at least a week. But I know your type. Try to stay in bed for another day or two, and eat and drink as much as you can. You are very low on plasma and red blood cells, and it takes time to get those back. I'm sure you are used to being Captain Superman or whatever, but for now, you are pretty much a ninety-eight-pound weakling. The wound is closed at least, and I sealed the capillaries with glue. You should be able to move around without reopening the damn thing, but if you rip out those staples too early, you are going to have a very bad time."

Sullivan could not help himself. "Honey, when you're with me, you never have a bad time."

Again, the doctor seemed unimpressed. She put her supplies back in her bag and turned a glower to her patient. "I've been with you for half an hour, and I'm already regretting it."

Sullivan let his head fall back against the side of the tub. "Yeah. I get that more often than not, too."

"Rest, Mister Sully. Doctor's orders. I assume the SOAP will pay me?"

Sullivan could not answer, because he had already fallen asleep.

CHAPTER SEVENTEEN

In a comfortable hotel room on the outskirts of Hubtown and far from the dingy brothels of Rosedale, Sharon Platt watched with her heart in her throat as Porter paced the floor. The gray-haired woman seated in a stuffed chair eyed him as well, her face a mask of quiet irritation.

"Are you sure, Maris?" Porter asked again, as if making the woman repeat herself could change the answer or its ramifications.

The older woman scowled. "I'm sure. That was no MINK. He took sixty-one staples without flinching. Doctor Platt will tell you that neuro-kinetics actually feel pain more acutely than normal people. I even worked slow and sloppy to see if I could get a yelp out of him. His pulse didn't even speed up. There was a SOAP, too. A big acromegalic with very little mandibular osteoplasia." She shook her head. "I'm damn sure."

"English!" Porter barked.

"The giant one showed none of the signs of baseline acromegaly." She gestured to her face. "Not like the trolls we see down here. His jaw wasn't deformed, and his forehead looked normal. No speech impediment either. It is a very expensive package, Porter." She shook her head emphatically. "And if the other one was a MINK, I'll eat my hat. It's them; you can bet on it."

"Aw, fuck. How did they find us?"

"They haven't found us, Porter. This place is enormous, and we are miles from them still. Obviously, they followed Platt to Rosedale."

Platt finally spoke. "I don't know how. We took the 'loop, we used fake identifications..."

"These are wardens, dear," Maris said with a warm smile for the terrified scientist. "They have access to tools and techniques the rest of us don't. You did your best and stayed ahead of them. That is good enough."

"Right," Porter breathed. "So GEED is closing in. The question is, do we need to adjust our plans?"

"We cannot move yet," Maris said. "We need at least another week. It's not safe for any of us out there. Less so with *him* so close."

"John L. Sullivan," Porter sighed with a growl in his voice. "Goddamn Super-GiMP himself."

"Language," Maris said. "That is not a word I care to have thrown around."

"Sullivan?" Platt shook her head, eyes wide with both fear and wonder. "It's Sullivan? You can't be serious!"

Porter answered. "You probably read about him in college. He's Mickey Sullivan's kid. You know... the mobster?"

Platt nodded. "I wrote a damn Ph.D. thesis on him. I consulted on his case to the GEED selection board, Porter. I know who he is."

"Yeah, but do you know anything about his dad?"

"Chimeras don't have parents," Platt fired back, and immediately regretted her pedantic reply. "But no, I didn't really look into Michael Sullivan much."

"Ol' Mickey wanted the most badass mob goon ever. Dropped about a billion bucks into a giant project with thousands of gene donors."

"There were more than sixteen hundred zygotes in his lot," Platt added. "His creche was winnowed down to fewer than forty embryos."

"All for one badass fetus," Porter added. "He was legendary among the criminals. A twelve-year-old as big as a man. Stronger than any two. He actually came here once before, when he was still with his father, I mean. Had to be maybe fourteen or fifteen. I saw him. He looked like a full-sized pro football player." Porter sniffed. "Mean kid, too. Broke a guy's arm for calling him a GiMP. Didn't say a word, just reached out and snapped it. His dad thought it was hilarious."

Platt shook her head. "He's a strange case. They've never unraveled his whole genome. The courts sealed the data to protect his privacy when GEED brought him in, but as a recognized expert on chimera DNA, I was able to see some of it. Nobody knows all the things that were done to his DNA." She shuddered. "He's a monster. They twisted him so much, it's a miracle he's not a serial killer."

Maris gave both of them a disapproving look. "Much of the world would say the same of your Emilie, Doctor Platt. John Sullivan may be many things, but in the end, he is merely another victim of his father's ego. We owe him the same compassion we'd give any other person in his position."

"Even though he hunts his own?" Porter made no attempt to hide his bitterness.

"He upholds the law," Maris corrected. "Because it is what he has been told he must do. It's all he knows. What was it you did before joining us, Porter?"

This seemed to touch a nerve. "Okay, Maris," Porter said with hands raised. "You win. Touché. I shouldn't be so judgmental. Got it. But we still have the issue of two First Class Wardens in the Complex with us while we are stuck here hunkered down. The people backing Sharon's project won't be far behind them, I might add."

"Agreed," Maris said. "Somebody shot Sullivan, and I can only assume that it has something to do with those backers."

"Yeah, about that. Any sign of Coll?" Porter asked.

"You would know better than me, Porter. You are the one with the contacts."

"Silk Road sent mercs in for the wardens, I know that much. That smells like Coll." He stopped his pacing and tapped his foot against the carpet. "But the scrap in the Mercantile was ugly. Those chumps got thumped pretty easy according to all the reports. You'd think Coll would have better guys. Plus, they moved really early. If they wanted you and the kid, doc, they should have waited to see if the wardens got close, first."

"I don't believe in coincidence," Maris said.

"A sound policy. I wonder if those were even Coll's boys at all. Naturally, we gotta assume GEED is compromised. Since we are sure the backers are using Coll, and it looks like Coll is using the Silk Road, then we can pretty much be sure that the backers are straight-up mob. Which mob, or mobs, I suppose, is anybody's guess right now. Either way, I got two real strong hunches about the current, ah, situation. First, it looks like the mob has bought themselves a GEED informer. Second, I think maybe the Silk Road is leaking the juicy bits to other interested parties." Porter rubbed his face with his hands. "I need to see if I can slow these wardens down. How bad was he hit, Maris? Any chance he'll be out for a while?"

"Not likely. If he's down for more than twenty-four hours, I'll be amazed. The wound was shallow, and he is very strong. Other than the pain and bleeding if he strains the wound, he'll be his usual self once he restores the lost plasma volume."

"Which will be very soon," Platt said. "He will heal fast."

"We got too many loose ends waving around. I gotta figure out how to put him down longer," Porter grumbled. "Him and the big one."

"Or you could try talking to them," Platt offered.

"What?" Porter and Maris spoke in unison.

"They want me. GEED won't be aware of Emilie's existence. If it gets Emilie somewhere safe, I'll turn myself in. Let GEED and Coll fight over me while Emilie gets away."

"Coll knows about Emilie," Porter reminded her.

"But he probably doesn't understand why she is important. Only a few people know what she is."

"We could offer Coll up to GEED," Maris said. "They would love to bring someone like him in."

"Wait a minute." Porter chewed his lower lip. "I'm starting to like this idea. So, maybe I do go talk to the wardens. I give just enough information to be helpful. Get them headed in Coll's direction instead of ours..."

"Yes," Maris said with an emphatic nod. "If anyone could be a match for Vincent Coll, it will be John Sullivan. Sullivan is smart, though. If what you give him is too thin or too manufactured, the plan is likely to backfire."

"Yeah. It's got to be solid stuff. Real leads he can actually run down. The trick is getting those leads to lead back to our other bad guys and not us," Porter said.

"Give him the Silk Road," Maris said. "He can't truly hurt them, but if Coll is using them to get people into the Complex, it will set the two against each other."

"Coll chases Sullivan while Sullivan chases Coll." Porter seemed to mull this over. "I got to say, I like it."

"What do I do?" Platt asked.

"You need to sit tight," Porter told her. "You are still safe here, and I ain't ready to hand you over to GEED. This close to Hubtown, you've got a lot of protection. Railroad influence over the Council is still pretty solid. Your job is to take care of Emilie and hang in there. As soon as it's clear, we are going to move you to a safer location. One with a laboratory."

"And a school? Emilie needs socialization."

"Absolutely. We just need a little more time to set things up. This operation has a lot of moving parts. Maris?"

"Yes?"

"I need you to mobilize some Railroad assets. If Coll is using the Silk Road, then I'm going to point Sullivan at the Teamsters. They work with the Silk Road more than anyone else." He saw the look on the older woman's face and held up his hands to stay her objections. "Yeah, I know the Teamsters have as much pull with the Council as we do. I'll be discreet, okay? Hopefully, it will look like GEED making trouble, or Silk Road pulling a move like they sometimes do."

"We have a lot of our own people on the Teamsters, too, Porter," Maris replied. "We need them to help GMPs get in and out of the Complex and onto other areas."

"You are going to have to get our people out of the way for a little bit. Use the Road Crew for now. They aren't as big, but they control intake from Rosedale already. They can handle it, and they'll appreciate the business."

Platt sat and listened to Porter scheme for another half hour. His worn boots paced a track into the carpet as he molded the bare bones of an idea into a plan that sounded far more complex than it needed to be. Then again, Platt possessed no understanding of gangs, mobsters, government agents, and mercenaries. Her life in the laboratory had not prepared her for this, and she had moved so far beyond fear at this point that she lacked the wherewithal to do anything more than sit and shiver. The world was larger than she had ever imagined, and the people in it were so much more complicated. She trusted Porter, though for the life of her she could not say why. She wondered if she should, and moving down that mental path sent electric tendrils of terror through her body. Platt resigned herself to believing Porter out of physical and emotional necessity. He had brought her to this place, and they seemed so close to getting somewhere far away from all the horror.

How far away is that, exactly?

Sharon Platt possessed the kind of intellect that had geneticists all over the world working themselves to death attempting to duplicate. Her brilliance had taken her far in life, though her intelligence was a curse as much as a blessing. Beneath her fear and confusion, a small but insistent voice asked a very basic question.

How do I trust any of these people?

The thought surprised her. No one had given her any reason to doubt they were trustworthy. Quite the opposite, in fact. If not for Porter and Maris, she would already be in the clutches of the mob or GEED, and Emilie's life destroyed either way.

That the Railroad was committed to the cause of GMP freedom and equality was not in question. More to the point, both Porter and Maris had the air of total zealots. Maris had as much compassion for a monster like Sullivan as she did for little Emilie, and that smacked of recklessness. Platt wanted to get Emilie away from both the mob and the wardens, too, but Emilie was an innocent child with no dangerous modifications. Sullivan was a different case altogether. She understood Sullivan's history better than anyone in the room, and the scientist in her refused to let idealism cloud her professional judgment. If evaluated without emotion, logic insisted that Sullivan should be caged. Or at the very least, leashed. She did not hate John Sullivan, but she was smart enough to fear him. It went beyond all the things he might do, or all the things he was capable of doing. The real horror lived in what it had taken to create him in the first place. Sullivan's creation defied every rule of ethics and violated every pretension toward decency. She pitied him the way one might pity a rabid animal right before putting it down.

Maris and Porter would never truly comprehend how much Michael Sullivan had invested and sacrificed to build the perfect criminal. They did not comprehend how awful and twisted the young Sullivan's life must have been, or how much the bastards had warped his brain to get the attributes they desired. A sudden and violent need to get away seized the scientist in a grip of burning terror.

Once again, the curse of her intellect shattered another poorly constructed conceit at the worst possible moment.

These people don't understand what's going on.

It felt so obvious, sitting in a chair watching the two Railroad leaders plan and scheme as if their little organization of do-gooders had a prayer in hell against the kind of Machiavellian machine that produced things like John Sullivan.

Or Emilie, she reminded herself. *Same machine. Different result.*

That concept chilled her swiftly heating blood. The distinctions between Emilie and Sullivan were large, and those distinctions were necessary for Platt to separate herself from those who had created the other chimeras. Without those differences, she might never sleep again. Even so, the machines were the problem, not the products, and this led to her next thought and a fresh round of crippling terror.

There is no way either GEED or the mob is letting us get anywhere. Sullivan's presence can't be a coincidence, either, can it?

Her mind refused to accept any of it. Yet, she could not shake the feeling that something was off about the whole situation. An accusation of paranoia flitted across her thoughts, and she considered it. Her own anxiety might be painting the shadows with dangers that did not exist, and her lack of familiarity with her circumstances cast her suspicions with more than enough doubt to calm the burgeoning panic souring her guts.

For the tenth time in as many hours, Platt resolved herself to trusting the Railroad and their ability to get her and Emilie somewhere safe.

Even if she herself could fathom no such place.

Genetic Equity Enforcement Division Expert's Notes for Case SUL-002-b

Dr. Sharon Platt, Ph.D.

Further sessions with GEED counselors are not recommended at this time. The subject continues to obfuscate on his emotional status, though I begin to suspect he does this as much to protect others as he does himself. Examiners made little progress in this latest session, but they were able to test a few theories I have developed. One such test leads me to a conclusion I shall enumerate below.

First, some background. I was able to locate several of his old combat instructors. Or I should say, I was able to discover who they were. First, there was a man named Scott Stevens. A former Olympian in both judo and Greco-Roman wrestling, Ph.D. in sports medicine, and a decorated veteran of the Third World War, it is easy to see why Michael Sullivan chose Doctor Stevens to lead the subject's physical and martial development. On top of his impressive resume, Stevens was six foot six and almost three hundred pounds at the time. Even with his significant physical gifts, I can now understand completely why the subject was unable to overpower his judo teacher.

There was also a four-time national pistol champion and a sixth-generation kali master. (This is apparently some kind of Filipino stick and knife fighting system. My knowledge of such things is sadly quite limited!) Sullivan was also extensively tutored by coaches from several highly-respected professional fighters' gyms, the names and disciplines of which are lost to me and not particularly important. What these people all had in common and what is significant is that to a man, they were all absolutely top of their class. The list is replete with champions, and so a theory is born.

I do not believe the subject ever beat any of these men at their own game, and I am convinced this was a deliberate choice on the part of Doctor Stevens. It is important to understand exactly how dangerous the subject was even at twelve years old. He was already as strong as a very strong adult, with reflexes to match. This alone would make instruction difficult, but the subject was never more than a hair's breadth away from being diagnosed as a full-blown psychotic. Doctor Stevens's approach to managing this was simple and, frankly, ingenious. He put the subject in situations where success was impossible, and then taught him to manage the frustration that came. It's not hard to picture the subject as a morose pre-teen proto-sociopath with the body of a professional athlete. The boy was likely quite arrogant and aggressive, as his testosterone levels were off the charts. He lacked empathy, and without a proper understanding of fear, I'd say his approach to strict discipline was rather less than optimal. Stevens would have been in quite a quandary were he not so formidable himself. I have virtually no understanding of how most martial arts instruction works. Given the nature of the board's request for my expertise, I must point out that I understand the mechanics of combat on the conceptual level only. Even so, I can imagine the subject hurling himself at these men, angry and malicious, only to be beaten soundly over and over again. It had to have been an infuriating experience for the boy.

I do not believe that the dopamine response the subject experiences when stressed is a good thing. The dopamine trigger is a rate-limiting mechanism to prevent panic or psychotic breaks, but the result is that the subject never learned to process any emotion stronger than mild irritation. There also remains the addictive nature of dopamine, locking the subject into a never-ending feedback loop of anger, frustration, and back to blissful calm.

Doctor Stevens's whole approach seemed to center around drawing out ever-increasing levels of intensity and forcing the subject to experience them in a controlled and supportive environment. Because his ability to handle higher levels of arousal would not be tested under normal circumstances, the subject was in real danger of never developing any coping mechanisms. This would leave the subject only one bad moment away from a catastrophic mental collapse at any given point. Any stimulus that pushed him beyond the rate-limiting step was going to cause a psychotic break, and Stevens appeared cognizant of this. Stevens's own notes said it best: "John Sullivan is a nuclear time bomb with an unreliable fuse."

Doctor Stevens surmised, and I agree with him, that no quantity of therapy or counseling is going to eliminate the subject's anger, nor will he ever learn to manage it organically. His anger is an artifact of his unique brain chemistry, and as such will be part of his life forever. That's the "bomb" part, and it cannot be fixed. What Stevens did was lengthen the "fuse" by forcing the subject to deal with the rage at its worst, over and over again. He did this while his physical development was still manageable and his emotional state workable. I suppose that technically constitutes a form of cognitive behavioral therapy, though I doubt the method will ever find mainstream acceptance.

How does this relate to the subject's performance in society? We could be witnessing the first signs of addictive behavior with respect to dopamine response. Also, I wonder if we are seeing his maturing brain's desire to experience normalized emotional responses. There is nothing wrong with his cognitive abilities, and the progression we are witnessing may be an inevitable part of his aging process. The concern I have is how he is going about doing this. Will the fuse hold? Is the bomb still there? These are questions I need to answer before we have a problem that cannot be solved.

With the approval of this board, I have located Doctor Stevens. I expect our conversations to be quite illuminating.

CHAPTER EIGHTEEN

Sullivan winced as he sat up.

The long wound down his side pulled against the staples, slapping the warden with a pain like a hundred bee stings. He looked around to find that they were back in the rented sleeping pod. How he had got there, he could not say.

"Feeling good?" Fagan called from the couch.

"The fuck you think?" Sullivan snapped. "I feel like I got shot. How long I been out?"

"Eleven hours. You ate about ten thousand calories, drank a liter of vodka, asked for a hooker, and promptly passed out." Fagan stood and walked to a closet. "So you know, just a regular Tuesday for you."

"Did I get laid?"

"Nope."

"Not even close, then."

Fagan opened the closet to reveal their captured mercenary. He was secured to a chair with thick bands of industrial tape. The tape covered his mouth, but his eyes were clearly visible, and they did not look pleased. Fagan picked up man and chair with one hand and brought them to the middle of the bedroom so Sullivan could see him without getting up. The trapped man grunted when the chair plunked to the floor, and Fagan growled, "Oh, shut up."

Sullivan viewed the mercenary through narrowed eyes. "He have anything to say, yet?"

"Keeps asking for a lawyer." Fagan reached down and tore the tape away from his mouth. The mercenary flinched hard. "Apparently, he knows his rights."

"Fuck you, fascist!"

Sullivan raised an eyebrow. "Fascist? That's a real highbrow accusation coming from a mercenary."

"It fits," the captive croaked. "And I ain't saying shit till I get a lawyer."

"Yeah." Sullivan wiped his face with his hands. "I'm going to go ahead and assume you haven't passed the bar yet."

"Seems probable," Fagan said with a knowing smile.

"Let me help you out," Sullivan said, rising from the bed. He was shirtless, though someone had managed to find him a pair of dungarees not soaked in his own blood. "We are not currently anywhere that recognizes your civil rights." He gestured to the dingy bedroom around them. "There are no lawyers. No procedures to follow. No Public Integrity Department with which to file a complaint."

"You're still wardens!" the captive blurted out. "You still got to follow the rules. Even down here."

"Maybe I do," Sullivan said with a shrug. "But that doesn't mean I have to protect you or help you."

The captive's face twisted into a bemused frown, though he remained silent.

"You are foreign agents fucking around on gang turf without respecting their rules. We kicked the shit out of your crew in front of a hundred witnesses. Left most of them dead or bleeding on the floor. According to our local guide, we are pretty much heroes right now." Sullivan did not know if this was true, but it might be, which was good enough for him. "Dipshit, we aren't here to arrest you. If I want to fuck your life up, all I have to do is send you out that door. You'll be dead in twenty minutes." Sullivan at last found a shirt, a gray short-sleeved number crumpled on top of an ancient dresser. He started to shrug into it, only wincing once or twice in the process. It was far too tight, but it fit without ripping, and that would have to do. "The way I see it, you want to help us out so we can help *you* out." With his shirt managed to the extent it was going to be, Sullivan reached for his boots. "Or I don't know, fuck it. We'll let your unhelpful ass go."

"It'll save us a ton of paperwork," Fagan added. He leered down at the captive. "I hate paperwork."

At last, the mercenary's facade began to crack. "What's the deal, then?"

Sullivan made a motion with his hands as if balancing two objects. "You talk, and if I like what you say, we'll have our local guide get you clear of the Complex. You lie or clam up, we send you out the door in your underwear."

"Please tell me you wore underwear," Fagan said with mock severity.

The captive chose not to answer this. He addressed Sullivan. "So if I sing to you fascist bastards, I get to walk out of here? That sounds a bit too generous."

Beaming benign affability, Fagan clapped the mercenary on the back, startling him. "What can I say? We really suck at being fascists. We could try harder, if that'll make you feel better. I only got a D-minus in witness torture at Jack-Boot Junior High, but I'll do my best..."

"Fuck you," the captive said, though his heart was not in it.

"Who hired you?" Sullivan asked.

"Usual channels," the man in the chair said. Sullivan's eyes told him that this was not a satisfactory answer, and he hurried to amend it. "My crew runs a lot of jobs for the SoA, and whenever there's a run in one of the complexes, it's usually a SoA job."

"Well, there's a goddamn wrinkle," Fagan said with a grunt.

"You aren't running a mob job?" Sullivan asked.

"I'm pretty sure it's SoA. I hear the mob hired Coll, and well, once you hire Coll, your shit is pretty much handled."

Fagan looked to Sullivan. "You figure the SoA are trying to jump a mob claim?"

"That'd be real damn ballsy, and a serious potential shit show." Sullivan turned to the captive again. "So the Sons of Adam are after what, exactly?"

"You, I guess," the man in the chair said.

"That doesn't make a whole lot of sense," Fagan remarked.

"Then they are after whatever you are after and figure you're the best way to get it. All I know is that the job was to bring you in, or bring you down."

Fagan snorted. It was a half-laugh, half-scoff kind of noise. "And they sent you six fuck-ups to take us down?"

"I'm kind of insulted," Sullivan said without humor.

The man in the chair shrugged against his restraints. "We got a piece of you."

"And we got all of you," Sullivan pointed out. "Now, where were you supposed to bring us, or what were you supposed to do with us when you got us?"

The captive paused while loyalty to his contract and fear of death competed for control of his facial expression. Fear won, and he said in a small voice, "We have a base just outside the Complex. Mobile command center, stuff like that."

"Where?"

"About twenty-five miles due west. Another forty guys or so, a couple of choppers, and some trucks. Send a drone, and you'll find it."

Sullivan's next question was interrupted by a loud knock at the door. A pistol appeared in Fagan's hand as if by magic, and Sullivan called, "Who is it?"

"It's Skip!"

"Check it," Sullivan said to Fagan.

The big man slid over to the door and cracked it enough to see out. He growled, "Who the fuck is that?"

"It's someone you really want to talk to," Skip replied, his voice muffled by the door.

Fagan looked to Sullivan, a question in his eyes. "He's got someone with him. What do you think?"

"In for a penny," Sullivan said back.

Fagan slid the bar back and opened the door. Skip walked in with a man in tow. The man was narrow and a touch disheveled. His green jacket was worn and patched, but his eyes were cool and bright. Fagan closed the door behind him and dropped a giant paw on his shoulder from behind, bringing the newcomer to a jolting halt.

"You armed?" the giant rumbled.

"Nope," the man said. "I know who you two are, so I didn't see the point."

"He came up to me while I was squaring you up with the Pale Horses," Skip volunteered. "Found me in the Mercantile while the stewards were hashing out the apologies. Says he has information you are going to want." Skip pointed at their new guest. "Says he's Railroad."

"Name's Porter," the man said. He squinted at the mercenary still taped to a chair. "That one of the guys who jumped you?"

"They tried," was Sullivan's even answer. "Looks like he's an SoA merc. You know you got anti-GiMP terrorists running around?"

"Those assholes always have something going on down here," Porter said. "He talking?"

"Little bit," Sullivan said. "What do you want to say?"

"Does your Roadie know the score?"

"He knows what he needs to know."

"Probably should take a walk, then, Roadie." Porter addressed Skip. "You don't want to hear any of this, you get me?"

Skip looked to the wardens. Fagan saved him. "Take the merc and get him clear of Rosedale. Is there a way to ice him for a couple of days?" He roasted the man in the chair with a smoldering glower. "In case we have more questions."

"Yeah, I can get him underground for a few days. Gonna cost though."

"Money, we've got," the giant said. "Take him and do whatever. If he gives you any shit, cut the gangs loose on him, and we'll go ahead and see how far he gets." Fagan gave the captive a knowing wink and added, "Go find Sully a shirt that fits, too. He looks like a stripper in that thing."

"Got it," Skip said. "I'll give you guys an hour or so." Skip cut the mercenary free of the chair with a pocketknife. "Come on, dipshit. I guess it's your lucky day. SoA boys don't last long in here when they get caught. Try anything, and you'll end up in the sewage plant. And I'm talking about your ass being stuck in the filters, get me?"

When the younger man had left with his charge, Porter turned his attention to the two wardens. "The kid figure out you're wardens?"

"Who says we're wardens?" Sullivan replied, his voice even.

"You're joking, right? I'm with the Railroad; I work with GMPs every day. You're John fucking Sullivan. You, my friend, are the most famous GMP ever. How you thought we wouldn't know who you were is kind of strange."

Fagan sounded ever so slightly dejected. "No one ever recognizes me."

Porter looked up at him. "We get a lot of trolls down here, and even the occasional SOAP like yourself. But chimeras?" He looked back to Sullivan. "You guys are pretty goddamn rare."

Sullivan did not rise to the bait, and changed the subject. "So what brings an admitted Railroad operative here, where two First Class Wardens such as ourselves might be inclined to make an arrest?"

"You won't arrest me. For the same reasons that mercenary ain't gonna give your Roadie any shit. The gangs run the Complex, not the Hegemony." He waved a finger back and forth, wearing a crooked smile. "GEED has no friends in here, and the Railroad has a lot of influence with the Council. Anyone finds out you two are with GEED?" He dragged the finger across his neck. "About two thousand angry GMPs will descend upon your ass faster than you can say 'Cognizant of Modification Advantage.'"

Sullivan allowed that this was almost certainly the case, and moved on. "So what? You here to tell us to fuck off? Nah. You could tip off the gangs about who we really are if you wanted to get rid of us. You didn't, so you want something. Spill."

Porter smiled even wider. "We got some problems, you and me. But I don't think our goals are so totally out of whack. May I sit?" He gestured to the chair only recently occupied by a captive mercenary. "I'm gonna sit." He sat. "Okay, here's the story. We've got your missing scientist; you've probably sorted that out on your own by now. The problem is that the folks who were funding her work?" He winced comically. "Yeah, they really want her back. They might have hired Vincent Coll to get her, and well, I think you understand what that means."

"They killed more than a hundred people already," Sullivan answered. He watched Porter's face for signs of surprise or confusion and found none.

The man simply raised an eyebrow. "You've heard of Coll?"

"My father is Mickey Sullivan. So yes, I've heard of Coll."

"Then you know a hundred is just the start. That's why I'm here."

"What are you offering?"

"The biggest bust of your career."

"You want me to handle Coll?"

"Bingo. Here's my pickle, Warden. Sons of Adam are using Silk Road channels. I can handle them because we deal with those assholes all the time. But Coll is a fucking nightmare. I doubt I have the resources to stop him. If he causes a massacre here like he did in Charlotte, the Railroad will be in deep shit with the gangs and the Council. That's no good for us. So I've decided to help you get the biggest, baddest, most infamous mob cleaner ever."

"We aren't here for Coll," Sullivan countered. "We are here to find and bust the people who funded that lab and killed those people so we can put them out of business. Coll is an afterthought."

Porter parried this easily. "Great. You want the killer? That's Coll. See? I'm helping already. But I can't give you the doctor. She's under our protection now, and you should be glad. If I let you take her, she'll be killed by the SoA or captured by the mob in a week."

This assertion drew Sullivan's face into a scowl. "Because?"

"GEED is compromised. All the usual channels were buzzing about wardens coming here right as you showed up. If you hadn't arrived so fast, they'd have been waiting at the gate for you. You got lucky, and that luck ain't gonna hold. The SoA are a bunch of right-wing asshats who couldn't find their own dicks with a map and a mirror. So if SoA knows you're here, you can bet Coll knows it, too. The minute you get her, *they* get her." He shook his head from side to side. "Ain't gonna happen. So I'm offering you Coll as a consolation prize. Get him, and you can probably figure out who is pulling the strings up there in Albany, too. Isn't that more important than one runaway scientist?"

"And the girl?" Sullivan asked, and this time he got the reaction he was looking for.

Porter twitched, no more than a tiny tic in the muscle of one cheek, but it was enough. "The girl is off limits too," was all he said.

"Tell me about the girl."

"Not my story to tell, Warden. But just like with the doc, if you get her, she's gone forever. Can't let that happen."

"It doesn't look like you have much to offer me, Porter," Sullivan said with a frown. "And if you know who I am, you've probably figured out that burning me to the local gangs will be just as much a problem for the Railroad as Coll would be."

"Maybe even more," Fagan added. "So perhaps you should start telling us what you've got, before we decide it's not worth it and attempt that arrest you don't think we can manage."

"What I have is lots and lots of intel, field assets, and influence. I might not be able to stop Coll, but I know who he'll be talking to. I can point you in that direction, and I can make sure you don't get hassled. Without my help, you will never see him coming, and if you're hoping he'll be stupid enough to stomp around the Mercantile with some hired goons, you're not as smart as people think you are. My deal gets you a huge bust, a chance at finding out who backed this whole mess, and insight into where your mole is. Your other option is to go it alone with every gang, GiMP, and mobster in this whole damn complex up your ass." Porter grinned. "Not much of a choice, is it?"

Sullivan kept his face blank while he considered it. The man was not wrong. If word got out they were wardens, they were as good as dead. Fagan's implied threat notwithstanding, getting killed did nothing to help anyone. He kept his eyes on Porter and asked Fagan, "What do you think, partner?"

"I think our job is to find out who backed that lab and killed all those people. Since we can be pretty sure it wasn't Doctor Platt, I'm happy to go after Coll, instead."

"Agreed," Sullivan said. "Okay, Porter, you've got yourself a deal. We'll leave off the doctor and the kid for now, but I expect a lot of good leads on Coll."

"Hey man, that's exactly what I want. The Railroad doesn't have a big fighting force or guys like you. We just want GMPs to have a chance at a life of their own. Coll will eat us for lunch without your help."

CHAPTER NINETEEN

"I don't like this."

Fagan's whispered warning fell on deaf ears. Sullivan replied with a harsh, "Nobody likes it."

"Don't snap at me, man. Just calling it like it is."

"At least the food's good," Sullivan offered by way of apology. "That shit from the Mercantile was gonna give me food poisoning eventually."

The KC Complex was arrayed in a series of concentric rings connected by hundreds of tunnels. Several rings inward from Rosedale, moving toward Hubtown, the two wardens sat in a diner booth absently munching on appetizers. This particular ring bore the lyrical moniker of 'D-ring,' as it was one of four interstitial layers of facilities separating the hub from the outer sections like Rosedale. Sullivan noted that being closer to the hub must have meant nicer facilities, as the design ethos shifted away from raw manufacturing and material handling. Two layers in from Rosedale, and the décor was much cleaner and less industrial in nature. As Sullivan had observed in other places, the same could be said for the occupants of the inner rings. The gritty, rough-hewn folks inhabiting the Rosedale section were far less prevalent here. Now, men and women in nicer clothes comprised the bulk of the passersby. Even the ubiquitous gangsters walked the corridors and wide open spaces of the repurposed manufacturing and office spaces wearing suits or slacks. The aesthetic jarred both the eyes and the sensibilities. If Sullivan squinted, he saw the same tired office drones, blue collar tradesmen, and bottom-level corporate stock one might find meandering the surface streets in any other city in the world. His native intelligence prevented him from disconnecting his impressions from the realities, however. These were not all laborers or office workers. He saw plenty of armed thugs, pimps, drug dealers, con artists, hucksters, and all species of riffraff under those facades, and the lie of it rankled Sullivan in the deepest part of his psyche. He sat in a lawless no man's land surrounded by people who would kill him as soon as look at him, and they all acted as if there was nothing wrong with that. No quantity of polish or make-up altered the true nature of life in the complexes, and the dishonesty he perceived in the dull pantomime he saw from his seat stank of desperation.

He shook his head at nothing in particular before shoving a greasy french fry into his mouth. Day three in the complex was starting to take its toll on his self-control. His wound itched all the time and stung miserably if he tried to move too fast. Even sleep was a chore in this place. The same cool white light seemed to be everywhere—a soft, unobtrusive illumination that precluded deep shadows and washed subtle contours into featureless planes. It was impossible to keep track of time in the Complex because there was no cycle of day or night to speak of, and the disorientation ruined any hope of familiar sleep patterns. Under normal circumstances, Sullivan needed very little sleep, but recovering from getting shot had necessitated a full day of bed rest and fluids. Fagan had done his best to get their room dark, but the twenty-four-hour nature of Rosedale business had meant a steady patter of noise and activity outside their rented pod's door. The bags under Sullivan's eyes told the story better than anything. However, a single day for recovery was all the time that could be spared. Despite his pain and his mood, even Sullivan had to admit that he felt as good as he was going to, and he left it at that.

Fagan interrupted Sullivan's sulk with a dejected, "When's the mark supposed to show up?"

"Any minute now, if Porter isn't jerking us around."

"You decided how to play this?"

This discussion had gone many rounds since receiving the tip, and Sullivan remained ambivalent. "We can go hard and bust him up. Not really official procedure, but it's likely to work quicker than the slow and quiet route."

"Good chance of bringing these Teamsters down on our heads, too," Fagan said.

"That, too." Sullivan rubbed his bleary eyes. "I figure we should probably do this one by the numbers. Dammit."

Fagan gaped, his face a melodramatic caricature of overwrought surprise. "What? What did I just hear? John 'Fuck The Rules' Sullivan wants to do something by the book?" Two giant hands clasped each other over his chest. "I don't know how to process this... I need air!"

"Fuck you," Sullivan replied, though the ghost of a chuckle ruined his affected belligerence. "If you tell anyone, I'll kill you."

"No one would believe me anyway," Fagan said with a rueful shake of his head. Though his expression soon hardened. "Look lively. Here's our guy, I think."

Sullivan gazed through the diner window, trying to appear nonchalant. As Fagan had indicated, a man in brown coveralls strolled toward their intersection. He carried a briefcase in his hand. The dingy black plastic case swung against a skinny thigh, clutched tightly in a white-knuckled grip.

Sullivan jerked his head in a brisk nod. "Sure looks like him. Now, let's see who he's meeting."

The man in the coveralls found a dark corner to lean against. Nowhere in this section of D-ring was all that dark, as the white-painted walls and pervasive cool lighting killed any opportunity for shadowy meeting places. Sullivan supposed the man simply wanted to be away from the stream of foot traffic and the occasional small vehicle that whirred along the main concourse.

Less than a minute later, another man approached. Sullivan suppressed a gasp of surprise when he saw the hunched posture and narrow shoulders. Fagan caught the twitch of his facial muscles and hissed in clipped tones. "Talk to me, partner."

"I fucking know that guy, Fagan. We arrested him in Chicago."

"Which one?"

"Mortenson. The little shit was trying to burn the data cards, remember?"

"How the hell is he out?" Fagan sounded perplexed. "He couldn't have been given bail, right? And why the hell is he here?"

Sullivan growled his response in a single word. "Horowitz."

Fagan replied with an uttered syllable of his own. "Fuck."

"Change of plan, partner. Skip the Teamster. I want Mortensen."

"Agreed," Fagan said. "But we need that Teamster, too."

"I'll take Mortensen," Sullivan said. "You need to grab the Teamster on your own."

"Are you improvising again?" Fagan shoved the last french fry into his mouth. "Because people tend to get hurt when you improvise."

"Trust me."

"We're doomed," the giant said, shaking his head and standing. "Let me get out there first. I'll find a spot to wait, and then I'll move on the other guy when he gets away from Mortensen."

"Got it. I'll be along in one minute."

Sullivan watched Fagan leave and experienced a moment of strange affinity for the big man. There was something tragic about Patrick Fagan. Fagan might be the physically strongest human being on the planet; he was certainly in the top ten. He was clever and loyal, tough and determined. Sullivan did not dole out compliments easily, though three years in the field with Fagan had forced the surly warden to acknowledge his partner's many exceptional traits. Sullivan had heard the man's whole story. Fagan could have escaped public service if his acromegaly had not been mishandled. Instead of curing it, Fagan's parents chose to optimize his condition, running them afoul of the Genetic Equity Act and condemning their son to a life of government employ. Somehow, the big man never turned bitter, and to this day, he maintained a very cordial relationship with his parents. Sullivan lacked the capacity to work out how that was even possible, though he supposed this was his failing and not Fagan's.

After one minute, Sullivan rose and paid the lunch bill with credits from his chit. He affected his best air of brusque indifference to those around him as he exited the diner, though his stride had a purpose he could not completely hide. He melded into the flow of foot traffic along the concourse and moved toward Mortenson and his accomplice in a lazy, meandering path. It was a struggle to keep eyes on the pair at all times. The crowd and traffic conspired to block his line of sight with every step. Sullivan lost sight of the men for a few seconds when a commuter van hummed by and obscured the alcove. When the obstruction had passed, Sullivan noticed that the meeting had ended and Mortensen was walking away at a pace too brisk to be unobtrusive. While making him easier to track, Sullivan had to increase his own pace to keep up. People began to ricochet off his chest and arms as he shoved himself through the sea of pedestrians.

Fortunately, Mortensen had eyes only for his escape. The little man walked with his shoulders hunched and his gaze fixated on a transport station and, Sullivan presumed, the next commuter van. He saw the briefcase in Mortensen's fist, banging against his leg as he half-walked, half-jogged toward the safety of the turnstile. Not liking his chances of following his quarry into a small vehicle, Sullivan abandoned stealth and closed the final thirty feet between himself and Mortensen at a jog. Mortensen was only just becoming aware of a commotion behind him when Sullivan's hand closed over the back of his neck like a vise, and the other locked onto the wrist with the briefcase with equal force.

"Walk normally, or I start breaking things," Sullivan rumbled into the man's ear.

Mortensen managed one reflexive jerk, an instinctive attempt to pull away, and Sullivan punished him with a vicious squeeze of the neck. A small yelp of pain and fear burst from Mortensen's lips, and he calmed.

"Okay, okay," he said. "You have me, I get it!"

"Walk."

Mortensen walked.

Sullivan maneuvered the man across the D-ring and back toward the tunnels leading to Rosedale. He paid for a tuk-tuk to give them a ride, and the two looked a most curious pair, riding the back of an electric tricycle like two kids on a date. The attention they drew irked the warden, though he supposed there was nothing to be done for it. Back in the dorms, Sullivan ushered his second prisoner in three days into their rented pod. Mortensen offered no resistance when Sullivan shoved him into the room and yanked the briefcase from his hands. He looked at the little man, taking in his disheveled appearance and poorly-concealed terror.

"Complex life a bit much for you?" he asked with a cocky smirk.

Mortensen sat on the bed. "It's quite different from Chicago, all right."

"How'd you get out?"

"You don't want the answer to that."

"Bullshit."

"Your department has some issues with loyalty."

"Who? Is it Horowitz?"

"Even I don't have that information, Warden. But I was released on her order."

"Where is Coll?"

Mortensen flinched. "I can't... I don't know."

"Sammy, I can smell a lie, and you fucking stink. The only reason you are here and dealing with the Teamsters is because Coll needs assets in here, and he needs the Silk Road to get them in. I don't need you to admit you are involved. I already know it. Try again."

"You don't understand. Coll is here already. He's not really looking for you, and you would be smart to avoid him."

Sullivan graced the man with a look oozing both disdain and condescension. Mortensen's shoulders rose and fell in an emphatic sigh. "But you won't. I wish you understood how dangerous your current path is."

"Enlighten me."

"I can't. I can only tell you that the things you are chasing don't lead to anywhere you want to be. I told you this in Chicago. Make your arrests, but stop chasing down my employers. It's both higher and deeper than you realize. There are things in motion that cannot be stopped, and you will only get crushed by this machine if you try to prevent this conflict or alter its course."

"What conflict?"

"Warden." Mortensen sounded tired. "That doctor you are looking for has made a discovery that will change the world. My employers know it, the Railroad knows it, and the Sons of Adam suspect it. Whoever controls her secrets will rewrite human history as they see fit. Your job? Your life?" Mortensen snapped his fingers. "Meaningless. The government?" He snapped again. "Merely an obstacle to be overcome." Mortensen leaned in to fix Sullivan with a worn and weary gaze. "The lives of everyone in the KC Complex?" Another snap. "Meaningless." He sat back on the bed. "My employers have called in all their assets. Your department is one of them. Large portions of the Ruling Council here in this complex are as well. So is the Silk Road. Even our lofty New Global Republic is compromised,

Warden. This is bigger than your investigation, and it will get you killed."

If the lecture was supposed to cow Sullivan, it failed. "It's the girl, isn't it? What does she have that's so valuable?"

Mortensen frowned. "I don't know. That information is too valuable for me to be trusted with."

"What's in the case?" Sullivan asked, jiggling the forgotten item.

"Intelligence, I presume. I don't get to look at what's inside."

Sullivan examined the lock. He turned the case over and frowned at the hinges.

"Tampering with the lock will destroy the contents," Mortensen warned.

Sullivan replied with an oily smile. "Guess I'll just have to leave the lock alone, then." Without losing his evil grin, Sullivan dug his fingers into the sides of the case and ripped the front panel off. A cascade of data cards and credit chits spilled onto the floor. A large pistol and two extra magazines landed on top.

"See?" Sullivan said. "Never touched the lock." He dropped the briefcase and examined the pile of debris. "Lots of local currency in that pile. That'll come in handy." He picked up the pistol. It was an expensive gas-operated model in ten-millimeter. A counterweight in front of the trigger guard and the conspicuously large magazines told Sullivan everything he needed to identify the weapon. "Shit, man. A Hudson H10 in full auto? Sexy!" He shoved the gun into his belt and picked up one of the data cards. "Let's go ahead and start looking through these, shall we?"

"Please don't," Mortensen said. His voice was devoid of hope or steel.

"Fuck you," came Sullivan's jovial retort. The warden began fumbling for his tablet and plugged the first data card into the black rectangle.

Mortensen watched with blank eyes for a minute and then asked. "What do you intend to do with me?"

"Well, I can't exactly arrest you down here, can I?" Sullivan watched as Mortensen blanched. "But I'm not particularly inclined to kill you, either." He looked back at his tablet. "Not as long as you are useful, anyway."

"I will try to be as useful as I can," Mortensen said.

"Who are these employers you keep talking about?"

"Oh come on, Warden. You haven't figured that out yet?"

Sullivan nodded. "I figured as much. Mickey still pulls all the strings, huh? Even from prison?"

"Prison is very different for people like your father."

"He's not my father."

"He would disagree. He has watched your career with great interest and great pride."

Sullivan looked up again, and rage burned in his glare. "Pride? Really? I find that hard to believe."

"Why not pride? You are exceptional. You have met or exceeded every expectation he ever had for you."

"Except the team I play for."

"If you believe that is the sort of thing that bothers Michael Sullivan, then you are a fool." Mortensen could not hide his smirk. "He owns your team, after all. No matter what you do, Warden, you are still working for your father. Whether you realize it or not."

Sullivan did not like it, but if all his other suspicions were accurate, the little man was right. Uncomfortable, he decided to change the subject. "Where is Coll?"

"I do not know. He is looking for the doctor and the girl. He will have figured out something has gone awry by now."

"Now who's acting like an idiot?" Sullivan's tone carried a warning. "This briefcase was meant for Coll, wasn't it? It's got everything he'll need to get his own hunt rolling. Not to mention a weapon that costs two-thirds of my monthly pay." He drew the aforementioned pistol and waved it around for emphasis. "How were you going to get this to him?"

"It's a dead drop over near Hubtown. I was supposed to collect this from a Teamster and get it to a warehouse near there."

"When?"

"I'm already late."

"Shit."

Mortensen nodded in agreement. "Like I said, he's probably aware something is wrong. He'll know you have me."

"So why isn't he kicking the door in?" Sullivan asked.

"Good question," the little man said. "I can't imagine he'll take the insult lying down. I assumed he'd be here to rescue or kill me before long." Mortensen's look of confusion seemed sincere, and that set Sullivan's jaw. Then realization hit the warden like a cannonball to the guts.

"Oh, shit. He's after Fagan!"

CHAPTER TWENTY

That he was cursed with incompetent idiots for help was something Vincent Coll had come to terms with years before. Mortensen should have been liquidated immediately upon his release from GEED custody, not banished to the KC Complex where he could continue to screw things up. Such decisions were not his to make, and now Coll was the one who suffered for it.

Far too cagey to trust the transport of his supplies to unsupervised screw-ups like Mortenson, Coll observed the handoff from a safe distance. Seconds later, he spotted the wardens. There was no missing them. Neither man had any business doing undercover or surveillance work. They gave sore thumbs a bad name, and Coll's professional pride took umbrage with their club-footed attempt at subtlety.

Sullivan was a well-known quantity to men like Coll, and the giant had been too obvious to miss when leaving the diner. While trolls were not so rare in the complexes, SOAPs were unique anywhere. It took a skilled eye to tell the difference, and Coll's eye was nothing if not skilled. He decided to deal with the SOAP first, owing mostly to the superior tactical challenge someone like that represented. Of course, one could not exclude the facts of John Sullivan's parentage from consideration, either. Discovering Sullivan's presence added a delicious wrinkle to a job already rife with interesting challenges. Mickey Sullivan would not look kindly upon Coll's work if his son ended up dead. Mobsters could be quixotically loyal to family sometimes. On the other well-funded hand, there were plenty of people who would pay very good money to the man who took John Sullivan out of the game. Coll could play to either side with equal facility, so he remained professionally ambivalent. No matter which way the winds of fortune chose to blow, the killer had already determined it would be better to deal with Sullivan after eliminating the giant, as Sullivan would require a very careful approach.

Coll stalked the big man, hanging back at least thirty feet while the hulking warden trailed the man in coveralls. Coll knew where the Teamster was going, so he could afford to be patient. His moment would come when the Teamster left the concourse and accessed a side tunnel that led nowhere interesting to anyone not involved in moving material between the rings. The space was wide, though lit only well enough to facilitate the cargo cars that slid along maglev tracks. Inside the tunnel, shadows stretched from every direction as all manner of devices and equipment for material-handling obscured the precious few recessed lights. Very few people moved around inside. A few dozen men in identical brown coveralls worked at various tasks. Other people strolled along the raised platforms running alongside the maglev rails. Some were supervising workers; others looked like they were up to no good. Everyone ignored everyone else.

Every few minutes, a cargo car would buzz past, crackling and spitting sparks from the electromagnets along the main central rail. Coll smiled when he saw the giant use the passing of one of these cars to mask his own entrance into the tunnel. Tradecraft was an art, and Coll appreciated good work when he saw it. He duplicated the maneuver himself and fell in behind his prey. With deep pools of inky blackness available, both Coll and the big warden were able to increase their speed. Coll chose a likely spot for an ambush, and set to ensuring his pace would have him in position at the same time as the giant. His choice was a junction of two tunnels with a complex switch-track system. The automated station routed cars to the correct rails via enormous overhead gantry. The space was open enough for Coll to move around, and the constant shuffling of cars and cranes would give him places to hide if things went poorly.

He used a maintenance walkway to shift his pursuit to the other side of the tunnel so he could bring himself abreast of the big warden. Forty feet of dark tunnel and three rows of maglev tracks separated the two of them, and Coll assured himself that the giant remained fixated on his own prey before making a move. Just as the big man sidled around the first corner of the intersection, Coll sprang into a full sprint. A cargo car obscured his path for an instant, just as he had planned. The cover allowed Coll to get within ten feet of his victim before something alerted the giant to his presence.

Coll aimed his first blow for the junction of the big man's jaw and skull, underneath the right ear. Such strikes tended to dislocate the jaw and render the recipient instantly unconscious, and this seemed the best method for dealing with someone far larger and stronger than himself. Out of pure instinct, the giant turned toward Coll at that precise moment. Coll's punch connected flush with Fagan's wide forehead. The hyper-dense skull, massive and thick thanks to advanced acromegaly, proved more than a match for Coll's knuckles. Within a tenth of a second, the pain lanced up Coll's arm in searing tendrils that traveled all the way to his shoulder. Coll crashed to the concrete floor with a snarl and rolled to his feet.

The giant staggered back as well. Merely surviving the punch did not render him immune from the spectacular quantity of kinetic energy it delivered. Stunned, the giant regained his traction with remarkable speed and glared at his assailant.

Coll stood tall. With the element of surprise wasted, he abandoned it to square off with the giant. He shook his injured hand with a rueful smile. "That's some hard head you got, buddy. I've never killed a SOAP before," he said, all but purring.

The giant cocked his head to one side, then the other, as if loosening a kink in his neck. "You gotta be this Coll fucker I keep hearing about." The big man stepped forward, bearing down on Coll as if beating him up was going to be no more interesting than completing the latest pile of paperwork. Coll let the warden draw his pistol with a smile. The giant replied with a smile of his own. "You are under arrest," he added.

"Sure I am," Coll said, and stood his ground. "Better take me in, then."

Fagan was not stupid. He knew he was being goaded into closing the distance. He also knew he outweighed Coll by two hundred pounds and was likely twice as strong. Still, he approached with professional caution. "Get on your knees," he ordered.

Coll knelt and put his hands on his head. "Like this?"

"That'll do." Fagan stepped close and dropped one huge paw on Coll's clasped hands to secure them. He angled his hip away, placing his body between Coll and the gun while he attempted to re-holster his weapon.

Coll uncoiled like a compressed spring.

Twisting without rising, Coll snaked around Fagan and grabbed for the gun. The big man was far too slow to stop him, but quick enough to prevent having his weapon stolen. Instead, Coll's fingers closed over the top of the frame. A deft flick of his thumb released the magazine, and the precious payload of caseless forty-five clattered to the concrete. As the metal box left the mag-well, a legally-required safety catch took the chambered round out of battery and rendered the gun a useless affectation.

Fagan neither mourned the loss nor did he dwell upon it. He leapt back to get clear of Coll and let a small smile turn the corners of his mouth. "I'd rather do it this way anyway," he said, shrugging out of his jacket.

Coll saw the thick arms and broad chest of his opponent and tilted his head. "Well, that's new. That's not the response I usually get from folks," he admitted.

"Welcome to my world," the giant said, and he charged.

Fagan's opening left hook missed Coll's head by less than an inch. The following right hook by even less. Coll spun and danced out of the path of a third punch with a wide grin. "My, my, my!" he crooned. "You *are* fast!"

Fagan stepped back, assessed his opponent, and advanced again. He opened with a jab this time, and Coll slipped it to fire a left hook into Fagan's ribs. Fagan twisted away from Coll's following straight right and parried the punch with a forearm.

"Reflexes need work, but still damn good for a SOAP," Coll said with a teacher's bland tone.

Fagan waded in again, though with more caution this time. He feinted several jabs, earning a derisive snort from Coll as he slapped each aside with contempt. When Fagan slid forward to sling a big right hand, Coll danced inside his guard and fired a kick into the giant's left knee. He followed it with a right hook to the body and left uppercut that snapped the slab jaw shut with a click. Under normal circumstances, Coll might expect this to end the fight. Fagan's guttural growl and giant overhand right disabused him of any such fantasies.

Coll stepped back, impressed. "Damn, Warden. I had heard they were sending their best men in." He shook his bruised hand again. "I can see they weren't exaggerating." He began to stalk his foe in a circle. First to the right, then to the left. He watched the warden's careful footwork and wary guard for exploitable mistakes, checked the expression on his face for signs of fear or confusion. He saw none of either. "I won't lie, big man. You do not disappoint."

"What can I say?" the giant quipped. "I'm a people-pleaser." Then he stepped forward again. It was a big step, nearly a lunge. Vincent slid to the outside to hit the exposed midsection some more when he realized his foe had changed his movement from a lunge into a tackle. With enormous arms spread out wide, there would be no getting clear of the giant's reach before being grabbed. Coll twisted and leapt, bringing his knee straight up to collide with the warden's face. It did not stop the forward momentum, and it did not prevent Coll from being crushed by the weight of his opponent. It stunned the man, however, and this allowed Coll to avoid those grasping hands and the horrific mangling they promised. Both men crashed to the concrete in a heap. Coll cycled his limbs like pistons, shoving and bashing at Fagan. Meanwhile, Fagan scrambled and clutched for a handhold on the elusive Coll. Coll kicked hard, not expecting to hurt the big man, but to give himself some distance. He made it to his feet before Fagan did, and he fell on the warden with a flurry of punches and kicks.

It felt like beating on a granite statue. The big man ignored most of these blows, absorbing the hits to focus on regaining his feet. This enraged Coll. Coll rarely fought anyone stronger than he was, and even then, he was accustomed to his punches garnering more respect than this. Normally, he enjoyed a good fight, but normally, his fights were much more one-sided. He found that he did not like this fight, and when the bulky warden sent him hurtling backward with the strength of a single arm, Coll began to lose his temper.

"Really squirrelly little guy, aren't you?" Fagan said, and spat blood from a split lip onto the floor. He added, "Stronger than you look, too. You a MINK? You seem like a MINK. I like bashing MINKs."

Coll attempted to suppress his growing rage. His voice betrayed him. "You've never fought anything like me." Coll advanced. "I'm gonna mount your hairy head on my goddamn wall!"

Fagan met Coll in the middle, accepting punches with muffled grunts while trying to land a few of his own. As each blow thumped against Fagan's body with little effect, Coll's movements grew wilder. His clean and methodical techniques collapsed into unsophisticated brawling as his cool demeanor melted under the heat of his growing frustration. Still, the giant came. Coll fought harder. A brutal combination of punches rocked the warden, three hooks and a straight right all landing flush. The big man stumbled backward into a stack of crates, toppling the pile. Coll pursued, then had to retreat as the giant rose with a cargo crate held aloft. With a roar, the big man sent the crate sailing for Coll's head. Coll threw himself to the side, and the crate crashed down where he had been standing. It shattered, littering the battlefield with construction materials and giving Coll an idea.

He dove for the pile and rolled to his feet clutching a three-foot piece of steel reinforcing bar. The warden was already upon him, so Coll swung blind with all his might. The improvised weapon hit something thick and meaty, and the tortured growl from his opponent told Coll the fight was now in his hands. He spun away, stepped back for some room, and brought the bar around again. This time, he had the luxury of aiming, and the bar caught the giant just above the knee. The warden went down with a yell, and Coll brought the weapon high for an attempt to bash the man's skull in.

The warden rolled away, and Coll missed, but he had the upper hand now and was not going to waste it. When Fagan scrambled toward the debris pile and a weapon of his own, Coll leapt and swung again, striping the big man's back and arms with cruel overhand blows. Fagan abandoned the pursuit and lashed out with a huge left fist that Coll evaded easily. Coll quartered the giant off from the pile and brought the bar down across Fagan's neck hard enough to bend it, and still the man came at him. On the next swing, the big warden managed to trap the bar between his ribs and arm. Momentarily confused, Coll tugged in an attempt to free his weapon. Fagan grabbed Coll by the throat with his free hand and squeezed. The imminent danger and pain sent a wildfire of fear and fury through Coll, and he wrenched the bar free with a savage yank. Unthinking, he drove the rough-cut end of the weapon through the arm choking him. The tip erupted from Fagan's bicep with a shower of blood and a roar of pain from the giant. Coll's world went topsy-turvy for an instant before he realized he was flying through the air. When he landed some twelve feet away, he saw the big warden on his knees, bleeding from a dozen wounds and covered in purpling bruises. His arm poured blood, matting the thick hair and painting him in garish streaks of crimson. His face was pale, the wide chest heaved in labored breaths. The injured arm hung by his side with both ends of the steel bar protruding at right angles to the bone. The intimidating warden looked weak and tired, and the sick monster inside Vincent Coll cackled with sadistic glee. His lips peeled back to show his perfect white teeth in an ugly leer.

"Here we go," he snarled.

Coll charged.

He rocketed a knee into Fagan's temple at full speed, then he turned and sent a heel kick into the big man's jaw. Punches followed, combinations of six or seven at a time, falling like hammer blows onto the shaggy head. The giant fought on. Slowed, weakened, and bleeding badly, the warden's resistance faltered in increments until he was reduced to swinging his arms in slow arcs, hoping to get lucky. Blood soaked the hair on his head and in his beard, his right arm hung limp at his side. Eventually, a brutal stomp to his knee sent the giant back to the floor. Fagan writhed and pushed, though it was obvious he lacked the strength to lift his massive body anymore. Seeing the helplessness of the man who had so completely infuriated him sent a cooling wave of relief through Coll. He paused to collect himself, running a hand through his disheveled hair and straightening the lines of his blood-spattered suit.

"Holy shit, Warden," he huffed, more than a little out of breath. "Now that was a workout!"

Fagan only growled and kept dragging at the floor.

"You, sir, should be very pleased with yourself. I haven't had a tussle like that in a very long time." Coll walked up to the writhing man. Still smiling, he grabbed the piece of steel still in Fagan's arm and ripped it free. Fagan screamed.

Coll leaned over and grabbed the big man by the head. He turned it so he could take a good look into his foe's eyes. The man was still conscious, eyes burning with hate for his tormentor. Coll smiled his approval. "Now, Warden," he cooed. "Let's talk about a missing scientist and a little girl, shall we?"

Fagan spat blood in Coll's face, reigniting the psychotic rage that had only just subsided. Coll turned the bloody steel bar in his hand and drove it through Fagan's thigh. The warden roared again, though he lacked the strength to do much more.

"Don't fuck with me, freak," Coll shouted. "I'll poke you so full of holes, they'll use your skull for a colander!" He ground the bar in a circle, widening the wound and dragging more pained gasps from Fagan. "I don't need you dead, so you can survive this if you talk. Where are they?"

Fagan's lips moved, and something soft and pained escaped.

Coll sighed in frustration. "Passing out, are we? Give me something I can use, and you won't die. Pass out without being helpful?" He gave the bar another twist for emphasis. "No promises."

Fagan's lips moved again, and Coll leaned in to listen.

He immediately regretted this. Fagan's forehead crashed against Coll's nose like a wrecking ball. A thousand flashbulbs went off behind his eyes, and a freight train of pain sent him stumbling backward. Coll's vision swam, and his knees wobbled as if the joints were rubber and not bone. Before he realized where he was, his ataxic staggering brought him to the edge of the platform, and he toppled from the walkway into the switchyard. Luck prevented his death when instead of landing on a maglev rail or impaling himself on any of the random pieces of equipment, he plummeted into the waiting belly of an empty cargo car. The impact drove the air from his lungs and left Coll semiconscious for several long seconds. When his senses returned, he tasted blood in his throat and felt a warm, wet river running from his nose and down his chin. Disoriented but focused, he staggered back to his feet just in time to get knocked down again when the car surged into motion. Scrambling up the concave sides of his prison, Coll made it to the top just as the platform and the wounded warden disappeared into the shadows.

Too irritated to even utter a curse, Coll slipped back down to the bottom of the car to wait for it to stop.

CHAPTER TWENTY-ONE

Something strange and uncomfortable surged in Sullivan's innards when they found Fagan.

The giant had managed to drag himself from the switchyard to the maintenance platform, and from there, he was able to force his bulk through a man door back onto the D-ring main concourse. He passed out shortly afterward, lying in an enormous pile of shaggy limbs, staining the side of the corridor with greasy streaks of thickening blood.

Finding his partner was not difficult. The fight had been relatively private, but rumors in the Complex spread at the speed of light. Both Porter and Skip had a read on the location within minutes of the outcome, and Fagan's emergence onto the concourse did not go unnoticed. Seeing the big man so broken and pale woke something new and strange in Sullivan. A sort of primal indignation narrowed his eyes. It was deep and hot, though it did not taste like the usual aborted fury or the ephemeral wisps of terror he was accustomed to. He did not think it was empathy. Empathy produced sadness, and Sullivan felt no sadness.

As he ran up to the bloody heap, his discomfort grew. Turning Fagan onto his back revealed a man covered in horrible bruises and two ugly puncture wounds. Fagan was quiet, his breath escaping in shallow wisps from broken and bloody lips. The heat in Sullivan's belly surged.

Teeth clenched, Sullivan tore strips from Fagan's shirt and tied off the holes in Fagan's arm and leg. A thin gasp of pain whooshed from the big man when Sullivan cinched these tight enough to stem the bleeding. "Sorry, partner," he mumbled. He turned to Skip and barked, "Get a fucking cart, or a car or something! And call that doctor lady!"

Skip bolted like a whipped spaniel from the unvarnished malice in Sullivan's voice. Sullivan heard it as well, though he had no tears to shed for Skip's feelings. His body burned, making his fingers tremble. The sensation confused the warden. The waves of heat, nausea, and what was that? Fear? Each took a turn at battering his concentration while the powerless Sullivan sat befuddled. He looked back to Fagan. The man still breathed, though each breath twisted his face into a grimace of pain.

"You with us, partner?" Sullivan asked.

An eye fluttered, not quite opening but acknowledging the question.

"You're going to be all right, man. Skip's getting us a ride so you don't have to walk."

The eye fluttered again, this time with a tiny twitch of the head.

Skip returned in that moment. Somehow, he had managed to procure a motorized freight cart. The front consisted of a large, low-slung, open-top box, and the operator rode behind it.

"How the hell we gonna get him in there?" Skip asked.

Sullivan did not answer. He gently sat Fagan upright, then pulled the heavy uninjured arm over his shoulder. "This is probably going to suck," he said. Then, as an afterthought he added, "Sorry." With as much care as possible, Sullivan dragged Fagan over his shoulder in a fireman's carry, then stood with the nearly five-hundred-pound man draped across his back. The giant covered Sullivan, making the warden look like a primitive hunter trying to lug a dead bear back to camp.

Skip gawked. "Holy shit..."

Sullivan walked over to the cart and placed Fagan inside as gingerly as he could manage. A few pained grunts wheezed from the injured man even so. The ride back to the Rosedale dorms began and ended in silence. Skip, being street smart, decided to avoid trying to engage Sullivan in conversation. The warden's smoldering glower played a significant role in cementing the wisdom of this. At the dorms, Sullivan repeated his feat of strength from earlier, carrying his massive partner into their pod with no more complaint than a man bringing in the groceries. Sam Mortensen, secured to the same wooden chair previously occupied by the mercenary, greeted the invasion with an expression of abject horror. Sullivan stomped past the man and deposited Fagan on the bed. The mattress fell short—the big man's feet hung well over the end—but there was no fixing that. Sullivan arranged the man's limbs so he could rest comfortably and propped the shaggy head up with a pillow. With Fagan on the bed, Sullivan pulled the big man's shirt and pants off to better assess his partner's injuries.

Skip verbalized Sullivan's impressions with a soft and horrified, "Holy fucking shit, man."

Sullivan narrated what he saw. He did not understand why. It felt detached and procedural, and this seemed to keep the strange and ugly emotional maelstrom in his brain from driving him any further from sanity than he already was.

"Guy or guys hit him with something." He pointed to the long linear bruises crisscrossing Fagan's chest. "Had to be metal. His bone and muscle are so dense, anything else would have broken."

"They worked him over with pipes?" Skip asked.

"Looks like re-bar. See the punctures? The edges were uneven and jagged. "Whatever it was didn't slice through his skin, it ripped through."

"Like the cut end of a piece of re-bar," Skip said.

"Exactly. Here's the thing: Suds is hardcore high-dollar GMP stock. His bones and muscles are way thicker than yours or mine.

Fucker who did that was strong." Sullivan peered closer at a bruise on Fagan's ribs. His frown deepened. "That one is from a fist."

"Yeah?" Skip did not seem to grasp the significance of this.

Sullivan elaborated. "You aren't getting it. Do you comprehend how hard you have to hit a guy like Fagan to raise a welt like that? Really fucking hard. There's dozens of them, too." Sullivan re-evaluated all the bruises and welts. He searched for the cooling fog of dopamine that would help him relax and sharpen his focus. It never came, though an unhappy realization did. "This was just one guy."

"So he got jumped by one guy, huh?" Skip nodded. "Lots of bad dudes in those tunnels."

Sullivan turned his glower to Skip, and the young gangster shrank beneath its intensity. "Bad dudes? Have you ever, in your entire life, met anyone stupid enough to go bare-knuckle with a guy like this?" He jerked a thumb over to the man on the bed. "What kind of guy looks at Suds, here, and thinks, 'Fuck yeah, I'll have a go at him?'" Sullivan shook his head slowly. "I'm not afraid of any living person in a fight, Skip, but even I don't push my luck with ol' Suds. So unless you've got honest-to-goodness monsters in there, we are well past 'bad dudes.' The bastard who did this is something else entirely." Sullivan collapsed into a chair. "Why don't you go find the doctor, Skip. I need a minute with my friend in the chair."

"Sure thing, Sully. I'll see if the Road Crew can get a line on Coll, too."

Skip left the room with a speed that betrayed just how badly he wanted to get away from all of them. Sullivan did not begrudge the young man his agitation. Things were spiraling out of control at a rate that even the warden found alarming.

"Fucking Vincent Coll," Sullivan growled toward Mortensen. "I get that he's a hard one, but this?" He shook his head in a slow, disbelieving arc. "What do you know about Coll?"

"Too much for my own good."

"Talk. I'm not even playing the warden thing anymore with you, Sam. Talk before I start to hurt you, because I am very confused and irritated."

Mortensen sighed. "What do you want me to say?"

"What is he? No bullshit, either." He pointed to Fagan. "That is not the work of some regular mob cleaner or a hopped-up MINK."

Mortensen did not answer right away. His jaw worked for a few seconds, and Sullivan could see indecision dance across his features. At last, the thin mobster slumped and answered. "Vincent is one of four very special chimeras. Each one specially designed for a specific role in what many hope will be a new world order."

The churning of Sullivan's guts increased in both violence and intensity. "What the fuck does that mean?"

"It means that many people believe the days of Genetic Equity and the New Republic are numbered. Enterprising individuals and organizations are already preparing for what comes next. There is a lot of money in global domination, Joh—" Mortensen caught himself. "Warden."

"So Vincent is what, exactly? A prototype for some new kind of GMP?"

"Exactly."

Sullivan wiped at his face with a dirty hand. "This is insanity, you know that? At best, one person per ten-thousand is modified for advantage. Probably a lot less than that. There are perhaps thirty chimeras walking the planet right now, too. This little revolution is off to a real shitty start."

Mortensen shrugged. "Maybe. But how many GMPs would you need to take over? How many regular people would it take to stop you if you tried? How many to bring down Vincent Coll? Isn't this fear why they made it illegal to modify embryos in the first place? The world is changing too fast for most people to understand what is really happening. A new type of humanity is being born every day, and nothing can stop that. Some people just want to make sure that the new world is profitable."

"Like Mickey Sullivan?"

"He is nothing if not a shrewd businessman."

Something clicked in the back of Sullivan's brain. "Am I one of these prototypes?"

Mortensen said nothing. He did not have to.

Sullivan fired a breath from his nostrils, less a snort and more of a huff. "Shit. I am, aren't I? Goddamn it. No wonder Mickey hasn't had me killed yet. I always wondered about that."

"He can be very sentimental, Warden."

"Bullshit. He's the kind of amoral bastard other amoral bastards want to grow up to be. He treated me like crap my whole life, and now I get why. I'm just glad he got caught. At least I can look forward to him dying in prison."

"There is that," Mortensen sighed. "If he does, in fact, die in prison, that is." Mortensen shook his head to dispel the thought. "He was advised against raising you as his son. But as I said, he can be sentimental."

"Tell me about this 'New World Order,' Sam."

"I don't know much. I'm not high enough up the food chain."

"Tell me what you do know, and fast."

Mortensen straightened as much as he could. "You could figure it all out on your own. After the war ended and the introduction of the Genetic Equity Act, a select group of enterprising individuals—"

"You mean mobsters, corporations, and dirty politicians."

"A select group of enterprising individuals decided that total prohibition of all modifications that grant an advantage was clearly stupid. The genie was out of the bottle, after all. They started to prepare for the inevitable failure of such a law and the ascension of GMPs to the ruling class."

"Because they want to control it?"

"They see this as inevitable, and simply want to profit from the transition."

"Who are they?"

"Oh, come on, John. As if I'd know that. I work for your father, and I know he is involved. Even so, I cannot even say to what extent he is involved."

"Enough to have me made at great personal expense."

Mortensen acknowledged the point with a nod. "At least that much."

"What about these prototypes? What's the deal with them?"

"They are potential product offerings. Several large biotech firms are developing them to serve the leaders of this..." he struggled for the right word. "...cabal? I presume they intend to market and sell them to the various factions that want to wrest control from the Global Republic."

"Them? You're talking about me, Mortensen. I'm one of these... things. I'm not serving anyone."

"Aren't you?"

Sullivan's face turned to stone, and his voice rumbled like distant thunder. "Just what the fuck does that mean?"

Mortensen smiled. His thin lips stretched in an ugly line. "Maybe you should ask your Captain Horowitz about that."

"I think I will, Sam. You better make sure she doesn't have anything to say that leads me to believe you aren't telling the truth."

"Why would I lie? Nothing you or I can do will change anything."

A knock at the door ended the conversation. Sullivan checked it see who it was, then opened the door to let Skip and the familiar old woman who had worked on Sullivan through. She eyed the warden with undisguised curiosity and asked, "How is your side?"

"Itches. Burns when I move too much. Otherwise okay."

"You heal very quickly, Mister Sully."

His reply was terse. "I'm just healthy like that."

The woman seemed entirely immune from his rudeness, and pushed past Sullivan to examine the man on the bed. "Well, I guess this place is better than that brothel. What happened to him?"

"He fell down some stairs."

The woman began to withdraw items from her satchel. Without looking at Sullivan, she droned, "The last time I saw you, you had been shot and there was a man tied to a chair. This time, a mere forty-eight hours later, I have a SOAP beaten half to death and a different man tied to a chair. You can go ahead and answer the question, Mister Sully, because my help is contingent upon understanding the risks."

"He was attacked."

"I had determined that already." She talked as she worked on Fagan. "I help plenty of people here in Rosedale, Mister Sully. I once worked on a troll that had been assaulted by four men with clubs. Three of the four attackers were dead, while the troll only suffered a fractured radius." Fagan exhaled when her fingers brushed the punctures in his arm with antiseptic wipes. "Mister Suds here is probably much more capable than one troll from the Tunnel Rats. I see marks from a fist and from a weapon. I do not see many fists, or many weapons. So, I am left to wonder exactly what kind of person did this."

"You're pretty observant for a Rosedale sawbones, Doc."

"Like you, John, I am much more than I appear."

Sullivan felt his eyebrows rise. "I guess so, Doctor...?"

"My name is Maris. 'Doctor' is not necessary."

"You're going to want me to leave the room again," Skip sighed.

"It's for your own health, kid," Sullivan advised.

"I'll go get some food. You guys need anything?"

"Food," Sullivan said.

"Lots of food," Maris added. "Suds will need a lot of calories over the next several days."

"On it," Skip said. "What about the douche in the chair?"

"Take him," Sullivan growled. "Put him on ice for us. I'll pay."

"Sure thing. You're the boss."

When Skip had left with Mortensen, Sullivan walked over to the bed. Fagan's eyes had not opened since his ride over from D-ring, and his breathing looked weak and shallow. "First off, how is he?"

Maris continued to work. She talked while plugging holes, listening to respiration, and checking limbs for fractures. "He is bad. He has lost too much blood, and in an acromegalic, that means a lot of blood to replace. He has a couple of broken ribs, though none displaced, thank the gods. He is lucky to be alive right now, though I can't promise he won't die eventually. I think he may be bleeding internally. He needs a hospital, not a rented dorm pod."

"They got hospitals in here?"

Maris shook her head. "Not any you would want to go to. The man who did this will be out there searching, and a SOAP in a hospital is not very hard to find."

"You know it was Coll?" This came out in the form of an accusation.

"I guessed. Your partner would not be so handily overcome by any normal person. We don't know exactly what Coll is, but his reputation is rather intimidating."

Sullivan felt the weight of his own weariness begin to pull on his shoulders. "So you know who I am, and I presume you know why I am here?"

"Yes, and yes."

"Which side are you on?"

"The side that saves a young girl from having to choose between a life of slavery and certain death."

Sullivan winced. "Good answer."

Maris finally looked up from her patient. "This has gone well beyond moving another GMP on to a better life, Mister Sully. The Railroad has accidentally grabbed a rabid tiger by the tail, and I can't figure out what to do with it. I can tell you that if I thought letting you have that girl would keep her safe, I would hand her over right now. But GEED custody will be a death sentence for the poor thing. I can't allow it." She returned to her ministrations. "On the other hand, the Sons of Adam also want her dead, and Vincent Coll is hunting her on behalf of the people who created her. The Sons of Adam we can deal with, as we always do. But Coll is another matter. Whoever holds his leash has infinite resources, and we cannot compete with that. He will find her, and a lot of people are going to die in the process."

"That's what Porter said."

"Porter was right. So where does that leave all of us?"

"It leaves us screwed. I can't trust you, I can't trust the gangs, and I can't even trust GEED." Sullivan looked at his hands in impotent frustration. There were no answers in those hands, only the potential for violence. They were big hands, strong hands. Useless hands. "What the hell am I supposed to do?"

Maris asked a loaded question. "What do you feel like doing?"

"That is never a question you want to ask me," Sullivan warned. "I've spent my whole life coming up with reasons not to act on the things I feel."

"Maybe you are focusing on the wrong feelings."

Sullivan eyed the old woman. "You sound like my shrink."

"Psychology was my original calling."

"Figures. Ugh. There are two things I want to do right now. I want to kill a lot of people, and I want to help my friend not die."

"Let's focus on the second one," Maris suggested.

"Thought you'd pick that one," he mumbled. "So I need to get him out of here and to a hospital that's safe?"

Maris nodded. “I think that is best, yes.”

A thought occurred to Sullivan. “What happens when I leave? Won’t Coll come after you?”

“A distinct possibility.”

“I’m going to need back-up. Time to go see the boss.”

CHAPTER TWENTY-TWO

Her hands full of file folders and take-out containers, Elaine Horowitz wrestled her keycard against the flat plastic surface of her apartment door scanner. A green light blinked with a welcoming chime, and the door latch clicked. A rough bump with her shoulder sent the door swinging, and she staggered through to the dim space beyond. The lights rose from pitch black to a comforting glow while the lean woman dropped her armload of supplies onto the black quartz countertop of her kitchen island with a sigh.

"Butler," she called to the empty air. "Give me the news."

A disembodied voice droned in a dulcet tenor, "Retrieving news." A thin screen rose from the counter with a soft hum, and a bland newscaster began to relate the day's events. Another Sons of Adam attack on a federal GMP work facility, another squad of leftover PRC commandos found in the jungles of Asia. The Global Republic finalized an expensive initiative to explore the chances of resource extraction from Venus. Yet another Biotech executive was caught laundering money for an illegal genetic modification facility somewhere in Europe. The committee for judicial oversight was considering a new limit on Genetic Equity Act sentences. Another pop star overdosed on whatever narcotic was currently in fashion.

It was always the same, and Horowitz grew bored and distracted almost immediately. Ignoring the newscast, she turned to her refrigerator to get a drink. She was doing a lot of drinking these days, and while she accepted that this was a bad thing, she could not find any drive within herself to correct it.

The assorted vegetables she had promised herself she would prepare and eat instead of take-out had wilted and turned black. The fetid aroma of decaying plant life felt like a reprimand. Vowing to do better next week, she grabbed a fruity malt beverage with a disgusted scowl. With the decision made, she turned back to the containers of Indian food she had picked up on her way home.

"This place makes the best goddamn tandoori chicken ever," John Sullivan said, picking through the now open container with a plastic fork.

Horowitz nearly dropped her drink at the sight of the big warden standing in her kitchen. He was still dressed for the Complex. A rumpled brown jacket over a dingy gray tee shirt, dungarees, and work boots. His beard was growing in, and his hair looked like it had been hastily shaved in a truck stop bathroom with a pair of cheap clippers several days prior.

As was her way, Horowitz regained her composure before anyone could see her lose it. Her scowl deepened into something darker and more dangerous, and she barked, "What the hell, Warden?!"

"I smelled the chicken, and I've been eating Complex food for five goddamn days." Sullivan said this as if it explained everything.

"What are you doing here?"

"I needed to talk to you."

Horowitz chewed her lower lip, a sure sign she was confused. "And you couldn't just call?"

"I wanted to talk to you privately. We've been struggling with that lately. So I figured four hours in a 'loop car wasn't so bad if it meant getting back here for a quiet little chat." He waved a finger in a circle, indicating the air around them. "Too many ears on the official channels, Captain."

Horowitz exhaled slowly and steadied herself. She had known this moment was coming, though she could not say if she was ready for it. "What have you figured out so far?"

"Less than I need to, more than I want to." Sullivan put the take-out box back down on the counter. Horowitz noticed he had devoured the whole thing. He dropped the fork into the empty container and fixed her with an intense stare. "Somebody has been telling my father's people where I am and what I'm doing. I also ran into Sam Mortensen in Rosedale. He's supposed to be locked up nice and tight. What kind of stupid coincidence could that be, right?" His face twisted, a frown angry and confused warping his features into a parody of his usual arrogance. "I don't believe in coincidence. Everywhere I go, the bad guys are one step ahead of me. It's like somebody out there wants me to fail, and it looks an awful lot like that person is you, Captain. I'm starting to wonder exactly which side you are playing for." He almost laughed in that moment and added, "I'm starting to wonder what team any of us play for."

"Where should I start?" Horowitz asked. "There's a lot to unpack here."

"The beginning."

She sighed. "Fine. Pass the curry fries if you haven't eaten them all yet."

Sullivan slid a container across the counter top without taking his eyes off the captain. She opened it and dumped some of the contents onto a plate. Drowning the fried potatoes in curry sauce, she stabbed a candidate with a plastic fork and started to chew. Sullivan was waiting, she knew, but she needed a moment to clear her head. Reading Doctor Connors's reports had made it very clear that saying the wrong thing right now could be catastrophic for both her plans and her health.

With a determined swallow, she began to speak. "I've been reporting to the Sullivan mob for about three years now, John."

The big warden stiffened but did not speak. Horowitz took this as a good sign. "I did not get a choice in this. I'm a captain, and I report to the director himself. There is no higher level for me to appeal to."

Sullivan's face betrayed his confusion, so she spelled it out. "The director of GEED is owned body and soul by your father. Nothing any of us does goes unreported. I had no choice."

"You could have blown the whistle!" Sullivan growled. "You could have fought them! I'd have helped!"

"And we would both be dead." She cocked her head and amended herself. "Or I would be, anyway. Mickey won't kill you for some weird reason. I'm not sure why, though."

Horowitz saw some of the tension leave Sullivan's shoulders and face, and her eyes narrowed. Sullivan knew something she did not, and this could be either good or bad news. The big warden shook his head. "I hear he's sentimental about me."

Horowitz doubted that was the whole of it, but she went on. "Every operation, every communication, everything we do goes through the Sullivan mob first. If I get out of line or if it looks like I'm not playing ball, they make sure I know the consequences. There are too many good wardens in the field for me to risk their lives, John. I did as I was told for their sake."

"So you did nothing?"

"No, you uncompromising son of a bitch. I did quite a bit." She abandoned her fries to wave an angry finger in Sullivan's face. "I used you the way they used me. I took their favorite weapon and turned it on them."

Now Sullivan's confusion seemed pure. Horowitz smiled, though the glee never touched her eyes. "Chicago. I sent you and Fagan there to observe and investigate, then I told the local MLEOs that GEED was on the verge of a big bust."

"You knew they'd jump the gun!"

"I counted on it, because I was pretty damn sure you couldn't resist charging in and ruining everything. Chicago MLEOs were never going to crack that place before they destroyed the evidence. You could."

She watched Sullivan's eyes widen as he realized the simple genius of her plan. "If you had just ordered me to bust the place, they'd have known ahead of time. So you sent me to observe and investigate, an order that wouldn't spook them."

"And when Chicago LEOs screwed up, you went in and found what I needed you to." She popped another fry into her mouth. "The director was pissed, but hey, it's not my fault you don't obey orders, is it?"

"I am rather impulsive."

"Exactly. Hartford was more complicated. I sent you to pick up Langley because lawyers know things and like comfortable lives. I thought he'd be a weak link."

"And I screwed it up?" Sullivan asked with a groan.

"All according to plan, John. If we picked up Langley on a CoMA, then he would be looking at a lengthy prison term and substantial financial reparations no matter what we offered him."

"CoMA cannot be pled down," Sullivan said with a nod. "But an NPK..."

"Yup. I offered him an NPK with no reparations if he submitted to WitSec and helped us out. Because you had fucked up the bust so badly, nobody could blame me for having to punt on the charge and send Langley into protection." She pointed at Sullivan. "You are lucky you did not get an official reprimand, by the way."

"Son of a bitch," was all Sullivan could manage to say.

"I got it all done before the director realized what was happening, and when it came down on me, I blamed you and your reckless bullshit. You are reliably unreliable."

"Wait a damn minute. Is this why you 'accidentally' mentioned Doctor Platt on that phone call? Were you warning me that there was a leak?"

Horowitz nodded. "Yes. I needed you to suspect me so you'd stop telling me what you were up to."

"It worked."

"It's like I know what I'm doing or something, huh?"

"Wow," the big man said with a shake of his head. "All this time, I thought you hated me. But you were protecting all of us by being such a jerk all the time."

"I never hated you, John. You are an intensely irritating man, but it's a miracle you are a man at all, given your circumstances. I needed to keep a firewall between the director and the rest of the squad. You were that firewall because everybody is aware of what an asshole you are, and I knew Mickey Sullivan wouldn't hurt you."

"Huh," Sullivan grunted. "I don't mind looking like a jerk, but looking like an idiot kind of stings."

Horowitz shook her head in disbelief. "You *are* a jerk, and if it makes you feel better, you're only an idiot compared to me."

"I'm sorry."

Horowitz had been poised to continue, but this stopped her cold. "What?"

Sullivan held up his hands. "I'm sorry I've been such an asshole to you. I don't like authority. I hate being told what to do, and being held to a higher standard of behavior really pisses me off. It felt like you were always up my ass over stupid things. It got really easy to just assume you were a bitch who hated me, so that's how I treated you. I hate apologies, too. So fuck you very much for making me do that, too." He tried to smile, but the face came out all wrong. "I especially don't like finding out that you were covering all our asses while I acted like the king of dicks. Mickey Sullivan's bullshit should be my burden, and you've been lugging it around all this time."

"We don't get to pick our own cards, John. It all comes down to how we play them."

"Hmph. I cheat."

"It's because you never bothered to learn how to play," she continued the analogy. "But then Charlotte happened."

"Wait. Tell me about Charlotte. What went wrong?"

Horowitz winced. "I figured they'd clean the place out. Sending you there was a logical next step. If I didn't do it, they'd suspect me of being up to something. I assumed you'd just find an empty building and some lame evidence of vaguely illegal activity."

"You didn't know about the girl."

"Nobody did, except the director."

"How did the Sons of Adam find me in Rosedale?"

"That I haven't figured out yet. When I heard Vincent Coll was involved, I tried to keep your movements as vague as I could. One of the best reasons to use you is that you never file reports, you don't follow protocol, and you never keep me informed of what you are up to. If I don't know what you are up to, I can't tell them. There was no way to hide that you were going to the KC Complex, though. You told me over an unsecured line. I had to slip you the Doctor Platt hint just to get you to shut up." Horowitz leaned in, her face beaming earnest concern. "You need to understand, John, that I have been on the side of the law from the beginning. The problem is that the law isn't on the side of the law right now. Where does that leave me? Or you? Or Fagan?"

"Fagan is in the hospital," Sullivan told her.

"What?"

"He ran into Coll in the Complex. Got worked over with a piece of rebar. He's hurt bad, Captain."

"Jesus Christ! He beat up Fagan? Oh god. How is that even possible? Is he okay?"

"He'll live, now that he's getting good medical care. It was close, though."

The captain pressed her palms to her forehead and breathed a long, exasperated sigh. "We need a plan."

"We need a goal," Sullivan corrected. "I don't even know what my endgame is anymore. Who am I even working for?" Horowitz felt as much as heard the catch in his voice. The effect was bizarre. The scruffy face and granite features of a very dangerous man were still in place. However, now they betrayed the indecision of a child lost in the woods. There were too many paths to choose from, and he had no idea which led home and which led farther into the darkness. As was always the case with Sullivan, any negative emotion flared into hot anger in short order. "Fuck!" It was nearly a roar, and his next words revealed the real cause of his roiling temper. "All these years gone by, and I'm still working for..." The lantern jaw flexed and worked, as if speaking the name was impossible. "... him! All my life, he's been there! Nothing I do matters because he will always be the guy pulling my strings!" Sullivan's fingers curled into white-knuckled fists. "The bastard. He thinks he can hurt whoever he wants to, kill whoever he wants to. Fucking *own* whoever he wants to..."

Horowitz said nothing. Sullivan was in a dangerous place, and she could see it. She looked for the signs of a dopamine surge, and sure enough, it happened. Sullivan stood in her kitchen like a statue while the incandescent fury in his mind fell victim to the quenching deluge of endorphins. As quickly as it came, the rage passed, leaving only a sick, unsatisfying tension to draw Sullivan's face into a tight mask of irritation.

He sent his gaze back to the captain. "You're the smart one. You tell me what I should do."

Horowitz could not say what she had expected from Sullivan under these circumstances. Being asked what to do came as an unpleasant surprise. "I don't know, John. I don't even know what I'm going to do."

"We have to stop them. Stop..." he waved his hands in frustration. "...this whole thing."

"We don't even know what they are after," Horowitz replied. "How do you stop the bad guys when you can't even tell what they are after?"

"They want that girl."

"But why, John? The why will tell us more than anything else."

"She's special. A chimera."

Horowitz was not biting. "You're a chimera, John. What's special about *her*."

"I don't know. I think the Railroad does, but they aren't talking." He swiped a dismissive hand across his face. "It doesn't really matter, though. They want the girl bad enough to send Vincent Coll, and they're so desperate to keep her secret that they didn't think twice about murdering everyone at a research lab."

Horowitz nodded in agreement. A strange sort of calm migrated across Sullivan's posture. The muscles in his neck and jaw no longer bulged, his shoulders rose and fell with his breathing in a natural rhythm, his palms rested lightly on the counter top. She had seen his bizarre mood swings before, and thanks to Connors, she now understood them. Sullivan's brain rewarded him for becoming angry with feel-good chemicals and increased neurological function, and she was seeing the process happen in real time. If it did not terrify her so much, it might have been fascinating.

He was still talking, not noticing her awestruck expression. "Coll will be after her, and we have to assume he will find her. The Railroad doesn't trust me enough to reveal her location, so I'm stuck chasing him."

"How much do they trust you?" Horowitz asked. "And why do they trust you at all?"

"Mutual self-interest. They need someone to handle Coll. I was available and looking for a big bust."

"Right," she said, bobbing her head slightly. "Makes sense. Coll is the best lead we're likely to get when it comes to tracking these mysterious backers. But here's my question: What do the backers want the girl for?" She watched his face, and the tiniest twitch of a cheek muscle gave him away. "You're onto something, John. I can tell. You have to tell me for me to help you."

"Mortensen got chatty while tied to a chair." When he saw the captain's bemused expression, he waved a hand. "Don't ask. Anyway, he talked about a 'cabal' of gangsters, corporations, and politicians trying to usher in a new world order of GMP supremacy. They think the Republic is doomed and want to be the big bosses when the GiMPs take over. They've been designing and producing new kinds of chimera embryos. Prototypes. This girl is probably one of them. Vincent Coll is, too." Sullivan paused, indecision slowing his narrative just long enough for Horowitz to guess the next part.

"Oh my God, John," she uttered. "You?"

"Yeah. Apparently, I'm part of it all. Or my creation is, anyway. This is where I need you, Captain. The stash from Chicago supposedly has all the information on this chimera program. I need that haul."

"It's all still in the evidence locker, John. CyberCrime has been working on the encryption, but it's very good. The important data is still locked up."

Sullivan nodded. "Can you get it to me without getting pinched?"

"I suppose I have to try either way."

"It's your call, Captain. You've been pulling this cart for long enough. I can do my part without you if you're tired."

Horowitz met the big warden's eyes with her own. Something in there prompted her to say, "Something's different with you, John. What happened in there?"

Sullivan surprised himself with how quickly he answered. "They almost killed Fagan. The only guy I haven't driven away or alienated in my whole miserable life. I didn't even think I could have a friend until I almost lost one. Now it turns out I had two friends, and I was too much of an asshole realize it. Most people don't understand me. I don't want to be this way. I don't want to be angry or mean or heartless." He looked down at his hands. "But I am. And I hate it. Do you know what's worse? I hate everything, so I'm not even special to myself."

His sincerity made the captain acutely uncomfortable. Sullivan was acting out of character, and this placed her in uncharted waters. His eyes had gone narrow, his voice sounded hoarse. Horowitz wondered if the psychotic break everyone feared was imminent. She lacked the training and experience to evaluate that possibility with any confidence, so she waited and listened.

"I can't be happy unless I get mad. And when I get mad, it makes me happy. But I can't get really mad, so I'll never be really happy. How fucked up is that?"

Horowitz did not know how or why inspiration chose that moment to strike, but she was grateful when it did. "John, who says that's bad?"

He looked up, confused.

"Vincent Coll and his goons killed a hundred and nine people in an attempt to kidnap an eight-year-old girl. Now you tell me the same people who hired him made you guys in a test tube so they could sell you to people who want to overthrow the government? This should be the happiest day of your life, Warden, because your ass is supposed to mad as hell!" She slammed a hand down on the counter for emphasis. "Congratulations, John. You now get to go straight to the people who are making you so goddamn mad and ruin their day. Anger makes you happy? That's wonderful! Anger turns most people into useless toddlers. It sucks and usually only makes things worse." An accusing finger jabbed at Sullivan's face. "But hey! Not you! Not John goddamn Sullivan. Anger turns you into the scariest fighting man in the world and puts a big old smile on your face!" The finger retreated, though the tension remained. "That makes you the perfect man for this job, Warden. You should be angry, and I'm fucking ecstatic that it makes you happy!"

Sullivan considered this, and some of the usual snark returned to his demeanor. "When you put it that way, it kind of sounds like I'm just being whiny. I guess you are right, though. I was made for this shit, literally."

"You *are* just being whiny. And while I don't envy you for what they've done to you, I can't say I'm not glad. The whole damn world needs you just the way you are right now." She straightened, the familiar steel returning to her spine and a reassuring scowl settling onto her face. "So go un-fuck yourself, Warden. Maybe the world is ending, maybe GEED is falling apart, and maybe that's unfair. But I became a warden to uphold the law and do the right thing. I don't care about the badge nearly as much as I do about that. Neither should you."

"There's the Captain Horowitz I remember." He, too, straightened his spine and settled himself. "Here's the thing. It's just like you said: GEED is out. Compromised. If I find Coll, I can't arrest him, because he'll be out in two minutes."

"I can't sanction murder—" Horowitz started, but Sullivan interrupted her.

"You don't sanction shit anymore, Captain." Sullivan caught the hard edge in his own voice and ground his teeth at the lapse. He tried again, this time with more tact than he was accustomed to. "Let's be honest, Captain. We are going way outside the lines on this one. Both of our careers are over if we don't get enough evidence to bury Coll, my father, and the director of GEED all at once."

"Not to mention our lives," Horowitz groused.

Sullivan conceded this point. "You ain't lying. I'm heading back into the Complex. We need those data cards, Captain. That's on you.

Have them copied. I'll set up a secure digital dropbox from inside the Complex for you to dump them into."

"How will we communicate?"

"I'll contact you."

Horowitz scoffed. "This plan is terrible. We are all going to die."

"Look on the bright side," Sullivan said as he headed for the door. "It's more of a plan than I usually have."

CHAPTER TWENTY-THREE

Sharon Platt paced the length of the shabby room she shared with Emilie. She lost count of the strides and turns, her mind locked in an internal moebius strip of fear and indecision. Terror had become a familiar companion since the day she fled, though every time she thought it had peaked, some new catastrophe revealed itself and invited her to enjoy new levels of dread.

"Auntie Sharon?" Emilie asked from the corner. "Are you okay?"

Platt stopped pacing. "Just thinking, Emilie. It's a grown-up thing. Sometimes, we get to thinking and forget what we are doing."

The child had been tapping at her tablet, playing some game or another. "Is it about me?"

Platt gifted herself an inward rebuke at the sincerity of the little girl's question. It was easy to forget just how perceptive Emilie was. The drive to enhance her intelligence and learning capabilities left her with excess mirror neurons. It was still unclear if this would make her smarter or easier to teach, but there was no question the child could read body language at an instinctive level.

"It's just because you are so special," Platt deflected, knowing Emilie would spot a lie at ten thousand yards. "You might be the specialest person in the whole world. It's very exciting."

"Because I won't get old?"

Platt almost gasped, grinding her teeth to prevent an overt display of shock and horror. Her efforts were wasted. Emilie barely looked up from her screen. "It's okay. I heard you talking to Mister Porter. Is that why the bad people are after me?"

Platt's heart fell to her stomach. All the effort she had expended to protect the child was for nothing. No eight-year-old should have to worry about things like mobsters or government agents, or the threat of being locked in a laboratory her whole life.

Emilie set her tablet in her lap. "I said it's okay, Auntie Sharon. I'm very smart, and I know you are, too. People tell me all the time how smart you are. It will be okay."

Platt felt the tears coming. She did not deserve this child's faith and trust. Her own complicity in Emilie's situation burned like a knife to the throat. "Oh, Emilie," she started to say, though there were no words to follow. She did not know what to say. After too long a pause, she managed to whisper, "I'm so sorry... This is all my fault."

"Yeah," Emilie said with a child's honesty. "But you can't change that now. And I hated the stupid laboratory anyway. This place is way more fun."

"I'll keep you safe, I promise!" Platt had no idea how she would keep so ludicrous a promise, but she substituted ferocity for conviction in this case.

"How?"

"I'm finding us the best help. Like Mister Porter and Doctor Maris. They are going to get us somewhere safer soon."

"Auntie Sharon?" Emilie's voice had taken on an almost patronizing timbre. "I don't think there really is anywhere safe. This Vincent Coll man is very bad. I can tell by how everybody talks about him."

Platt's mouth worked wordlessly for a few seconds. When the words came, they were not as strong and confident as she supposed they should have been. "How... how would you know that?"

"Doctor Maris is super afraid of him, and she is super smart like you. Mister Porter is not very smart, and he's not afraid of him at all. I notice that dumb people are usually really confident when they oughta be more scared."

"What?" Platt said. "Porter is as afraid of Vincent Coll as any of us."

"No, he's not. I can tell. I think Mister Porter thinks he has a good plan for taking care of Vincent, because he isn't worried one bit."

"Well," Platt said without confidence. "I suppose Mister Porter has seen and done a lot of scary things. I guess he's just used to it."

"See?" Emilie said, picking up her tablet again. "You don't have to worry so much, then."

The girl's logic was damnably coherent, yet it failed to alleviate Platt's anxiety. "I suppose you're right, kiddo."

A knock at the door interrupted their conversation, and Platt opened it a crack to find Porter waiting in the hall.

"We've found somewhere to put you guys that's a little more hidden and a lot more comfortable," he said by way of greeting. "I think now is the time to move you. The, uh... situation..." his eyes flicked over to Emilie for a millisecond, "...is stable enough for the moment."

"You mean Vincent Coll is too busy to chase us?" Emilie said without looking up.

"What the fuck?" Porter blurted.

"She's really perceptive," Platt explained. "Neuroplasticity."

"Damn," Porter said with raised eyebrows. "You ain't kidding!"

"We'll grab our stuff," Platt said. "Come on, Emilie."

Porter waited in the hall while the pair stuffed what few things they had into a couple of backpacks. When they were ready, Porter led them down the hall and out of the safe house.

Hubtown did not look or feel like the Rosedale section of the KC Complex. Bright lights worked into the vaulted ceilings washed the floors and walls with a warm and friendly glow. The concourse winding between various structures had been built to be wide and airy. The subterranean nexus was designed to evoke the sensation of being outdoors even though it sat almost a thousand feet underground. The air moved in a gentle breeze, cool and fresh, piped in from the surface by giant fans and circulated by hundreds of thousands of artfully concealed vents. No small quantity of effort had been put into making the complexes feel comfortable and pleasant because its denizens rarely got to go outside during the war. The workers and administrators had been too critical to the war effort, and the pure impregnability of the complexes is what had kept them safe from bombardment. Even so, the industrial origins of the place lurked just beneath the clean white surfaces. The occasional whiff of ozone, the buzzing of a transformer, the tinny echoes of faraway sounds broke the spell with enough regularity to make Platt jumpy and nervous. Porter appeared immune and Emilie too wide-eyed with youthful curiosity to care.

Porter talked as he led them along a bustling concourse. "We found a good place in the old heavy weapons research ring. You'll have equipment, space, and in time, some staff. We've been vetting the people still working there. You know, making sure they are sympathetic to the cause and discreet, stuff like that. It's a little remote, which is a bonus." He ushered the pair up to a row of tram cars. "We'll take the rails. It's a hell of a walk otherwise, and I don't like having you guys out in the open." When they had settled inside, he smiled at Emilie. "There is also a very nice education center one tram stop over. You will have kids to play with, Emilie. How does that sound?"

"Sounds fun," Emilie said. She looked up at Platt. "Will I go to school?"

"I'm not sure if any school is going to be challenging enough for you, Emilie," Platt answered with a smile. "But I'll make sure you get lots of opportunities to play with the other kids."

"How were you able to arrange for all this?" Platt asked. "I can't... you know... pay for any of it."

"Well," Porter said with a sly smile, "I may have made some arrangements on your behalf. The main Council of gangs that runs the KC Complex is going to want you to help out with research and medical services." He saw Platt's face darken and held up his hands, "Hey, hey, hey! Chill out, okay? It's not like topside, Doc. You won't be sewing up murderers or designing new drugs or shit like that. Lots of people come through the Complex to avoid the Genetic Equity Act and the Hegemony, all right? Some of them have very unique medical needs. The Council was real happy to hear that The Railroad now has better capabilities for working with those folks is all. Now they can attract more GMP assets to KC than the other complexes. You make us more valuable, and that means you got influence."

Platt allowed herself to be placated by this, though her lack of agency in the matter precluded any sort of meaningful protest. "Okay," she said, her voice devoid of confidence. "How far is the ride?"

Porter gave her a reassuring smile. "It's about forty minutes. The facility is under the Lenexa terminal. With no big war-wagons coming out of the KC Complex these days, that terminal is not exactly hot territory. It's remote, quiet, and out of the way. We had to negotiate with the Grease Monkeys for use of the only good lab space, but I got some guys who smoothed that over."

"You seem to know an awful lot of people," Emilie remarked.

"I've been around a long time, and I've met lots of folks, kid," Porter replied with a throaty chuckle. "But I don't want to give you nightmares, so I can't tell you about all of 'em."

"Did you ever meet Vincent Coll?" Platt asked.

Porter responded with a sharp look. "Like, in person?"

Platt nodded.

Porter looked conflicted. His eyes darted to Emilie. "I ain't sure if that's the sort of thing that..."

"She can handle it," Platt said. "At this point, I think she gets it all better than I do."

"I've met him," Porter confessed. "I don't really want to talk about my previous life, but yeah, I've bounced off of Coll once or twice."

"Is that why he doesn't scare you like he does Doctor Maris?" Emilie asked.

"Oh man, kid." Porter could not hide the nervous catch in his voice. "Coll scares me all kinds of bad! He's got to be the baddest man I've ever known, and I've known some very bad men." Porter attempted his best fatherly expression and failed. "Maris is a super-smart lady, but she isn't used to a problem that can't be reasoned out, y'know? Coll is not the sort of thing that you reason through. He's kinda like a hurricane. You don't handle him; you ride him out. I've been around enough guys like Coll to know how to survive them, is all. Guys like that go after a goal, and they don't stop until they get the job done. The only way to manage them is to kill 'em, give 'em what they want, or convince 'em they want something else more."

"Oh," Emilie said in a strange whisper. Her eyes darted back to her tablet and left Porter hanging onto the limp end of the conversation. After realizing Emilie was done talking about Vincent Coll, he looked back to Platt with raised eyebrows.

"That's one precocious little kid, Doc."

"Yes," Platt said. "Yes, she is."

The rest of the ride proceeded with uncomfortable silence. The aura of relief was palpable when the passenger car hissed to a smooth stop at a lonely platform. That same aura dissipated like morning fog when Platt at last took in their surroundings. Porter had not exaggerated the desolate nature of the location. The dirty slab of stained concrete stood alone and dim against a gray wall. Words stenciled at eye level in bright cyan directed them to either the factory floor, the R&D section, or administration depending upon which colored lines they chose to follow. No other people moved along the painted walkway that paralleled the tram rails, and no sounds but the slapping of their own feet against the cement met their ears. Platt shuddered, the eerie quiet and overwhelming sense of isolation overcoming her thin layer of outward calm.

Porter led them along the red line marked as "R&D." Even he seemed affected by the emptiness. His pace quickened, strides gaining length as he ushered his charges toward their unseen destination. The guide line led them into one of the ubiquitous walkways, this one a long white-walled hallway tiled in a happy sky blue.

"Porter," Platt finally spoke up. "Slow down! She's only eight."

"What? Oh. Sorry."

"Is there really nobody here?" Platt asked when they had caught up.

"I had the Grease Monkeys clear the section so you could be moved safely," he replied. "As a precaution."

This seemed reasonable to Platt, and she again marveled at just how much influence Porter and the Railroad appeared to wield within the Complex. She felt Emilie's tiny hand stiffen in hers, and a sharp tug pulled Platt's attention to the little girl.

Emilie's face was pale, and her eyes wide with terror. She tugged again, pulling Platt to a halt with a strength that surprised the older woman.

"What's the matter?" Platt asked.

Emilie stared with undisguised fear and confusion at Porter's retreating back. Platt matched her gaze, trying to make out what Emilie was getting at.

At the sound of Platt's question, Porter turned. Looking befuddled, he asked, "What's the hold-up ladies? We gotta get you two under cover, here."

Emilie whispered, "He's lying."

Platt froze. It took her far too long to process all the horrible things those three syllables meant for her and the little girl. She hesitated less than one second, or just long enough for a whole universe to fall apart before her eyes.

"Run," she said to Emilie.

The girl ran.

Platt stayed behind the tiny body as it sped back down the hallway. She might have outrun Porter if not for her need to protect the child. As it was, Porter caught up before they made it to the tram platform. With no other options, Platt threw herself at the man and tangled herself in as many of his limbs as she could. Both went down hard. Platt fought with the ferocity of a mother bear and the residual athleticism of a former competitive gymnast. Porter scrambled like a frantic man whose last chance for freedom flew further out of reach with each passing second. It made for a rather even contest.

Emilie turned to the struggling adults, her tiny face wracked with indecision. "Run!" Platt screamed to Emilie. Porter lashed out at her, thrashing and pulling at her hands. "Get away! Go!" Platt kept screaming while she fought against the escalating desperation of Porter.

"Auntie Sharon!" the little girl pleaded, tears running down her cheeks.

"Go!" Platt yelled back. Porter dragged an arm free and tried to club her in the head. He missed, and Platt shouted, "Find Maris!" She did not know if Emilie would be able to do that, yet it was all she could think of. She saw the girl hesitate, and knowing it was an unforgivable lie, she promised, "I'll catch up!"

At last Emilie turned and sprinted to the tram station. Platt saw the tiny body bolt to a passenger car and leap inside. Just as it started to move, something like a vise clamped over the back of her neck and raised her bodily from the floor. Porter stopped fighting in that same instant, and the scientist's head spun until she found herself upright and staring into the burning blue eyes of Vincent Coll.

Coll was wearing a dark gray suit, and he held each of them by the neck. The cloth stretched taut over his arms as he hoisted both man and woman onto their tiptoes with the strength of a single arm for each. Porter clutched at the hand holding him, his face locked into a sick and frantic snarl. Platt realized that while Coll held her tightly by the back of her neck, he gripped Porter by the throat. The sleeve of Coll's gray suit groaned against the bulk of his forearms, and cords of muscle writhed across his wrists and the back of the hand she now understood was choking Porter.

"Oh Porter, Porter, Porter," the big cleaner tutted. "I've never seen the job a guy like you couldn't figure out how to screw up." The sound of straining cloth told Platt that Coll had just ratcheted up the pressure. "Your job was so stinking simple, man. I told you what would happen, didn't I?"

Porter began beating at Coll's forearm, swatting the powerful limb like it was a vending machine that owed him a beverage. Platt watched in horror as Porter swung harder and harder, urgency swelling with each fruitless swipe at the steely arm. A strange gurgle emerged from the dying man's lips, accompanied by a stream of foamy spittle as the struggler's impotent intensity surged and broke like a wave against the cliff that was Vincent Coll's ire. In just a few scant seconds, grim comprehension dawned across that purpling face. The pale rider had arrived in a smart gray suit, and it was time for poor Porter to settle his earthly accounts. When he at last accepted that he could not prevent the inevitable, Porter despaired as only the dying can. Platt wondered if breaking the man's spirit had been Coll's goal all along. The look on his face beamed nothing short of ecstatic bliss at the sight of a man watching the approach of his own death. Without warning, the smug matinee-idol smile twisted into something ugly and sadistic. Coll's arm spasmed, and a savage surge of crushing power crumpled his victim's trachea like an empty beer can. Coll dropped his gasping and heaving victim to the floor, where Porter slowly asphyxiated over the next sixty seconds. Curled into a fetal ball, hacking and drooling, Porter died wheezing a long, silent scream. The last light of consciousness in his eyes dimmed with agonizing lethargy. He never blinked, leaving his blank gaze to stare into the uncaring face of a madman well past the point where his brain stopped functioning.

Only after witnessing the long and unpleasant demise of the Railroad man did Coll's attention swing back to his other captive. Platt had gone ghost-white, her pupils dilating as shock and panic overrode her nervous system. Coll scowled at her appearance, shaking his head in disgust. "Oh, come on, Doctor! The bastard betrayed you! Sold you out for a clean slate and some stake money! Don't tell me you feel sorry for him!"

Platt's expression never changed. Locked in his grip, her reason buried beneath an avalanche of fear and horror, she breathed, "You're a monster!"

"I suppose I am," mused the man with a cocky smirk. "But that doesn't mean we can't be friends, does it?"

Genetic Equity Enforcement Division Selection Board Expert's Notes for Case SUL-002-c

Dr. Sharon Platt, Ph.D.

My conversation with Doctor Stevens was as enlightening as I imagined it would be. The amount of energy and resources it took to find him was rather surprising, I must say. I was unaware of his current status as a protected witness, so my access was very limited. For his protection, I am only including a limited transcript of our conversation.

Even at the age of fifty-one, Doctor Stevens is an imposing physical presence. He seemed to remember his time with the subject fondly, though his opinions with regards to Michael Sullivan are blunt and unprintable. I have transcribed relevant parts of the interview below:

PLATT: Tell me about the first training sessions with John Sullivan.

STEVENS: At first, I didn't believe he was twelve. He was so damn tall, and he had way too much muscle mass and density. But I brought him out onto the mat to see what he could do. Apparently, they had started with some other instructors, but they all quit.

P: Because of the boy's behavior?

S: Yeah. The kid was rough as hell. Spoiled brat, really. He hated to lose and was prone to temper tantrums when things didn't go his way. Classic narcissist with latent sociopathy; you know the type.

P: I do. Did he take well to your instruction?

S: Nope. Came at me hard right off the bat. Didn't want to drill or practice, didn't like authority or discipline. I'd tell him to do something, and he'd tell me to fuck off.

P: How did you address this?

S: I told him if he could kick my ass, I'd let him have the afternoon off.

P: I'm going to assume that this did not go his way?

S: Hell, no. Kid was big for his age and strong, but he was still twelve and mostly untrained. I put him in an ude garame and held him there until he sang, "I'm a little teapot."

P: I'm sorry, what?

S: It's a thing where I bend his arm the wrong way. And, yup, I made him sing before I let go of his arm. Had to reinforce how helpless he was so he'd comprehend his stupidity. Didn't work. He came right at me again. This time, I made him recite the alphabet backwards before I let him up. We repeated this for about two hours. Then I told him that class was over and I looked forward to the next one. He was too tired and pissed off to keep going, anyway. I had made my point.

P: How did the next class go?

S: More of the same. He tried different tricks, tried to bite, or gouge my eyes, stupid shit like that. Hell, I fought for bronze against a guy from Azerbaijan, so the kid was not getting anything over on me. This went on for about a week. Finally, I asked the kid if he ever got tired of losing. You know what he said? He said, "I'm not losing, I'm just figuring out all the ways to not win." Snarky little prick even then. But then I asked him if he even understood what he was doing wrong, and if he didn't, then how did he expect to figure it out? He told me to fuck off, and I told him I looked forward to the next class. This is where it gets fun. The next class, I'm doing my thing. I go to toss him with an easy o goshi, and the little shit hits a tani otoshi to counter it! I win the scramble and choke him out anyway, but I was pretty impressed.

P: I don't know what any of those words mean, Doctor.

S: Sorry. I tried to throw him, and he used the correct counter move to throw me instead. He had been studying videos and reading books on judo behind my back, Doctor Platt.

P: Rather than accept your instruction, he tried to learn on his own? The font of all the knowledge he wanted was right there before him, and he chose spite over his goal?

S: Nope. Spite *was* the goal. He didn't give a shit about judo. He just hated me. That's when I started to get a handle on how essential anger was to his entire thought process. I decided not to fight that. I had read his case study; I already figured that him being mad was just going to be a thing we dealt with. A lot of modern psych types—no offense, Doctor—

P: None taken. My degrees are in biochemistry, biomedical engineering, and genetics.

S: Damn. Wow. Anyway, a lot of psych guys automatically assume being mad is a problem. I don't buy into that. I'll tell you something: I've never won a competition without getting at least a little mad. Mad at myself for screwing up, mad at the other guy for being too good, hell, mad at the universe for giving me a broken toe. There's a whole truckload of sympathetic physiological reactions that come with anger that are very helpful and positive when employed in the right way. Any fighter in the world will tell you that.

P: I agree. My work with GMP soldiers has sold me on the potential.

S: I've read some of your stuff. Good work.

P: Thank you. Now, the subject has always spoken very fondly of you in his limited psychiatric sessions. At what point did you get through to him?

S: The subject has a name, Doctor. John stopped actively resisting training after about three months of getting his ass kicked. Once he realized his tantrums were useless, he moved on to trying to beat me on his own. Watching videos, reading books, things like that. Finally, he figured out that he needed my knowledge and instruction to get what he wanted.

P: Which was to beat you up?

S: Exactly. He really hated me for the first year or so.

P: Did this concern you?

S: No. By the time he had the skills to beat me, he would have learned what he needed to know about his own mental state.

P: And what was that?

S: That he was never going to beat me mad. He needed to be cold as ice to take me. His technique would have to be dead-on, his focus laser-like, and his head totally in the game. I knew he was genetically engineered for it. If you really look at the profile, his tantrums were technically *against* type. He's not supposed to lose his temper. He's supposed to get mad, stay mad, and still be cold as a Michigan Christmas. He was acting out because he's kind of a dick is all. I taught him to deal with it.

P: Fascinating. Did he ever beat you?

S: Three weeks before GEED found him. He got me good and clean. I was very proud.

P: How did you take it when GEED finally brought him in?

S: It felt great. I always knew what he was, but Mickey Sullivan had managed to avoid getting exposed, and I was not brave enough to cross him on it at first. But I watched that kid grow and develop for four years. I trained him and trained with him every single day. You think he can wrestle well? You should see him handle a gun or in the boxing ring. He could bench press more than six-hundred pounds and run the forty in three-five flat. Leaving something like John Sullivan in the care of that [EXPLETIVE REDACTED] mobster was going to be a disaster. How did I feel? Hah. Doctor, I called it into Genetic Equity myself. To hell with Mickey Sullivan. That [EXPLETIVE REDACTED] piece of [EXPLETIVE REDACTED] can go [EXPLETIVE REDACTED] himself with a rusty [EXPLETIVE REDACTED] right up his [EXPLETIVE REDACTED] [EXPLETIVE REDACTED].

P: Really? I was not aware of that. You tipped off GEED?

S: I had no choice. John is not a bad kid, and he didn't deserve to be treated like a prize bull. I figured the best thing I could do was use my time with him to try to undo the damage his father was causing. I had to teach him that his anger is a tool he can learn to use, not a disability his [EXPLETIVE REDACTED] of a father could exploit. I always figured at some point, he'd need to be separated from Mickey, but I needed to make sure he could handle his emotional issues well enough to not end up sedated in a psych hospital first. Once I felt good about that, I tipped off the feds, and I've been running ever since. He's not crazy, Doctor Platt. Maybe a little rough around the edges, but he won't break. You can bet on it.

At this point, I am forced to concede that John Sullivan is probably stable enough for government service. Obviously, he will need to be carefully monitored, and his case may need to be re-examined if his behavior changes. It is this expert's opinion that despite his bizarre neurological circumstances, there appears to be no immediate risk of psychological collapse. He will make an excellent warden, and his gifts will be an asset to society in this role.

CHAPTER TWENTY-FOUR

John Sullivan returned to Rosedale with a head full of questions. Some of these queries had obvious answers, though he avoided these out of a pressing need to not go on a homicidal rampage.

Returning to his pod only presented him with more questions, and yet another catastrophe to deal with.

"Is that who I think it is?" he asked Maris. The old woman was sitting in the chair previously occupied by Mortensen, and on the messy bed, a small blond girl slept.

"It is."

"I thought you said that you weren't letting me near her?"

"Things have changed, Warden."

"Talk."

Maris explained that Emilie had appeared on her doorstep a sobbing mess, wailing about Porter and Doctor Platt. "Somehow, the child memorized the route back to me, even from as far away as the Lenexa terminal," Maris said. "Her recall is fantastic."

"She have any other tricks?" The question was loaded. "Good memory is one of genetic engineering's holy grails, but I can't imagine that's enough to set all this in motion."

Maris acknowledged this with a solemn nod. "She does, but it's probably better if you don't know the rest."

"I won't get old," Emilie said from the bed. "My tellow-mares don't get messed up."

"Kid's awake," Sullivan quipped.

"I noticed," Maris replied, her tone equally dry. Then she smiled at the girl and in a warm and motherly tone said, "Emilie, this is Warden Sullivan. He is here to help us."

"Auntie Sharon says the wardens want to take me away."

Maris knew better than to lie to the girl. "They uphold the law, dear. It is a silly law, and we all hope it will go away soon, but that does not make the wardens bad people."

The girl sat up, bleary-eyed, grubby-faced, and tear-streaked. "Are you here to take me away, Warden Sullivan?"

The question hit Sullivan right in the guts. That strange sensation burbled upward from his midsection and soured the back of his throat. It tasted like fear and sadness mixed. The word *empathy* came to his mind, and again, he dismissed it. Empathy was wrong. He did not feel the child's anxiety, but he did understand it. Whatever this was, the feeling was his. It came from within himself.

The girl still awaited his answer. She watched him with a bird-like expression, searching for the truth in words he had not even spoken yet. "I'm here to arrest Vincent Coll." He dismayed at how easy he found obfuscation.

Emilie looked right at Maris, and real fear widened her eyes. "He's lying, too!"

"What?" Sullivan asked.

The old woman's eyes sparkled. "Emilie is very intuitive, Warden. Maybe you should re-examine your answer."

"I *am* here to arrest Coll!" Sullivan insisted, and then he too realized the lie of that. "Dammit," he grunted. "No, I'm not. I'm here to kill him, I guess."

Emilie relaxed, apparently satisfied. "That's the truth."

"Yeah, yeah, kid. Don't rub it in, all right?"

"Do wardens kill people a lot?" The child's question bore no recrimination, and the strange fear clobbered Sullivan again.

"We're not supposed to," he answered. He realized in that moment that he had no idea how to talk to children. "I don't try to, anyway. But it happens all the time." He did not attempt to bend the truth this time. "I'm not sure I have a choice anymore."

"That sounds like a very sad job. You should quit."

The child's response was staggeringly naive, simplistic, and starkly indicative of how poorly the girl understood the world she had been thrust into. She did not understand what had been done to her. She did not comprehend the things evil people planned for her future. She had so much more fear, anger, and sadness left to endure before the world discarded her used-up husk that it made Sullivan want to spit on the floor to get the taste out of his mouth.

And just like that, he figured it out.

Sullivan understood. He was experiencing his own horrible childhood in the doe-eyed face of an eight-year-old girl. He saw every unforgivable thing his father had done to him. He relived the countless hours of pain, rage, and loneliness of his youth every time their eyes met. The weight of age and wisdom sharpened the sting, turning a hot flash of anger into an excruciating third-degree burn. He knew everything that was coming her way. Even worse, only he would ever truly comprehend the terrible fate in store for this child. All the torment of his warped existence, all his damage and derangement, every bit of his personal hurt would be hers soon enough. It was inevitable, and he hated that fact more than he had ever hated anything in the world. John Sullivan was not experiencing empathy for Emilie at all. This feeling, this gut-wrenching fear-sadness, was sympathy. He *knew* how she felt, how she was going to feel, and how much the world was going to damage her. That knowledge hurt like nothing he had ever endured before. Everything he had ever heard or read about sympathy told him it was a good thing, a nice thing. This did not feel good to Sullivan. It felt awful.

Fortunately for him, sympathy, like all his other emotions, soon morphed into a boiling anger. The dopamine followed, and this time, he welcomed the relief it brought.

"I think I just might, kid." The calm suffused him with a new clarity. "Now, tell me about your telomeres."

Maris answered this one. "It appears that Emilie is a legitimate mutant. Doctor Platt stumbled upon the mutation while trying to improve the embryo's potential for recall and neuroplasticity. It's entirely random."

"Stop avoiding the question."

Maris frowned. "It's like she said. Emilie is not going to age normally."

"She's immortal?"

Maris shook her head. "If she was immortal, we wouldn't need your help, Warden. She is going to age very slowly is all. She can still die in all the normal ways, lucky her."

"How long?" He did not need to specify what he was asking.

"Platt thinks two hundred years, easily."

Sullivan nodded, keeping his reaction internal. "That is kind of a big deal, Maris."

"Yes, we thought so, too."

"I suppose you will want me to go get the doctor, then?"

Maris returned his nod with one of her own. "It is what I would like, yes. What do you want?"

Sullivan suspected the question was a test. "Clarity. If I can even manage a rescue, what the hell do I do with the doctor when I get her?"

"There is that," Maris agreed. "You could arrest her and bring her in to GEED custody, of course. She is still young. I'm sure the government will find good use for her services after her prison term is over."

"Except my father and his partners will kill her before that happens. Or arrange for GEED to lose her somewhere along the way."

"Well, yes," Maris said. "It's almost certainly a death sentence for the poor woman. But that is the law, and you are a warden."

"Did you leave the psychology profession, or did they throw you out?" Sullivan snapped. "Because you suck at this."

The old woman did not take the bait. "We are all at the same crossroads, Warden. Circumstances have forced my hand, and now I lay all my hopes and dreams for Emilie at your feet. I don't care if you arrest me. I'm old, and there are others ready to take my place. My work will continue without me. However, Doctor Platt is young, and Emilie is just a child. They're the ones who will plague your conscience, not me."

"You make it sound like me doing my job makes me guilty of other people's crimes." A dangerous edge crept into his voice, and Sullivan let it stay. "Isn't that sort of thing why you hate the Genetic Equity Act so much?"

Maris acknowledged the riposte with a gesture of surrender. "Fair play to that, Warden. You are not the one doing the harm. You merely serve the ones doing the harm, is all. But before you wash your hands of all responsibility, make sure you understand something, Warden Sullivan." Maris narrowed her eyes. "The world will not tolerate Emilie's existence. It's not ready yet. Those who won't try to kill her for being an abomination will want to exploit her for her gifts." A crooked finger jabbed his direction. "Exactly like they have done with you, John Sullivan. If you bring this girl to your masters, you are giving her to the same corrupt bastards who have made your life a living hell since the day they pulled you from the creche." She leaned back. "Perhaps it won't be you to pull the trigger, but I don't see how you are any less responsible at this point. You no longer have the luxury of ignorance." She held up a hand to forestall his interruption. "I'm sorry, but that's how it is. With knowledge comes responsibility, and for that, I am truly sorry."

"You sound real choked up about it, lady."

"It's better this way. You are a chimera. You know the stakes intimately. No matter what you choose, you will at least understand the choice better than any of us will."

"Choice?" Sullivan's face burned. "You call this a choice?" He looked back to Emilie, who had been watching and listening in that curious manner of hers. "They took my choices away from me at birth! I had to eat through a tube until I was three because I was starving all the time. They put me on anti-psychotic medication until I was fifteen so I wouldn't kill someone every time I got upset. Do you know what the first toy my father ever bought me was? A goddamn gun!" Sullivan pantomimed shooting himself in the head. "I was inches away from being a legitimate psychopath... and the asshole gave me a gun to play with!"

"So let's just talk about choices then!" He locked eyes with Emilie. He was angry at her naivete. He resented the innocence she got to enjoy, was jealous of the childhood he had been denied. "Here's the reality of your future, kid. Rich assholes are going to want to poke and cut you every day of your life until they figure out how to copy your DNA. Other assholes are going to spend their every waking moment trying to kill you because they hate anything their tiny brains can't understand. Nobody will love you, although a lot of people will pretend to if they think it will help them get what they want out of you." He tore the Hudson H10 from his belt and shoved the pistol into the old woman's lap. Maris recoiled as if a venomous snake had appeared, and Emilie whimpered. "Okay, Maris. You want a choice? Pick up that gun right now and blow my brains all over the fucking wall, or blow the kid's brains all over the wall. Either way, my problem is solved! That's the kind of goddamn choice we are talking about!"

"John!" Maris hissed. "Too far!"

"Not far enough!" He whipped his head back around to Emilie, who had started to cry. "But wait, there's more! Your Auntie Sharon lied to you, kid. Get used to that. She took money from the same people who want to hurt you so she could chase her dreams of scientific discovery. She never asked what you wanted, and she never stopped to wonder what your life would be like before she bent your genes any way she saw fit. I know because that's what they did to me." Now he spun back to Maris. "Oh, that reminds me! Guess who else is part of our little family of genetic freaks?"

The woman's face had gone coldly angry. Sullivan did not wait for her reply. "Vincent fucking Coll." Sullivan smiled when the look of shock finished wiping her scowl away. "That's right. He's just like me and poor little Emilie, here. We're all just product offerings for the next group of megalomaniacs who want to run the planet. You didn't know that?"

"No, I didn't," Maris said through clenched teeth. "But it doesn't change anything. It only makes your choice that much more important!"

"Maybe not. Maybe you aren't understanding just how stupid your little speech about 'choice' is. The only choice I've ever made for myself was not putting the barrel of a gun in my mouth and ending it all. You tell me, how is now any different?"

Maris shouted her reply, startling both Sullivan and Emilie. "Because this time there is nothing to stop you from doing what you want to!" She calmed herself with visible effort, though this did not keep the icy condescension out of her words. "As long as someone else made your decisions, you got to ignore the consequences. Your whole life, you have traded your free will for the comfort of blaming others. You blame your father, or GEED, or your own genes, so you never have to face the consequences of your actions. That's not freedom, that's cowardice." She smiled at his visceral reaction to the insult. "But not anymore! Now you know that they are all liars, and you can't count on them to take the fall for your lack of mental fortitude. Boo hoo, right?" She ticked the examples off on her fingers. "GEED is corrupted, so you can't lean on your status as a warden to guide you. Your father is a mobster, and you owe him no consideration at all. The Railroad? Who are we to you? I wouldn't trust us if I was in your shoes. Your big friend is not here to tell you what to do or think, either. All of your usual crutches are gone, but that means your constraints are gone, too." Her motherly smile returned. "Whether you like it or not, the choice and its consequences will fall on you alone. Do what you *feel* is right, John." She handed the pistol back to him with shaking hands. He took it from her trembling fingers, his own grip tentative. When she was sure he would not drop it, Maris added, "It's time to be the man you want to be. Forget about what they tried to make you into, and just do what you feel you must."

It seemed like the world had shrunk to the size of the room and the weight of the gun in his hand. He turned the pistol over, looking at it like it might go off at any moment. "You don't mean that. You don't know what I feel. You don't even know what I am."

"Neither do you, idiot. Stop running from this. Stop running from this monster you imagine you are. It's childish." She clapped her hands together like a teacher rebuking a particularly dull student. Sullivan blinked. "Playtime is over." Maris sat on the chair with an eyebrow raised and her chin jutting. "Who is John L. Sullivan?"

"You really are a shitty psychologist if you think you're going to get into my head that way."

Maris snorted. "Oh, trust me. I've been in your head, Warden. Largely empty and stinking of brandy, I might add. By the way, did you know Doctor Platt did one of her doctoral theses on you?"

"What?"

Maris noted his confusion and barreled on. "She did, you know. When she mentioned that, I went and looked it up. Her work is excellent and very thorough. The genetics were beyond me, obviously. I can't tell an allele from a peptide. But I was a professional psychologist, and I think I picked up on something most people missed." Maris shook her head from side to side. "Everyone believes Michael Sullivan was trying to create some kind of super-mobster in his own image when he dreamed you up."

"I expect I am a huge disappointment," Sullivan grunted.

"Wrong!" Maris crowed. "I'm telling you right now, they're all dead wrong. That man spent a lot of money creating a very specific kind of person, and I think he got exactly what he ordered." She leaned into the next part. "Do you hear me? I'm telling you that you are precisely what you are supposed to be. Frankly, I can't believe you haven't figured it out for yourself, yet."

"Figured what out?"

Maris looked at Sullivan from beneath scrunched brows. "Do you know who the original John L. Sullivan was?"

"There's an original?"

Maris nodded an emphatic affirmative. "Oh, yes. They called him 'the Boston Strong Boy.' He was the last heavyweight bare-knuckle boxing champion and the first gloved champion around the turn of the twentieth century. By all accounts, he was extremely strong, tough as a tree, fast and agile, too. More than 450 fights and, the legends claim, only one recorded loss. They say he was an amiable man. Perhaps he loved women and whiskey a bit too much for his own good. Most accounts say he was easy to get along with, but not at all averse to hurting people who crossed him. He absolutely hated authority, of course." The woman paused to gauge Sullivan's reaction, then asked, "Any of this sound familiar?"

It did. "So you think Mickey wanted an old boxer?"

"No, you idiot. He wanted a fighter. A man who would never know fear in battle, a man who craved the thrill of combat. The kind of bruiser who might walk into any bar in the world, spit on the floor, and announce that he could kick the ass of anyone in the room. Then go and do it."

Sullivan's face fell. "John Sullivan really did that? In random bars, I mean."

"Often."

"That does sound like something Mickey Sullivan would respect."

"A lot of people would respect that. The world could use a few people with courage, conviction, and maybe a bit of pugnacity. Is *Warden* Sullivan that kind of man?" She held out her hands. "I think so. Maybe. I guess we don't know yet. Nobody has given you the chance to see for yourself."

Sullivan could find no flaws in the woman's logic, and much of what she was saying rang with the uncomfortable note of inconvenient truth. He *was* pugnacious, he did enjoy a good fight, and he was neurologically incapable of excessive fear or anger. The harder he examined the whole picture, the stronger the old woman's points got. He thought about what Horowitz had told him. Fear and anger made most normal people behave like fools. Why would he ever want that? As it stood, fear and anger made him better at everything he loved. For the life of him, he could not come up with a good reason to apologize for it. It all made a perverse kind of sense. Viewed in this light, his wasted years trying to experience fear and anger the way normal people did now bore an unflattering resemblance to the cowardice Maris accused him of. This led to a more profound realization. A pair of thoughts crossed his mind, each spinning off into thousands of dire fractals and turning the blood in his veins to liquid nitrogen.

I am not a mistake or a failure. I am a successful prototype. Followed by: *This is all going according to his plan, isn't it?*

Only one more question needed a satisfactory answer before Sullivan made up his mind. "Why are you doing this? Why are you trusting me?"

"Two reasons." Maris held up two fingers, then tapped one with her other hand. "The first is that I am convinced you are every bit the fighter your father wanted you to be. What is coming will take both courage and compassion to win. What Coll did to your friend hurt you, and that means you have compassion, even if you don't recognize it. You also know what will happen to the girl if she is caught by any faction, so I am counting on that compassion to help you make the right choices. As for courage? I don't believe for one second you are afraid of the battle saving this girl will be. I think you can win it, too."

"And the second reason?"

"The second reason is simple. You frighten both your masters and your creators. Compassion is for your comrades, courage is for the battle, but fear?" Thin lips peeled back to reveal the bright white of bared teeth. "Fear is for the enemy."

Sullivan smiled at the smoldering ferocity behind the old woman's words and added, "Fear and bullets."

"Those, too."

"Are you going to rescue Auntie Sharon?" Emilie asked, finally speaking up.

"What do you think I should do, kid?"

"You should rescue her and kill Vincent Coll." The adults looked at the child, Maris aghast and Sullivan amused. "What?" Emilie said, noisily wiping her nose with the back of her hand. "It's the truth!"

CHAPTER TWENTY-FIVE

Sharon Platt opened her eyes slowly.

Part of her hoped that the light would reveal her room back in Hubtown, or even better, her apartment in Charlotte. To her eternal dismay, she saw neither. The fog of unconsciousness burned away to reveal the dim interior of some abandoned weapons laboratory, and her terror returned with a vengeance. Against her will, memories assembled themselves in the correct order to remind the doctor of where she was and how she had arrived in such bizarre and dire circumstances. She relived the death of Porter and her subsequent abduction in frantic stop-motion. The movie in her head paused to linger on the most horrific and gruesome bits before hurtling off at triple-speed through shock-filled transitions.

Coll had carried her back from the tram platform. She remembered bouncing uncomfortably on his shoulder as he loped down the white halls and pattered over the beige tiles. When he placed her on the floor of this room, a burst of desperation overtook Platt, and she had bolted for the door with a speed even she could not believe was possible. Coll had found this amusing, and her escape ended abruptly when he plucked her from the floor and sent her skidding back into a cabinet. That was the last thing she remembered, so Platt assumed she had either hit her head hard enough to get a concussion, or she had passed out from the overwhelming shock. She could not say which, and she could not say how long she had been out.

Her eyes found her captor at the other end of the room, standing by a sink. He was shirtless, and she saw him washing his hands and forearms. His back was to her, and the urge to flee surged within

Platt's chest once again. Without conscious thought, she shifted to coil her legs beneath her. Coll heard the noise and tutted. "Oh, I would not try it, Doctor Platt. If you keep trying to run off, I'll have to break your legs just to get anything done around here."

Platt considered the possibility he was bluffing, then remembered how easy it had been for Coll to kill Porter. She sat back against the cabinet.

Coll dried his hands on a thin towel and turned to face his captive. Platt observed the absolute perfection of his physical construction, marred as it was by a recently broken nose. She noted it with a scientist's abstraction, appreciating the craftsmanship of whichever genetic engineer had manipulated Coll's genes. A wave of disgust followed. Someone just like herself had turned a regular baby into the horror that was Vincent Coll. A person had sat down at a terminal and warped an innocent child with all the same detachment Platt had employed to produce Emilie. For the thousandth time, Platt wondered who the real monsters were in this case.

"How are you feeling, Doctor?" The question was deliberately absurd, considering her situation, and she did not answer. Coll continued as if she had. "Sorry for the rough treatment and all that, but you have caused our employers quite a bit of trouble. I'd like to finish this job without having to hurt you, but that's really up to you."

Platt doubted this very much. She shrank back against her cabinet and hugged her knees to her chest. There was no point in pretending there was anything to talk about, so she remained silent. Coll took two steps in her direction, then crouched down to look her in the eye. His were blue and intense, centered in his model-perfect face. The chiseled brow line scrunched with concern that appeared sincere.

"I understand that you aren't feeling very chatty, Doctor. It's been a very hard week for all of us. Unfortunately, I kind of need you to help me out, here. You see, I've got friends that were able to get me into this place, but those Railroad types have this stupid Council of theirs sewn up pretty good. I'm all alone, and if I can't figure out how to find that little kid of yours, well..." Coll managed a surprisingly convincing look of chagrin. "Well, then I might have to start hurting a lot of people."

Platt tried not to flinch at this remark, but her body betrayed her fear.

Coll smiled. "That's how this stuff goes, Doc. Now, I understand that you don't want to help me. You've got some weird pie-in-the-sky notion that the Railroad is going to get you two somewhere safe where you can live a life of bliss or whatever." His smile turned sad. "But come on, Miss Three Ph.Ds. You know damn well that's not ever going to happen. Your little Emilie is the most valuable thing on the planet, and folks are starting to talk. Porter couldn't sell you out fast enough once he found out how close I was. The Sons of Adam are hunting her, too. They don't want to take her, Doctor Platt. They just want to kill her. Have you considered that?"

She had, and the implications of what Coll said were not lost on her.

"For someone who's supposed to be all kinds of smart, you've been stupid and reckless, Doc. The people who financed your work are extremely angry, and they have infinite resources. There is no place on earth they can't find you. That *I* can't find you. The best thing you can do for yourself and that kid is to come back in and finish the job you're paid to do. I have it on good authority that all will be forgiven. Your lab, your stipend, everything will be returned. You can go back to a normal life."

Finally, Platt found her voice. "What happens to Emilie?"

"She stays with you."

"In a laboratory, as a guinea pig?"

Coll's scowl dripped condescension like a leaking grease bucket. "Oh, don't play high and mighty with me, Doctor. It was never going to be any other way. You knew that the second you noticed her unique mutation."

Platt discovered an ember of defiance beneath her overwhelming terror. "If that was the case, *Vincent*, neither of us would be here."

Coll laughed out loud. He appeared genuinely amused by her temerity. He extended a hand to her surroundings and then clapped softly. "Oh? Do tell, Doctor Platt! I can see your devious plan was years in the making!"

Platt shrank under his derision. He was right, of course. She had done a rather poor job of running, and her own complicity in Emilie's plight could not be ignored.

"You signed on to do a job, Doctor." Coll was scolding her now. "You were to create a product for your employer to bring to market. You can't change the terms of the deal just because somewhere along the line, you grew scruples."

"She's a person! How can you say that?" Platt realized the question was stupid the moment it left her mouth.

Coll rose and took another step to loom over her. "How can I say that? What the hell do you think I am, Doctor? Look at me!" He spread his arms. "What am I?"

Platt did look. This time with a critical eye toward what she was seeing. There was no body fat to speak of anywhere on the man, and the telltale signs of myostatin inhibition and excess testosterone could be found in every line of his physique. The skin looked tight and thin, with engorged veins in his biceps and neck darting like lightning bolts across his tan skin. Platt's professional inspection picked out all the subtle touches that made Coll's body distinct from more common genetic modifications. His hypermuscularity came without excessive bulk, and she suspected that careful attention had been paid to balancing testosterone levels, human-growth hormone production, and androgen receptor sensitivity. She had not witnessed the extent of his speed and coordination yet, though she suspected his neuro-muscular proprioception had to have been modified as well. It made no sense to limit his mass, otherwise. He carried no signs of acromegaly or other skeletal deformities, which was quite impressive for someone with so much muscle.

The reason was obvious, and Platt despaired. "You're a chimera," she said flatly. The realization took the dagger of self-reproach firmly lodged in her heart and gave it a rough twist.

"Correct!" he said with an unhinged grin. "I am a top-of-the-line product just like that little brat of yours. Funded by people just like your employers and created by a scientist just like you."

The dagger torqued again, and Platt tasted bile in her throat. Nevertheless, his revelation sent her mind to working on the problem of her captor. She detected something else now that she was really looking for the signs. Coll's pupils were dilated, his breathing a touch shallow. She noticed a slight tic in the muscles of his cheek, as well.

"No, that's not right," she said, suddenly confident. "You're not at all like Emilie. You have aggression markers. Your t:c ratio is off, isn't it?" Then inspiration struck, and she could not stop herself from saying it. "You're like Sullivan, aren't you?"

Coll's fist struck the cabinet next to her head with a crash. The thin metal buckled like tinfoil, and Platt squeaked in terror. Coll's veneer of civility dissolved like wet tissue, and the inhuman snarl from his lips teetered on the fringe of true insanity. "Don't you *ever* fucking compare me to *him*!" His nostrils flared, his face inches from hers. "That moping bitch isn't fit to hold my dick while I take a piss! He's a fuck-up! A failure!"

Coll's sudden rage suffused Platt with a strange and paradoxical calm. Watching his devolution into tantrums gave her hope. Coll was not a foe she had to defeat, but a puzzle she had to solve.

"I don't know, Vincent. He sure looked like a success to GEED when they found him."

Coll spun away from her. "Sullivan? A success? Hah!" The last word came out as a harsh croak. "Only if you don't know what he's supposed to be."

"And that is?"

Wide shoulders rose and fell in a big, cleansing breath. Platt noted the conscious effort it took for the man to reassert control of his voice. "First of all, John L. Sullivan isn't even his name. So get that out of your head right now."

"Really?" Platt prodded.

"No, Doc. It's the model his dear old daddy ordered up."

Platt did not know what he was talking about. When the man turned and saw her bemused expression, Coll explained. "John L. Sullivan is what they called his, uh, genetic profile. It's a marketing thing. The real John Sullivan was some famous fighter from a long-ass time ago." Coll waved his hands in exasperation. "Some tough drunk who could throw hands better than anyone. Fucking Johnny-Boy was designed to be an enforcer, Doc. A product rich pricks ordered up when they needed a problem solved with muscle." Coll shook his head. "But Daddy's little angel never really fit the mold. His brain isn't right. He's supposed to mean and hard, not mopey and sarcastic."

"And you?" Platt asked. "Is Vincent Coll your name? Or is that a product designation too?"

The tic reappeared, so obvious now that she knew to look for it. "Vincent 'Mad Dog' Coll was the nastiest hitman in all the Irish mobs of the twentieth century, Doc. What the fuck do you think?"

"Fascinating," was all she could manage to say in the moment. "So you would be what got ordered when?"

"When you need every motherfucker in your way dead and buried."

"So they made you insane," she stated, and waited for his reaction.

Coll's face went dark, and he spoke with a hushed intensity. "Who the fuck are you calling insane, Doc?"

"Vincent," she spoke calmly, like a parent explaining the concept of death to a child. "Your testosterone-to-cortisol ratio is all over the place. I can see it. I can only assume that your creator deliberately gave you psychotic tendencies. The PRC did the same to thousands of their soldiers."

"I'm not like that!" Coll nearly screamed it. The hint of fear told Platt she had struck a nerve.

She leaned into it. "No, certainly not. You are too well-designed to go berserk. I wonder if they used the same dopamine trigger that keeps Sullivan from snapping."

At the mention of Sullivan, Coll's cheek twitched. "Fuck that, Doc. I'm not a psycho. But I'm not soft like Sullivan, either."

"Probably some other rate-limiting step, then," Platt mused. "Are there other... uh... models?"

Deep into his narrative, Coll did not notice he was being manipulated. "Plenty. Your Emilie is one, too. They wanted some sort of administrative or tactical genius package out of her." His face twitched again, and the leer reasserted itself. "But they got something way better in the end, didn't they?"

Platt did not bother to argue that, and she tried to change the subject. "Who are they? Who is doing all this?"

Coll swung his head back and forth. "Who? Everybody that matters, that's who. The mob, the big corporations, hell, half the world government is probably in on it. There's a whole thing going on above our heads, Doc. The world isn't what you think it is. The people we see running everything aren't really running anything. The real power on this planet has nothing to do with the New Global Republic or the old governments. It's about who has money and influence and the muscle to hold on to both. Me, Sullivan, cute little Emilie? We're the next generation of that muscle. That's what this whole shit show is all about, Doc." He attempted his best disarming grin. "We are the latest thing, the state-of-the-art in what my boss calls 'urban pacification.'"

"That's..." Platt had no words for what she was feeling. "That's insane!"

Coll's indifference stood in marked contrast to Platt's shock and horror. "I hope you're getting the point, Doc," he pressed on. "That girl is just the latest model to come out of R&D, and the people who want to sell it are not going to just let her go. You want to help her? Then you better help me bring her back in."

"I could just let GEED have her." Platt knew the threat had no teeth, yet she tried anyway.

Coll scoffed. "We own GEED. She'd be in our hands forty-eight hours after processing." He sniffed. "We would have just let the let the wardens bring you both in, but the bosses wanted secrecy, and fuck me if GEED can do anything without a lot of noise, right?" Coll's rage had passed as quickly as it had flared up, confirming her suspicions about his latent psychopathy. "Not to mention their operations are a matter of public record." With greater calm, Coll's more urbane mannerisms returned. "So you see, Doctor, the best thing for you both is to come back in without making this any harder than it already is."

"Well," Platt said. "You've got me already, but the Railroad still has Emilie. She's probably a million miles away right now."

"I guess I'll just go home, then?" Coll said with a sarcastic chuckle. "Come on, Doctor. I think we both know that's not the case. How would your friends bargain for your release without the girl?"

"They'd never give you Emilie, not even for me."

"Of course, they won't, but they'll need to try to trick me in order for their rescue plan to work."

"What makes you so sure they'll even try?"

"Because the Railroad will want the knowledge locked in your brain, Doctor. And Sullivan?" Coll inhaled sharply and let out a very satisfied sigh. "Well, I know that screw-up better than he knows himself. Right now, he's probably moping over being betrayed by GEED and letting his friend get hurt." Coll found his shirt and shrugged back into it. "But trust me, big, bad John Sullivan isn't going to leave you out here to swing. I guarantee it. He's a pansy who will run from his responsibilities, sure. He'll run from his father, absolutely. Hell, he'll run from pretty much anything that makes him feel bad." Coll finished buttoning and grabbed his jacket. "The only thing that idiot won't run from is a fight. He is going to come right for me because that is all he knows how to do."

"Isn't that what he was made to do?" Platt asked.

"Damn straight," Coll replied.

"Doesn't sound like a failure to me, then."

Coll looked down on Platt, and his ice-blue eyes betrayed the glacial confidence of a man unaccustomed to failure. "Remember you said that after I kill him."

CHAPTER TWENTY-SIX

"That is a stupid idea, and I hate it."

The tremble in Skip's voice eroded the conviction of his otherwise plain statement.

"Do tell," Sullivan replied. Though his delivery made it clear he was not entertaining alternatives.

"There is no way I am gonna follow an eight-year-old kid and a fucking warden all the way across Hubtown and into the Lenexa Terminal. I could get killed just for talking to you!"

Skip had not taken the news about Sullivan's identity well. This is why the young man was currently laying on his back with Sullivan's foot pressing on his chest. His attempt to flee the sleeping pod had been simultaneously brief and anticlimactic. That he sustained no serious injuries in the abbreviated struggle indicated an improvement in either Sullivan's mood or his own personal luck. He remained unsure which.

Sullivan leaned in to catch Skip's eye and bared his teeth. "Well, Skip, there's a real solid chance you could get killed for not talking to me, too. The good news is that nobody's really sure if I'm still a warden or not. I am so far off the reservation at this point that I can't even see the smoke signals anymore."

"You don't get it, man! Every gang between Rosedale and Lenexa will want to kill you if they even smell a badge. There's a ton of Teamster territory between here and there, and they're tight with Silk Road contacts. Your mob cleaner obviously has the Silk Road for backup, so we're fucked that way, too."

"That's why we need you, Skip," Sullivan said. "I thought the Road Crew gang managed the mass transit system around these parts."

"Yeah, we do."

"Well, Skip, I find myself in need of some transit."

"It can't be done man," Skip insisted. "All this Coll fucker has to do is let it get out that you are a G-man, and you're dead." He paused, considering the situation with a befuddled look. "Come to think of it, why the hell hasn't he done it already?"

"Discretion," Sullivan said with an easy shrug. "He knows what I can do. He knows what GEED is capable of. If your gang-bangers come for me, I'm going to make a huge ruckus, and then GEED will make a huge ruckus. Even corrupted, there is no way GEED can allow a warden to get killed in a massive gang battle within one of the complexes without some kind of response. Doing nothing would expose their corruption. And there *will* be a massive battle. You can bet your scrawny ass I'll make sure of it. Coll knows I won't go down without a bunch of noise, and so we are stuck dancing around each other and trying not to wake the neighbors. Probably because the mob hasn't told those neighbors that the most valuable GMP ever created is wandering their halls. Honestly, Skip, you should be falling all over yourself to get us out of here; you'd only be helping yourself."

The young gangster considered this. "Fucking let me up, man," he whined at last.

"You try to run again, and I'll thump you," Sullivan said as he removed his foot.

"Yeah, yeah, yeah." He gathered his feet beneath him and rose on wobbly legs. He tried manfully to fix Sullivan with a burning glare but withered under the barely-restrained violence just behind the eyes of the warden. He cleared his throat, "Uh, so this girl," Skip pointed to Emilie. She was still on the bed, still wide-eyed with fear, still listening with unsettling intensity. "That means the Council doesn't know how crazy important she is, right?"

"I sincerely doubt the Council has any idea what is going on. I'm guessing that whoever needed to be bribed has been bribed, and that's the extent of it. As long as Emilie is in the KC Complex, Coll's employers are going to move heaven and earth to keep her a secret from anybody who actually has power in here."

"Probably a good call," Skip said. "The Council may not have loads of power outside the Complex, but inside?" He shook his head. "They may as well be gods."

"Exactly why everyone is tip-toeing so delicately around the issue."

"Your plan is still shit, though."

Sullivan raised an eyebrow. "Do tell."

Skip straightened his rumpled clothes. "So Coll wants this girl, and he's already got the scientist, right?"

"Yes."

"Well, he ain't got to do shit, then. He knows you got to come to him."

"My plan sort of hinges on that exact premise, Skip." Sullivan struggled to hide his irritation.

"I don't know what they teach for strategy in no fancy warden schools or whatever, but doing exactly what the bad guy knows you're gonna do sounds stupid to this lowly hustler," Skip said with transparent derision. "Maybe I don't know what I'm talking about, but it seems like you've got some advantages you aren't using."

"Oh, I can't wait to hear this."

"Anyone ever point out that you're kind of an asshole?"

"All the time, kid."

"Imagine that," Skip harrumphed. "Okay. First thing: You don't gotta go hunt this guy down personally. All you need to do is get the gangs to do it for you. How deep does your infinite well of GEED cryptcoin go?"

"As deep as I want until they figure out I'm in the wind and cut me off."

"That's good. Now, I know it looks like we got all kinds of organization and rules down here, and we do, but there ain't nothing down here so sacred that cash won't trump the rules. Hell, the Silk Road counts on that. For enough 'coin, we can get the Road Crew and the Tunnel Rats to find Coll and scope his safehouse out first."

Maris, who had been silent up to this point, finally spoke up. "The Railroad has some people with... skills... that can help. We don't really do this kind of..." She faltered, not familiar with the terms for what she was describing.

Sullivan helped. "Wet work?"

A disgusted frown creased her wizened features. "You really call it wet work? What exactly makes this sort of work 'wet'?" She shuddered and cut off any reply. "Wait. No. Never mind. Don't answer that. I don't want to know."

"I didn't invent the term."

"Ugh. Anyway, a few of our wayward brothers and sisters have training and experience in..." she winced. "Wet work."

"See?" Skip said with a smug curl of the lip. "You got scouts, and you got soldiers. This already sounds better than your plan to walk right into whatever trap this guy has set up for you."

"Not so fast, smart guy." Sullivan was not convinced. "First, Coll dropped Suds with his bare hands. That means nobody down here should be getting anywhere near him, experienced or not. Second, nobody in the Railroad is going to work with a warden."

"They will if I ask them to," Maris said. "And let's be honest, John." She used his given name with a hint of irony. "Are you really still a warden?"

Sullivan scowled. “It’s all I’ve ever been, but I suppose you have a point. I don’t even know what a warden is anymore.” Though everyone could see he was avoiding the question, they let it pass. Sullivan returned to his original point. “I still don’t want any of your people trying to take on Coll. He’s... different.”

“He’s like you, you mean?” Skip asked. Sullivan’s answering glare put Skip on his heels. The youth held up his hands in surrender. “Oh, come on, man! I ain’t never seen a GiMP like you, pal.”

“Skip?”

“Yeah?”

“You have a bad habit of asking questions that can get your dumb ass killed.”

“Dropping the subject, then.”

“Smart kid.” Sullivan pinched the bridge of his nose between a thumb and forefinger. “Okay, then. I like the thought of some recon. Great. Wonderful. Skip, your job will be to find Coll and get as much info as you can on how he’s set up. Maris?”

“Yes?”

“I’ll take some of your crew, but they’ll be on extraction duty only.”

The woman’s blank gaze dragged an exasperated sigh from the big warden. “They’re going to rescue the doctor.”

“What will you do?” Maris asked.

“I’m going to give Coll exactly what he wants.”

“Emilie?” Maris sounded horrified.

“No,” Sullivan said, looking at the woman as if she had grown a second head. “Jesus, I’m not a monster! He wants the girl, but first he needs to figure out where the girl is. That’s what he wants right now.”

Skip’s smile went from ear to ear. “Now I get it! Coll knows you got to come to him, and he thinks you’re out here on your own. So if you dangle a little cheddar for him to sniff at...”

"Exactly," Sullivan said with a nod. "He wants the girl, so let's let him think he's found a way to get her."

"Without actually giving her to him?" Maris said.

"Obviously," Sullivan grunted. "We only need him to believe that it's a real shot."

Skip pointed to Maris. "Then, while the big boys are off killing each other, the Railroad guys are gonna sneak behind him and grab that doctor lady."

"Exactly," Sullivan said. "Coll will not expect the Railroad to be working with a warden. It's too far-fetched. Hell, I don't really believe it myself. He's forcing me to come to him because he thinks I'm alone, and it's the best way to avoid spooking the Council and GEED. It's probably why he picked Lenexa," Sullivan added at the end. "It's nice and remote."

Skip finished the thought. "He figures you gotta go get him all by yourself, so he camped in a spot where you can have a nice little dust-up without causing a big mess." He shook his head. "Not a terrible plan, really. We should use it against him. There are spots out that way that would work real nice for a mousetrap."

"So let's pick a good one and set it up. Skip, you can make as much money on this as you want. I'm okay buying your loyalty. However, if I think for one second you are going to turn on us..." his eyes finished the threat, and Skip nodded.

"I get you, big man. I've seen your expense account. You don't gotta worry about me." A nervous chuckle escaped his mouth. "Besides, uh, the Railroad folks have a reputation for dealing with folks who interfere with their work."

Maris beamed a grandmotherly smile at the young man. "Such a nice boy," she cooed. Somehow, this appeared to intimidate Skip more than Sullivan did.

Sullivan approved. "Good for you, Maris. Glad to hear it. For this to work, I need to know where Doctor Platt is being held. Then we have to get Vincent away from her so the Railroad team can grab her. Can the gangs do all this without spooking him?"

Skip actually laughed at this. "That's the only part of this idea I'm sure will work. Gangs don't give a shit about conspiracies or mob wars or secret projects. They care about making money." Skip acknowledged the irony of selling his own loyalty with a wink before moving on. "All we gotta do is find whichever gang set him up in Lenexa, then buy them off. Tin Knockers, Tunnel Rats, Silk Road, whatever. As long as your bankroll is bigger, you win."

Maris snorted. "He speaks truth, John. Any gang in the KC Complex would sell their mothers for the right price. For enough money, the only thing that will stop them from selling out Coll would be fear of his masters."

"And since they aren't showing their faces," Skip said, "that fear really won't play at the street level."

"I guess that leaves only one thing," Sullivan said. "Can you keep Emilie hidden, Maris? It needs to be somewhere even you and I don't know, in case this goes bad."

The old woman nodded a brisk affirmative. "Of course. I have been hiding GMP children in this complex since the Genetic Equity Act was passed. He won't find me if I don't want to be found. He knows that. That's why he turned Porter."

"Perfect," Sullivan grunted. "Once you get the girl stashed, meet me back here."

"Why?" Maris seemed genuinely confused.

"Someone has to draw Coll out of his hole," Sullivan said with a shrug. "It can't be me. Coll will smell the trick a mile off if we use me for bait. We need someone he thinks can get him to the girl."

"Wait." The confusion had become terror. "You want *me* to be on this mission? Like, out there?"

"What's the matter, Maris?" Sullivan's voice held a sadistic growl wrapped in a thick layer of evil humor. "You too good for a little wet work?"

CHAPTER TWENTY-SEVEN

Sullivan stepped off the tram and into the blackness of the unlit tunnel, and Maris followed.

The local Tunnel Rat detachment had arranged for his tram car to stop between stations on a rarely-used section of track. An additional pile of cryptcoin ensured the pair would be alone and unnoticed for this, and they slipped from the thin shaft of blue light spilling from the open door of the car to disappear into the deep shadows unseen. Moving along the sides of the tram tunnel, Sullivan lightly dragged his fingers across the rough concrete surface until they brushed a metal hatch. Finding the handle, he flipped the latch over and hauled the metal door open to reveal a small, thin, and uninviting scuttle. Sullivan had no love or appreciation for tight spaces, yet he wriggled his way inside without hesitation. A muttered expletive from Maris informed him that she anticipated the climb with as much enthusiasm as he did. Sullivan's shoulders scraped the walls of the tight gap, forcing his arms against his sides. He had to grasp the knurled rungs of the greasy ladder like a praying mantis and shuffle his way up each step to avoid bashing his knees the whole way.

Revelations about his provenance sent wry thoughts through his head as he climbed. The most apropos being that for tasks like this, they really should have built a stealthier model of chimera. He wondered if anyone had designed a ninja configuration to compliment the pugilistic version he embodied. With no predisposition toward woolgathering, he abandoned these musings long before he reached the top of the shaft. A round hatch at the end of his climb yielded to his shove with the squeal of rusty hinges. It opened into a mechanical space, a high mezzanine filled with air filtration, recirculation, and climate control machinery. Metal boxes the size of houses thrummed and hissed as millions of cubic feet of air whisked to and from various spaces to be heated, cooled, or filtered as needed. Pumps lay aligned with military precision along one wall, moving water and other fluids around with a quiet, keening wail. This was the very heart and lungs of the Lenexa terminal. All gangs considered this sacred ground, and no one dared molest the essential machinery up here. Sullivan had no intention of breaking this rule. He merely planned to exploit the neutral territory's dearth of prying eyes. He reached back to help Maris exit the scuttle. In the dim light, he could just make out the grim set of her jaw as she tried to mask her growing fear and exhaustion.

"You all right?" he said in a hushed voice.

"I'm fine," the breathless woman said.

Without acknowledging her lie, Sullivan crossed the mezzanine with long and silent strides. Maris followed with her own shuffling steps as she struggled to match his pace. At the far end, he held up a hand to halt the woman. He drew the Hudson H10 from his belt and checked the weapon for readiness. Satisfied, he pushed the door open and swept into the dark space beyond. Like a stalking cat, he moved through what appeared to be a locker room with his gun in a firm, two-handed grip. When he had checked the room for danger and found none, he at last signaled for Maris to follow. At a door marked "Exit" in cleat white letters, Sullivan stepped across the threshold and found himself in what had once been a maintenance workers' dormitory.

A wide-open rec room lay spread out before his eyes. Tables and chairs sat stacked neatly against the walls, and several large monitor screens hung like flat black paintings on the pale gray background. "We're in," he grunted back to Maris. "Looks like nobody saw us."

"Thank goodness for small favors," the woman huffed. "Let's find the room."

While there were quite a few easier ways to get to this place, the circuitous route had ensured that nobody had witnessed their approach. The dormitory slept empty and alone for the moment, and the two stalked through its empty halls with only the pattering of their own feet to keep them company. Sullivan had been assured that the dormitory was used only during equipment maintenance cycles. No gang was allowed to set up permanent residence so close to the equipment. Skip explained that the Grease Monkeys usually maintained the life-support machinery on this side of the complex. However, the Tunnel Rats, Glow Worms, Tin Knockers, and Throttle Jockeys all took regular turns, if only to prevent one gang from asserting control over such important equipment. The choice to use such a hotly-contested and highly-volatile space had not been made lightly, and now the desolate atmosphere scratched at the edges of Sullivan's frosty calm. He ignored it. The main area lights sulked in recessed coves, and inky shadows from the minimal emergency illumination stretched in all directions. The shifting shapes and intersecting swathes of light and dark disguised the shape and dimensions of the space. Sullivan imagined a hundred ways they might get ambushed and killed. His rational mind accepted the unlikelihood of such a disaster, and he disregarded the twinge of apprehension struggling beneath the crushing sheet of genetically-engineered calm. They were well and truly alone, so worrying seemed a waste of time.

"Sleeping pods are through there," Maris said. Her finger stretched out to specify another darkened hall. "That's our spot."

"Ready?" Sullivan asked.

"Now you want to know if I'm ready? Now?"

"I suppose it doesn't really matter at this point, huh? Skip's already leaked the intel, so if you plan on getting squeamish..." he made an apologetic gesture, "I'll have to knock you out and tie you up."

Her silence was all the answer he needed. With a non-committal sniff, Sullivan turned and gestured for the woman to make her way inside. She stepped past him, clad in a countenance of rigid determination. Turning back to fix him with an inscrutable glare, the old woman shook her head. "I hope this plan of yours works, John," she said. "Because I don't think I am cut out for wet work."

"I promise you that it will probably work."

"Dear God. You really are an asshole."

"I get that a lot," he said. "Now sit tight and be ready with that clicker. I'll be close by, but that doesn't mean he can't sneak past me."

"I know my role."

"Right." Sullivan hid a mean smirk and turned away from her. His own apprehensions returned as he moved back through the darkness. The bait was in place, and all that remained was for him to be ready to spring the trap. He found his way to the mezzanine, assuming Coll would employ the same approach to avoiding discovery as he had. The element of chance to this part irked him. If Coll came up this way, Sullivan would have a shot at the target before Maris ever knew what was happening. If Coll chose to take the direct approach and come up through the main concourse, Sullivan would miss his chance and have to attack while Coll interrogated Maris. Both versions worked, but only one kept Maris out of the line of fire. Sullivan had never met Vincent Coll. He had no idea what kind of man he was or how his mind worked. His choice to set up in the mezzanine was a coin flip. Only luck would decide the outcome of this gamble, and the only kind of luck John Sullivan had ever known was bad luck.

Settling in behind a droning air handler, Sullivan chewed his lip. A strange intensity had been building in his emotions over the last several days, and the implications worried him. Without warning, his universe had shifted away from the familiar pillars of career, booze, and women, and he harbored nagging suspicions as to why.

My mind isn't right. Something is happening in my brain.

It had started as little things like the growing need to test his ability to experience fear and anger. Then there was the sudden deterioration of the emotional barriers in his personal life. Now, he felt a bizarre need to protect an eight-year-old girl he hardly knew and was sure he did not like, simply because he did not want her life to be like his.

I'm changing. But why?

Looking back on the last ten days made Sullivan feel like a man out of time and place, a hapless spectator to some other life. This person's life he did not recognize. This person possessed a clear focus and eschewed distractions. It had been days since his last drink, he realized. More than a week since he had been with a woman, too. Examining the recent past revealed more strange behaviors barely acknowledged at the time.

He tried and failed to find the exact moment that he gave up on pretending his career meant anything. In the attempt, he discovered that his blistering anger over Emilie's situation had taken care of any lingering doubts along those lines. Even with that knowledge, he could not pinpoint precisely when the change occurred.

Even his anger betrayed him. The familiar smoldering antipathy had transformed somewhere along the line. Normally a blunt object he used to lash out at anything in his path, his ever-present desire to hurt people had been filed to a sharp point and turned inward. Instead of punishing the world and all those living in it, his anger gouged at his own conscience. He hated it. He *feared* it.

The moment of self-reflection brought a wave of panic. The overwhelming urge to run saturated his thoughts like a dense fog. It would be a simple matter to arrest Maris, grab Emilie, and return to

GEED a hero. Then he could go back to drinking, fighting, and rutting his way to an early grave as he had always intended. Sullivan considered this option with a seriousness that shamed him. He did not like what it said about him as a person, yet in the quiet solitude of the dark mezzanine, the dark ruminations came unbidden. After far too long, and with much reluctance, Sullivan discarded the idea and abandoned all hope of taking the easy path. If he pretended nothing had changed and acted like the good little warden he was supposed to be, Horowitz would despise him, Fagan's injuries would have been for nothing, and the world would slowly descend into tyranny under new and terrible masters. To his eternal chagrin, Sullivan admitted that with enough whiskey, a man like him might be able to live with all that. However, a small, still voice in his head chose this moment to speak up for what he already knew to be true. If John Sullivan walked away now, that little girl's life would be exactly as his had been. The very thought of it spiked his adrenaline and set his heart pounding. Horowitz, Fagan, Platt—all of them had made their choices, and he took no responsibility for their fates. But not Emilie. She had no choice, and the world did not care. She would spend her life suffering through no fault of her own unless somebody with the power to change it took action. He would have given much for that somebody to be anyone other than himself, though he had to admit no such person existed. It would be him or nothing. If he failed that girl now, the bad guys won, and his father got to destroy another innocent child.

He made himself a promise to do this one thing right. Not because he cared so much if the world burned, but because he could not accept the destruction of yet another helpless child. He doubted there was enough whiskey in all the world to drown that kind of guilt. The very existence of this internal dispute told Sullivan that something in his neurochemical matrix had shifted, and he supposed this was as good a time as any to see what it was like to not be an asshole for once.

It was an emotionally confused and intensely conflicted Sullivan who detected the first signs of the plan going awry. Their strategy hinged upon Coll operating more or less alone in the Complex, and this was the first of several assumptions that proved to be erroneous. Lost in his own thoughts, Sullivan almost missed the creaking of the scuttle hatch as it opened. The weak flickering of a headlamp swung across the pervasive blackness of the mezzanine and sent white flashes reflecting off the surfaces of the air handlers. Sullivan's senses snapped into focus, and he readied his pistol for his one good chance at Vincent Coll.

Vincent Coll did not emerge from the scuttle. The head that poked up through the hatch lacked the square-jawed symmetry and flawless skin Sullivan expected to find. The stranger finished climbing and stepped into the mezzanine. He was holding a weapon of some kind in both hands, though it was far too dark for Sullivan to determine the exact type. Another man followed, and another after that. They kept coming until six armed men stood whispering around the scuttle. Sullivan's vantage point was too far away for him to make out the furtive conversation that ensued, though he guessed the general thrust of it. When the intruders reached a mutual accord, they began to creep his direction through the mezzanine.

Sullivan spat a silent expletive under his breath at the wrinkle. It seemed Coll had managed to secure some assets inside the Complex after all. A thousand questions whipped through his mind in the few moments it took for the men to close in on his position. He had no good answers for any of them, though he supposed these goons might have some insights. He debated signaling Maris to abort, then opted not to. If he managed to take these men down quietly, it might draw Coll out. If this was a feint, then Sullivan could still swoop in to aid Maris once he finished with them. The slight sting of guilt rode along with this decision. He was gambling with the old woman's safety. She did not seem to fear death, though. If Maris thought dying at the hands of Vincent Coll would save Emilie, she would not hesitate. Sullivan decided to respect her commitment and keep the mission running.

For once, he did not court the fire of rage before acting. It was in the usual place, rolling and heaving beneath the ever-present layer of soothing detachment. It would be there if he needed it.

CHAPTER TWENTY-EIGHT

Carlo Santino assembled his strike team as soon as they had all emerged from the scuttle. When everyone was accounted for, he scanned his surroundings as best he could given the limitations of his equipment. He swept the deck from left to right with his headlamp, pitting one meager beam of light against the army of shadows cast by the assorted machinery around him. He learned little of use other than that the area was big, dark, and full of weird machines.

"Can't we get this shit moving yet, Santino?"

Santino resisted the urge to brain the idiot with his shotgun. Instead, he looked back over his shoulder to scowl at the gnarled man just behind him. "You wanna move faster, huh? How fast should we go, smart guy? Don't forget that it's pitch black, and we happen to be surrounded by ambush spots where a goddamn super-GiMP killer might be hiding. Go ahead. You make the call."

The other man wilted. "I'm just sayin' this is gonna take forever if we don't pick it up."

Santino sighed. "Okay, Wilson, you take left, and Coates, you have right. Blane, your ass is up front with me since you are in so much of a fuckin' hurry. Sawyer and Granby, you guys lock in behind Wilson and Coates, but not too close. I want two goddamn meters between everybody at all times."

"How big is a meter?" Blane asked.

"Three feet, you fucking idiot," the man moving to the left flank said.

"Fuck you, Wilson," Blane said. "I'm an American, and we don't use no metric bullshit."

"You are a moron," Wilson said, and settled into his slot.

"Stow it, boys," Santino said in his best command voice. "Stay on me. The old bitch is supposed to be holed up in one of the sleeping pods. Our intel says she probably has the girl with her. If she does, we are clear to execute on sight. If not, well, then we'll need her alive. So don't get trigger happy. Now, the local gangs will eat us for lunch if they find out we are messing around up here, so watch your fire. If we run into that freak GiMP, you can go to town, but for fuck's sake, check your targets. It's dark up here, and I don't want to die because Blane can't figure out who the bad guy is."

He neither asked for nor received acknowledgment from his team. He turned, checked his shotgun one more time, and started picking his way through the darkness.

"You maybe wanna kill that light?" Wilson asked. His own light, mounted to the side of his carbine, remained dark.

Santino snorted. "Fuck that. If he's up here, he's seen us already. Fucker can probably see in the dark. If he's not, it doesn't matter if the light's on or off. Might as well see where I'm going."

To both men's chagrin, the relative tactical advantage of using the lights never came into play. Sawyer's disappearance went completely unnoticed. No one noticed the shadow detach from behind a large metal box, and no one noticed the muscular arm when it clamped across Sawyer's face and dragged him backward to disappear into the silent blackness. Granby thought he heard something like a struggle. Since he did not see anything, and he did not want to sound like a jumpy rookie, he kept his mouth shut. His suspicions heightened his overall sense of alertness, so when he felt the first crushing pressure of a forearm across his throat, he managed a panicked screech that lasted barely a quarter of a second before both oxygen and blood stopped flowing to his brain.

Granby would never know it, but his cry succeeded in alerting his team. Blane spun toward the sound, his reckless turn sweeping every remaining man with his muzzle. With a snarl, Santino slapped the muzzle down before Blane let loose with a volley of panic-inspired gunfire. The leader fixed Blane with a fierce glare and pressed a finger to his lips.

Coates and Wilson dropped to crouches behind some compressors and covered their fields of fire without a word. Everything fell deathly quiet for several long seconds. Santino played the light from his headlamp in a wide circle. At last, he discovered the two missing men and bit down on a roar of frustration. He channeled the fire in his gut into a shouted challenge. "Come on out, GiMP. You're still outnumbered four to one. Don't make this any harder than it needs to be." He pointed to a brown metal expansion tank and gestured for Blane to take cover. Blane complied with less grace than was strictly professional.

"Three to one," a voice boomed from the darkness.

Santino spun to find Coates had gone missing while he directed Blane. "On me!" he barked to Blane and Wilson. Then to their tormentor, he called, "You're not shooting? I guess that means the gangs don't know you're up here, either, huh?"

"Maybe I'm just enjoying myself."

Santino tried to pick out the voice's location while moving to a more defensible spot. The rows of equipment bounced sound in all directions, and the team leader could make neither heads nor tails of where the reply had come from. He and his remaining two shooters eventually closed up back to back to back in the space between two very large air handlers. The giant sheet metal boxes were ten feet tall and close to forty feet long. The three men were effectively trapped in a metal canyon, though Santino accepted the risk because he figured the enemy would have to come from one of only two directions to get them. From a tactical perspective, the maneuver made sense. The limited access and narrow corridor would condense the fields of fire into something more than manageable for the remainder of his fire team.

Santino leveled his shotgun down one end of their canyon. "Come on, then, you GiMP sonofabitch," he taunted. "Come have some more fun."

Santino squinted down the axis of his shotgun barrel toward the shadows at the end of their canyon. "Just pick a direction, you bastard," he whispered. "Pick one and make your fucking move, you freak."

The team leader did not realize it, but Sullivan had already chosen his direction of attack. A direction Santino had neglected to consider. Something struck the leader from above like a falling tree. Two hundred and sixty-five pounds of bone and muscle drove the man flat against the deck and sent his shotgun skidding across the floor. All the air in his lungs burst outward in an explosive grunt of surprise and pain, then hands like clamps seized him by the scruff of the neck and sent him upward once again.

At the top of his rise, Santino finally got a good look at the enemy. He did not know what he had expected from the legendary GiMP, but the grizzled, scruffy, and dead-eyed thing he faced was definitely not it. Santino's impressions mattered very little, for John Sullivan was in a killing mood, and Carlo Santino had presented himself as a viable target for his poor humor. Carlo Santino's last thoughts were desperate and unfocused as the floor loomed large in his view, though no small amount of his remaining time was spent lamenting the error of not looking up at least once before picking a defensible position.

The superhuman might of the genetic monstrosity sent the team leader back into the metal surface with speed and force well beyond anything his tiny, brittle, all-too-human vertebrae could survive. He died in a flash of light and the intermittent firing of disconnected nerves.

Sullivan, for his part, had no idea if his slam had killed the team leader or not. He saw the man lying still and quiet, and that was good enough for the moment. He moved on from Santino without a second thought and dove for the next man he intended to kill. Sullivan had watched the team for long enough to determine who the real shooters were and who were the weak links. He wanted Blane alive, and the condition of the rest did not matter much. He counted on Wilson to hold fire until there was a target to shoot at. Blane, he figured, would start blasting as soon as he panicked. This was something Sullivan suspected would occur without much provocation.

He was right. Instead of Wilson exploiting the narrow canyon to secure a clean field of fire, Blane rose and tried to hit moving shadows with undisciplined one-handed shooting. He nearly shot Wilson in the ensuing chaos, and the more seasoned operative had to waste a full second getting Blane's muzzle clear of his own chest. Wilson shouldered his useless teammate to the side with a shouted expletive and brought his carbine up to put the beam from his mounted flashlight on the enemy. If not for the wasted time dealing with Blane, Wilson would have had at least one clean shot at Sullivan. Instead, the shaft of light from his torch caught only the whipcrack-quick streak of a thick arm. Sullivan's hand struck the carbine aside, and a booted foot connected with Wilson's chest like a car crash. Wilson felt the sickening crunch of ribs breaking followed by a wildfire of burning pain across his chest. He wanted to gasp or scream, but the act of inhalation doubled his agony, and he passed out from pain even as his feet left the floor. This was for the best. The impact of his body against the metal side of the air handler displaced those fractured ribs and tore a hole in his left lung. He was not dead when his body slid to the floor, but he was dying, and that was the sort of ordeal best endured unconscious.

Blane had given up all pretense of composure and started firing. The noise was deafening. He cycled the trigger of his borrowed pistol as fast as his finger could twitch, dumping fifteen rounds in five seconds. His bullets struck the floor, the sides of the machines hemming him in, the ceiling of the mezzanine, and many other surfaces. The copper and steel-jacketed projectiles bounced and tumbled, they threw sparks and gouged furrows, they ruined everything they touched. They all missed Sullivan, though.

Blane backpedaled as he fired, letting his muzzle flashes light the way while his legs scampered away from the specter that had reduced the six-man team to one lone shooter without firing a shot. He thought only of escape and survival, all lofty philosophical and ideological positions abandoned at the first sign of serious opposition. His back struck something solid, and he whirled to see what sort of immovable object had blocked his escape. Something terrible and strong grabbed his wrist and yanked the gun from his hand. In that moment, Blane suffered an instant of perfect clarity, and his soul wailed in defeat.

He was done.

He was trapped in the clutches of John L. Sullivan, the genetically-modified son of the most powerful mobster on the planet—a state-of-the art chimera with capabilities no one really understood. Goddamned Super-GiMP himself.

Blane tried to yank free and despaired at the sheer inexorable power of the hand crushing his wrist. He swung his left fist like a club at his captor, missing by a wide margin. With a casual, contemptuous, humiliating ease, Sullivan spun Blane in a circle, twisted his arm behind his back, and sent him to his knees with a rough boot to the back of his knee. Sullivan's other hand reached around and lifted his chin with a rough yank, and Blane felt the humid breath of his enemy on his ear when the man spoke.

"Do you have any idea how fucked you are, little man?"

Blane did not answer at first, befuddled as he was by the question. When he realized Sullivan was waiting for an answer, he bobbed his head as best he could within Sullivan's iron grip.

"Start clucking, little chicken, and I might just let you out of here with your head attached."

Blane did not know what to say, and panic kept his lips pressed together.

"Who hired you?" Sullivan prompted. "Was it Coll?"

"No!" Blane blurted. "We're... I mean we were SoA! Silk Road tipped us off you were up here!"

"SoA?" The question managed to emerge both confused and angry at the same time. "You're SoA?" Then another question followed, one more relevant. "Silk Road tipped you off? I thought they were helping Coll?"

"How the fuck should I know, man?" Blane whimpered. "Silk Road isn't like a single group. Lots of them were willing to sell you out. Coll, too," he added. "As long as you talk to the right folks, you can get whatever you want from them."

"Where's Coll now?"

"What?"

"Coll!" Sullivan snarled. "Is he after the girl?"

"I don't work for Coll! I don't know shit! But if we know she was up here, then he does, too."

"Of course he does," Sullivan said. "We wanted him to come."

Sullivan was not a gifted strategic thinker, though he was capable of impressive intuition under the right circumstances. "Oh, fucking hell," he spat. He spun Blane around to face him, then hoisted the trembling man aloft by the throat. "Silk Road didn't tell you shit, dumbass. That was Coll trying to flush us out. He sent you up here to die, you goddamn idiot."

Blane did not answer because he was being strangled to death a foot off the floor. His eyes began to glaze, and the intensity of his struggling faded with each passing second. Realizing that the man was dying, Sullivan dropped him. In a fit of bizarre calm, Sullivan found that he had no desire to kill the man. The coughing piece of human garbage at his feet was a GMP-hater and a terrorist, yet Sullivan could not dredge up enough animosity to finish him off. The pathetic man stirred more pity than anything else. He was so much... less than Sullivan. Slower, weaker, stupider. Blane represented the very worst of humanity, and for the first time in his life, Sullivan understood why many people feared and hated the genetically-modified. Understanding brought more of the sympathy he barely understood, and the writhing leviathan of anger deep in his psyche calmed. With calm came clarity. Why would Vincent dupe the SoA into a suicide mission?

He spun on a heel and bolted for the dormitory. He burst through the door with a crash to find a wholly terrified Maris inside frantically mashing the panic button clutched in her hand.

"Don't bother," he nearly shouted. "It's me. We gotta move!"

"What's happening?" Maris asked as she rose.

"Vincent is on to us. I think your rescue team is in trouble!"

CHAPTER TWENTY-NINE

Vincent Coll loved this part.

He missed his Hudson H10; however, the old Russian 12.7mm anti-materiel revolver his contacts had dug up proved to be a highly satisfying weapon to use. The recoil slammed the pistol into his hand and threatened to send the weapon flying with every shot, though this could be forgiven when one considered the results. The first man struck by the half-inch bullet did not so much die as he exploded. The round impacted high on the left side of his chest and removed his arm with a gory spray of blood and bone fragments. The shock of traumatic amputation and the subsequent loss in blood volume put that man down instantly and scattered his team like startled crows.

Coll's grin was irrepressible as he slipped from the cover of a fortified lab station and slid to another pre-constructed bulwark of office furniture to re-engage.

Coll found it almost amusing that Sullivan thought it possible to beat him at his own game. His very DNA had been manipulated to produce the perfect hitman, and this included a lot of time and money spent on making Vincent Coll devious on a level a clod like Sullivan was incapable of even comprehending. Sullivan's trap was a joke, and Coll had seen through it more or less instantly. His own plan was a work of art, and things were already aligning perfectly. The first reports of return fire began to pepper the place he had until recently occupied, and this brought his attention back to the matter at hand.

His opponents were competent and well-trained, and possessed good discipline. Coll respected that. That they were hopelessly outclassed was not his fault. As he assumed they would, the first two flankers peeled off under covering fire to move abreast of where he had been. This brought the pair of gray-clad assaulters directly past his vantage point, and Coll killed them with a single round each. The giant pistol treated body armor like so much tissue paper and rendered torsos into gooey piles of ruined organs. Coll bolted before the corpses hit the floor and tore off under a hail of gunfire through an open door adjacent to the lab. Ricochets and chips of tile whipped by his face as he dove through the exit and slid along the tiles. He regained his feet like an acrobat and disappeared through a side door into an office.

Secure in the knowledge that his enemies would have to proceed down the narrow killzone of the hall, Coll popped the cylinder out of his revolver and slid three more rounds in to replace the ones he had spent. Closing the weapon back up, he poked his head out to see how close pursuit was. Two men in military-style garb had posted up to either side off the hall door and were sweeping the corridor with the muzzles of short carbines. When they noticed his head, a burst of gunfire raked his hiding spot. Coll ducked his head back inside with a chuckle and waited for the barrage to stop. When the chattering ceased, he crouched, leaned out, and squeezed off a single round with one fluid motion.

The bullet struck the door frame at the end of the hall and passed through the light metal with almost no deflection whatsoever. Through the frame, through the wall board, and through the hapless soldier crouched just beyond the bullet sped, unconcerned with the interference of the various types of interior construction material it encountered along the way. He did not see the hit, though the choked scream of a dying man told him all he needed to know about the efficacy of his ludicrous pistol. Another peek from his hiding spot, and he saw the other soldier leap back and grab his fallen buddy. He sent two more bullets through the walls, just to back the pursuers off, then he moved again.

It had all been so easy. As soon as Sullivan's pet Roadie had started making inquiries, Coll's misinformation campaign had begun. With no practical way to keep his location a secret, he had not even tried. What he had allowed his pursuers to believe was that he was alone and unsupported. Naturally, as long as his employers had money, the Silk Road would always be able to provide assistance. The same gangland indifference to morality that allowed Sullivan his latitude did the same for Coll. The Railroad was never going to let the girl's location get out. When he heard news of a secret safe house in the mechanical space, he figured out Sullivan's game without too much difficulty. Coll knew a trap when he saw it, and nothing in life pleased him so much as turning the tables on a foe.

Getting his Silk Road contacts to manipulate the Sons of Adam took very little time and even less effort. Zealots made for excellent cannon fodder. He had not known exactly who or what would come for Platt, so he had planned for the worst. A good-sized squad of ex-military GiMPs seemed about right. With any luck, his whittling of their numbers had set a hook in the squad. They certainly seemed committed to running him down at this point. His next fighting position was through a door at the end of the hall. On the other side lay an open production floor. Coll assumed it had been used for final assembly of large war machines, as the wide open space looked desolate and spare when compared to the other production facilities and their dense distribution of machinery.

At a sprint, Coll made his way across the open factory floor. A sprint from Vincent Coll was impressive, and he slid the last ten feet like a baseball player and came to a halt behind a gantry platform. His pursuers burst through the door forty yards away and fanned out in a manner that looked distressingly professional. He fought the temptation to squeeze off a shot. Making a kill shot at forty yards with an antique revolver would not be too much of a challenge, though the returning hail of gunfire would pin him down. He had moves to make still, so this would not do.

When the men stopped filing through the door, Vincent finally got a count of his attackers. Seven men remained; gray-faced and dead-eyed, they scanned the dim interior of the production floor for the enemy. Vincent let them come. Seven well-trained, well-armed, and probably genetically-enhanced opponents represented a credible challenge in a straight shootout, even for Vincent Coll.

As expected, the seven moved along the edges of the production floor. They picked along the workstations, cranes, and other sundry equipment that lined the walls in a leap-frog fashion. Three men darted ahead of the rest, heads hunched over their weapons and sweeping the shadows for opposition. The remainder watched from cover for signs of ambush. The squad avoided the open space in the middle of the room for obvious reasons. The empty space held nothing of use to them and presented a clear field of fire to the enemy. Vincent approved of their maneuvers in a distant sort of way. He was no military tactician, so the flawless execution of the sweep came as more of a curiosity to him. There was a flaw in their manner that Vincent knew how to exploit, and he decided the time had come to demonstrate this.

The men were pursuing their enemy as if engaged in urban warfare. They moved with speed and precision, methodically clearing each potential hiding spot while pushing the foe further along and away from familiar territory. Their mistake lay in the misapplied conceit that they were pushing Vincent anywhere he did not want to go. Vincent was not a lone operator hiding in a foreign urban labyrinth. Vincent Coll was a skilled hunter leading his prey into a carefully prepared trap.

When the squad had completed half a circuit around to Vincent's hiding spot, the first hidden mine detonated. One thousand metal spheres rocketed outward, driven by a shaped charge of high-yield plastic explosive. The man unlucky enough to trip the mine died instantly, torn to bloody pieces of meat and bone by the steel wind. The man moving with him took a total of eleven hits, though he had the good fortune to be shielded by the body of his teammate. He went down hard and bled like a leaking bucket onto the concrete. His hands pulled at the floor, dragging his perforated body like an inchworm toward the safety of a nearby tool cabinet. A third man was thrown several feet back and slid to a stop, pouring blood from his side, though he rose quickly to lurch back into the shelter of a nearby work station.

Vincent's lips peeled back from his gums to reveal perfect white teeth. He allowed that three casualties out of a possible seven was pretty good for one mine, then he raised his pistol and fired. The cylinder of his revolver held five enormous rounds of 12.7 millimeter caseless. Designed to stop vehicles or penetrate light armor, each bullet did the job of five or six smaller ones, so Vincent applied them with a judicious touch. He cycled through all five like a metronome, sending the bullets through cover and into bodies with as much precision as the poor light and fog of war allowed. The lightly wounded man screamed and fell down on his face, his weapon clattering to the floor at his side. Another man shouted in shock and pain before slumping against the wall with open eyes unblinking and a hole in his chest the size of a fist.

Then the squad retaliated. Long, sustained bursts of concentrated fire crisscrossed Vincent's hiding spot and sent him to the deck with a demonic cackle. The tools and terminals along the gantry control panel shattered with blossoms of orange sparks and a shower of plastic and metal fragments that rained down on the killer below. Vincent did not care. Vincent was reloading. Reloading and counting his kills. One dead from the mine, another badly hurt. Two dead from his pistol. That left three remaining shooters, and these odds Vincent could accept. He snuck a single eye out from behind the gantry platform to get a fix on the targets. Their muzzle flashes made it easy to see where all the shots were coming from, and he could not resist trying a shot off-hand. Vincent had been *made* to shoot, and his enemies were powerless before his skill. The big pistol lurched and boomed, and somewhere across the factory floor, a man screamed when the cabinet he was using for cover failed to stop a bullet from pulping his guts.

More return fire sent Vincent back behind his gantry platform, though his feral grin had widened by several degrees. There was a primal madness to a proper gunfight that Vincent found intoxicating. He reveled in the simplicity of it all. All he had to do was point at his enemy and twitch one little finger. He enjoyed the noise of it, the chaos of it, and most of all, he bathed in pure carnal delight at how good he was at it. It never occurred to Vincent Coll that one of these men might have the skill and grit to put him down. These were not cowards, nor were they unskilled. None of that mattered to Vincent. They were merely men, and he was so much more than that.

Suffused with psychotic glee, Vincent bolted from behind the gantry platform toward the two remaining shooters. Their muzzles rotated to track him, but their bullets stayed just behind his hurtling form as their reflexes lost their race with Vincent's speed. He dove across a gap to roll to his feet behind a wide column. Now, less than twenty feet separated the combatants, and Vincent swore he could smell the fear and indecision from the other side. He heard their breathing, fast and shallow. He smelled their sweat, saturated with the slick sweetness of mortal terror. He imagined he could even hear their thoughts, cluttered and desperate. Vincent trembled with ecstasy, guzzling the salty tang of murder from the very air like it was fine wine. It tasted like blood and honey in his twisted fantasies, and the part of him still present in the here and now whispered a silent warning. This would be a supremely bad moment to have one of his little episodes. Not while there was still work to do.

Vincent waited another three seconds. It had to be long enough to make the pair uncertain enough to try moving. As he suspected, his enemy's fear did not make them stupid. One man began to pepper Vincent's column with covering fire. This kept Vincent's head down so the other could move. The tactics were solid, as there was no way for the shooter to know that Vincent could hear his partner move to flank his position.

Vincent crouched low and waited. The flanker slid out to his right and moved swiftly to another column parallel to Vincent's. This maneuver would have been perfect if Vincent was not already aware of what the man was up to. The flanker, behind his own column, now had a clean shooting lane on Vincent's position while his partner held his head down. Or he would have, if Vincent had not moved.

When given the choice between defending a fortified position or charging the enemy, Vincent Coll's preference was clear. This was not to say he was stupid; just tactically aggressive with a healthy portion of pragmatic bias. In this case, the best and most practical way to deal with two shooters at once was to separate them. By closing the distance, he had encouraged the men to do just that, and they had obliged like the good little soldiers they were. Now, the time had come for Vincent to have some fun. He charged the man laying down the covering fire just as the flanker settled into the safety of his column.

The column providing the flanker with cover now obstructed his field of fire, leaving Vincent and the other man to shoot it out alone until he managed to reposition himself. One on one, Vincent Coll would bet his skills against any living human. His first advantage was the sheer surprise the entrenched shooter experienced at the sight of his pinned foe's sudden burst of violent action. The unavoidable delay between realization, comprehension, decision, and action that the shooter's mind and body experienced was his second great advantage. On a good day, Vincent Coll's reflexes were twice as good as his opponent's. Today was a very good day, so Vincent's weapon was up and spitting death an eighth of a second before the other man had even started to press his trigger. Finally, and most importantly, Vincent Coll was a preternaturally good shooter. Taking his shots at a dead run, using a weapon he was not entirely familiar with, and firing bullets large enough to bring down aircraft, the killer put four rounds through the workstation where the enemy hid. Only two actually struck the man, and of those hits, only one was solid. One proved sufficient, and his foe staggered back in a spray of blood before collapsing into a blank-eyed heap on the concrete.

In his zeal, Vincent had forgotten his weapon held only five rounds, not the traditional six. When he spun to send a bullet into the column where the flanker still hid, the click of his hammer striking the transfer bar replaced the earth-shattering boom he had become accustomed to.

He did not have the time to reload. Vincent sprinted for the column. As he flew toward his final foe, he saw the muzzle of a carbine peek around the slate-gray slab. His vision sharpened to a single pinprick, and he watched the flanker's pupils dilate as he squinted down the barrel of his gun. Vincent perceived the first twitch of a metacarpal and realized he was out of time. Snarling, he dove into a low slide just as a three-round burst belched yellow and orange fire over his head. Each bullet passed without biting flesh, though Vincent would not have cared either way. The sudden increase in stress pulled him deeper and deeper into a psychotic rage, swamping his brain in competing neurotransmitters. The millisecond of fear and uncertainty where he did not know if he was going to get his man or his man get him passed like a glacier through the chaos of his mind. But pass it did, and in its wake remained only the pure, radiant wrath of a man no longer in control of his own actions.

Vincent's slide brought him past the column, where he snagged the flanker's ankle in passing. Rising, Vincent pulled the foot from the floor and upended the enemy with the strength of a single arm. The man crashed to the floor on his back. He had the presence of mind not to try to get up. The carbine swung forward to align its muzzle with Vincent's chest. Vincent brought a heavy foot down on the man's wrist, breaking several of the bones there and sending the gun sliding out of reach. The hapless shooter tried for his sidearm with his good hand, and Vincent dropped a knee onto his chest and seized the arm before the weapon cleared its holster. Vincent forced the limb backward across his thigh and dislocated the elbow with a snapping sound far louder than one might have expected. The shooter screamed and bucked, trying to shimmy away from Vincent, though his two injured arms made the attempt an awkward, flopping mess. Vincent slid his knee off the man's solar plexus and shifted to sit astride his torso. The shooter looked up into the face of his tormentor, and his eyes grew wide.

Vincent Coll was gone.

His eyes were empty black chasms, his pupils so dilated that his ice-blue irises were all but gone. He was snarling so hard that angry lines stretched across the skin of his face. Each twitching contortion bent his perfect features deeper into a twisted, inhuman death mask. He grunted and hissed like a reptile while his hands secured unbreakable grips on the man beneath him.

And then the blows came. The first rendered his man unconscious, and that was a blessing. Vincent did not care about precision or target selection. The parts of his brain where his years of training and experience lived had clocked out for the day, leaving something ugly and primordial behind the wheel. He roared as he pummeled, shattering the bones of the face, fracturing the collarbone, shifting vertebrae. The man beneath him had been dead for more than a minute before Vincent stopped punching the mushy sack of meat and blood.

When his fury had spent itself, Vincent stopped and looked at his hands. They were stained crimson up to his forearms, and a tooth had lodged between his first and second knuckles. "Damn it," he whispered, and yanked the offending tooth from his skin. He stood, legs shaking slightly, and shook his head in disgust. "Goddamn it," he repeated.

Then he went looking for a survivor to question.

CHAPTER THIRTY

Sullivan ran.

Part of him was well aware that running would make no difference. If Vincent really had been created from the same mold he was, then the Railroad's extraction team was almost certainly dead by now. He and Vincent were not like regular people. It seemed so obvious, and Sullivan had taken this for granted his whole life. Somehow, he never truly understood what it meant to be this thing he was. Protected by his own ego, he never even considered what other people saw when they looked at him. Sympathy, it turned out, was a virus. It spread through all his carefully constructed conceits like typhus, infecting him with guilt and shame.

They had every right to fear him. This last bit stung on several levels, because the anxiety made perfect sense. He represented the most terrifying thing in human history: a paradigm shift. Humanity rarely waltzed into a new era with grace. Human rights, democratic rule, civil rights, nuclear power—anything that changed the established order was resisted by those afraid of what came next. In every case, the future proved inexorable, and those unwilling to move forward ended up crushed by the weight of history. To the masses, Sullivan was the next doomsday weapon, the new god, or the latest advance in AI. Everything was going to change because of him. That was what humanity saw in John Sullivan, and that was why they were afraid.

Sullivan did not blame them. Sympathy again. It stripped him of the single-minded arrogance that had always protected him from the responsibility that came with his condition. Horowitz and Maris were right, and he grew weary of repeating that to himself. They were right, Vincent had tricked them, and a bunch of good people were going to die because of it. The old John Sullivan would have no problem pointing out that Vincent Coll was the one doing the killing, and that humanity's inability to accept progress was not his cross to bear. To his everlasting chagrin, the new John Sullivan had sympathy, and this meant he felt responsible for every death he might have stopped were it not for his own stupidity.

So he ran.

He ran, and he counted dead bodies. He found the first dead man in the laboratory section where Platt was supposed to have been held. The one-armed corpse lay in a puddle of congealed blood, and Sullivan swore under his breath at the unnecessary level of carnage. Another dead body lay near the door, also ripped apart by a giant bullet. He checked each as he found them, even knowing they would all be dead. He examined Vincent's carefully laid out fighting positions, noting the professional way in which he had funneled the enemy into his shooting lanes. He also took note of Vincent's marksmanship. The man lived up to his reputation. He found the dead men on the production floor, as well as two unexploded mines set up to trap those foolish enough to wander about.

It was the last body that sent Sullivan's quiet frustration to a place of deep and unreserved malice. The man had been brutalized beyond recognition. The beating had proceeded well past the point of death. His own upbringing had brought him close enough to the edge for him to recognize the work of someone who had gone over it. Sullivan saw the work of a madman, the mark of a true psychopath. The old John Sullivan might have been afraid of what that meant for himself. He might have feared for his own sanity. Now, Sullivan understood that he would never be like Vincent Coll. Somewhere along the line, he had developed a conscience, and he began to suspect where that might have been.

The mangled mess on the floor lacked eyes, so it could not stare back through Sullivan. This did not stop him from standing over it. For a moment, Sullivan wondered what he should do, and as quickly as the question was asked, he answered it. Instead of searching for the anger buried below the surface, he sought out the cleansing balm of the corresponding calm. His mind turned sharper, and his senses expanded. Looking around the scene of the battle, he picked out relevant clues and information. Most importantly, the trail of bloody footprints leading away from the dead body splayed at his feet.

It seemed such a stupid mistake for Coll to make. Leaving a trail from the scene was the kind of oversight a guy like that did not make. No such oversights had occurred in Charlotte, and the rusty brown prints meant one of two things.

Either Vincent was in the throes of a psychotic break, or this was an invitation into a trap. Sullivan's brain worked these possibilities over and found both explanations to be equally plausible. It did not matter, he realized. He needed to follow them in either case. Vincent was the only one who knew where Platt was, and that meant Sullivan had to run the bastard down. He followed the tracks at a trot. He hoped that getting on the trail quickly would prevent Coll from setting up any of the same traps that had served him so well against the Railroad. It occurred to Sullivan that Coll might not realize he was being stalked. This felt too much like hope, and Sullivan discarded the thought as wishful thinking.

The trail led down a narrow hall that connected the production floor to several offices. Sullivan slowed out of a sense of caution. He checked and cleared each potential ambush location before moving on. The footprints grew harder to spot with each yard of travel, and searching for each ever-fainter imprint began to eat up precious time. The path pushed onward past the row of offices and several locker rooms. Past these, the trail brought Sullivan to a dim concourse with a single tram rail and platform. His breath quickened at the sight. If

Coll had boarded a tram, then he might be anywhere. Relief washed over him when he saw a blood stain on the handle of a maintenance door just beyond the boarding platform. Sullivan drew the H10 and took a deep breath before pushing through the door.

The space beyond was dark. Wide enough for small material-handling equipment, Sullivan assumed its purpose to be movement of raw materials to the production zones. Though no expert on industrial process, Sullivan felt certain that even when not in use, there should have been at least a minimal quantity of safety lighting. He had found Vincent's trap.

To simply step inside the tunnel would be suicide. He decided against it.

"Coll!" he bellowed into the darkness. "Might as well come out, because I'm sure as hell not going in there!"

His voice bounced off the walls, echoing back in a series of taunting repeats. Sullivan waited by the entrance but not in it. After several long moments, a voice called back. "I wondered if you were smarter than you looked."

"Where's the doctor?" Sullivan shouted. "Give her to me, and you can walk away!"

The laugh that came back was throaty and rich. "Oh, come on! I'm giving you some credit for intelligence here, Johnny. The least you can do is return the favor!"

"I know you aren't here to kill me, Coll," Sullivan replied. "And you know I'm here to bring in the doctor. We can be reasonable. Mickey Sullivan won't take kindly to the two of us murdering each other in the dark. We're big investments, right?"

"So Mortensen blabbed, huh?" Coll sounded amused. "Your daddy isn't the only one with skin in this game, Johnny. Plenty of others don't appreciate your career choices. Mickey will get pissed if I drop you, but a whole bunch just like him will give me a bonus for it."

"Well, I'm sure as hell not walking through your tunnel of terror here, Vinny. I have the girl, and you have the doctor. I think we have ourselves an impasse, pal."

With a loud click, three rows of blue-tinged emergency lights flickered to life along the floor and ceiling of the tunnel. It stretched out before Sullivan for a hundred feet and stood twenty feet wide. Streaks of black ran along the dirty concrete, leftover tracks from the endless passing of rubber-wheeled vehicles in decades past. Large bay doors were situated at the halfway point, and another big bay sat at the far end. From the shadows cast by the loading dock stepped the silhouette of a man. He moved under the row of lights along the ceiling and turned his face up to where Sullivan could see it. With a broad smile, he unbuttoned his blood-blackened jacket and let it fall. From the small of his back, the man drew an enormous revolver. Slowly, and with theatrical flair, the man opened the cylinder and up-ended the pistol to let the bullets fall to the floor. When he was done, he tossed the pistol to the side and held out both hands.

"Let's negotiate, then!" he called. He pointed to the gun in Sullivan's fist. "Your turn."

Sullivan trusted this about as much as he trusted an angry swarm of hornets not to sting. However, charging down the hall with guns blazing against a man he had every reason to believe was his equal felt stupid. That Coll had disarmed first meant that he had something up his sleeve, either literally or figuratively. Of this, Sullivan was certain.

"Oh, come on now, Johnny!" Coll implored. "I'm unarmed! Either try to gun me down where I stand, or drop your piece, and let's sort this out like professionals." Sullivan saw the white of his teeth even at this distance. "But if you shoot me, the good doctor dies."

"That does rather limit my options," Sullivan said. He held up his own pistol, dropped the magazine, and cleared the chambered round. Then he placed it on the floor. "Satisfied?" he asked.

"You asshole!" Coll sounded incredulous. "Is that my Hudson? Fucking Mortensen. I should have iced that useless idiot when I had the chance."

Sullivan took that for a "yes" and started walking toward Coll, hands outstretched to the sides. "Meet me in the middle, Vincent."

"Yeah, sure. Whatever," Coll agreed, and mirrored Sullivan's careful approach.

Sullivan suspected he might be playing into Coll's hands. This was not just a hitman. If Mortensen's information was to be trusted, this was the perfect hitman. There had to be a trick in play for Coll to let him so close. Sullivan stretched his senses as far as he could with will alone. He battered his mind for options. Why would Coll choose this place? The tunnel was wide enough to move in but narrow enough to prevent any fight from turning into a running gun battle. There were no easy exits, and the walls looked like solid concrete. They were essentially locked in a box, and Sullivan did not understand why. It might make sense if Coll had a hidden pistol, though he could not know if Sullivan had one too. There was no clear advantage. A shootout in here between men like Coll and Sullivan virtually guaranteed both parties an ugly death. Sullivan turned his attention to the bay doors as he neared the halfway point. He considered the possibility Coll had backup hidden behind them, then dismissed the idea. The doors would open too slowly. Sullivan would be out of the tunnel before anyone on the other side got a clear shot.

Then he remembered the production floor and stopped. Coll had been moving more slowly and stopped as well. They faced each other at a distance of less than thirty feet. Coll cocked his head with a bemused expression at the broad smile splitting Sullivan's features. With an exaggerated swing of his legs like a man clearing a low fence, Sullivan stepped over an invisible beam of infrared light.

"Come on, Vinny. Trip mines? In here? Half a chance you'd have gotten yourself with that."

"I hoped you'd just walk on by the thing. If necessary, I was going to use your wide ass as a shield."

"Anything else up your sleeve?"

Coll shrugged with a sly smirk. "That'd be telling, Johnny."

"We still have our impasse," Sullivan reminded him. "You kill me, you'll never find that girl.

"You keep assuming I'm stupid, Johnny. I know you have no clue where the kid is. You wouldn't have come if you did. You're a sap like that."

"So why do you want me at all?"

"Here's the thing, Johnny. I work for lots of folks. All the big players want that little brat. However, on the subject of one John L. Sullivan, there is quite a bit of debate. Some want you dead. If you had been blown up just now, I'd be collecting from them. But you didn't get blown up, so now I'm gonna try to make my money from the other side."

Sullivan raised an eyebrow. "Really? Now I am curious."

"Your dad wants you back in the fold, Johnny. You think Mortensen knew all that shit 'cause he's reliable?" Coll scoffed. "Your dad put him in here knowing you'd find him. He was *supposed* to spill to you. You wouldn't have believed any of it otherwise. The whole plot he mentioned? That's not just something that is gonna happen. It's fucking going on right now." Coll grinned at Sullivan's blank expression. "The time is now, Johnny. The Republic is a sham, and the folks really running shit are all done pretending otherwise. The kid forced everybody's hand because her mojo is the kind of shit that changes everything. She's the next big thing."

"What do you mean it's all a 'sham,' Coll."

"There is no Republic, shit-for-brains. Two-thirds of the elected members are owned by a handful of powerful mobsters and a couple of big corporations. They've been producing GiMPs and then funneling them into government service for almost thirty fucking years. Don't you get it?"

Sullivan did get it, and his jaw dropped. "An entire race of superhumans, separated from the normals, and galvanized by three decades of discrimination..."

"And they're all working for us," Coll added, "whether they know it or not. We own GEED, too."

"Every scientist we've arrested, every GiMP criminal..."

Coll nodded. "All of them pissed off and hating the society that marginalized them for the crime of being born. The big boys are going to cut them loose on the members of the Republic that don't fall in line. They will be our army, John. And you and I are meant to be the generals." Coll saw the conflict race across Sullivan's face, and his tone grew soothing. "You don't have to fight this. You don't have to be some kind of hero. It's already happening. Hell, most of it has already happened. It's done. You can't change shit." Coll scratched his head and added, "Hell, I'll be honest with you, John. I'd rather have you on board myself. There are only four of us right now, and I don't trust half these yahoos not to screw this up. We'll need you for what's coming."

"If it's so inevitable, why would you need me?"

"The girl," Coll said. "She's too valuable. Her arrival pushed the timetable up by a lot. We were holding out for another five years or so to build up numbers. The ranks are a touch thin at the moment. You know, from a global takeover standpoint."

Sullivan's head shook from side to side. "Christ, it really is a hegemony, isn't it?"

"Yeah," Coll agreed with a laugh. "Except it's not exactly the hegemony they all thought it was. It's not norms ruling over the GiMPs or even the Republic over the rest of the world."

"It's us over them," Sullivan sighed.

"It was never going to be any other way, Johnny. Homo sapiens do not play well with each other when one side has the advantage. The Cro-Magnons wiped out the Neanderthals, the GiMPs are replacing the norms..."

"And us chimeras will rule the GiMPs?"

"That's the plan. Once we have the secret of that kid's DNA, a whole new crop of humans will inherit the planet. Might as well be part of the winning team." Coll's face never wavered. "Because it's going to happen whether we like it or not."

"Two weeks ago, I might have gone along for the ride, Vincent. I resent the norms as much as any GMP forced into government service. But I think I'm going to have to decline the offer."

Coll darkened. "You can't be fucking serious, John. You don't have a chance if you don't go along. Your father will—"

"My father can go to hell!" Sullivan spat. "I'm through running, Coll. Maybe you're right. Maybe I can't beat this, but do you know what I can beat?" Sullivan shrugged out of his jacket. "I can beat your ass. Because I am John L. Sullivan, the greatest bare-knuckle brawler ever born. I can lick any man in this room, and damned if I don't see anyone but you in here. When I'm done with you, I'm going to go see my old man and kick his ass, too. After that?" Sullivan tore his grimy tee shirt off and started to walk down Coll. "I guess we'll just see how far I get, won't we?"

"I didn't really want shit to go like this, but if the big, bad hero wants to go down swinging?" Coll tore his own shirt away. "Have it your way, tough guy."

CHAPTER THIRTY-ONE

The two men met in a flurry of blows.

The first pass proved inconclusive. Neither man got the better of the other, and both took as many hits as they delivered. Coll's combinations came with fury and force, and Sullivan matched each with a stoic and dangerous indifference. Coll's left fist clipped Sullivan's jaw, but a counter-punch slammed into the hitman's ribs like a sledgehammer. Coll fired two overhand rights in response, both landing against Sullivan's high guard. Coll backed away from three alternating hooks and nearly stumbled when a chopping foot sweep spoiled his steps.

The killer found his footing just as Sullivan surged forward to take advantage. Coll exploited his foe's exuberance by rocketing an uppercut to the man's chin that landed flush and lifted him from the floor. Now Sullivan was on his heels, and Coll charged. Every muscle and sinew in his body burned with the fire of his savagery. Cortisol, adrenaline, acetylcholine, and norepinephrine drenched his brain—all unencumbered by the regulating influence of serotonin and encouraged by liberal quantities of testosterone. Vincent Coll lived for this feeling, basking in the heat of his unhinged mental state and all the superhuman might it granted him. He knew it was monstrous. He understood that it controlled him far more than he would ever control it. He possessed the wisdom to indulge the monster only when necessary, but this did not stop him from loving every second of it.

The heavy impact of his knuckles against the unforgiving density of Sullivan's muscles assured him that this was one of those times when letting the demon out was a good idea. He rained punches against Sullivan's defenses with wordless grunts, bashing over and over again at the big man's guard. There was no pain when his knuckle bounced off the hard bones of Sullivan's forearms or when his wrists bent against the mass of his triceps. When Coll grew tired of this, he kicked at Sullivan's midriff, nearly crowing with glee when his foot connected. Sullivan folded in half and collapsed, and Coll fell upon him in an instant. He started with kicks to the body. Over and over, he drove his feet into Sullivan's flanks, missing as much as hitting. He did not care. He could kick forever if he wanted to. He would kick until there was nothing left of John Sullivan but soft, formless mush. He saw blood ooze from the ugly gash in Sullivan's side and exploded into maniacal laughter. The coppery tang of it filled his nostrils and tickled the back of his throat. He felt the hot, sticky warmth as subsequent kicks soaked the legs of his pants with warm liquid life. The blood seeped rather than flowed from the long gash. The wound was not deep, but the mere presence of blood was all it took to send Coll spinning off to new heights of psychotic frenzy.

At last, Sullivan rolled away from the kicks and got his feet beneath him once again. Coll snarled at the mistake, only realizing once Sullivan had risen that he should have done more to hold him down. It did not matter. Vincent would knock him down once more and start the fun all over again. They locked eyes for a fraction of a second, and the killer took heart at Sullivan's transparent frustration. The man before him radiated malice in the terawatt range, and Vincent soaked it in like a flower drinking sunlight. The madness was his world, his backyard, and his house. If Sullivan wanted to pit his dark side against Vincent's, that suited the killer just fine.

"Come on then, Johnny-Boy" he growled. "Make your daddy proud!"

Sullivan's face turned a full shade darker, and a delighted Coll charged in again. The unbowed Sullivan stepped up to meet him. Like the ocean battering a cliff, Coll's fury crashed against the obstinate slab of granite that was his foe. Sullivan took it all and gave it back pound for pound. The killer felt no pain when a fist like iron clubbed him in the ribs, and his answering jab bounced off Sullivan's skull like a ping pong ball. It seemed impossible, but Coll's anger swelled in the face of Sullivan's obstinance. His refusal to go down and stay down grew more infuriating with each passing second. As Coll's rage increased, so did the violence of his assault. Ignoring defense, Coll hurled himself at Sullivan. The bold move must have surprised his foe, because Sullivan failed to exploit his lack of care. Tangling up Sullivan's arms with his, Coll sent a vicious head butt straight down the middle and smashed Sullivan's nose into a bloody mess.

Sullivan spat blood and saliva into Coll's face and returned the favor with a head butt of his own. Coll took it across his mouth, and his lower lip burst against his teeth. Snarling like a wild animal, Coll leaned in and bit Sullivan's neck as hard as he could. He tasted hot blood for a second before the world went into a spin when Sullivan hurled him to the side. The killer sailed across the tunnel to slam into the wall. He rose slowly and warily, assessing his enemy with a feral sneer.

Sullivan watched his foe rise and swallowed blood. He saw the confidence in Coll's face, his smug approval bordering upon certainty. To his surprise, he agreed with his foe. Sullivan was not going to win this fight. How could he? Coll was faster and meaner. He enjoyed full investment in all his emotions, even the bad ones. Coll could fight like this for hours and never feel a thing, and Sullivan knew in the darkest part of his soul that he could not compete with that. His body ached, his wounds wept. For the first time in a long time, the creeping weight of exhaustion dragged at his limbs, and he sucked air like a forge bellows. Coll smiled like a moray eel and licked blood from his lips.

Despite giving everything he had and dishing out as much punishment as he took, the madman across the tunnel looked ready to go another ten rounds. Sullivan slapped a hand over the bite mark on his trapezius and marveled at Coll's devolution into insanity. The killer understood his own madness, and his surrender to it made him invincible. Sullivan remembered that feeling, and this sparked another, much more useful memory. He remembered an angry young man trying to beat a wise old fighter with nothing but muscle and senseless ferocity. It had not worked then, and it would not work now.

Sullivan took a deep breath and exhaled. He willed the anger to go away. It did not. Coll charged.

Sullivan met the onslaught with a barrage of fists. He was back on his heels in an instant, losing ground to Coll's furious assault. Coll kicked at his bleeding side, clawed at his face, and bashed at Sullivan's defense with an unending hail of overhand punches. Sullivan's feet slid, and thunderclaps of pain in his chest told him that one of Coll's shins had made contact with his ribs. For a moment, his breath failed him, and Coll put two more punches into his head.

Sullivan crashed to the concrete. Coll fell on him before he could get up, though Sullivan recovered enough to protect his head from the killer's renewed assault and pull him into a closed guard. Sullivan lay on his back with Coll trapped between his legs. This allowed him some control of his foe's position and power, sparing him the full fury of Coll's assault. It did not matter. Coll postured up from his knees and punched downward. His eyes burned with satanic glee, and Coll cackled like a hyena as he pummeled. Sullivan's resistance grew slower; his attempts to escape weakened with each passing second. Both men acknowledged it was merely a matter of time before enough of Coll's blows landed to put Sullivan out.

Sullivan recognized what he saw in his foe. It was a reflection, a glimpse of what might have been his fate. Vincent Coll was just John Sullivan without control, and for a second, he was jealous. Coll got to feel his anger. He could embrace it. He could indulge it. It made him powerful.

Sullivan would never have that. The paradox maddened him. He had been taught that rage was not the answer, but he could not stop being angry, either. He was trapped, a prisoner of his own broken neurochemistry with no concept of how to escape this unending cycle. As defeat loomed large in his mind, despair came with it, and by accident, Sullivan did the one thing it had never occurred to him to try.

He surrendered.

With nothing left to lose but his life, Sullivan decided not to care one way or the other about his mental state and just let it happen. Over the next three seconds, he felt many things. He felt them all strongly, and he did not care. A detached calm overtook Sullivan, and he discovered that the barrier between himself and his anger was not a barrier at all. The mere act of ignoring it caused it to disappear. To his surprise, underneath it was nothing. No hidden rage, no deep psychotic urges, no violent monster scratching at the walls. Nothing. The wet blanket hid nothing at all, and he doubted it ever had.

Sullivan almost laughed at his own stupidity. He did not have to overcome his anger, or embrace it, or come to terms with it. The truth was much simpler than that. He just was not that angry. Irritated, frustrated, grouchy, sarcastic, rude, and impatient, sure. Yet even in the midst of this fight, battered and bloody, he was not filled with rage at all. It bothered Sullivan that his stubborn nature had kept him searching for the solution to a problem he did not have. What he was feeling in this moment, in all his moments of violent intent, was his body behaving exactly as it had been designed to. This is what he had been created for, and the lack of emotional intensity was a feature, not a bug.

He did not search for a clear head. He did not have to. His thoughts slid into order without any resistance. The transition was not something he did; rather, it was something he *allowed to happen*. The tunnel grew quiet, time seemed to slow, and the bestial mien of Vincent Coll snapped into perfect focus once again. Sullivan could count his own heartbeats, sense the rush of blood through his veins, feel the individual bones and muscles as they moved beneath his skin, and he *understood*.

The old John Sullivan might have missed it, but now he perceived the slight shift in Coll's weight as he prepared to drop another blow. Cold as ice, Sullivan twisted his hips at the perfect instant to unbalance the killer and dragged Coll's body to the side. Coll bounded away from Sullivan, and both men rose to their feet. Coll panted like a hound, though his eyes sparkled with unrestrained glee.

Sullivan wiped blood from his mouth and met the deranged look with his own slightly unhinged sneer. "Okay, Vincent," he said to the thing across the tunnel. "Round two." Then he took one calm, careful, and perfectly-controlled step toward the man.

Vincent lunged. Deep within his own mind, Sullivan saw and calculated. From his viewpoint, it was obvious just how ludicrously fast Vincent was. That he had ever tried to match that speed now seemed patently stupid.

Coll was going to get hands on him. He took that to be inevitable. His foe's superior speed forced Sullivan to fight from his heels. Normally, Sullivan would find this frustrating. Now, it was merely data. He knew how to fight reactively, thanks to losing endless matches with Stevens all those years ago. The gnarled old grappler was a master at setting traps for overzealous opponents with great physical gifts and poor impulse control, and Sullivan had walked into every one of them before learning his lesson. Now, Sullivan set a trap of his own.

Sullivan squared up and left his guard open down the middle. As he suspected, Coll's tactical thinking had lost much of its sophistication, making the gap far too tempting to ignore. Even knowing it was coming, the punch very nearly connected. Sullivan did not try to block; rather, he angled his head away and took only a glancing hit off his shoulder. Coll followed the overhand right with a haymaker left, leaving his left side exposed from the neck down. Sullivan put a left hook into his solar plexus and followed it with a second left hook to the face. This re-broke Coll's nose and sent the killer staggering in a spray of blood. Sullivan tried an overhand right, but he was too slow. Coll had already moved out of the line of fire. The blow fell short, and the snarling hitman was on him once again. This time, Coll led with a soccer kick toward Sullivan's groin. Sullivan angled his thigh just in time to prevent a disaster, and then weathered a series of overhand punches. One slipped past his guard and opened a cut on his cheek. The pain set fire to his anger, and the urge to chase it flashed across his mind. He ignored it and dismissed the reflex without judgement. He re-engaged Coll with the same emotional intensity a butcher showed to a side of beef.

Coll hit him twice more while he tried to find an opportunity. Sullivan let it happen, giving ground by degrees and letting Coll's confidence grow. He angled his left side away, presenting the weeping wound on his flank to the enemy and tempting Coll with an easy takedown. He took the bait. Coll feinted a jab and lunged for Sullivan's fabricated opening. Driving into the injured ribs, Coll wrapped a leg around Sullivan's heel and tried to throw the big warden to the floor.

Too late, Coll felt Sullivan's weight shift. Too late, Coll felt the column of muscle that was Sullivan's leg stiffen. Too late, he felt his own feet leave the floor. The trap was sprung.

Vincent Coll did not sail through the air. In truth, that would have been a better outcome. Sullivan's arms gripped him like bands of steel, and when Coll returned to the earth, it was head-first and underneath the descending mass of John Sullivan.

Coll's vision exploded with dancing spots of colored light. When his senses snapped back to focus, the crushing weight of Sullivan pinned his back to the floor. Coll's head screamed in agony, leaving his legs to kick and scrape in useless agitation. Sullivan shifted to wrap an arm around Coll's neck, keeping his weight heavy on the killer while switching to a side headlock. Coll scratched and swatted at Sullivan's eyes, but the big man's grip and posture prevented these attacks from doing more than annoy. The two men sidled and writhed across the concrete as each struggled to improve their position. Sullivan cinched his hold tighter in tiny, controlled increments while Coll bucked and thrashed like a snake in the claws of an eagle. At last, Sullivan trapped Coll's arm against his own neck and squeezed.

No quantity of psychotic mania or genetic modification will keep a man awake when there is no blood flowing to his brain. Skilled fighters understand the difference between zeal and technique and when to apply them. Coll never internalized this in his training, and his anger was replaced by confusion when twilight descended over his eyes and a soft static filled his ears. Confusion became sadness and disappointment as perception retreated behind a descending gray fog. Just before he passed out, the pressure lessened, and Coll heard a distant voice say, "Where is Doctor Platt?"

Coll said nothing at first. The rage that had fueled him thus far was gone, blasted from his brain by head trauma and lack of oxygen. He had lost the fight, and he knew it. Now, it was time to think about escape. After a second, he croaked, "Let's deal."

"You talk or you die. That's the deal," Sullivan said without releasing his hold. The blood flowing from his broken nose dripped down onto Coll's face in hot spatters. "I'll find her either way. This is just faster."

"You'll kill me either way," the beaten man countered.

"Not my style. You know that. Make a call, asshole. Start talking or..." Sullivan resumed choking for several seconds, and Coll heaved in protest.

When Sullivan let up once again, Coll coughed blood from his smashed lip and gasped. "Okay! She's in the old chemical storage locker! Lab 241B!"

"See?" Sullivan said. "Was that so hard?"

"You gonna let me up? Or are you a liar?"

"Are you a liar? Is she really there?"

"Check my phone, or call your pet Roadie."

Sullivan released his hold and stood up with a smooth motion. Vincent was much slower to rise, and even so, he immediately sank to his knees to retch stomach acid all over the floor.

"You've got a nasty concussion, Vincent," Sullivan chuckled. "You should learn to take a fall." He fished Coll's phone out of his discarded jacket and slid it over to the man. "Show me."

Coll swiped across several screens to bring up a live feed of a woman tied up and gagged inside a dark closet. "241B" was clearly stenciled on several surfaces. Satisfied, Sullivan kept a wary eye on Coll's heaving back as he called and spoke briefly with Skip. Then he returned the phone to his pocket. "My people are checking the lab. If you aren't lying. I'll let you walk away right now."

"You're not going to arrest me?" Coll asked.

"What would that do? I couldn't even keep Mortensen behind bars. You'll just walk."

"And you aren't going to kill me?"

"I told you. That's not my style. We'll get another crack at each other, I'm sure."

"What is your style, then?" Coll asked. He again rose to his feet, still unsteady and still bleeding from the face.

"I haven't decided yet. Now, here's the real question, Vinny. What are you going to do? Try to kill me again, or try to recruit me?"

"Well, one thing's for sure," Coll tried to sound jocular. He was unsuccessful. "I sure as shit ain't gonna try to kick your ass again."

"I guess you can be taught."

"But here's the thing, Johnny. I got one group of guys that expects me to bring back an immortal mutant kid, a super genius, and a dead warden. I got another that expects me to bring the kid, the doc, and a live warden. One side or the other needs satisfaction."

Sullivan sighed. It was deep and long and very tired. "Here's where you reveal that you have a secret trick to play and thus secure your victory, right?"

Coll shrugged. "Sorry, man. It's just business." He held up his phone. "Anyway, in about ten seconds, twenty or thirty Silk Road dipshits are going to grab that sexy doctor chick, because I might have let it slip that a GEED warden was chasing a GiMP messiah through this section, and that certain parties would pay handsomely for retrieval of said messiah. If I timed it right, they'll bump into your pet Roadie and that nice old Railroad lady while they try to get the doc out. They'll hold everyone until they can torture the location of that kid out of one of them. I'll have time to pick them all up later." He held up his hands in surrender. "What can I say? Those assholes will believe anything if you phrase it right. I didn't even have to pay them. I just implied there was a reward. These mercs don't care where the money comes from or how they get it." He wagged a finger in Sullivan's face. "You're good and fucked, John. Now, which is it gonna be? You coming along as a dead warden or a live one?"

"You really thought this through, huh?"

Coll nodded. "I wasn't sure I could take you, so I bought insurance. Hardest part was figuring out how to get you to let me have my phone back so I could send her location to them." He affected a look of innocence. "Oh, you thought I was showing you her location? Johnny-Boy, I was showing *everybody* her location. Thank god you are such a sap for the ladies, right?"

The smug look on Coll's face lacked some punch considering the greenish hue of his skin and the mangled mess of his lip and nose. Even so, his confidence faded at the sound of Sullivan's chuckling.

"That's the thing about these merc types, Vincent. You said it yourself. They don't care where the money comes from or how they get it. You'd be amazed at how affordable a double cross is when the other guy only pays in promises."

"What the hell are you talking about?" Coll said, his voice low and dangerous.

"Your mercenaries don't work for you, Vincent. They work for me. My 'pet Roadie' had them all sewn up before we even started." He scolded the battered hitman like a schoolteacher. "You can't just tell amoral assholes secrets like that and not expect them to talk. Every gang in here knows something is up. How hard do you think it was for someone with a GEED expense account to outbid your cheap ass? You telling them where to find the doctor only means I get her even sooner." Sullivan smiled, and it was an ugly, angry thing. "If you aren't bluffing, I expect Doctor Platt will be safely in our custody any moment now." Sullivan's phone chimed on cue, and he did not even bother to check it. "Wonder what that could be?" he asked.

Coll's face fell. "You son of a bitch..."

"Technically, we don't have mothers, Vincent. You know that."

Where Coll found the strength for his lunge, Sullivan could not say. Suffering from a concussion and fresh from a thorough beating, Vincent Coll hurled himself at Sullivan without warning. A tribute to the laboratory that created him, his charge covered the ten feet separating the men in the blink of an eye. If Sullivan had not known it was coming, the outcome may have been different. But he did know, and his sidestep left his assailant with a lot of momentum and no target to transfer it to. Coll's feet slid awkwardly along the concrete as he tried to regain his footing. When he at a last came to a halt, he turned just in time to see John Sullivan's smiling face an inch from his.

"Watch your step, Vinny," he suggested helpfully, and then shoved Coll hard with both hands.

Vincent Coll was still trying to decipher this cryptic piece of advice as he stumbled backward. Perhaps it was the concussion that slowed his comprehension, but when his calf broke the invisible beam of infrared still attached to the detonator of his own mine, he had still not figured it out.

CHAPTER THIRTY-TWO

Sharon Platt thought she had run out of feelings.

Since escaping the massacre in Charlotte, her emotional range had collapsed into alternating intervals of fear and guilt. When the strange mercenaries pulled her from Coll's storage locker, she did not care if they were there to kill her or rescue her. Any ending would have sufficed so long as it was an ending. They brought her to the tram station without telling her anything. They rode in silence for more than an hour before the car stopped somewhere in Hubtown. From there, the men marched her to an old residential block and brought her to what had once been a lavish administrator's apartment.

She did not know what she expected to happen when she arrived, but seeing Emilie curled up on an easy chair was not it. Only when she saw the little blond head did Platt realize how much she had despaired of ever seeing the little girl again. Her mind went from the gray fog of defeated depression through the shock of disbelief, past the fear of hope, and on to pure elation in ten seconds. She ran to the girl and wrapped her tiny frame in a crushing hug, delighting in the child's squeals.

"Oh my God, Emilie! Are you all right? Did anyone hurt you?"

"I'm fine, Auntie Sharon," the girl said. "Maris and Mister Sullivan took care of me after Porter tried to—"

Platt interrupted. "Sullivan? John Sullivan?" The fear returned just as quickly as it had fled.

"It's all right," came a voice from behind her. Maris entered the room looking thin and pale. "Mister Sullivan has taken care of Vincent Coll. We are safe." She turned to the brace of mercenaries escorting Platt. "You've been paid?"

They nodded.

"Then you may go," she said.

Having recognized her icy tone as a flat dismissal, the men left.

"What the hell is all this about Sullivan?" Platt asked.

"Mister Sullivan is the reason you are alive and Emilie is not currently in the clutches of your former employers. He went to great pains—literally—to help us. You should be thankful for his help."

"He's a warden, Maris! What happens when he's done playing with Coll and comes for us!" Platt nearly shouted. "What does he know? Where is he now?"

"Everything. In the bedroom." Maris seemed pleased with her answer.

Platt blanched ghost-white. "In the..."

The door to the sleeping compartment opened, and a nightmare stepped through the threshold. Platt knew most of everything there was to know about John Sullivan, and somehow none of that knowledge had prepared her for what she saw. He was as big as she expected. The leviathan stood tall and thick and wide all at once. He had no shirt, and the swollen muscles of his chest and arms strained against his skin as they had in all the medical photos she had studied. All this was as she expected. It was the reality of his present state that shocked her. A long, jagged, and angry gouge ran up one side of his torso. His nose was purple and swollen, bearing a noticeable kink despite the thick tape across the bridge. Both his eyes were blackened, and the right side of his neck bore what appeared to be a deep bite wound that had yet to be dressed. She saw deep, mottled bruises across most of his body, several of which still displayed the clear and angry raised outlines of somebody's shoe. He had been beaten badly and for a long time by someone or something as fundamentally alien as he was.

She found herself drawn to his face. More expressive than the blank stare of the young man in her medical journals, the man looking back at her carried decades of abuse and struggle in his battered features. His eyes were clear and angry, his face bent into a malicious scowl. He had shaved his head at some point, though the sandy stubble gracing his scalp told her it had been at least a week ago. This was not the maladjusted teenager she had done a thesis on, and this was not the hard-nosed young man applying for warden status. Platt had no words for what she saw now, and considering all the work she had put into becoming the expert, her ignorance frightened her.

Emilie broke the spell. "Mister Sullivan! You're awake!" She ran from Platt to Sullivan and extended her tiny hand in a child's version of a proper handshake. Sullivan grasped it gingerly and let her shake it, looking as confused as everyone else in the room. "Mister Sullivan is not a hugger," she explained to the slack-jawed doctor. "Maris says his brain is weird."

The cold eyes turned down to look into the beaming face of a small child who obviously had no idea how precarious her existence was. The corner of his mouth twitched. "Yeah kid, you aren't wrong about that. You okay?"

"Yup!"

"This the doc we're all worked up over?"

Emilie nodded. Maris answered. "John, this is Doctor Sharon Platt. Doctor Platt..." she gestured toward the mangled behemoth, "John Sullivan."

Platt did not know what to say. Her lips parted, but nothing came out. Sullivan waited for a polite five seconds before speaking. "Lady, you and I need to have a very long conversation. If all you can do is stare with your mouth open, then this is going to take forever."

"John! She's been through a lot!" Maris scolded.

The frosty glare turned to the old woman. "My heart bleeds. No, wait. That's my side, my nose, and my neck. Yeah. I'm real low on giving a shit right now."

Emilie gasped at his blatant use of profanity. Sullivan muttered, "Sorry, kid."

Platt responded by reflex, and in hindsight, virtually any other reply would have been better. She was a scientist to her core, and what came out of her mouth came out naturally. "He can't feel empathy under stress. The right supramarginal gyrus is prioritized so it..." Platt began to suspect she was talking too much, and her voice trailed off. "...over-represents in his decision making..."

All eyes in the room turned to Platt, who suddenly realized she was being very rude to a very dangerous person no more than six feet away from her. She tried to save herself. "It's not a bad thing! He, uh... I mean, you... are capable of making good decisions under high levels of mental arousal because oxytocin never gets a chance to influence your thoughts. It just means affection and, uh... empathy don't, uh... work... right?" Her voice had trailed off again at the end. The hole she was digging got deeper with each word, and she abandoned the train of thought far too late to save herself.

"Is that right?" Sullivan's voice took a dangerous tone. "And you know this because?"

"Perhaps you'd like to start over, Doctor Platt?" Maris offered. "John, I told you that Doctor Platt wrote one of her doctoral theses on your case. She is a recognized expert on you. Isn't that flattering?"

Sullivan did not appear flattered. He appeared even angrier than usual. "Fucking. Charming." Then he said to Emilie, "Sorry, kid."

"You swear a lot," she observed. "Are you going to arrest Auntie Sharon?"

The broken face and all its quiet anger fixed Platt with an intense stare. "I don't think so."

"Why not?" The scientist did not understand what was happening. "I don't—"

"Things aren't the way they look, or whatever." Sullivan seemed to understand how useless and cryptic his answer had been. "It's complicated, and that's mostly your fault, but also not your fault." This answer fell short as well, and the man's frustration became apparent. "I can't bring you back to GEED because GEED is in the pocket of the same people that hired Coll and financed your work."

"What?"

"The mob, a couple of big corporations, some rogue governments. It's a whole goddamn thing. They're all working to replace the Global Republic with their own race of GMP leaders. Coll told me the whole setup was already in place and running things. Based on what I know about GEED, I'm inclined to believe him. All that's left is to dissolve the Republic itself." He pointed to Emilie. "When they found out about the kid, everybody jumped the gun. What she's got, everybody wants, and that's made all of them impatient. They don't have the numbers they need to wipe the slate clean, but they're starting anyway because apocalyptic paradigm shifts are fun, right?"

"Coll told you this?" Maris asked. "Why?"

"Part of his job was to recruit me." In response to their shocked faces, he added, "I'm supposed to be one of their four horsemen or whatever. Special chimera designs that people can order up and use to pacify the masses. They want me back in the program." He gestured to his abused state. "Some of the jerks want me dead, others want me back on the payroll. Obviously, I declined. The severance package sucks, too."

"Where is Coll now?" Platt asked, her fear rising.

Sullivan looked at the doctor with incredulous eyes and spoke as if explaining nuclear physics to a chimpanzee. "Well, Doc, I sure as hell didn't arrest him, if that's what you are asking. Most of him is on the floor of a transport tunnel in Lenexa. The rest of him is kind of splattered over the walls and ceiling."

"For the love of..." Maris sighed. "The child, John!"

"It's okay," Emilie said. "He was an asshole."

"Emilie!" Platt cried.

"It's the truth!" Emilie whined back. "He wanted to take us away, and he hurt a bunch of people. So I told Mister Sullivan it was okay to kill him. Was that bad?"

The child's blatant misreading of her rebuke shocked Platt into snorted laughter. "Not this time, Emilie. But let's watch the language, okay? Mister Sullivan has kind of a potty mouth."

"I'm an asshole, too," he agreed.

Platt shook her head in bemused disbelief. She had another question for the big man, and she feared the answer. "What are you going to do with us?"

She held her breath while waiting for his reply. He did not make her wait long.

"Doctor, I honestly don't know. I don't even know what I'm going to do with myself. I have friends in GEED still. Friends who aren't dirty. I'm supposed to get a whole bunch of sensitive information on what's going on from them soon. I'll know better once it's in my hands. In the meantime?" He shrugged and winced when the motion aggravated one of his many injuries. "I'm cut off. The people behind all this have probably figured out that I'm onto them. If I go back to GEED, I'm as good as dead." He curled a lip toward Maris. "I guess I'll need help from the Railroad. Imagine that."

"We owe you a great debt, John," Maris replied with a nod toward Platt and Emilie. "You will have all the help you need. What we can't give you is a plan."

"Too bad," Sullivan said. "They've got me running right now. That's better than dead, but it's not my style. I'd rather be on the offensive." He held up his hands in defeat. "Right now, I need information, and for that, I need mobility."

"That can be arranged," Maris replied. "Our network is vast. Can the Railroad rely on you as well?"

"Fair's fair," he said. "Until I can sort out GEED and expose this..." he fished for the appropriate word. "...whole thing, I'm pretty much at your mercy."

"What about Emilie?" Platt asked. "If they found us in here once, they can do it again."

"Let them come," Sullivan growled from deep in his chest. "I'd rather fight them here."

Platt and Maris both let their eyebrows climb. Maris asked the question on both their minds. "*You* would rather fight them here?" A gnarled finger wagged at him. "Have you taken a shine to our little Emilie, John?"

"She's just a kid, Maris. What they'll want to do to her is awful. They'll use her hard and break her spirit if we let them. They'll ruin that kid without a second thought, and I've already lived that nightmare once." He tapped his head. "They put a monster up here and then taught it to hurt people. I get what they were after now. A product. A tool. Not a human being." His finger moved to point at Emilie. "That's what they want from her, too. She doesn't get to be a person in their world, just a boutique genetic template they can sell. These people are worse than animals, and they deserve what I'll do to them if they come after her."

"I see," Maris said, folding her hands in her lap. "You wish to punish the people who hurt you by keeping them from Emilie. Is this your chance to strike a blow for your miserable childhood?"

Sullivan glared at the woman. "Maybe. Something like that."

"So it's not that you feel a kinship with her situation, or that by helping her, you might be reclaiming a part of yourself?"

"Maris?"

"Yes, John?"

"You have got to be the worst psychologist that ever lived."

"You've mentioned that."

Sullivan's shoulders sagged. Some of his irritated tension melted away, and the loss seemed to bother him. Platt realized that a new and dangerous struggle was going on in his head, and part of her wanted to study it. When he spoke, frustration replaced the rudeness that had been there before. "It doesn't matter why I'm doing this. At least not to me, all right? Stuff that never used to bother me is pissing me off, and the things that used to piss me off seem stupid now. The world is about to end, and I don't have time to explore my feelings. I'm just trying to stay focused on the next steps."

Maris nodded. "What are the next steps?"

"I need answers. My father has some of them."

The old woman scowled. "You're saying you want to break into a maximum-security prison and interrogate a powerful mob boss?"

"He's in minimum security. They only ever got him on the illegal genetic modification stuff. Either way, my old man has a lot to answer for is what I'm saying," Sullivan replied with the fire of deeply-held conviction. "I'm done running from him, and I intend to get those goddamn answers." He turned from the group and started toward the bedroom. "After that? We'll just have to see."

When the door closed behind his retreating back, Platt looked up from Emilie and over to Maris. "I don't believe it... he's... he's..."

"He is a victim of his father's ego and a world that does not understand him. He will need you, Doctor Platt. He will need you because you *do* understand him. I'm telling you, something is changing, and he does not like it. I can't tell if it's psychological or neurological, but I know he's afraid and can't admit it."

"He's dangerous..."

Maris shut her down with a raised hand. "Yes, he is, Doctor Platt. But God help us, he is also our only hope."

Epilogue

Resident 456-65 of the Great Oaks Federal Minimum-Security Correctional Facility shoveled a forkful of scrambled eggs into his mouth and gave the mushy morsel a thoughtful chew. He followed this with a big bite of his wheat toast and a substantial swallow of orange juice.

"How's breakfast?" his guest asked.

"It's prison food," the convict answered. "But it ain't half bad, really."

"I'm glad your time here has not been too onerous, then," the guest replied. "I hear that all your special requests have been given the proper level of consideration."

"Within reason," the prisoner said. "But I'm twenty years into a hundred-and-ten-year stretch. All in all, I'd say I have it pretty damn good. I got my own room. There's plenty of stuff to watch on InfoNet. Plus, I get three squares a day, lots of exercise, and the occasional conjugal visit." He shrugged. "Could be worse, really." Another loaded fork disappeared into his maw, and without finishing the bite, he added. "But you ain't here to talk about my living arrangements. What's the word?"

"Vincent Coll is dead."

Resident 456-65 paused in his chewing for a second, then resumed with a dismissive nod. "Told you that was gonna happen. You built a goddamn psycho animal and then cut him loose. It was just a matter of time before he got his ticket punched." He swallowed. "Doesn't matter how tough or mean you breed 'em. If you don't make the guy smart or resourceful, he's just gonna end up dead.

There's no gene for bulletproofing." The fork descended to the tray again. "Who got him? GEED? Local cops?"

"Technically, it was GEED who brought him down. Specifically, Warden John Sullivan."

The fork fell to the table, and the man in the orange jumpsuit met his guest's eyes with a look both amused and bemused. "Johnny dropped him? That, my friend, is fucking hilarious."

His guest did not agree. "The others do not find it quite so humorous."

"That's because they spent too much money on gene manipulation for Coll and the others when they should have focused on training and aptitudes. We're making the next generation of human being here. These idiots act like we're building toasters. I told them to spend more on developing the person as a damn whole, and it looks like I've just been proved right. They don't like it when I'm right and they're wrong."

"They want to discuss next steps. There is a consensus that the time to begin phase three is now."

"Well, I can't do much from in here about that."

"Steps are being taken. You will be re-sentenced to 'time served' within the next few months."

"You think that new law is gonna pass?"

"Mister Sullivan, we have ensured it."

"Mister Sullivan is my dad. You call me Mickey, all right?"

Also by Andrew Vaillencourt

Hegemony

Sullivan's Run

The Fixer

Ordnance

Hell Follows

Hammers and Nails

Aphrodite's Tears

Dead Man Dreaming

Head Space

Escalante

The Fixer Omnibus

Watch for more at www.AndrewVaillencourt.com.

About the Author

Andrew Vaillencourt would like you to believe he is a writer. But that is probably not the best place to start. He *is* a former MMA competitor, bouncer, gym teacher, exotic dancer wrangler, and engineer.

He wrote his first novel, 'Ordnance,' on a dare from his father and has no intention of stopping now. Drawing on far too many bad influences including comic books, action movies, pulp sci-fi and his own upbringing as one of twelve children, Andrew is committed to filling the heads of readers with hard-boiled action and vivid worlds in which to set it. His work pulls characters and voices born from his time throwing drunks out of a KC biker bar, fighting in the Midwest amateur MMA circuit, or teaching kindergarteners how to do a proper push-up.

He currently lives in Connecticut with his lovely wife, three decent children, and a very lazy ball python named Max.

Read more at www.AndrewVaillencourt.com.

Made in the USA
Las Vegas, NV
09 August 2023